THE
CONGRUENT
MAGE

Book Six of the Congruent Mage Series

The Congruent Mage Series

The Congruent Apprentice

The Congruent Wizard

The Congruent Dragon

The Congruent Emperor

The Congruent King

The Congruent Mage

www.CongruentMage.com

The Xenotech Support Series

Xenotech Rising

Xenotech Queen's Gambit

Xenotech First Contact Day (novelette)

Xenotech What Happens

Xenotech General Mayhem

www.XenotechSupport.com

Dedication

To my readers and listeners with my thanks
for their patience as it's taken so long for
this book to be finished. You're the best!

Cover and Map designs by Dan Paulson
Glyppo illustration by Tori "Ishy" Smith

ISBN-13: 978-0-9978319-7-9

Spiral Arm Press
1725 Carlington Court
Grayson, GA 30017

www.SpiralArmPress.com

Glyppo

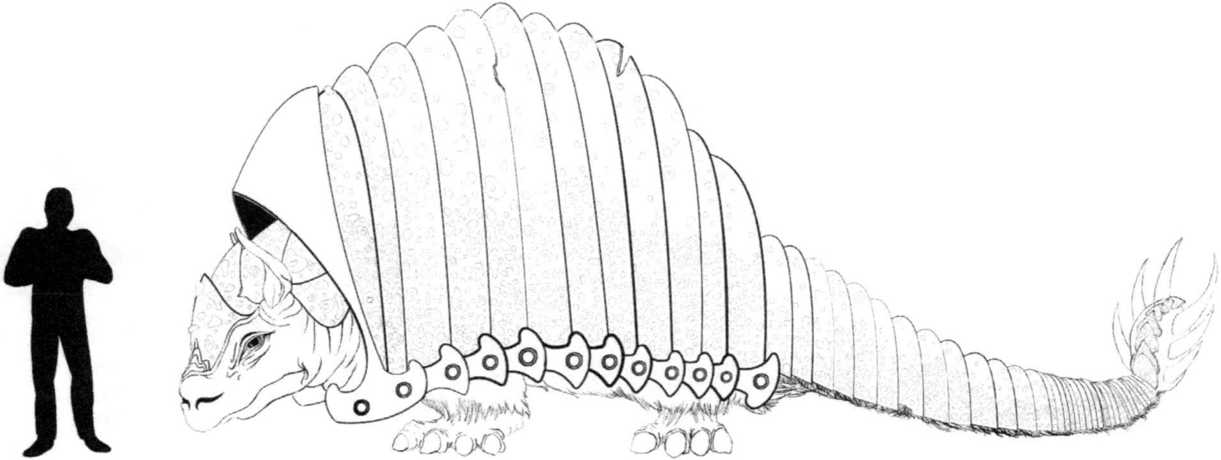

Prologue

"Why are you neglecting Eynon's education?" Astrí asked Damon as she shifted the down comforter covering them and spooned against her husband.

He didn't reply until she poked his rib, provoking a sleepy and reluctant *"Wha...?"*

It was late and the two of them were relaxing in an oversized bed after a delightful chance to *reconnect,* as Astrí liked to call it. The bed nearly filled the chamber, one of four rooms in the luxurious suite Laetícia had assigned them in the Governor-General's palace in Nova Eboracum. It was quite a few steps up from the humble quarters where they'd slept when they'd been masquerading as Côbb and Réah, servants working in the stables and kitchens, while spying on Emperor Sírénae and her minions a few days earlier.

"Listen to me," Astrí insisted. "I don't understand you."

"That's nothing new," said Damon with only a hint of teasing in his voice.

Astrí shifted to put the soles of her chilly feet on Damon's calves.

"Cold cold cold *cold!"* the old wizard protested. "Stop that!"

"It's only what you deserve," teased Astrí, keeping her feet in place. "First you nearly got Eynon killed by sending him out to basilisk country to find his magestone..."

"Nûd was keeping an eye on him," Damon responded.

"You should have been watching him, too," said Astrí.

Damon sighed. "I was, my love. But don't tell anyone. It's bad for my curmudgeonly image."

"Hah!" said Astrí. "You weren't a curmudgeon when I married you."

"Of course I wasn't," said Damon. "I was too young to be a curmudgeon. When you're under fifty, you're irascible."

"And you're *still* irascible, but that's not my point," said Astrí. She was about to continue then paused before resuming. "You're changing the subject," she said at last.

"It took you long enough to notice," said Damon, moving his legs away from Astrí's feet.

"You're doing it *again*," said Astrí. She touched her magestone with her free hand and summoned cold, then put the palm of that hand in the small of his back.

"Brrrrr!" exclaimed Damon. "That was cruel!"

"No," said Astrí. "Cruel is how you treat your would-be apprentices."

"Uh huh," said Damon. This wasn't the first time Astrí had criticized his training technique.

"Why do you send apprentices out to the hot springs and basilisk-beset mud pots on their own, before they've learned any magic?" asked Astrí.

"I've told you before," said Damon. "Because that's where the best magestones are."

"You could *take* them there and protect them while they searched," said Astrí.

"But then how would I know if they were clever enough to be worth my time?" asked Damon. He turned his head to look back over his shoulder. "I do rescue apprentice candidates who've been turned to stone," he said. "And sometimes I save them *before* they're petrified."

"No sense in getting the master-student relationship off to a rocky start then," said Astrí.

Damon took a deep breath. "I wouldn't want to take a new apprentice for..."

"If you say *granite,* I'll put my cold hand somewhere more sensitive than the small of your back," said Astrí.

"Fine, fine, I'll play *gneiss,*" said Damon. "Seriously, though, if I don't give would-be apprentices a chance to show their capabilities under pressure, how will I know if they're worth the time it will take me to train them?"

"Which brings us back to my original question," said Astrí. "Why are you neglecting Eynon's education? Back when you were taking apprentices more frequently, you'd train them for several years, not a few days."

"True," said Damon.

Astrí draped her arm across Damon's chest and felt his rapid heartbeat. "I was about to complain about you putting me off again," she said, "but you're reacting like you're worried about something. Does my question upset you?"

Damon sighed. "I'm not upset, my princess," he said. "I'm afraid."

"Not afraid of *me*, I hope? Afraid of Eynon?"

"No," said Damon. "Afraid *for* Eynon."

"What do you mean?" asked Astrí.

"It was clear from the first time I met him that Eynon wasn't an average apprentice candidate," said Damon. "He was naive, but far more powerful than he realized."

"Given all the feats he's accomplished since then, I think that's obvious," said Astrí.

"It was also quite apparent that Eynon didn't have a clue about what wizards can and can't do," said Damon. "He was a near-total innocent. I gave him a few of the basics—shields, fireballs, lightning, flying— but was afraid if I started teaching him more advanced lessons, he might have tried to fit himself into *my* idea of wizardry, not figured out his own."

"That was quite wise of you," said Astrí.

"Thank you," said Damon. "I do *write* epigrams, not just collect them."

"Epigrams aren't *necessarily* wisdom," said Astrí.

"That's a given," said Damon. "If I were truly wise, I wouldn't have driven you away with my irascibility."

"That's all water over the Great Falls," said Astrí. "We're back together now. I think you're easier to put up with now that you're a curmudgeon."

"One of the joys of aging, to counterbalance the aches and pains," said Damon.

"I could make you a potion to help with that," said Astrí.

"Just being with you is medicine enough," offered Damon.

"That's sweet," said Astrí. "Thank you. Do you think you'll be giving Eynon more lessons now that he's made so much progress on his own?"

"Maybe," said Damon. "I don't know when I'll have a chance, though. He's talking about taking time to explore the Imperium with Merry, visiting all the sights he's read about in Robin Goodfellow's *Peregrinations*."

"After they get back, maybe you can take *me* to tour the Imperium," said Astrí.

"I'd love to," said Damon. "Especially now that our daughter and her fellow wizards have figured out how to gate across the Ocean. I'm not enthusiastic about long sea voyages."

"Neither am I," said Astrí. "How long before we can go?"

"At least a year," said Damon. "I'll take my role back as Master Mage of Dâron for that long—but don't tell Eynon. I want to retain my cantankerous reputation and surprise him."

"If you must," said Astrí. "Continuing as Dâron's master mage will be fun. We can live in my suite in the palace in Brendinas."

"Isn't that next to your mother's rooms?" asked Damon. "She never liked me."

"You stole her daughter from her," said Astrí. "Now that I've been keeping her company for more than a decade, I can assure you she's mellowed. Mostly."

"Good," said Damon. "Mostly."

"Pleasant dreams," said Astrí.

"With you beside me, what else could they be?"

Chapter 1

Too Many Glyppos

"Watch out for its tail!" shouted Merry as she floated high above an open spot in the jungles of central Valentia.

Eynon wasn't able to fly up out of range but did generate a spherical shield of solidified sound in time to save himself from the full force of the nearest glyppo's blow. The great armored beast was the size of an elephant and resembled a cross between a giant pillbug and a colossal opossum—with the addition of a long, muscular tail ending in a spiky, mace-like tip. The young mage heard the whistling sound of the tail's motion, saw the spikes approaching his shield, and felt the impact send him sailing toward the edge of the clearing. Unfortunately, another glyppo noticed Eynon's approach and used its tail to *thwack* the wizard off in yet another direction where he bounced off a third glyppo's plate-covered side and rolled across the clearing's floor, coming to rest perilously close to a fourth one of the immense creatures.

"Do it again!" cried the high piping voice of Tertia, the third child and second daughter of Laetícia and Quintillius, the leaders of Occidens Province. All three children, watched by Aleña, were safely above the fray on top of a rock outcrop that bordered one side of the clearing. Chee and Ace, Eynon and Merry's familiars, were with the children, mostly enjoying their attentions.

"Are you hurt, Eynon?" asked Seconda, Tertia's older sister. She leaned over the edge of the outcrop to peer inside Eynon's transparent bubble of solidified sound.

"Of course he isn't," said Primus, the girls' older brother. "He's a master mage. It would take more than a few thwacks from a roll of glyppos to do him any harm."

"A *roll* of glyppos!" piped Tertia. "That's as much fun as a *scurry* of squirrels."

"But more dangerous and painful," added Seconda.

"Owwww..." moaned Eynon. He was flat on his back at the bottom of his protective sphere, holding his head with both hands.

"Cheeeee!" cried Chee at high volume, causing Eynon to try to cover his ears while still rubbing his temples.

"You should have braced yourself," said Merry.

"You should have *helped* me," Eynon replied.

"But then it wouldn't have been nearly so entertaining for the children," said Merry.

"A glyppo is going to smack Eynon again," Tertia told her siblings.

"I'll brace you," said Merry. She generated a pattern of forces like a dozen interlocking spiderwebs inside Eynon's bubble moments before the nearest glyppo lifted its tail, shifted its posterior, and swung the spike-covered tip of that appendage with enough power to spin Eynon all the way to the base of the outcrop.

"Th-th-thank you..." said Eynon, waving weakly up to Merry. "Do you have any healing potions? I think I'm going to need one."

"Stop fooling around," came an authoritative voice from above. Valentius was standing on a flying disk behind Magister Callidus observing the scene. "I asked you to *solve* our glyppo problem, not just annoy the oversized beasts. How are we supposed to get crops planted when these single-minded armored eating machines are monopolizing all the clearings?"

"I'm sorry, Governor-General," said Eynon as he slowly got to his feet inside the solidified sound sphere. "I got too close to one when I started to inspect it."

Tertia piped up to continue Eynon's tale. "Then the glyppo thwacked him and another did and another and..."

"That's enough, little one," said Aleña. "Let the grownups talk."

Valentius smiled at his wife and the children. "I saw what happened, Tertia. Magister Callidus made me distance-seeing lenses. I can understand why you thought it was funny."

"Because it *was*," teased Merry as she eased her flying disk over to join Valentius and Callidus.

Eynon gave his head a few shakes to clear it and rose to meet them, dispelling his shield when he was well out of thwacking range. "I suppose there was a bit of humor in it if you weren't the one being knocked around." Eynon brought his flying disk next to Merry's and nodded to Valentius and Callidus.

Merry leaned close and whispered to Eynon. "Are you hurt? Should I give you a healing potion?"

"I'm fine," Eynon replied. "I feel like I just spent an hour inside a bell being rung, but the only thing injured is my dignity."

"Good," said Merry. "You've managed quite well without dignity so far." She reached out and squeezed his hand. Eynon made a face at her that provoked a laugh.

"Young love," remarked Valentius. "Isn't it grand?"

"I'm sure Aleña thinks so," said Magister Callidus. He raised an eyebrow, causing Valentius to add his laughter to Merry's.

"Now that everyone has been amused at my expense," said Eynon, holding back a smile, "what is the problem posed by the glyppos beyond their mere presence?"

"Their presence *is* the problem," said Valentius. "And there's nothing *mere* about a glyppo."

"The largest are ten feet tall and mass more than fifteen tons," added Callidus.

Eynon whistled.

"Where did you find something big enough to weigh one?" asked Merry.

"We made a scale from solidified sound," said the magister. "It took a dozen of my best mages to craft the upright and crossbar while more coaxed the glyppo onto the platform and still others filled a box-construct with water as a counterweight."

"I'm impressed," said Eynon.

"It was quite an elaborate undertaking," said Valentius. "With its own comedic moments as our mages struggled to immobilize its tail."

"I expect so," said Eynon. "And I'm glad to know I'm not the only one providing opportunities for amusement." He extended his arm to point down at the glyppos in the clearing. "It's clear that they're huge. But you have tens of thousands of legionnaires," he continued.

"Are you saying you can't get your troops to poke them with pikes until they move out of your way?"

"It's those thwacking *tails*," said Magister Callidus. "It takes a wizard to block them and we can't afford to assign my mages to such duties if we want to use them for all the other things it takes magic to accomplish. There are a *lot* of glyppos here. You could have warned us."

"I didn't know," said Eynon.

"Rōlin and Peregrína didn't say a word about them," said Merry.

"That's neither here nor there," said Valentius. *"We* still have to deal with them. They're monopolizing the most fertile cleared land for planting."

"I think you've got that wrong," said Eynon. "I may not know much about glyppos, but I do know a lot about cows and glyppos seem like just another sort of big herbivore to me. The glyppos are *creating* the fertile cleared land."

"What do you mean?" asked Magister Callidus.

"I get it," said Merry. "The glyppos graze on all the plants in a section of jungle, expanding clearings..."

"And their dung fertilizes the newly cleared ground," said Eynon. "That should improve your crop yields."

"Only if the glyppos move elsewhere," said Valentius. "As you've seen, it isn't easy to herd them."

"Do they have any natural predators?" asked Eynon. "They'd have to be big. Are there any dragons native to Valentia, for example?"

"The island doesn't seem to have native dragons," said Magister Callidus. "Xaxidiánus has flown it from end to end and didn't spot any—though there are quite a few of your western dragons here with us as imports."

"Look!" called Primus from below.

"You'll really want to see this," shouted Aleña from the top of the outcrop.

Chee and Ace added to the obvious excitement below with *chee-chee-chee-chee* and loud barking.

The three wizards and the governor-general focused on the clearing where one of the glyppos was about to knock over a tall slender tree with long, wide leaves. Eynon generated distance-viewing lenses of solidified sound and saw the tree supported dozens of green, pear-shaped fruits that looked somewhat scaly.

An angry *basso* bellow came from the edge of the jungle near the tree and a strange new creature entered the clearing. It was a shaggy upright monstrosity larger than a cave bear, with claws on its forelimbs as long as legionnaires' swords. It was nearly as tall as the glyppo, though not as massive. Still, it made up for its lack of relative size with ferocity. It threw itself at the glyppo, raking the beast's armored sides with its claws.

"Now I understand," said Merry.

"Understand what?" asked Eynon.

"Why glyppos have such thick armor," Merry answered.

Eynon nodded and watched as the glyppo rotated away from the newcomer and *thwacked* the shaggy giant with its spiked tail. Its attacker shrugged off the blow, bellowed again, and circled toward the glyppo's head where its claws could do more damage. The glyppo literally turned tail on its clawed attacker and retreated to join the other glyppos, seeking safety in numbers. With one final roar of triumph, the shaggy creature ambled to the tree and began pulling green, pear-shaped fruits from its branches, consuming them with evident pleasure.

The three wizards took advantage of the relative peace in the clearing to descend and join Aleña and the children on top of the outcrop.

"That answers one of your questions," said Magister Callidus as he stepped off his flying disk.

"The one about natural predators?" said Eynon.

"Obviously," Callidus replied. "I think we now have an effective way of *herding* glyppos," he remarked to Valentius.

"Using the green fruits to attract the shaggy clawed beasts?" asked the governor-general.

"They're called *megatheres,*" said Primus.

"Who says?" asked Tertia.

"I do," said Primus. "I made it up."

"I like it," said Eynon.

"They're quite tasty," said Aleña as she crossed to hug Valentius.

"The megatheres?" asked Eynon with a smile.

Merry poked his ribs.

"The green fruits, silly," said Seconda. "When they're ripe their insides are like green butter."

"I like them spread on toast," said Tertia. "Momma made some for us."

"Speaking of toast—and bread—I'm glad Laetícia was able to arrange grain shipments from Alexandria through a narrow gate across the Ocean," said Valentius.

"Fercha, Laetícia, and Mafuta have done an excellent job expanding the range and reliability of trans-Ocean gates in the last few weeks," said Magister Callidus.

"Their gates are helping us keep our people fed until we can plant and harvest," said Valentius. "Even if the wheat did have to be handed through the gate one *modius* at a time."

"Well, *I'm* glad I finally had a chance to meet your family," said Aleña. "I'm so pleased your father recovered."

"He's too stubborn to let a little thing like an assassination attempt using poison kill him," said Valentius. "Seeing me wed *and* meeting his talented new daughter-in-law for the first time helped boost his spirits."

"Your mother and aunts didn't waste time on asking when we'd start a family," teased Aleña. "Your father's chief minister seemed equally concerned."

They think it will be easier to confirm me as Southern Emperor when my father steps down if I have children of my own," said Valentius.

"I thought Roma's Imperium didn't believe in hereditary rule of its four empires," said Merry.

"The Imperium believes in selecting the best, most competent, and most experienced people as emperors of its four divisions," said Magister Callidus. He winked at Merry. "It just so happens that being the son or daughter of a serving emperor can do a lot to boost one's competence and experience."

"I... see..." said Merry.

"Just be glad you're a mage and don't have to succeed your father as baron," teased Eynon. "Political machinations are more complicated than wizardry."

"Says the man who's the master mage of Dâron," said Merry. "You have to worry about wizardry *and* politics."

"Don't remind me," said Eynon. "At least I can hope Damon can be convinced to take the title back long enough for us to see the wonders of the world across the Ocean."

"*After* you find out what happened to Emperor Sírénae and Magister Umbrose, her spymaster," said Valentius.

"And Celéri," added Callidus. "I expect she will be your biggest challenge."

"You're probably right about that," said Eynon. "Any thoughts on where to find her?"

Chapter 2

At the Tempest Isles

"What do you mean you can't teach me without your magestone?" protested Celéri. "How stupid do you think I am?"

With some effort Magister Umbrose left his expression neutral. "This isn't a question of relative intellects," said Umbrose from the rock where he sat with his hands tied behind him. "I can't show you how to work magic without my magestone."

"If you can't teach me, you aren't much use to me," said Celéri. She shifted to find a more comfortable position seated on a somewhat higher rock.

"Things are what they are," said Umbrose. He shrugged his shoulders as best he could with his hands bound.

"Things are what I *will* them to be," insisted Celéri. The powerful young mage tossed a fish to Thraxa, her bloodthirsty snow-gryffon familiar. The beast snatched the offering out of the air, swallowing it in one gulp, and shifted to sit in the sand at Celéri's feet.

"Can you will the sun to rise in the west?" asked Umbrose. "Or command the tides to stop their rise and fall?"

"Don't bother using reason to argue with her," said the woman on the rock next to Umbrose. Sírénae Accipiter, the Siren Hawk, former Emperor of Roma's Western Empire—now deposed—was looking exhausted and ragged in a torn and tattered purple tunic. Her hands were tied and her face, arms, and back showed scratches and puncture wounds from Thraxa's beak and claws. "She still thinks it possible to be both emperor and senior magister."

"Be thankful I *don't* hold such thoughts," said Celéri. "If I did, you'd be dead. But as things stand, you may have value for me as a figurehead."

"Isn't your uncle, Admiral Pixo, better suited for that role?" asked Sírénae.

"My uncle is busy sailing my—once *your*—personal legion from Occidens Province to join us here at the Tempest Isles," said Celéri.

"Whether or not he'll be a better choice for my figurehead leading the legion remains to be seen."

"He's as wooden as the figurehead on his flagship," said Sírénae. "I couldn't even trust him not to attack half his own fleet."

"You know very well conditions were foggy when that happened," said Celéri. "It's not that you've demonstrated outstanding military prowess yourself. You allowed a rag-tag alliance of barbarian kingdoms to execute a Fabian strategy of non-engagement for months, then lost almost all your legions to Valentius."

"That last part is an unfair accusation," said Umbrose. "Your own actions had a lot to do with Sírénae's legions changing their allegiance."

"My wheeled gates should have worked," said Celéri. "They did work delivering tens of thousands of soldiers to the battlefield. We should have won the Battle of the Abbenoth."

Farther down the beach along the curve of the great harbor of the Tempest Isles a dragon groaned. Mégàrotáxus sprawled half on the hot sand, half in the cool water. His head thrashed from side to side as he suffered from disorientation sickness—a painful affliction caused by gating dragons, so they no longer know *where* they are.

"Not blasted likely with you in command!" grumbled Sírénae. "You have no more experience in military command than a common cowherd. If you hadn't *ad hoc* gated me and that poor dragon to the Rhuthro valley and left us there, I could have won a victory."

Celéri heard Mégàrotáxus give out an anguished bellow loud enough to send a dozen nearby seagulls into flight. She knew he was immensely powerful and second in size only to Xaxidiánus among the invading Roma dragons. Unfortunately, Xaxidiánus had turned traitor and joined the Orluin Alliance along with Magister Callidus and all but one of *her* legions.

"Sorry, big fellow," she whispered to herself. "I need a dragon to project my authority."

"It wasn't kind of you to gate Mégàrotáxus a second time, transporting him here when he hadn't recovered from your first gating," said Umbrose. "It will be days or weeks until he recovers—if he ever does."

"You're giving lessons in compassion now?" asked Celéri. "I'm sure all your many victims over the years will be surprised to hear you've grown a heart inside your empty chest."

"Expedience isn't cruelty," said Umbrose. "I did what I did to serve my emperor—and while I would torture men and women to extract information, I would never intentionally harm a dragon."

Celéri laughed. "Hah! If you hadn't captured me and hung me by my wrists in a dungeon you might be more believable." She constructed a sphere of solidified sound around Umbrose's head and kept it in place until his face turned blue. He glared at her but didn't beg for air and Celéri finally dispelled her construct. "I'd asked you to do your worst when I was in your power" she said. "Do you recall how you answered?"

"I'm sure I offered you a glass of wine and a honey cake," said Umbrose with mock sweetness.

"Stop trying to sell me Trajan's Bridge over the Tiber," said Celéri. "Your reply is permanently engraved in my memory. *'Young wizard, you don't know what you're asking. If I did my worst—or perhaps my best—you'd never live to see tomorrow's dawn.'*"

"A bit melodramatic, but that does sound like something you'd say," noted Sírénae.

"Shut up," said Umbrose. "It works more often than not."

"Much as I enjoy watching trapped rats squabble, there are more important matters at hand," said Celéri. "The two of you can draw on your vast stores of wisdom and expertise to advise me on my next steps, thus justifying your continued existence."

"I'd like to continue to exist," said Umbrose.

"As would I," said Sírénae.

"Good," said Celéri. "Now that that's established, what can we do to improve our current strategic position with only five thousand legionnaires, a small flotilla of ships, and a dragon?"

"Kidnap Gwýnnett, Túathal, and—I suppose—that far from bright wizard who follows Gwýnnett around," said Umbrose.

"Hibblig," said Celéri. "He makes me feel like I'm sucking on lemons."

"That's the one," said Umbrose. "Gwýnnett will provide us with potions to control key leaders of the Orluin Alliance and we can use Túathal to destabilize Tamloch."

"Perhaps," said Celéri. "What about Hibblig?"

"He can keep Gwýnnett happy," said Sírénae. "And serve as a willing test subject for her potions."

"With whatever will he has remaining," said Celéri.

"We also need allies by the thousands," said Sírénae.

"Who do you have in mind?" asked Celéri.

"The *Southern* Clan Landers," said Sírénae.

"Excellent!" said Umbrose. "They're perfectly situated to destabilize Dâron while Túathal is doing the same to Tamloch."

"How do we push Occidens Province off balance?" asked Celéri.

Umbrose and Sírénae exchanged a glance. "By taking something Laetícia and Quintillius value above all else," said the spymaster.

Sírénae nodded. "Precisely," she said.

"What would that be?" asked Celéri.

"I'll keep that to myself for the present," said Sírénae. "If I tell you everything I plan *now*, it will reduce my bargaining power when it comes to justifying my continued existence."

"What about that annoying northern kingdom—Bifurland?" asked Celéri.

"They're seafarers," said Sírénae. "Your uncle, the admiral, will have to keep them off balance."

"He may be up to it," said Celéri. "Though we'd have to do his thinking for him."

"True enough," said Sírénae. "I think *we're* up to *that*."

"Ahem," said Umbrose. "If I'm to deliver on *my* part in this enterprise, I'll need my magestone."

"Never!" said Celéri. "You'd find a way to kill me."

"That may have been true earlier, but matters have changed," said Sírénae. "Now Umbrose and I *need* you. You're a very powerful wizard and can help counter the mages who oppose us."

"Particularly Eynon," said Umbrose. "That young wizard is immensely talented. I've only met one other mage anything like him."

"Who?" asked Celéri.

"You," replied Umbrose.

Celéri smiled at the spymaster's compliment then promptly wiped that expression from her face.

"So you can see—given your power—that *we* need you and you need *us*," said Sírénae. "If we don't stand together, we have next to no chance of success."

"Yes, but what *I* say goes," said Celéri.

"Behind the scenes only," said Sírénae. "For our new plan to work, I remain emperor, with Umbrose as my spymaster and you as my master mage."

Umbrose nodded, but Celéri had reservations. "In private, *I* make the final decisions," she insisted.

"Understood," said Sírénae. "We plan together. We come to a mutual agreement on our course of action and work together to implement it. But we *will* defer to you as the final authority, won't we Umbrose?"

"If we must," said the spymaster.

"We must," said Sírénae.

Umbrose slowly nodded assent.

"Good," said Celéri. "On that basis, I'll go forward—but aren't we forgetting something?"

"What would that be?" asked Sírénae.

"The little matter of Valentius and nearly forty legions on that southern island," said Celéri. "If we start moving against his allies, he'll respond with overwhelming force."

"I thought that part of our plan was obvious," said Umbrose.

"Not to me," said Celéri. She tossed a fish to Thraxa and watched the snow-gryffon devour it.

"You'd get there in time," said Sírénae. "Once the key pieces on our *shah-mat* board are in place, we have to kill Valentius."

Chapter 3

Consulting Cartographers

Rain was falling in Three Mountains Valley when Eynon, Merry and their familiars arrived via Eynon's *ad hoc* gate. The young wizards promptly generated shields of solidified sound to keep them from getting wet and climbed the three steps to the back porch of the sturdy log structure called Travelers' Rest.

Ace shifted to his flying form and Chee hopped on his back to soar and explore. Rain didn't bother them and there might be large bugs and other tasty morsels to be found.

Merry lifted her hand to knock on the door but before her knuckles hit wood Peregrína opened it and hugged them.

"I heard your boots on the porch," she said. "There's no need for either of *you* to knock. Whenever you visit, just step inside and call for us. You're always welcome! Come in, come in."

"Thank you," said Eynon, smiling at the thin woman with wavy brown hair.

"You're so *nice!*" said Merry. "And your magestone setting is *so* pretty!"

Eynon looked at the back of Peregrína's right hand and admired the oval blue magestone resting there, held in place by a delicate glove of interlaced silver links.

"Who's there?" called Rōlin from somewhere deeper inside the house.

"Eynon and Merry," replied Peregrína. "I'm going to make birch bark tea. Come join us."

"I'll be right with you," came Rōlin's voice. "I'm just finishing up that detailed map of Valentia I promised Valentius."

Peregrína laughed and the room seemed brighter. "It's such fun to see the way his face gets red when we talk about *his* island," she said as she removed pieces of aromatic bark from an earthenware crock and put a kettle on to boil. "The poor man seems embarrassed over the legionnaires insisting it should be named for him."

"It must have been a challenge updating all your maps with the new name," said Merry.

"We have special spells for that," said Peregrína as she handed four mugs to Eynon for him to put on the kitchen table.

"Spelling spells?" teased Eynon.

"Not quite," said Peregrína. "Rōlin's grandfather figured them out. There's a master scroll with the names of all the places on our maps. When a name changes, we just have to change it on that scroll and it updates everywhere."

"That's impressive," said Merry. "Did you change the name of Nova Eboracum to Sírénaeopolis Magna?"

"We thought we'd wait on that," said Rōlin as he bustled into the kitchen. "And now we're spared that bother."

"Thank goodness," said Eynon.

"I'm glad we could do our part by pointing out a potential place for the invading legionnaires to settle," said Rōlin. He stepped close to Peregrína and kissed her cheek. "Do we have any cakes or tarts to have with our tea? It's hard work drawing maps with such fine detail, and I'd love something sweet."

"I haven't had a chance to bake yet today," said Peregrína. "And neither have you, as you well know."

"Will these do?" asked Eynon. He pulled a box from his backpack and opened it to display its contents.

"Currant biscuits!" exclaimed Rōlin.

"Not just *any* currant biscuits," said Merry. "These were made by Queen Carys herself."

"We're honored," said Peregrína. "Please sit down—the water is boiling."

"I saw that you're finally alone again," said Eynon, waving toward the back porch and the land beyond. Not long ago the land near Travelers' Rest had been filled with refugees from Dâron, Tamloch, and Occidens Province escaping Sírénae's invading legions.

"We have more neighbors now, but they're not in our backyard," said Rōlin. "Most settled east, west, and south of us. The majority of the refugees decided to go back to their original homes, but some stayed. They say they like it here—though they may change their minds after they go through a western winter."

"I expect you're right," said Eynon, remembering how cold it had been when he'd accidentally fallen through a gate at Fercha's tower and found himself in Melyncárreg in what passed for spring in the high mountains west a few months ago. For that matter, he'd noticed there were still patches of snow in shaded spots near Rōlin and Peregrína's home when he'd gated in.

They all sat at the table, Merry and Eynon together on one side across from their hosts. Peregrína added sticks of bark to their mugs and filled each with boiling water. While they waited for the flavor to infuse the liquid, they each took a currant biscuit—though Rōlin took two. The older wizard broke off a small corner of biscuit and held it up to his bushy beard, where Lléwys, his small squirrel familiar, snatched it. Rōlin popped the remaining portion of that biscuit into his own mouth.

"My husband's busy chewing, but *I* can still ask questions," said Peregrína. "I doubt this was purely a social call. What brings you here? How can we help?"

"It was Merry's idea to see you," said Eynon. "We were visiting with Valentius in Valentia…"

"I'll tell you a story about that later," said Merry. She grinned and bit her biscuit.

"As I was saying, when we met with Valentius he gave us a mission," said Eynon.

"He wants you to find Sírénae and Umbrose and Celéri," said Peregrína.

"How did you know?" asked Eynon.

"It only makes sense," said Rōlin. "You're certainly the best mage to deal with Celéri, and I expect Sírénae and Umbrose will be with her."

"They're two steps ahead of us," said Merry. "I told you it would be wise to talk to them first."

"That *is* why we're here," said Eynon. "We need your cartographic expertise to help us figure out where Sírénae, Umbrose, and Celéri are hiding."

"You don't need us as cartographers," said Peregrína. "You just need our help with thinking it through. There are only a limited number of places they can be."

"Such as?" asked Merry.

"I won't tell you what *I* think," said Rōlin. "It's much better if you figure it out yourselves."

"You're as bad as my father," said Merry. "By which I mean as *good*."

"Let me try to reason it out," said Eynon. "Check me if I'm wrong. We heard from Laetícia that Sírénae's personal legion and a good number of ships are missing from Nova Eboracum."

"What does that tell you?" asked Peregrína.

"That they're probably not hiding underground like we did," said Eynon.

"Unless they're trying to trick us by sailing their ships away," said Merry.

"Even if they are, the ships have to find safe harbor *somewhere*," said Eynon. "Can we track *them?*"

"The Ocean is vast," said Rōlin. "It might have been worthwhile if you'd started within a day or two of them leaving the city."

"Maybe we can convince Viridáxés to search for them," said Merry. "He can cover a lot of territory."

"Dáx isn't leaving Zûrafiérix and their eggs except to hunt," said Eynon. "He's heard about Kârkingórēx and his interest in Zûra."

"That's out then," said Merry. "What about Xaxidiánus and your friends the western dragons?"

"They're helping Valentius," said Eynon. "His job is hard enough without me asking *him* for resources."

"You're a very considerate young man," said Peregrína. "I don't think you need to follow the fleet, though. Your reason should be enough. Think it through."

Eynon shrugged, then nodded and put his chin on his knuckles in a classic thinking pose.

Merry put her elbows on the table and rested *her* chin on the arch her interlaced fingers formed.

"Pass me another currant biscuit," said Rōlin. "This may take a while."

Peregrína refilled Rōlin's mug with hot water, passed him a third biscuit, and took a second one for herself.

"They didn't go south," said Eynon after a long pause. "Valentius is south, and they'd want to stay out of his way."

"Agreed," said Merry. "And they didn't go north or..."

Merry's words were drowned out by what sounded like drumming or thunder, loud enough to shake the rafters.

"Are the elk herds or wisents migrating again?" asked Eynon, remembering a similar sound on a previous visit when he'd been trying to work particularly delicate magic.

"I think we should brace ourselves," said Rōlin.

"Is he back?" asked Peregrína.

"It sounds like it," said Rōlin.

Outside the sturdy structure of the Travelers' Rest they heard a bellow that sounded like a combination of the bugles of two dozen lovesick flathorns, ten wisent bulls huffing their authority, and an anguished dragon with a toothache. Seconds later something massive slammed into one wall of the kitchen, knocking chunks of plaster stuck between the building's logs onto the floor and filling the air with fine dust. All four wizards instinctively covered the tops of their mugs with protective barriers of solidified sound and Rōlin acted quickly to cover the remaining currant biscuits as well.

"What was *that?*" asked Merry.

"It wasn't a wisent, that's for sure," said Eynon.

"It's Maddox," said Rōlin.

"What's a *maddox?*" asked Merry.

"Not *a* maddox. Maddox is the name we gave him. The polite name, anyway," said Peregrína.

The kitchen shook with another solid impact. Eynon imagined it must be what it felt like to be on the other side of a castle door from a battering ram.

"We'd better get out there and talk to him," said Rōlin. "Follow me."

The four wizards left through the back door, boarded their flying disks, and rose until they were above the roof line. As soon as they gained a bit of altitude, Maddox was visible.

The beast was huge and built like an elephant but lower to the ground. It was covered in shaggy fur like a wisent in winter. He had big sad eyes and a mouth that seemed to smile at rest. Maddox stood higher than Eynon was tall and must have massed as much as two wyverns the size of Rocky. His most striking characteristic, however, was a single giant horn at the end of his snout. It was much larger than the one on the animal depicted under *rhinoceros* in Robin Goodfellow's *Peregrinations*.

"Stop that!" shouted Peregrína before Maddox could slam into their home again. "You're damaging my kitchen."

Maddox looked up, saw the wizards, and waggled the tip of his horn back and forth in greeting. His tail—something like a tufted riding crop—moved in excited circles.

"Hello, Maddox!" called Rōlin. "Good to see you. Any luck finding a mate this season?"

The big creature's head moved left and right in negation.

"I'm sorry," said Rōlin. "You might try farther north and west. That's where others of your kind are most likely to be."

This prompted more horn wagging and tail circling.

"These are our friends, Eynon and Merry," said Peregrína. "They can be your friends, too. Would you like that?"

The response from Maddox was definitely positive.

Merry descended first and rubbed Maddox's eye ridges, which seemed to make him even happier. Eynon did the same on the other side.

"Get the thing," Peregrína told Rōlin. "I think he'll like it—and it will save us from being surprised again when he returns."

"Yes, dear," said Rōlin. He flew toward the back door and returned shortly with a gold circlet that sparkled with magestone dust. "This is for you," Rōlin told Maddox. "It's a decoration for your horn. Would you like to wear it?"

Maddox bellowed in joy and Rōlin slid the circlet over his horn until it was firmly in place near the base. He accepted more eye ridge rubs from Eynon and Merry, then nodded his massive head in farewell and plodded off toward the northwest.

When Maddox was out of earshot, Peregrína spoke. "It's a tracking device," she told Eynon and Merry. "That way we can locate and alert Maddox if we ever discover more creatures like him."

"Like those cloisonné pins Celéri gave us," Merry said to Eynon.

"That makes sense," Eynon replied. He gave Peregrína a puzzled look. "Why is it important to tell Maddox about others like him?"

"Because we think he may be the last of his kind," the slender cartographer answered.

"We've done a lot of traveling and we've never seen any similar beasts," said Rōlin.

"That's so sad," said Merry softly.

"It is," said Eynon. "We'll start looking, too."

"That's very kind of you," said Peregrína. "I think he's lonely."

"Maddox stops by and gets our attention twice a year as he migrates," said Rōlin. "He does it the same way each time."

"Now that we can track him, we should be able to avoid damage to our home," said Peregrína. "Let's see if the dust has settled and we can finish our tea while you finish thinking."

"That won't be necessary," said Eynon. "We've figured it out."

"We have?" asked Merry.

"Yes," said Eynon. "It's time to go. We just have to collect our familiars. Thank you *so* much for your hospitality and the chance to meet Maddox."

"Anytime," said Rōlin.

"For the hospitality, anyway," said Peregrína. "There's no guarantee on seeing Maddox again."

"Understood and appreciated," said Eynon. "I may be back soon to talk to you about *On Wizardry: A Recipe Book of Magic* and its sequels. I need to do more formal study of magecraft if I'm going to be a master mage."

"After we find Sírénae, Umbrose, and Celéri," said Merry.

Chee and Ace chose that moment to join them, swooping out of the sky from the north. The raconette was covered in soggy cobwebs and Ace had a bit of bat's wing stuck in his teeth. Both were dripping wet from the rain, which was increasing.

"Where have you two been?" asked Eynon.

"I don't think we want to know," said Merry.

"Safe travels, wherever you're off to next," said Peregrína.

"Come back soon," added Rōlin.

"Where *are* we off to next?" Merry asked Eynon.

"Nova Eboracum," he replied. "We need to talk to Laetícia."

Chapter 4

At the Palace in Brendinas

"Not that way," Dârio told Nûd. "You want to guide your sword, not strangle it!"

"I'm trying," said Nûd. "But I'm afraid I'll drop it."

"Let your sword be an extension of your arm," said Dârio. "Make your motions fluid. Slide my sword away from yours—don't block at right angles or you *will* drop it."

"Show me, please," said Nûd.

Dârio nodded and took his stance. Nûd did likewise. The kings and cousins crossed blades, sending the chiming of metal striking metal echoing around the high-ceilinged Great Hall. Dârio helped Nûd practice parries that would move his opponent's sword out of position while maintaining control of his own.

"Does that help?" asked Dârio after they'd engaged and disengaged a dozen times.

"It does," said Nûd. "And my hand doesn't hurt—or not as much, anyway."

"That's because you're holding your sword, not gripping it like the leg of a pig you've just caught for dinner," said Dârio.

"Are you done scuffing up the floor for now?" called Jenet from one of four chairs arrayed around the fireplace at the opposite end of the hall where she was sitting with Bonnie. "We've got things to talk about."

"You're looking a lot better," Bonnie remarked to Nûd, increasing her volume so her voice would carry the length of the Great Hall, even though the largest room in the royal palace in Brendinas had excellent acoustics. She grinned. "More like a skillful dancer and less like an unfortunate farmer who's just been struck by lightning."

Nûd laughed, sheathed his sword, and started the long walk needed to join Bonnie and Jenet. "I hope that's a compliment—which I'll gladly accept, my love."

Dârio waved his own blade at Jenet and gracefully advanced down the hall beside Nûd, practicing attacks and parries against an imaginary opponent as he went. "What's on your mind, Earl Marshall?" he asked Jenet as he draped himself over one of the empty chairs.

"Personal business, not Earl Marshall business," said Jenet.

"Would you like us to leave to give you privacy?" asked Nûd, who now stood next to Bonnie's chair.

"Stay," said Dârio. "I have a good idea what's on Jenet's mind, and it affects all four of us."

"Correct," said Jenet. "We have royal weddings to plan."

"Oh!" said Nûd. "I'd hoped we could get married at Melyncárreg without much fuss."

"Think again," said Jenet. "That might have been possible when most of us were still in the west, but now that the majority of our citizens have returned to their homes, things are different."

"No plan of battle survives confrontation with the enemy," said Dârio. He turned to look at Jenet and was dismayed to see her frown.

"I'm *not* your enemy," said Jenet.

"I didn't mean it that way," said Dârio. "I meant that..."

"I know what you meant," said Jenet. Her serious face suddenly shifted to show her hidden amusement. "It's just that planning royal weddings can be complicated and we need to think about how to make them best work to our benefit."

"It's all so overwhelming," said Bonnie. "Can't we just elope?"

"Kings and future queens can't elope," said Jenet.

"My grandmother did," said Nûd.

"She's a wizard," said Jenet.

"*I'm* a wizard," offered Bonnie.

Dârio waved his arm to Nûd, palm down. "Please sit, cousin. This is going to take a while."

Nûd sat next to Bonnie and held her hand as Dârio continued. "I think our partners were discussing matters while we were practicing."

Jenet gave Dârio a knowing smile and nodded.

"Will it be one ceremony or two?" Dârio asked. "And if one, where would we hold them?"

"How could it possibly be one ceremony?" asked Nûd. "Wouldn't we have to have separate ceremonies, one in each kingdom?"

"Maybe not," said Jenet. "Two ceremonies would be twice as expensive and you and Dârio are cousins. We also want to remind everyone that both kingdoms are part of the Orluin Alliance and will be working closely together in the future."

"I see what you're thinking and it's out of the question," said Dârio. "Quintillius and Laetícia are our allies, but we can't be married in Nova Eboracum. It would make us seem like client kingdoms of Roma's Imperium."

Jenet turned to Bonnie. "I told you he would say that, didn't I?"

"You did," said Bonnie. "I'm not nearly as good at predicting what Nûd will say."

"You didn't grow up with him like I did with Dârio," said Jenet. She reached over and playfully tapped Dârio's shoulder. "Care to make any more guesses, my liege?"

"If she's calling you that, you're in trouble," said Nûd.

"Stop pointing out the obvious and help me think," said Dârio. He rubbed his chin. "It needs to be somewhere that's neutral territory, neither Tamloch nor Dâron..."

"You're on the right track," said Jenet.

"What about Melyncárreg?" asked Nûd.

"It's too smelly and too far away," said Dârio.

"Distance doesn't matter as much with Eynon's new mobile gates," said Nûd.

"But I haven't come up with a way to stop the sulphur fumes yet," said Bonnie. "Sorry."

"What about Three Mountains Valley?" asked Nûd.

"That's not a bad idea, but it's more of a reminder of where we were, not where we're going," said Jenet.

"And it's not very romantic," said Bonnie softly. "Not that being romantic is all that important, I guess."

"It's important to me," said Nûd. "I only plan on getting married once and want it to be special." He squeezed Bonnie's hand and she squeezed back.

"If all the political and symbolic dimensions are equal, I'm perfectly fine with somewhere romantic as well," said Dârio. "You've found somewhere, haven't you?"

"I might have," said Jenet.

"Where?" asked Nûd. "It can't be Valentia, which is beautiful. That would have the same problems as Nova Eboracum."

"You're getting close," said Jenet. "It *is* an island—but one a lot smaller than Valentia."

"Not Bucket Island," said Dârio. "Viridáxés and Zûrafiérix wouldn't tolerate the massive disruption our weddings would cause, especially when they're protecting eggs."

"I wouldn't dream of disturbing Viridáxés and Zûrafiérix," said Jenet. "Try again."

"I've never been there, but it's said to be *very* romantic," said Bonnie. "And a bit damp."

"I remember Damon and Astrí going someplace romantic," said Nûd. "But I don't remember them mentioning an island there."

"What are you talking about?" asked Dârio. "You've all made my head spin."

"Don't *fall* over," teased Jenet.

"The Great Falls," said Dârio after slapping his palm against his forehead. "They're on the border between Tamloch and Dâron."

"Plus, the Inn at the Falls is neutral territory for parties afterward, if it rains," said Jenet.

"Enough wizards will be attending that it won't matter if it rains," said Nûd. "They can take turns creating canopies of solidified sound."

"I could help," said Bonnie.

"Not on your wedding day!" said Jenet.

"Where's this island you're talking about?" asked Nûd.

"Between the curved falls and the straight falls," said Jenet. "We could have the ceremony there, with views of both."

"Sounds like we'll need canopies of solidified sound even if it isn't raining," said Dârio,

"Probably," said Jenet. "But that's just a detail. Do you like the idea of getting married at the Great Falls?"

"I do," said Nûd.

"I do, too," said Bonnie. "I like the idea of getting married somewhere romantic. Can we do it soon?"

"Soon is a relative term," said Jenet. "We can't make it happen in days—but can probably pull everything together in weeks if we keep the guest list down to a few hundred..."

Bonnie gasped. *"A few hundred?"*

"...for each kingdom, plus our allies," Jenet continued. "With luck, we can hold it under a thousand."

Bonnie clutched Nûd's arm and went pale.

Jenet ignored Bonnie's unspoken protestations and turned to Dârio. "Are there any guests you want to make sure are invited?"

"I'm sure you've already identified the people I want to attend," said Dârio. "I'm more concerned about the individuals I *don't* want there."

"Gwýnnett and Túathal's names are definitely *not* on the guest list," said Jenet. "We'll even be posting guards to make sure they don't crash the weddings."

"Valentius marooned Gwýnnett and Túathal—and Hibblig without his magestone—on an isolated and uninhabited island south of Valentia," said Jenet. "It's not likely they'll escape and cause us problems."

"I consulted with Valentius on the choice of island, with advice from Rôlin and Peregrína," said Nûd. "It's mostly just sand, sea turtles, and caimans."

"What are caimans?" asked Dârio.

"Scaly, semi-aquatic lizards with bad tempers and lots of teeth," Nûd responded.

"I guess Gwýnnett will fit right in," said Bonnie. She laughed, then covered her mouth. "I'm sorry, Dârio. I didn't mean to insult your mother."

"Don't worry, he does it all the time," said Jenet. "Just be thankful you won't have her as your mother-in-law."

"Given the miles between here and that caiman island, at least she'll be a *distant* relation," teased Nûd.

"It can't be far enough," said Dârio. "How are they guarded—do you know?"

"I do," said Nûd. "Rōlin told me. Kârkingórēx and Brünedíxés are assigning that job to one of their fellow western dragons on a rotating basis. I think it's considered a punishment detail."

"Rightly so," Dârio replied. "It sounds like matters are in good hands, so back to the wedding planning?"

"Yes," said Janet. "Are we agreed that the island between the straight and curved falls is a suitable venue?"

"Before I agree, what's this island called?" asked Nûd.

"Goat Island," said Bonnie.

"Will we be temporarily relocating its eponymous denizens for the duration of the ceremony?" asked Dârio.

"I love it when you show off your vocabulary," said Jenet. She leaned over and kissed Dârio's cheek. "It proves you were paying attention to our tutors' lessons."

"I was paying attention to your younger sister Linette paying attention to her lessons," teased Dârio. He grinned and kissed her back.

"I suppose I deserved that," said Jenet.

"The kiss, or the teasing?" asked Bonnie.

"Both, I expect," said Jenet. "Don't worry, the goats will be relocated, and the grass will be raked and mowed before things get started."

"I supposed there will be plenty of opportunities to step in it *after* the wedding," said Nûd.

"You've managed to avoid such things so far," said Bonnie. "Keep it up." She copied Jenet and kissed Nûd, but on the lips, not the cheek.

Nûd returned the kiss enthusiastically.

"Keep it up," Dârio repeated, putting a somewhat different emphasis on the words. "There's still time enough before dinner for us to adjourn to our quarters, get cleaned up, and enjoy *other* amusements."

Jenet stood, pulled Dârio to his feet, bent his head down, and kissed him thoroughly. "What sort of amusements did you have in mind, my liege?"

"You're in trouble now, cousin," said Nûd.

"I am indeed, cousin," Dârio replied as he and Jenet walked across the polished wood floor toward the closest exit.

"Shall we see what sort of trouble *we* can get into?" asked Bonnie.

Nûd could see her face was flushed and could sense his was as well.

"Of course," said Nûd. He offered Bonnie his elbow, but she surprised him by tugging him onto her flying disk and sailing down the length of the Great Hall until they reached the royal balcony.

Nûd opened the door to the king's private quarters and welcomed his future queen inside.

Chapter 5

On the Beach

"Here's your magestone," said Celéri as she tossed Umbrose the iron chain and the serrated disk of obsidian hanging from it.

Umbrose nodded to Celéri and slipped the chain over his neck, hiding his magestone in the folds of his wizard's robes.

"See that you don't give me cause to take that from you again," Celéri commanded. "Now, how can we find out where Gwýnnett and Túathal are being held?"

They now sat on crude chairs in a shaded spot under the broad canopy of an ancient juniper a hundred paces away from the pink-sand-covered beach of the Tempest Isles' Great Harbor where seals and sea turtles were basking. It was far more comfortable than the trio's former position on boulders of sharp coral in the hot sun. Umbrose and Sírénae were unbound but uneasy, because Thraxa stood between them, claws out, ready to enforce their good behavior. Farther around the arc of the beach, Mégàrotáxus lay nearly unconscious, still sleeping off the effects of disorientation sickness.

Umbrose put his hand on his chest and felt his magestone for reassurance. "I'm not sure," he said. "Callidus seems to have done a thorough job of identifying my agents among his wizards. He and his minions must have confiscated their magestones and communications rings."

Umbrose is wrong to call them minions, thought Celéri. *We were respected subordinates, not nameless underlings.* "What about your cadres of spy-wizards?" she asked.

"Most left with your uncle's fleet to join us here," said Umbrose. "The others were rounded up by Callidus."

"It's too bad about the ones who were captured," said Celéri. "But it will be good to have more wizards here in the Tempest Isles. Maybe they can help hunt down and capture some of the two-legged local residents I've heard rustling about at night."

"And excellent idea," said Sírénae. "We could use new slaves for quite a few projects. Building us a palace, for example."

"Don't get ahead of yourself," said Celéri. "I'd be happy with a dry hut—or even a cozy cave."

"I'm not fond of caves," said Sírénae.

"That's right," said Celéri. "I'd heard the last cave you'd approached was far from dry." She flashed the other woman a smile and quickly returned her face to a neutral expression while enjoying the mental image she'd constructed of Sírénae, in her golden armor, caught in a huge wave of water streaming out from a cave in Dâron's southern provinces. "I wish I could have been there to see it for myself."

"Just as well you didn't," said Umbrose with a glance at Sírénae. He saw that her face was red and not from the sun.

"Getting back to your intelligence resources..." said Celéri to the spymaster. "Do you have *anyone* available to contact?"

"Not at this point," said Umbrose. He slowly shook his head, then wiped his palms on the gray fabric of his wizard's robe.

"That's unfortunate," said Sírénae. "We need information only spies in Valentia can provide us." The doubly-deposed emperor glanced at Thraxa and extended a hand to stroke the snow-gryffon's feathers but stopped the motion and withdrew it when she saw the predatory look in Thraxa's eyes. Her former pet was hers no longer.

"Do any of the legionnaires have your rings?" asked Celéri, waving her hand to Umbrose.

"They do—or did," Umbrose replied. "None of them have answered my calls."

"Blast!" said Celéri. "Frost and fire! Thunder and lightning!"

"There *are* ways to learn what's happening," said Umbrose.

"We can go there in person and recruit new spies," said Sírénae.

"If so, I have some creative ideas on how to get us there quickly," said Celéri.

"I look forward to hearing them," said Umbrose.

"First, we have to *ad hoc* gate back to Celériopolis Magna," said Celéri.

"You mean Sírénaeopolis Magna," said Sírénae.

"Given our current circumstances," said Umbrose, who waved his arm to take in the empty extent of pink-sand beach before them, "I think Nova Eboracum is more appropriate."

"For now," said Celéri and Sírénae simultaneously.

Umbrose shook his head and didn't bother to hide his amusement. "How will returning to the capital of Occidens Province help us get to Valentia any faster than flying or sailing there directly?" he asked.

"You expect them to have permanent gates to Valentia at the governor-general's palace, don't you?" said Sírénae.

"Correct," said Celéri. "I knew you had to have something inside your skull that did more than hold your ears apart."

"You're too kind, *child*," replied Sírénae. "But we can't just *ad hoc* gate into the palace. The portals to Valentia will be heavily guarded."

"Don't worry, *grandmother*," said Celéri. "I have that figured out. We'll be going in the front gate."

"Grandmother?" said Sírénae. "Why you supercilious, egotistical..."

"Pot. Kettle," said Celéri, cutting her off.

Thraxa squawked and extended a talon toward Sírénae.

"If we could please return to the problem at hand," said Umbrose. "Once we get to Valentia, we still have to gather news and recruit informants."

"That shouldn't be a problem," said Sírénae. "Once we're on Valentia, we can carefully tease out information from legionnaires at taverns," said Sírénae.

"How can there be taverns already?" asked Celéri. "They've barely been on that thrice-blasted island for a fortnight!"

"There are *always* taverns," said Sírénae. "The legions erect them before they put up their tents."

"I suppose you're right about their priorities," said Celéri. "But have you given thought to how we might enter taverns in Valentia and remain undiscovered?"

"The matter never entered the empty space inside my head," said Sírénae, giving Celéri a feral look that rivaled Thraxa's. "I certainly can't," she continued. "My face is far too well known—but you could, and Umbrose is a master of disguise."

"That possibility never entered the empty space inside *my* head," said Celéri. "And I'd never considered using a disguise to get us into the governor-general's palace, either." She glared at Sírénae. "I suppose I could probably manage enough of an illusion to adjust my own appearance—and yours as well—with my feeble abilities."

"Enough. Let's stop shooting verbal crossbow quarrels at each other. It's not productive," said Sírénae. "I'm sure you could disguise us both. You're a very powerful mage."

"Hah!" said Celéri. "I'll stop *quarreling* if you will." She frowned at Sírénae. "However, I must admit that whenever you compliment me my shoulders tense, expecting to feel a blade between them."

"That's sort of thing is Umbrose's style," said Sírénae. "I'm more of a spear under the sternum sort of person."

"You can tell yourself that if you want to," said Umbrose. "But I know better."

"So much for my illusions of your cordial professional relationship," said Celéri.

All three laughed. They were surprised to hear exclamations of a different sort a moment later, however. Down by the waterline, a dozen seals began to bark and waddle frantically toward Sírénae, Umbrose, and Celéri, followed and then passed by sea turtles who were making surprising speed away from the beach.

"What's gotten into them?" asked Sírénae.

"I suppose we'll find out soon enough," said Umbrose.

Thraxa squawked and moved her attention back and forth between Celéri and the water. The young wizard stroked Thraxa's feathers and focused her attention on the shore where a large ripple indicated a massive creature was approaching beneath the surface.

"Umbrose. Shields!" Celéri shouted. The spymaster followed her instructions as Celéri stepped onto her flying disk and rose thirty feet to have a better view of whatever was coming. She didn't have long to wait.

A massive wedge-shaped head first emerged from the water, followed by a long, thick neck and the powerful shoulders of some unusual sort of dragon. The beast snapped at the fleeing seals and caught an unlucky one in its toothy jaws. The other seals and turtles sought shelter behind the shields Umbrose had raised as the giant creature brought more of its bulk up onto the beach.

The strange new dragon emerging from the Ocean differed in several ways from dragons Celéri knew, like Mégàrotáxus. Larger even than Xaxidiánus, it was colored like a sea wolf, with a black back and white belly. Its wings were quite small, like elongated flippers, and it had a dragon's typical row of bony plates sticking out at angles along its neck instead of a sea wolf's tall dorsal fin. It's limbs were a dragon's legs, but instead of terminating in claws and talons like an eagle's, this creature had webbing between its claws.

The most striking difference between the creature and a typical dragon, however, was its tail. Where most dragons have tapering, pointed tails, this one's tail stayed broad for most of its length and featured horizontal flukes like a whale's.

"What *is* that thing?" asked Sírénae.

"I don't know, but I'm calling it a whale dragon," Celéri called down.

"That seems appropriate," said Umbrose. "I never saw an illustration of anything remotely like it in Robin Goodfellow's *Peregrinations.*"

"I have another suggestion," said Sírénae.

Celéri arched one eyebrow. "Do tell," she said.

"Leviathan," said Sírénae.

Celéri clapped her hands. "That's a much better name."

Sírénae lowered her head then raised it, acknowledging the compliment. "Seadragon might work as well."

Celéri nodded. "That's good, too."

The three of them couldn't look away from the sight of the leviathan stretching its toothy jaws around the seal. It then lifted its head, and they watched the body of the seal slide down the creature's thick neck. It made a noticeable bulge, like a rat being digested by a snake.

Thraxa was screeching and flapping her wings. Before Celéri could countermand the movement—*if* she could countermand it—the snow gryffon launched herself toward the leviathan with her claws out to attack. Like a mongoose the size of a mouse attacking a cobra, Thraxa was drastically outweighed by her opponent, but made up for that disadvantage with ferocity. She focused the swipes from her sharp claws and pecks from her hooked, pointed beak on the leviathan's vulnerable eyes.

The beast swung its head from side to side, trying to avoid Thraxa's strikes, but the snow gryffon was highly maneuverable in the air and the leviathan wasn't moving at its top speed with a seal in its gullet. One of the creature's frantic movements ended with its snout smacking the bottom of Celéri's flying disk, sending the young wizard sailing off it and toward the trees up from the beach.

Celéri quickly threw up a spherical shield to minimize the shock of impact with the ground but was pleased to see Magister Umbrose intercepting her fall and lowering her gently to the sand with constructs of solidified sound.

Thraxa, meanwhile, was proving to be such a challenge for the leviathan that the creature retreated and slid back into the water of the Great Harbor with a tremendous splash. The snow gryffon screamed in triumph and flew down to join Umbrose, Sírénae, and Celéri by the ancient juniper.

"That was exciting," said Celéri. "Thanks for the assist, 'Brose!"

The spymaster barely hid a wince from Celéri's shortened form of address. "It's what partners do," he replied.

"Thraxa kept things from being even more exciting," said Sírénae.

The snow gryffon was crowded against Celéri, rubbing her beak against the young wizard's torso and accepting Celéri's hands stroking gratefully on her fur and feathers.

"What happened to those seals and turtles?" asked Celéri. "I want to give Thraxa a treat for her noble defense. Weren't they right behind your shields, Umbrose? Where did they go?"

Umbrose didn't answer and turned to stare into the shadows of the forest.

"They did not go back to the water," Sírénae asserted. "I was watching the beach."

"Perhaps the seals and turtles were taken by the locals," said Umbrose after returning his attention to the others. "If the leviathan visits this beach frequently, it may be a common hunting strategy."

"It might be at that," said Celéri. "I still need a treat for Thraxa. Could you find me a good-sized fish, please, Umbrose?"

"Gladly," said the spymaster. He rose on his own flying disk, floated fifty feet—out of leviathan range, he hoped—over the surface of the Great Harbor. Umbrose then generated a net of solidified sound that he dropped into the water, pulling it up a few seconds later with several large fish in its mesh. After he delivered his catch to Thraxa, Celéri thanked him again.

"I really appreciate your help," Celéri said. "In more ways than one."

"How so?" asked Umbrose.

"I think I know," said Sírénae. "It has to do with how long our conversation lasted."

"Correct," said Celéri. "After we'd finished talking, I'd planned to go swimming."

Chapter 6

The Dough-Ring Man

Eynon and Merry stood on the back porch of Travelers' Rest, avoiding the cold rain coming down hard, like thousands of sharp, insistent needles. With a gentle motion, Eynon shifted Chee's front paws off his eyebrows. "Shall I *ad hoc* gate us directly to Laetícia's tower?" he asked Merry.

"No," Merry replied. "I don't know your plan, but we don't want to just show up on her doorstep unannounced. That would be rude. Remember, I want her to teach me how to be a spymaster someday."

"I could gate us directly into Laetícia's office, if you think that would impress her?" said Eynon.

"Don't be ridiculous," said Merry. "That would demonstrate *your* talents, not mine." She reached down to rub Ace's ears and the rockhound reacted by starting to shake off the water his fur had collected. Merry quickly surrounded Ace in a bubble of solidified sound and watched the rockhound's puzzled expression as a high percentage of the water droplets he'd tried to lose immediately returned.

"Let me help," said Eynon. He moved Ace off the porch on a long finger of solidified sound then generated a much larger bubble around him. Merry dispelled her bubble and both humans were amused as Ace shook more energetically than Rowsch, Doethan's giant hound familiar, coating the interior of the large bubble with muddy liquid.

"Thank you," said Merry. "But I could have handled it. Can you *ad hoc* gate us somewhere in or near Nova Eboracum, but *not* Laetícia's tower?"

"Of course," said Eynon. "Would you prefer the amphitheater where we interrupted that play rehearsal, the island in the harbor holding the New Colossus statue, or somewhere else?"

"Can you gate us in a few hundred yards in the air above the city?" asked Merry. "There's a person I want to talk to—if I can find them. And I'd also like to pick up something to bring to Laetícia."

"I'd be glad to—but do we even know if Laetícia is even in the city?" asked Eynon. "With her children in Valentia, she could be anywhere."

"That's another good reason to ask a few questions before simply popping into her office," said Merry.

"I think you have an ulterior motive to visit the province's capital," said Eynon.

"I... might," said Merry, smiling at one of the reasons for her interest in their new destination.

"You want more of those dough rings, don't you?" said Eynon. "You kept raving about them and once I tried them at the party after the treaty signing, I could see why."

Eynon watched Merry run her tongue around her lips. She seemed to be indulging memories that were more gustatory than amatory. "Well..." she said.

"We'll find you dough rings then," said Eynon. "Once that desire is satisfied, maybe you'll tell me why we need to talk to Laetícia."

* * * * *

Looking down from the high vantage where they'd gated in, Merry and Eynon were both impressed by the number of people bustling about on the streets of Nova Eboracum. After months in caverns and days in the West before the invaders' threat was defused, seeing so many people at once took getting used to. Of course, the capital of Occidens Province was two or three times larger than Brendinas and hundreds of times more densely populated than the Coombe or the Rhuthro Valley, so it was understandable the two of them would be taken aback by the crowds.

Massive, thick-walled apartment buildings, some five or six stories tall, lined many of the city's broad boulevards. Awnings extended out from ground-level openings in the buildings' walls, shading shops for diverse merchants selling clothing, leather goods, perfumes, jewelry, and more.

Half the shops sold food or wine or both, and many offered the sour-smelling sorghum beer popular with legionnaires from the native land of Quintillius along the upper Nile. Hundreds of people, channeled by the buildings, swarmed along, shopping, chatting, or just moving purposely from one place to another.

"They look like ants," announced Eynon.

"They *are* ants," said Merry. "Dispel your distance-viewing lenses and look again."

"Sorry," said Eynon. "Do you see what you're looking for?" he asked after following Merry's recommendation.

"I see *who* I'm looking for," Merry answered. She grabbed Eynon's upper arm and line-of-sight gated them both to an intersection next to a familiar man selling three varieties of dough rings from long poles. His eyes went wide when he saw Merry and Eynon seem to materialize out of empty air, then his mouth turned up in a broad smile.

"I remember you, young wizard," said the man. "You liked my brother-in-law's cooking."

"I like your dough rings even more," said Merry.

"That's good to hear," said the man. He adjusted his poles to keep his stock in balance. "Who's your friend?"

"This is Eynon," said Merry. "He's a wizard, too."

"I gathered as much from his robes," said the dough-ring vendor. His smile grew even broader in welcome, then his expression turned to puzzlement as he noticed the wizards' two familiars.

As if unaware of the merchant's attention, Chee climbed down from Eynon's shoulder, intent on stealing a dough ring. Eynon intercepted him and chided him by wagging a stern finger. The raconette, chastised but unrepentant, jumped from the cobbled street back to Eynon's shoulder and from there to the top of a sign for a shop selling meat pies.

Chee decided to use his new perch to watch the humans' comings and goings, ever alert for opportunities to snag snacks. Ace shifted to his flying form and launched himself up from Merry's side in search of prey—probably pigeons—in the concrete cliffs above them.

The dough-ring man followed the movements of the two unusual familiars with interest, but once they'd left his proximity, he returned his attention to the two wizards. "Would you like some of my wares, my friends? I now have poppy-seed dough rings along with plain and sesame."

"I'd like a dozen of whichever variety Laetícia and Quintillius favor," said Merry.

"That's not as simple a matter as one might hope," said the dough-ring man. "The usual order from the palace is eight plain and four sesame. I add an extra plain since nine is much easier to divide by three than eight, so my assumption is our Governor-General and our Master Mage prefer sesame."

"I'll take a dozen sesame then," said Merry.

"None for the little ones?" asked the dough-ring man.

"They're in Valentia," said Eynon.

"Interesting," said the man. "Once the gates there are open for travelers, I might want to spend the winter there if it's as warm as I've heard."

"It's quite warm," said Eynon. "If you made dough rings there, I'm sure you'd soon have loyal customers."

"I'll take it under advisement," the man replied.

"Where *are* the gates to Valentia?" asked Merry.

"Sure knowledge of such information is not given to a poor purveyor of street food such as myself," said the dough-ring man.

"But..." said Merry.

"If I *were* to venture a guess from what words pass by my corner, I would say they are in a garden inside the palace walls, along with the gates across the Ocean," said the man. "Not that I ever thought I'd live long enough to witness such marvels."

"Thank you," said Merry. "May you continue to enjoy a long and well-informed life."

"Thank *you*, young wizard," said the dough-ring man.

"You're so well informed you'd do well as an agent in Laetícia's network," offered Eynon.

The man leaned one of his poles against his shoulder long enough to place a finger alongside his nose for a moment. "That's kind of you to say," said the man, "but so unlikely it doesn't bear repeating."

Eynon narrowed his brows and looked at Merry. He was about to speak but closed his mouth when Merry's elbow poked him in the ribs. "Is Laetícia currently in her tower?" she asked.

"From what I've observed of the attitude of the legionnaires guarding the palace gate, I'd say both Laetícia and Quintillius are in residence," said the dough-ring man. "There's a lot to be done to undo the harm done to the city and province by the invaders."

"Very true," said Merry. "It sounds like I'll need to buy out your entire stock of dough rings. Let's have a baker's dozen of sesame for the Governor-General and Master Mage, an assorted dozen for the gate guards, and the rest for Távi's contingent of enterprising urchins."

"I'll see to it," said the dough-ring man.

"And my associates and I will be glad to assist," said Távi who seemed to pop out of the crowd of passing pedestrians to occupy a spot at the merchant's right elbow. A dozen children of indeterminate ages and genders surrounded the dough-ring man and began to transfer dough rings from poles to loosely knit mesh bags removed from the man's belt. All had big smiles in dirty faces, though their hands were clean. They worked quickly and efficiently, so less than a minute later Merry and Eynon each held a bag of dough rings and the remaining dough rings were nowhere to be seen.

The urchins then disappeared into the flow of bodies nearby until only the memory of their smiles remained. Before Távi could do likewise, Merry put her hand on the youth's shoulder.

"What do you hear from inside the palace?" she asked. "We're especially interested in news concerning the whereabouts of Celéri, Umbrose, and Sírénae."

"You'd learn more if you asked me about Thraxa," Távi replied.

"Sírénae's snow-gryffon?" asked Eynon.

"Aye," said Távi. "The emperor and Umbrose were going to use the bloodthirsty beast against Celéri, but once their eyes met Thraxa became Celéri's familiar. She turned the tables on the two of them and took Umbrose's magestone."

"I would have enjoyed seeing *that,*" said Merry.

"I did," said Távi. "It was hard to tell who to root for in the struggle."

"I wouldn't have been cheering on any of them," said Eynon. "But I suppose I'm pleased Celéri wasn't tortured. Did she gate out with Thraxa and the others?"

"They were there, then they weren't, if that answers your question," said Távi.

"I suppose it does," said Merry. "Did she happen to mention where they were going?"

"No," said Távi. "That surprised me, because Celéri loves the sound of her own voice."

"We'd noticed," said Eynon. He grinned at Merry, and she linked her arm in his, remembering their previous encounter with Celéri at Applegarth.

"If you're interested in learning more about where they might have gone, you should ask me about what my mates heard down by the docks," said Távi.

"What did they hear down by the docks?" interjected the dough-ring man to hurry things along.

"The invading sailors said they were going back to the last place they'd been," said Távi.

"Really?" mused Merry. "I wonder where that might be? Nárbo across the Ocean, perhaps?"

"I don't think so," said Eynon.

"One of my youngest associates heard something odd that might be of use to you," said Távi. "It made no sense to her."

"What was that?" asked Merry.

"Two sailors were complaining about having to cross the stream," Távi answered. "It seemed strange, since they were about to sail the Ocean."

"We have friends who might understand it," said Eynon.

"Please tell me what it is when you find out," said Távi. "The little ones are asking me about it constantly."

"Are we there yet?" said Merry.

"What?" asked Távi.

"I was just remembering who I used to annoy my father when we traveled down the Rhuthro to Tyford," said Merry. "I'm surprised he didn't throw me overboard. Don't worry, we'll tell you once we have an answer for you and your little ones."

"Thank you," said Távi. "Now look at that falcon!" Távi pointed at the top of a nearby apartment building.

When Eynon, Merry, and the dough-ring man looked back after realizing Távi had distracted them, the clever youth was gone.

"Thank you again for the dough rings," said Merry.

"Yes, thanks so much," said Eynon. He looked at the mesh bag he held and realized, too late, that he and Merry hadn't specified reserving any dough-rings for themselves.

The dough-ring man tapped the toe of his booted foot on the cobbles and cleared his throat.

"What is it?" asked Merry.

"There remains the matter of payment for my entire stock," said the dough-ring man. "Last time, you and that older wizard—Doethan, I think his name was—paid with magic."

"I remember," said Merry. "My palm had a circular burn from the coin I'd enchanted to keep things cold for you."

"I'm sorry, good wizard," said the merchant. "My brother-in-law has said he'd love to have some heat magic to help him cook if I ever ran into you again—and here you are."

"Heat is more your department," Merry told Eynon. "Please make him a cook stone."

Eynon looked around for something suitable to work with and noticed a broad cobblestone that stuck up two inches higher than its neighbors. He used a plane of solidified sound to shave off the top of the stone, leaving it level with the street, then willed heat into the slice of cobble with his red magestone.

Concentrating, as if pulling something from his memory, Eynon bound four phrases to it, leaving it cool to the touch. "Here's a cook stone for your brother-in-law," Eynon informed the dough-ring man. "The *Stone Hottest* command should help him quick-fry meats and vegetables for the busiest times at his dining establishment and the *Stone Hot* level will keep soups and stews simmering."

"Once again I'm in your debt," said the dough-ring man. "Please come by my brother-in-law's taverna for a complimentary meal whenever you're in Nova Eboracum."

"Thank you," said Merry. "I remember how good everything tasted. Unfortunately, we can't stop by now. We have places to be."

"Safe travels," said the dough-ring man. He consolidated his now empty poles and dipped them like spears to salute Merry and Eynon.

Merry nodded and looked overhead at the artificial cliffs formed by the tall apartment buildings. "Ace!" she shouted. "Time to go!"

The rockhound emerged from shadows high above and circled down to assume his usual position beside Merry. A few feathers were stuck to his fur.

Chee jumped from the meat pie shop's sign back to Eynon's shoulder, munching on an apple.

"Where did you find that?" asked Eynon.

"He didn't steal it, if that's what worries you," said the dough-ring man. "One of Távi's urchins tossed it to him."

"Good," said Eynon. To himself he muttered, "I hope the urchin didn't steal it."

Merry turned to Eynon. "Now that we're all back together, let's get on with our mission. Snap to it and *ad hoc* gate us to Laetícia's tower."

"No," said Eynon.

"What do you mean, *no?*" asked Merry.

"You've forgotten we have to *walk* to the palace," said Eynon. He held up his mesh bag. "I have dough rings to deliver to the gate guards."

Chapter 7

Laetícia and Tembóku

Laetícia smiled when she saw the face appearing in the circle of the communication ring linked to her old mentor in magic across the Ocean. Her smile didn't last long.

"I have bad news," said Tembóku, the gray-haired Southern Empire wizard.

Behind her old friend Laetícia could see familiar books and potions on shelves in Tembóku's study. It gave her comfort to know some things atop a slender tower in the Southern Imperial capital of Alexandria had not changed.

"Worse than what we've already endured?" Laetícia asked. She peered into the communication ring's shimmering interface, which sparkled with interference. The ring's magic was challenged by working over a third of the circumference of the globe.

"Probably not," Tembóku admitted. "But it's a different sort of challenge."

Laetícia sighed. "Tell me, 'Bóku. I'm ready to listen."

"You remember Gertrude of Mainz, the governor of the Rhineland?" said Tembóku.

"An ambitious woman, protege of Sírénae and the Northern Emperor, Flavia Drusila," said Laetícia. "Valentius warned me about her."

"With good reason," said Tembóku. "Everything I'm about to tell you is happening against the backdrop of imperial politics."

"That's a given," said Laetícia. "I'd thought we were mostly free of such intrigues here until Sírénae arrived, but Quintillius and I knew we were only fooling ourselves."

"Your talents are clearly wasted on that distant frontier posting," said Tembóku. "Unfortunately, my news will require you to fully exercise of those talents."

"Against Gertrude of Mainz?" asked Laetícia. "That shouldn't be a challenge. She's no Sírénae, or Flavia for that matter."

"In this case, she might as well *be* Flavia," said Tembóku. "You probably heard from Valentius that Flavia wants Gertrude named as the new Emperor of the West in return for *her* support of Valentius taking over his father's imperial seat?"

"Yes," said Laetícia. "But since Valentius has promised to lead the legions in Valentia for five years instead of immediately stepping into his father's boots, I'd thought that would have defanged Flavia's venomous scheming."

"It did the opposite," said Tembóku. "Flavia is determined to twist enough togas to win Gertrude the purple by any means necessary. Once Gertrude is Emperor of the West, she and Gertrude will work as a block to thwart any attempt by Valens in the South and Phraátēs in the East to support Valentius. If the two outcomes don't happen at the same time, Valens will never be Emperor of the South."

"I have confidence in Valens and Phraátēs," said Laetícia. "They'll find a way to thwart Flavia and her puppet."

"They think they have," said Tembóku. "But the solution is complicated—and requires sacrifice."

"Citizens of the Imperium aren't strangers to sacrifice," said Laetícia. "The situation is unfortunate, but how does it affect us here on the other side of the Ocean? Flavia's arm would have to be long indeed to threaten us here."

"Flavia plans to wield the long arm of imperial duty," said Tembóku. "Valentius is defenseless against his own nobility."

"Has Flavia taken hostages on the Isles of Dogs then?" asked Laetícia. "Is she threatening members of Aleña's family?"

"Nothing so crude—or on so small a scale," said Tembóku. "Gertrude is holding the reins of imperial power in the West on an interim basis, pending her confirmation by the First Citizen and the other three emperors."

"Of course," said Laetícia. "But her interim appointment is only valid for half a year, or until a suitable new candidate is chosen."

"True," said Tembóku. "We have other candidates to offer as Western Emperor, but the promise Valentius made to the legions now under his command allows Flavia and Gertrude to manipulate Valentius *and* his father."

"I don't understand," said Laetícia.

"Gertrude wants her legions back," said Tembóku.

For a moment, Laetícia was uncharacteristically speechless. Her eyes shifted left and right while her mind raced along countless paths without reaching a firm destination. She pressed her lips together and shook her head. The clack of the beads woven into her braids was reassuring. After a pair of deep breaths, she spoke. "Now that Valentius has accepted them back into imperial service, that is her right."

"Yes," said Tembóku.

"And Gertrude, at Flavia's urging, can use the promise Valentius gave his legions to prevent him from succeeding his father *unless* Valens and Phraátēs support her as emperor," said Laetícia. "Valens can keep his promise if he's immediately made Southern Emperor by transferring those legions to his command there, but only after promising Gertrude and Flavia major concessions to allow it."

"You've got most of it," said Tembóku.

"Most?" asked Laetícia. "What more is there? This is a disaster! Flavia will become in fact what Sírénae was exiled to prevent—a person in control of half the Imperium."

"I told you Valens and Phraátēs had a solution," said Tembóku.

"What is it?" asked Laetícia. "I can't see how to avoid Gertrude as Western Emperor."

"Valens and Phraátēs think another, highly respected candidate for the job—someone with an exemplary career as a provincial governor, previous experience working in the Western Empire, and an outstanding military record would be far more acceptable to the First Citizen than Gertrude of Mainz," said Tembóku. "Her accomplishments to date have been, shall we say, uninspiring. Without pressure from Flavia..."

"She'd be an unlikely candidate," said Laetícia. "I see what you mean, but I don't know anyone on the other side of the Ocean who comes close to being the paragon of Roma virtues you describe."

"Keep thinking," said Tembóku. "The individual Valens and Phraátēs want to put forward has a nimble mind, willing to seek alliances. He's also a devoted family man, with three young children."

Laetícia's mouth fell open. She closed it and pressed her lips to a thin line. "No," she said. "It won't work. He and Valentius are distant cousins. I'm Valens' niece. It would be as bad as Flavia controlling Gertrude."

"No, it won't," said Tembóku. "As you said, he's a *distant* cousin. He's still better than Gertrude by five days of forced marches. The First Citizen knows that—and he's the deciding vote."

"What about balancing men and women in control of the Imperium?" asked Laetícia. "This would be four men to one woman."

Tembóku laughed. "As if anyone expects him to rule on his own without you beside him. That's part of what will sell the plan. Not every man has such a skilled woman and wizard as a partner."

"But we'd have to move to Nárbo!" Laetícia protested.

"The lavender fields are lovely in the spring," teased Tembóku. "And with the new gates across the Ocean, you could still visit Occidens Province and support this Orluin Alliance you've somehow stitched together."

"I didn't..." Laetícia began. "I mean I helped, but..."

"Victory has many parents," said Tembóku.

"Failure but one, I know," said Laetícia. "But our work here isn't done yet. We haven't found Sírénae or Umbrose or Celéri. They're Roma. I feel like they're my responsibility."

"I think you'll find your alliance partners quite capable of dealing with that unpleasant trio," said Tembóku. "And don't worry— when it comes to choosing a new emperor, deliberations more closely resemble a Tortoise than a Hare."

Laetícia sighed. "When we first arrived in Occidens Province I dreamed about such things—then imperial power seemed to lose its attraction as we settled into our new lives."

"That's part of what will make you two better for the job," said Tembóku. "The First Citizen remembers the lessons taught at the School of Good Governance about selecting people for leadership roles who are too eager to seek them."

"I know," said Laetícia. "You're right. I just don't know how I'm going to break it to Quintillius. We've been so happy here."

"I wouldn't worry about your husband's reaction," said Tembóku. "But I'd definitely wait before informing your children."

Chapter 8

The Governor-General's Palace

Eynon and Merry smiled when they saw the guards standing on alert at the main gate to the Governor-General's palace. The two young wizards had walked the few blocks from the intersection where they'd met the dough-ring man to the gate in the palace's well-engineered stone walls. Chee was still on Eynon's shoulder and Ace, in his dog form, was beside Merry, without any telltale feathers stuck to his fur.

"Hail and good greetings, Antica!" said Merry. "It's good to see you again. I'm afraid I don't have an entry token."

"Nice to see you again," said the senior guard, a veteran legionnaire with a lined face and bright eyes. Two younger guards stood nearby. One, a tall man with a wary expression, moved a few steps back and stood at stiff attention, pointedly not looking at the new arrivals.

"We brought you something," said Eynon as he held out the mesh bag with the dough rings. "I hope you like them on your breaks, even if you can't eat them on duty."

"Are you trying to bribe a Roma gate guard?" asked Antica. She lowered her chin a few degrees and gave Eynon a stern look.

"Just trying to do something nice for our friends," Eynon replied.

Antica took the dough rings from Eynon and turned to the two younger guards. "What do you think?" she asked. "Do these look like a bribe to you, Propitia? And what about you, Stultio? Should I confiscate them and toss this pair in the dungeons for trying to corrupt Roma legionnaires?"

The young woman pulled her shoulders back, making the plates of her lorica clank. "I think we'll have to thoroughly inspect their offering," Propitia replied. "Perhaps with butter—or with soft cheese to spread on them. That's the only way we can properly evaluate their potential crime."

Merry grinned at Propitia. "I think you'll find them quite satisfactory—they're fresh from the dough-ring man himself."

"I knew we should have picked up some soft cheese," said Eynon, as much to himself as to anyone else. He was remembering the fun of making soft cheese back on the village dairy farm in Haywall, including boiling milk, adding vinegar, stirring until the curds separated, then straining the curds and stirring them more until the cheese was smooth.

Merry noticed Eynon wasn't paying attention any longer and nudged him in time for him to see Propitia nod, confirming his statement.

The young legionnaire leaned over and inhaled the aroma of the dough rings her senior officer was holding. "Soft cheese would have been quite nice, but I can pick some up when our shift is over," Propitia noted. "In the meantime, I think we can let them pass with a stern warning, if you agree," she said, offering a small bow to Antica.

"I do," Antica replied. "You're shaping up to be a fine guard, Propitia—and demonstrating excellent judgment—but please get butter as well as soft cheese."

Propitia made a fist with her right hand and brought it to her sternum with a snap, causing Antica to almost show a smile. "Always glad to butter you up," she added, thereby changing Antica's potential smile into a real one.

Merry shifted her attention to the other young guard who was only a few inches shorter than Quintillius. "You're Stultio?"

The guard nodded slowly, remaining at attention.

"Doethan told me about you," Merry continued. "You're looking remarkably fit. Running ten times around the city must have been good for you."

Stultio's dark face suddenly turned a few shades darker. "It's not something I'd like to repeat, good wizard," he said softly.

"I expect so," said Merry.

"I think Stultio has learned the importance of being polite to visitors," said Antica.

Stultio tapped the butt of his long pilum against the cobblestones to confirm the truth of his superior's words.

Eynon moved his hands to his chest, catching Stultio's eye. "Hard-won lessons can be the best teachers," he said, earning half a smile from the young legionnaire.

"Is Laetícia in her tower?" asked Merry. "We didn't contact her ahead of time and aren't sure."

"I believe so, good wizard," said Antica. "She and the Governor-General were in the gardens inspecting the new gates a few hours ago."

"Excellent," said Merry. "We just came from Valentia and saw their children. They were visiting with Aleña and Valentius."

"I'm sure their behavior was exemplary," said Antica.

Eynon laughed, then covered his mouth.

"Pay close attention to your senior officer, legionnaires," said Merry to Propitia and Stultio. "Keeping a straight face while stretching the truth is an important skill to master."

"We'll bear that in mind, won't we Stultio?" said Propitia.

Stultio's eyes rolled up to examine the sky before returning to stare at a nearby wall.

"Be back in a minute," said Eynon. He created an *ad hoc* gate and he and Chee disappeared with a small *pop*.

Merry turned her head, considering the various places he might have gone. She made a bet with herself about what he'd be carrying when he returned.

"Does he do that often?" asked Antica. Her eyes narrowed as she looked at the place where Eynon had been standing.

"What? Disappear?" Merry replied. "Not that often, or at least not without taking me with him."

"It must be amazing to gate anywhere you want to," said Propitia. "I want to see Roma Mater and visit the wonders of the world."

"Join the legion, see the world," muttered Stultio.

"What was that?" asked Antica.

"Nothing," Stultio answered.

"Being able to *ad hoc* gate can be disconcerting at times," said Merry. "I can only line-of-sight gate."

"What's that?" asked Stultio, who had suddenly forgotten to remain silent.

"This," said Merry. She was suddenly behind Antica, waving her arms, then back where she'd been standing.

"Can you gate wherever you want?" asked Stultio.

Before Merry could answer, Antica said, "I expect she can only gate to somewhere she can see..."

"Which is why she called it line-of-sight gating, not gating wherever you want," teased Propitia.

Stultio clamped his lips together and tried to stand as straight and unmoving as his pilum.

Before any of them could take another breath, Eynon reappeared.

Chee announced his reappearance with a loud, "Chee chee chee *chee!*" and Ace barked.

Merry smiled to herself—Eynon was holding two small crocks, as she'd expected.

"Butter and soft cheese from the Coombe?" she asked.

"From Haywall's dairy," Eynon replied. "Now you won't have to take time out from your day to get some." He handed the crocks to Propitia.

Merry took a thin copper coin bearing the image of King Dârio from her belt pouch and concentrated for a few moments, binding it to the cold of the far north with a small congruency. She flipped the coin to Stultio, who quickly shifted from his rigid posture to catch it before it could fall to the cobbles. "That should keep the crocks cold," she said. "It should also help you all have cold water to drink in the future."

"You're very kind, good wizards," said Antica. "We all thank you for your generosity."

Propitia and Stultio nodded their agreement, though Stultio was trying to figure out how to transfer the cold copper coin to his other hand without losing control of his pilum before it froze to his palm.

"Would you like me to send word of your arrival to Laetícia and her security team?" asked Antica, remembering her role as senior gate guard.

"That would be appreciated," said Eynon. "We'll walk to the base of her tower through the gardens. I want to see the fixed gate across the Ocean."

"It's not much to look at," said Antica.

"Many wondrous things are not," said Eynon.

"True enough," said Merry. She waved toward Eynon. "For example, who'd ever believe an unassuming young man like my companion was the master mage of Dâron?"

"I would," said Antica. "I was at the ceremony where the Orluin Alliance treaty was signed."

Eynon shifted from foot to foot. Merry noticed his discomfort with her praise, and Antica's acknowledgment of Eynon's title.

"Which way is the gate across the Ocean?" she asked.

Antica indicated a direction with the point of her pilum. "It's on the right, near the back of the gardens," she said. "You can't miss it—there are three wizards and a dozen legionnaires guarding it."

"I can't bribe them with these," said Eynon, patting the second mesh bag of dough rings on his belt. "They're for Quintillius and Laetícia."

"We'd best be on our way," said Merry. She took Eynon's elbow and tugged him toward the Governor-General's palace gardens.

When they were two-hundred steps away from the three guards, Eynon leaned down and fiercely whispered in Merry's ear. *"Now* will you tell me why we have to talk to Laetícia?"

Chapter 9

Caiman Island

"I'm tired of turtle meat," said Gwýnnett, shaking Hibblig's shoulder and distracting him from his inspection of the sand, stones, and shells on the beach. "Catch me a fish," she ordered.

"Catch your own fish," Hibblig replied. "I'm busy."

Túathal was seated on a rock nearby, working on the carapace of a dead horseshoe crab with a clamshell. He glared at Gwýnnett and gave the carapace a sharp blow before giving his own response to her order. "Yes, why don't you wade out and catch your own dinner?" he asked. "Better yet, *be* dinner for one of those caimans pretending to be logs on the far side of the cove."

Hibblig looked up and frowned at Gwýnnett. "The sharks are hungry, too," he said. "We don't have a boat and I'm not interested in going for a swim and trying to spear a fish, though you're welcome to." He shook his head and made a face like he'd just bitten into a crabapple. "Be thankful you've got sea turtle meat, *princess*. At least they move themselves out of the water and we can cook them in their own shells."

"Not that you've done any of the cooking since we were exiled, Your Highness," added Túathal.

"I've never cooked anything in my life," Gwýnnett protested.

"Except for cooking up potions and poisons," said Túathal.

"Well..." Gwýnnett began.

Hibblig cut her off. "Perhaps it's best if she *doesn't* do any cooking."

"Agreed," Túathal replied.

Hibblig smiled to himself, appreciating that the former king of Tamloch had stopped speaking in rhymes once Gwýnnett's assorted elixirs were no longer in his system. A few weeks of sun, fresh air, and exercise appeared to have done Túathal's mental health quite a bit of good as well. The ex-monarch's delusions hadn't been in evidence for several days now. As if to prove his improved status, Túathal asked a sensible question.

"Are you looking for something to supplement tonight's turtle stew?" the former king asked the mage without a magestone.

"No," answered Hibblig. "At least not intentionally, though if I find anything edible, we can certainly toss it in the shell-pot."

"What about my fish?" said Gwýnnett.

"I thought we'd already covered that," said Túathal. "Go set a snare for one of those tailless beavers we've seen inland or bash one of those big blue lizards, why don't you?"

Hibblig, pleased to have recovered his will after Gwýnnett's potions had left *his* system, offered suggestions of his own. "Look for ripe fruits, or birds' eggs—and if you must have fish, make a pole and see what you can catch from the edge of the cove. There are hooks and spools of fishing line in the supplies Nûd and Dârio left for us."

"Couldn't one of you do it for me?" asked Gwýnnett.

"Do it yourself," said Hibblig as he picked up a small object from the beach, held it to his eye, then shook his head in disgust and tossed it into the water.

"You'll have to start carrying your share of the load," said Túathal. "I'm tired of you claiming a privileged status because you're a princess. I'm a king, after all, and I'm not shirking."

Gwýnnett leaned forward and tried to make her voice sound husky. "I thought I'd do my part after dark."

Túathal shook his head in disgust. "Once was enough," he said. "For that matter, given how things turned out, once was probably one time too many."

Hibblig snorted. "I may change my mind later, but for now I'd rather share a bed with one of those toothed logs than sleep with you, princess. I prefer to control my own mind instead of being a prisoner to your potions."

"Be that way," said Gwýnnett. "I'll go look for edible plants." She turned her back on the two men and marched off toward a thick stand of trees a quarter mile inland from the shore.

When Gwýnnett was too far away to overhear, Túathal spoke to Hibblig. "Do you think we need to worry about her finding something she can use for one of her potions?"

"Yes," said Hibblig, "but I don't think she'll kill us immediately—we're too useful for that. We'll have some time, I think. I expect it will take her quite a while to identify the properties of the local plants and compound a potion to make us suggestible."

"I'll watch your back if you'll watch mine," said Túathal.

"That would be wise," said Hibblig. "If I thought it was practical, I'd tie her to a tree at night so she doesn't slit our throats for some imagined insult."

"I thought you felt we were too useful to her for Gwýnnett to take such drastic action..." said Túathal.

Hibblig bent down and picked up something else that caught his eye—a shiny pebble peeking out of the sand. "Do you want to bet your life on that?" he asked.

"I see your point," said Túathal. The deposed king finished worrying the tail spike off the horseshoe crab and tested the tip with his thumb.

"That looks useful," said Hibblig. "A proper poniard, if you add a handle. I'll have to find a crab and get one for myself."

"Don't bother," said Túathal, kicking a second dead crab at his feet. "I'll work yours free next. You can add the handles."

"Why are you doing something nice for me?" asked Hibblig. "It makes me nervous."

"Reluctant allies are allies nonetheless," said Túathal. "Dârio—my *son*—told us there aren't any dangerous land animals here, if we stay out of the way of the caimans, but I'd feel more secure if we were both armed."

"Gwýnnett is a dangerous animal," said Hibblig. "All three of us are dangerous, for that matter. Why would you want to make *me* more so?"

"Because unlike Gwýnnett, I know that a wizard without a magestone can become a wizard again with a new one," said Túathal. He waved the spike toward the pebble Hibblig was inspecting. "Did you find something?"

"I think so, yes," Hibblig replied. He stepped close to show Túathal what he held. The pebble looked melted, like the obsidian the Roma wizards preferred for their magestones, but instead of being black, this bit of stone held a rainbow of reflective colors. "I saw a stone like this in a wizard's collection at the Valley of Towers. She told me it had been formed when a great rock from the sky came crashing down in far ancient days."

"Will it do?" asked Túathal.

"I think so," said Hibblig. "The wizard who had one was right. I can sense this stone was formed by tremendous energies and I'm sure I can craft a setting for it and bind with it."

"How can I help?" asked Túathal.

Hibblig rubbed his chin with one hand while holding the sparkling pebble up to his eye with the other. "Distract Gwýnnett," he answered. "Preparing a new magestone and crafting a setting are challenging tasks that require intense focus. Gwýnnett is like a thoughtless cat—she could easily jostle my elbow at the wrong time and ruin things."

"I could tie her to a tree?" Túathal suggested.

"She'd scream," said Hibblig. "I wouldn't be able to concentrate."

"I could gag her as well," said Túathal.

"It's easier if I just find a private spot on my own," said Hibblig. "While I'm gone, see if you can find me a big sea turtle shell to use as a flying disk."

"You *will* come back for me, won't you?" said Túathal.

"Reluctant allies are still allies," said Hibblig. "And you still have those caches of gold and gems buried at various spots around Tamloch. With treasure in hand, we can both disguise ourselves and catch a Roma ship across the Ocean."

"An excellent idea," said Túathal. "How does a comfortable villa on the Dalmatian coast sound to you?"

"A far sight better than a hut on this benighted shore," said Hibblig.

"You should leave now," said Túathal. "I'll make excuses for Gwýnnett. Do you plan to take her with us?"

"We can figure that out later," said Hibblig. "Find a turtle shell big enough for three of us, just in case."

"I will," said Túathal. "Now go. The sooner you start, the sooner we can leave. We don't know how often that western dragon—"

"Brünedíxés," said Hibblig.

"—will be back to check on us and bring more supplies," Túathal continued. "Take this with you," said the former monarch as he handed Hibblig the tail spike. "It might be useful."

"Good luck putting up with Gwýnnett," said Hibblig as he trudged away up the beach in the opposite direction from Gwýnnett's earlier path."

"Good luck crafting your new magestone," said Túathal. The former king watched the heavily muscled once-and-future wizard walk away. *It will be useful having a wizard around to transport my treasure,* he thought. *And maybe he can help me take one last shot at my son and nephew before we leave for the Dalmatian coast. Who knows, I might even reclaim my throne.* He shook his head slowly and reached down for the second horseshoe crab. *No, that's not a sane expectation,* he considered. *I'll have to watch myself to avoid such thinking.* He methodically began to work the second crab's tail spike free, amusing himself with thoughts of how he might use the tail spike on Gwýnnett in the future.

* * * * *

It took Gwýnnett's eyes several seconds to grow accustomed to the dim light under the trees. She took a deep breath through her nose, trying to identify any familiar smells amid the many new and unusual scents. Gwýnnett would love to identify old friends from her personal pharmacopeia among the Caiman Island's flora, but wasn't overly optimistic, given the decidedly different climate here. Still, she might find something useful. With the right plants she could easily blend new potions to beguile Hibblig and befuddle Túathal once again.

She looked back over her shoulder, concerned about what Hibblig and Túathal might be discussing in her absence. Gwýnnett wasn't nearly as helpless and scatterbrained as she'd presented herself to be to her companions and prior paramours, but it served her long-term aims for the one-time wizard and deposed king to underestimate her. After watching Hibblig examine pebbles on the beach, Gwýnnett was particularly concerned about him making a new magestone and leaving her here—with or without Túathal. *I don't know which option would be worse,* she considered, while resolving to persuade Hibblig to take her with him when, or if, he left the island. *For that matter, who knows when that western dragon will be back?* she mused. *I wonder if dragons are susceptible to flattery—or pharmacology?*

Gwýnnett collected three ripe fruits—the kind with leathery yellow skin, sweet, if stringy orange flesh, and hundreds of spherical black seeds. She tucked them into a large pocket formed by tucking one of her skirts into her waist like she'd seen peasant women do at the markets in Brendinas. Gwýnnett had fond memories of incognito forays into those markets for potion ingredients before her life had been so unfairly transformed.

In a clearing, Gwýnnett saw one of the big blue lizards basking on a pink coral block and stunned it with a well-thrown rock the size of her fist. Taking a few quick steps closer to the creature, she grabbed it by its tail, lifted it high, and smacked its head against the block with enough force to kill it. She examined the lizard closely, noting its sharp teeth and lamenting the absence of venom sacks that could have proved useful. Few animals on the island—at least few land animals—seemed to use poison or venom. Her *son,* Dârio, and his cousin Nûd—the new kings of Tamloch and Dâron—had warned her and the others about the perils of the seas around the island.

Beyond the obvious threats like the caimans, there were stinging jellyfish, sharp-spined sea urchins, huge rays with barbed tails, and sharks five times the size of a man. She'd seen large sharks' teeth in the sand that made her reluctant to do more than dip her toe in the waters of the cove. She'd cajole Túathal into disarticulating one those horseshoe crab tail spikes for her and talk him into skinning the lizard while she was at it. Gwýnnett would offer him one of the fruits she'd collected as an incentive.

Past the clearing was a tall, broad tree with small, yellow apple-like fruits. She paused to inspect its spade-shaped leaves before plucking several of the *apples* for future in-depth examination. As she pulled a leaf off the end of a thin branch, she saw a drop of white liquid, like heavy cream, exude from the end of the branch.

Gwýnnett had enough respect for plant toxins not to taste the liquid but was curious to learn more about its properties. She found a sliver of palm frond and used it to transport a spider from its web on a nearby bush to the end of the branch. When the liquid touched the spider, the thick sap immediately froze it in place, then began to digest the arachnid's body. The position of the spider's legs made it seem like the creature was in agony. Gwýnnett smiled. She found a clam shell and used it to collect sap from several branches, wrapping the shell in large leaves and tucking it into a separate pocket formed from her first underskirt, along with several of the small *apples* for later research.

A productive walk, thought Gwýnnett. She started making her way back to the cove by a different path, resolving to change her default mode of behavior from whining to charming henceforward, mentally rehearsing phrases and actions that would change Hibblig and Túathal's perceptions of her value. A bright flash of red at eye level on tall bush ahead dropped her out of her reverie and focused her attention on what was before her. She approached closer and saw familiar broad green leaves formed like eight fat fingers with their veins marked in crimson. "Hello, old friend," she said. "I'm surprised to see *you* here."

A dozen bright-red barbed seed pods of the castor plant, one of the most poisonous varieties of flora Gwýnnett knew, joined the *apples* in her underskirt.

A productive walk indeed.

Chapter 10

In the Milking Barn

Signý and Amber, Bifurland's queen and master mage respectively, found King Bjarni holding the udders of a shaggy cow in the milking barn on his farm north of Bjarniston. Princess Sigrun and her best friend Rannveigr, both twelve, were near at hand, milking adjacent cows. The girls kept very quiet, hoping the adults would forget their presence and allow them to overhear whatever news had prompted Signý and Amber to come to the milking barn instead of waiting for Bjarni to return to his royal farmhouse. The cow Bjarni was milking grumbled a plaintive moo that echoed around the barn.

"Is he mistreating you, Huppa?" asked Signý. "Didn't he warm his hands first?"

"What are you going on about, my love?" asked Bjarni. "It's your own sudden arrival that's made her unhappy."

Sigrun and Rannveigr exchanged a quick glance, then bent their heads down to stare into their milking pails.

"He's done it again," said Signý.

"Who's done what now?" asked Bjarni, though he shook his head slowly from side to side, anticipating her answer.

"Harald Magnússon has sent a new emissary," said Signý. "Probably to renew his demands we swear fealty to Nordland."

"That's not going to happen," said Bjarni.

"I know that, and you know that, but Harald doesn't seem to know that," said Signý.

"Yet," said Bjarni.

"The emissary is in the guest house," said Signý.

"Then I guess we'll have to meet him," grumbled Bjarni.

Amber nodded.

"That would be wise," said Signý.

Bjarni snorted and muttered something too soft for the others to hear, though his tone made his mood obvious. "You didn't have to restate the obvious," he told his wife. "Harald has ten times our ships and twenty times our population."

"We've remained independent for a thousand years," said Signý. "And we have strong allies now. We can do it for another thousand."

"Still," said Amber, "it would be discourteous to keep the Nordland emissary waiting."

"He can wait until I've finished milking Huppa," said Bjarni.

"Moooo..." the cow confirmed.

"We can milk her," said Sigrun. "Huppa likes us."

The cow repeated her previous comment.

"Don't be bossy," Bjarni told the cow. Then he laughed. "Very well, girls," he told Sigrun and Rannveigr. "You can take over and I'll head for the guest house." He rose and his daughter took his place on his milking stool.

"Wash your hands first," said Signý.

"I think not," said Bjarni. "Let the emissary shake the hand of a king who works for a living instead of one who plants his ass on a throne in a gilded hall."

"I'd advise using the walk to the guest house to tamp down your temper," said Amber, speaking more words than usual.

"Because it would be wiser to hear him out before you try to kill him," noted Signý.

"What makes you think I would do such a thing?" asked Bjarni.

"You were going to kill the king of Tamloch on your flagship when sailing up the Brenavon several months ago," said Signý.

"That's different," Bjarni protested. "I thought he was a spy."

"I heard he'd said he was a strawberry merchant, from Dâron's southern provinces," offered Rannveigr.

"Dârio was king of Dâron, not Tamloch, then," contributed Sigrun as she milked Huppa.

"He's so handsome," added Rannveigr.

"Jenet certainly thinks so," said Signý.

"If we could please get back to the immediate matter of Nordland's diplomatic emissary..." said Amber with an expression resembling a thundercloud.

"There's nothing diplomatic about any of King Harald's previous emissaries," said Bjarni. "And we just got through dealing with *one* invasion from across the Ocean. We don't need another."

"Would you like me to see if Laetícia is free to join us for the meeting?" asked Amber. "It might be a good idea to remind him we don't stand alone this time."

"And we can't count on kin-strife in Nordland to save us," said Signý, "though your grandsire promising gold to Olav the Bloody's nephew Magnús if he tried for the throne was well worth the expense."

Bjarni took a deep breath, then another. "I'll stay calm and hear what he has to say."

"I'll try to do the same," said Signý.

"Let's see how long that lasts," said Amber.

"Did anyone else come with the emissary, Mother?" asked Sigrun.

"His knarr docked in Bjarniston this morning," said Signý. "There's a wizard with him."

"And twin boys, about your age," added Amber. "I think they're the emissary's sons."

"Well now, that gives the stew a different flavor," said Bjarni. "I can't see why an emissary demanding our fealty would travel with his young sons." He glanced down at his daughter and his niece who were pointedly attending to milking. "Sounds like the two of you will want to join us at the guest house when you finish with Huppa and Búkolla."

"We'd planned on that already," said Rannveigr, grinning at Sigrun.

"I'm sure you did," said Signý.

"If this is a friendly meeting, rather than an occasion to deliver an ultimatum, perhaps I *will* wash up first," said Bjarni.

"Good," said Signý. "And you can change your tunic, too."

"Yes, my love," said Bjarni.

"I wonder what the emissary wants to talk about?" asked Sigrun.

"That's a very good question," said Amber. "From recent conversations with Laetícia I may have some guesses."

"You can share those guesses with me while I wash up—and change my tunic," said Bjarni.

"And we should hurry," said Signý. "We shouldn't keep Prince Flóki waiting."

"A prince!" said Sigrun and Rannveigr in unison.

"Harald's younger brother," said Signý.

"You could have included that *minor* detail at the very beginning," said Bjarni.

"Yes, but if I had, the girls wouldn't have been able to concentrate on their milking," said Signý with a smile.

Bjarni hugged Signý and all five of them carried full pails of milk to the cold room.

"Let's get on with it then, my husband," said Signý. "If we're quick, I'll have time to braid your beard."

* * * * *

Prince Flóki Magnússon, brother of Nordland's king, Harald Magnússon, was a tall man of middle age with reddish-blond hair and a neatly trimmed beard extending from his chin to his sternum. His luxuriant mustache was waxed and curled, and his ice-blue tunic was covered with elaborate embroidery. As he paced from one side to the other of the largest room in the guest house, avoiding the table and chairs placed near the fireplace, his long stride only allowed him ten steps from wall to wall.

His two sons, Selr and Otr, paced together at right angles to their father's path, adjusting their course to avoid collisions. The boys were twelve or thirteen and resembled their father, except for their lack of beards, mustaches, and perhaps a foot of additional growth.

Knútr, the slender, gold-robed wizard sent by King Harald, stood by the door, constructing and disassembling a small, highly detailed illusion of a dragonship with a red sail from solidified sound. A gray raven perched on Knútr's right shoulder offered critical *caws* of comment before each cycle.

"What's keeping King Bjarni?" grumbled Flóki.

"Patience," Knútr counseled. "It's not like we'd made an appointment to see Bifurland's rulers—and this is a working farm."

"I begrudge every wasted minute," said Flóki. "Who knows what's happening across the Ocean?"

"I've told you we still have time," said Knútr. "Not a lot of it, but—with luck—enough."

"I saw four big barns when we walked up," said Selr. "One is clearly a hay barn and one smelled like cows."

"Another smelled like sheep—and goats," said Otr.

"What's the fourth barn for?" asked Selr.

"It smelled funny," noted Otr.

Knútr answered instead of Flóki who was focused on the floorboards and avoiding collisions with walls. "I think it's a dragon barn," said the wizard. "Bifurlanders are rumored to have a few gold dragons only twice the size of warhorses."

"Like the ones the Roma took from us ten years ago?" asked Selr.

"Along with all our eggs," complained Otr.

"I expect," said Knútr.

"Blasted Roma try to take everything," said Prince Flóki whose hands tightened into fists as he walked.

"Don't go too far down that path," said Knútr. "Your ancestors and mine did much the same to build up Nordland's wealth."

"Through honorable battle and raiding," said Flóki. "That's different."

"Not to those whose wealth was taken," said Knútr. "Take deep breaths. You can't serve as an effective emissary if you're ready to chew on your shield."

Otr was about to speak, but Selr shook his head and tried to help their father find his balance. "Do you think we could see the gold dragons?"

Selr joined in. "I'd like to see them too, Father."

"We'll see," said Prince Flóki. "It will depend on how things go when we speak to Bifurland's king and queen."

As if on cue, footsteps sounded on the paving slates outside the guest house. Flóki, Selr, and Otr stopped pacing and turned to face the door, which opened to admit five people. Bjarni and Signý were wearing their royal finery in Bifurland's colors of black and gold.

Sigrun and Rannveigr had not only managed to put on new dresses and aprons, they were also wearing strings of Baltic amber beads between polished-gold oval brooches decorated with entwined patterns of knotwork dragons. The girls had somehow found time to braid their long blonde hair as well—Rannveigr with thirteen strands and Sigrun with fifteen. Amber was the last to enter, closing the door then turning to nod at Flóki and Knútr.

Selr and Otr didn't notice the Bifurland master mage's presence—all their attention was devoted to staring at the girls.

"Close your mouths, boys," whispered Knútr. "You don't want the young ladies to think you've lost your wits."

"It's too late for that," teased Flóki under his breath.

"Welcome to Bifurland," said Bjarni, extending his hand to the new arrivals. "I'm Bjarni, and this is my wife, Signý."

"Flóki Magnússon," said the Nordland emissary. He smiled when he saw that the four young people hadn't waited to be introduced, but were already clumped together, talking rapidly. Flóki waved in their direction. "Those are my twin sons, Selr and Otr. Please forgive them, but it's been weeks since they've met anyone near their own age."

"Our daughter is Sigrun, and her cousin is Rannveigr," said Signý quietly. "They're at that stage when they alternate between having no time for boys and thinking *only* about them."

"My young Seal and Otter are at a similar stage, allowing for the change in genders," said Flóki.

Selr broke away from the clump of young people and approached his father. "Sigrun and Rannveigr want to show us the dragon barn," he said. "Can we go with them to see it? We'll be careful."

"You can go," said Flóki. "But stay out of trouble."

"No promises," said Otr as the young people left the guest house without a backward glance.

The two wizards watched them leave and smiled at each other, exchanging names.

"Sit," said Bjarni, waving toward the table. He nodded at Amber and the mage stepped into a storage closet and emerged holding a jug and five mugs.

"Talk always goes better with mead," said Signý.

"That's been my experience," said Flóki. "And Bifurland's mead is famed on both sides of the Ocean."

"You don't have to waste time telling me my cow is beautiful," said Bjarni.

Signý put a hand on her husband's shoulder, then pulled the stopper from the jug and filled the mugs. The scent of wildflower honey filled the room.

Everyone drank. Prince Flóki put his mug down and wiped sweet liquid from his lips before using them to form a smile. "It's not your cow I'm complimenting, it's your bees—and now I see I didn't need to prevaricate to praise your mead. It's the best I've ever tasted."

"Thank you," said Signý. "Now what brings you across the Ocean?"

"You're here for a reason," said Bjarni.

"Obviously," said Flóki. His eyes moved from Bjarni to Signý to Amber and back to Bjarni. "You know about the delicate balancing act Nordland has been performing for the past two centuries...?"

"Don't take me for a fool," Bjarni grumbled.

"Everyone knows that Nordland only continues an independent existence on the sufferance of the Imperium," said Signý. "If not for the tribute you provide and the way your raiding can be a useful threat when the Imperium wants to justify tax increases..."

"That's all part of our great game, playing one empire against the other to help us survive," said Flóki. "But now..."

"You fear your independence will soon be over?" said Amber.

Flóki nodded. "The Western Empire has already taken two provinces from the south of the Dane Mark. Gertrude of Mainz wants to take the entire peninsula to demonstrate her fitness to wear the purple as western emperor—and her friend Flavia Drusila of the Northern Empire is supporting her."

"It's an unenviable position," said Knútr.

Bjarni glanced over at Amber before speaking to Knútr. "I see understatement is a common trait for mages in Nordland as well as Bifurland."

Knútr didn't respond except for a thin-lipped smile shared, in sympathy, by Amber.

"My brother sent me to ask for your help," said Flóki. "We need dragonships and warriors and *dragons* if you have them."

"We do," said Bjarni.

"Wizards, too," said Knútr. "As many as you can spare."

"We have our own ships, warriors, and dragons, plus more besides—we have allies," said Signý. "Have you heard of the Orluin Alliance?"

"Bifurland, Occidens Province, Tamloch and Dâron coming together to hold off deposed Emperor Sírénae's invasion?" asked Flóki. "I'd heard of it, but found it hard to believe, since I'd also heard rumors of huge dragons larger than Roma blacks."

"The great dragons exist," said Amber. "And so does the alliance."

"Good," said Flóki. "With your aid we may remain our own kingdom, and..."

"And what?" asked Bjarni.

"And I won't have to ask a second boon," said Flóki.

Bjarni and Signý looked at the emissary. One of his hands we balled into a fist and the other was reflexively clasping and releasing the handle of his mug. Bjarni motioned for him to continue.

Flóki tilted his mug back and drained it, slamming its base down on the table so hard Signý was impressed the mug didn't shatter. "I was told to ask you," he said. "If our best efforts fail and we lose to the Imperium, could the people of Nordland unwilling to live under Roma's rule find new homes with you in Orluin?"

"I don't see why not," said Bjarni. "There's plenty of empty land to the west."

"How many people are we talking about?" asked Signý.

"Let's not get ahead of ourselves, Your Majesty," said Amber. "I think we need to consult with my friends Laetícia and Quintillius first."

"Those names sound Roma," said Knútr.

"They are," said Amber. "But they're also our allies—and far from fond of Gertrude and Flavia."

"Tell me more," said Knútr.

"Yes, please do," said Flóki, "And maybe later you can show me the dragon barn..."

Chapter 11

Assumed Identities

Celéri stood with her arms around Thraxa's neck, speaking to the snow-gryffon reassuringly. "I won't be gone long, dear one, so you'll just have to amuse yourself here on the Tempest Isles while you wait for me to return."

"You won't have to worry about the leviathan eating her, at least," said Sírénae. "We all saw how she drove that beast off."

"I'm not concerned about something eating *her*," said Celéri, "though I do want to make sure she has enough to eat."

"Left on her own she may find a few of the locals to amuse her," said Umbrose. "If you call rending them limb from limb with her beak and claws amusing."

"Thraxa follows her nature," said Sírénae. "I expect any human residents of the Tempest Isles will keep their distance."

"What if Admiral Pixo and the fleet arrive while we're away?" asked Umbrose.

"Pixo knows enough to feed Thraxa from a distance," said Celéri. "And he'll have mages with him to keep her away from his legionnaires and sailors."

"Should we warn your uncle about the leviathan?" asked Sírénae.

"The beast didn't bother us when we were here earlier," said Celéri. "It might avoid ships in large numbers."

"There are far fewer ships in Pixo's fleet now than when we sailed from Nárbo," said Umbrose. "We don't know how many ships will be enough to discourage the monster."

"I'm not worried," said Celéri.

"You should be," muttered Sírénae softly.

"What was that?" asked Celéri.

"Nothing important," Sírénae replied. "I was just tallying up the likely number of loyal ships in Pixo's fleet and considering their drafts and tonnage."

"I'd expect you to use your fingers and toes for counting, though that would only get you up to twenty," said Celéri. "I wouldn't think someone like yourself to have the mathematical training given to wizards."

"In that you would be wrong," said Sírénae. "Legion commanders are thoroughly trained in mathematics—for calculating troop strengths and more importantly, for ensuring the legions have the supplies they need to fight."

"I'll concede you may have been taught arithmetic," said Celéri, "but I doubt you have knowledge of transfinite numbers or non-Euclidean geometries."

"I leave that to my wizards," said Sírénae.

Umbrose spoke before the unproductive one-upmanship could continue. "Pixo and his people can wait here for us to return from gathering news in Valentia."

"Perhaps his wizards can brew up a few barrels of healing potions to help Mégàrotáxus recover from disorientation sickness," said Sírénae. "I don't like to see my dragons suffer."

"*My* dragons," said Celéri. She patted Thraxa's flank to emphasize her *familiar* connection to the snow-gryffon as well.

"Can we get on with it?" asked Umbrose. "As I understand things, I'll be disguised as Eynon and you'll be his frequent companion, Merry. How will you disguise Sírénae? As Merry's canine familiar?"

Celéri laughed. "While it would be appropriate for Sírénae to be a dog, I have other plans," she said. "You will be Eynon, Sírénae will be Merry, and I will be Nyssia, one of their friends I met gathering honey in the Rhuthro valley. If anyone asks, Eynon and Merry's familiars are elsewhere."

"You expect the gate guards to just admit our disguised selves to the governor-general's palace, then?" asked Umbrose.

"Yes," said Celéri. "They're well-known allies. I want to be Nyssia in case the guards give us trouble. She is, shall we say, quite distracting."

"We can always *ad hoc* gate back here if we have problems with the guards," said Umbrose. "Please remind me why we don't just gate *inside* the palace?"

"Because our goal is the gate to Valentia in the gardens, and we don't want to risk running into Laetícia, Mafuta, or one of the other senior Occidens Province wizards *in* the palace," said Celéri.

"Who could easily be in the gardens as well," grumbled Sírénae *sotto voce.*

"What did you say?" asked Celéri.

"Nothing," said Sírénae.

Umbrose, who *had* heard what Sírénae had said, abruptly changed his appearance to that of a tall, somewhat gangling youth of sixteen wearing sky-blue wizard's robes. "If we're going to do this, we'd best do it quickly..." said the ersatz Eynon.

"Fine," said Celéri. She stroked her hand down Thraxa's head to her body, transitioning from feathers to fur, then stood up and moved next to Sírénae. Soon two young women—a blonde and a redhead—replaced the wizard and former emperor. "I'll *ad hoc* gate us to a room above one of my favorite tavernas not far from the main gate to the governor-general's palace," said the woman disguised as Nyssia. "Now."

* * * * *

The trio from the Tempest Isles suddenly appeared in the room above the taverna, startling a couple who had not yet gotten far in removing their garments. The couple made a hasty exit, sharing well-selected epithets in the process.

"I won't ask why you're acquainted with such an unsavory location," Sírénae informed Celéri.

"Some of us prefer *willing* lovers," Celéri responded.

"I'd recommend leaving for the gate before the individuals we interrupted tell someone working for the taverna and the owner comes up to investigate," said Umbrose.

"Not that there's much any mere taverna owner could do about us," said Celéri. "I'd blast any anyone to cinders with a fireball if they tried."

"Setting the taverna alight in the process, which wouldn't help our attempt at subterfuge," said Sírénae. She moved to the door and beckoned to Umbrose. "Come along, my young, handsome lover."

"Must you say such things?" asked Umbrose. He shook his head and scowled but followed Sírénae out of the room.

Celéri paused to admire her appearance as Nyssia in a mirror beside the door, then joined them.

It only took a few minutes to walk to the palace gate. On their way, all three of them were struck by the change in the energy of the city's streets since its original population returned. Instead of a displaying a melancholic lethargy from lack of food and no obvious enemy to fight, Nova Eboracum's cobblestoned thoroughfares were now filled with pedestrians striding about their business, merchants selling their wares from carts on every corner, and legionnaires marching purposefully on their official duties. Wonderful smells filled the air: baking bread, bubbling stews, and what must be a whole wisent slowly roasting over a spit nearby.

Celéri, Sírénae, and Umbrose had more pressing concerns than hunger, however, and ignored the tempting odors along their path. When they reached the gate a tall young guard, obviously from the southeast of the Southern Empire, saw them and did a double take.

"Uh..." said the guard, reflexively blocking their way with his pilum while looking like someone had smacked him on his helmet with the flat of a short sword.

"We're here to gate to Valentia," said Sírénae/Merry. "Let us pass and tell us the fastest route to the portal."

Celéri/Nyssia looked up at the guard, smiled, and reached out to touch the arm that held his pilum. "You're a big one, aren't you?" she said.

The guard moved a step back and stood stiffly at attention, shifting his pilum and striking its butt on the cobbles. "State your business," he said, attempting to make it a command—and failing.

"If you'd been paying attention," said Umbrose/Eynon, "you'd know Merry already told you what we want."

"Yes, but you were just here and..." the guard began.

"What's your name, legionnaire?" barked Sírénae/Merry, sounding much more like an emperor than a wizard.

"You *know* my name," said the guard.

Umbrose/Eynon coughed to remind Sírénae she should be acting like Merry, but Sírénae's next words made things worse.

"How can you expect me to remember the name of every gate guard in the city, you impertinent fool?" she complained.

"But you brought me *dough rings,*" said the guard. "And soft cheese. You even teased me about Antica commanding me to run ten times around the city's walls."

"I think this big strong man has been standing out in the hot sun too long, don't you, Eynon?" said Celéri/Nyssia. "He needs to come into the shade where I can feed him peeled grapes and spiced wine..."

"I can't *do* that," said the guard, looking like his boots were two sizes too tight. "I'm on duty."

"Just point us in the direction of the gate to Valentia and we'll leave you to your work," said Umbrose/Eynon. "Nyssia can come back and see to your comfort when you're off watch."

"Nyssia?" said the guard. "I know you, Eynon, and Merry, of course, but who are *you,* Nyssia?"

"I'm their friend," said Celéri/Nyssia. "I'm a member of the Dâron royal guard." She licked her lips. "I'm very good with swords—maybe you can show me yours later?"

"Wait a minute," said the guard. "Where's Chee? And Ace? They were with you earlier? And why are you back on *this* side of the gate again?"

"Took him long enough," muttered Umbrose/Eynon to himself. "Just our luck those blasted barbarian wizards were here ahead of us."

Sírénae/Merry grinned at Umbrose then turned back to the guard. "Chee and Ace are off amusing themselves," she said. "And we want to amuse *ourselves* in Valentia, where it's warm. Let us pass and go back to your daydreams."

"Something isn't right here," said the guard. "Captain Antica! Propitia!"

Two more guards—an older and a young woman—suddenly stepped out from an antechamber beside the gate and appeared beside the first guard, the rapid clacking of their hobnails sharp in the late morning air. The older of the two new arrivals was clearly the guard captain.

She wiped a dot of spreading cheese from the corner of her mouth and moved her hand to the hilt of her gladius.

"What seems to be the problem, Stultio?" asked the guard captain.

"Hi Eynon. Hi Merry. Your dough rings were delicious," said the female guard. "Did your visit with Laetícia go well? Why are you back at the gate?"

The older guard gave the female guard a look that made Umbrose think *she* would soon be doing laps around the walls of the city for speaking without permission. Umbrose readied a spell in case their circumstances grew worse. Then he saw Celéri/Nyssia preparing to cast a fireball and knew there was a high likelihood they soon would be. As he saw it, there were good odds a century of Quintillius's legionnaires and a dozen of Laetícia's battle wizards would be at the gate in minutes if Celéri threw her fireball or the guard captain had time to raise a general alarm.

"Why are you back at the gate?" the guard captain asked, eying the imitation Eynon, Merry, and Nyssia warily. "You were just here. Did Laetícia send you? And who is *this* woman?"

"That's Nyssia," said Stultio. "She's a member of Dâron's royal guard."

Umbrose hid his amusement under his professional mask while speculating Propitia wouldn't be making her run around the city walls alone. He stepped close to Celéri/Nyssia and draped an arm over her shoulders, hoping to calm the young wizard's rising temper. *A fireball at the gate won't help us get to Valentia,* he thought. "Take a deep breath," he told Celéri softly. "Charm them, don't char them." Umbrose saw Celéri give a slight nod before she pulled away and approached Antica.

"Laetícia is fine," said Celéri/Nyssia. "And Stultio is right. I am a member of Dâron's royal guard. She sent my friends Eynon and Merry to Brendinas to fetch me so I could brief her on King Nûd's plans for upcoming joint maneuvers."

"I hadn't heard anything about joint maneuvers with Dâron," said Antica.

Umbrose could feel frustration growing in Sírénae and magical energy building in Celéri.

Sírénae spoke again, further eroding her disguise as Merry. "Do Quintillius and Laetícia inform a mere gate guard about all their upcoming operations with their allies?" she asked, making each word a sharp knife.

"They do, actually," said Antica. "As guard captain I have a seat at the table for the governor-general's daily briefing."

"This is ludicrous," said Celéri/Nyssia. "Let us pass so we can get to the gate to Valentia and be about our business."

From Celéri's tone, Umbrose could tell that *charring* was close to winning out over *charming* the gate guards.

"This still doesn't feel right," said Antica. "I'll have to bring in a wizard…"

Umbrose was seconds away from summoning globes of solidified sound around the guards' heads to cut off their air when a very tall young wizard in purple robes stepped out of the gatehouse.

"Did I hear you say you needed a wizard?" asked the new arrival.

"*Salve* Felix!" said Antica. "I'm glad to see you." She waved toward Umbrose, Sírénae, and Celéri. "Could you please…"

Felix turned in the direction Antica had waved, and his face lit up with a grin. "Eynon! Merry! And Nyssia, isn't it? I'm *so* glad to see you!"

"Glad to see you, too," said Umbrose, who knew of Felix as one of Mafuta's recent students.

"Are you here to see Laetícia?" Felix asked.

"We're looking for the gate to Valentia," Sírénae/Merry replied.

"You and Eynon were just through it," said Felix. "I'm surprised you just don't *ad hoc* gate back."

"I wanted to show Nyssia the palace gardens," said Umbrose/Eynon. "And it's easier to take a fixed gate with a passenger," he added, indicating Celéri/Nyssia.

"I understand," said Felix. "Come along then. Don't worry about these three, Antica. I'll take them to the gate to Valentia. The path there can be like a maze because it was originally designed as one."

Umbrose relaxed and sensed that Sírénae did as well. He could tell that Celéri was calming as well and much less likely to blow up the gatehouse with a petulant fireball.

Antica, Stultio, and Propitia wore troubled faces as they watched Felix lead Eynon, Merry, and Nyssia toward the palace gardens.

Felix wasn't ill at ease, however. He had something really important to discover.

"Tell me, Eynon," said the tall Occidens Province wizard. "How's your sister? Does she ever ask about me?"

"All the time," said Umbrose/Eynon with a smile. "All the time."

Chapter 12

Dragon Games

Felix talked non-stop as he escorted Umbrose, Sírénae, and Celéri, disguised as Eynon, Merry, and Nyssia, to the fixed gate to Valentia.

"The gate comes out half a mile from Portus Aleña, the name of the main settlement on the island," said the tall young wizard from Occidens Province. "I'd heard that Valentius wanted to name the proto-city Nova Alexandria, after his home, the capital of the Southern Empire, but the legionnaires he leads had taken his wife Aleña into their hearts and insisted the settlement be named for her. It's on the north shore of the western part of the island and is supposed to be mostly just tents for now, but a few public buildings are under construction using blocks of coral limestone, at least from what I've been told. I haven't been there yet myself. Mafuta has me so busy working on projects for her and for Laetícia that I haven't had a chance to go anywhere or do anything and I'm so glad I ran into the three of you at the gate because it gave me a good excuse to postpone carrying messages to Bifurland and the Northern Clan Lands and tell me again about Braith. Is she still back in the Coombe and is she really asking after me?"

Umbrose/Eynon said, "Braith confided that she wants to take you into a dark corner of the hay barn and..."

Celéri/Nyssia started laughing. "Don't believe a thing he says, Felix. He's just teasing you."

The expression on Felix's face changed from sunny to gloomy in the interval it would take to say *tempus fugit*. His dark face turned even darker as he blushed, realizing how much he'd been hoping the prospect of Braith in the hay barn had been true.

"What sorts of messages will you be carrying to Bifurland and the Northern Clan Landers?" asked Sírénae/Merry.

"I don't know exactly," said Felix. "They're sealed. But I've heard lots of speculation about candidates to be the new emperor of the

West to replace Sírénae Accipiter and wonder if they might have something to do with that. Do you have any idea where she and her spymaster might have gone?"

"I don't have a clue," said Sírénae/Merry, hiding a smile. "And I've got no idea why barbarians would need to be informed of such things anyway."

I can guess, thought Umbrose. *And I expect Sírénae can as well. Quintillius must be a leading candidate and Laetícia must be alerting her friends in the Orluin Alliance.*

"Are any messages going to Dâron and Tamloch?" asked Umbrose.

"Oh yes," said Felix. "Doethan was visiting Nova Eboracum—Princess Ruth is fond of dough rings—and gladly volunteered to carry messages to Nûd in Brendinas before returning home to Riyas where he can deliver the message for Dârio."

"I'm sure we'll learn about the content of the messages in due course," said Celéri/Nyssia. "And someone will have to replace the disgraced Western emperor, after all." She smiled when she saw the scowl flash across the false Merry's face.

"We'd best be on our way and not keep you from your work for Mafuta and Laetícia any longer," said Umbrose/Eynon. "Please give our best to them both."

"And please give *my* best to your sister," Felix replied. "I hope your trip goes well."

"So do I," said Sírénae/Merry. She entered the gate with an imperious stride and Umbrose and Celéri followed close behind her.

The gate guards greeted the false Eynon, Merry, and Nyssia warmly, remembering their "previous" visit, and pointed them down a packed earth path they said ran from the gate to the main legion encampment. Sírénae and Celéri managed to avoid antagonizing the guards and the disguised trio set off on the path.

Umbrose could see they were close to a lovely bay, with what looked an excellent anchorage. *That explains the Portus in Portus Aleña then,* he mused.

"I thought Felix would never shut up," said Sírénae once they were two hundred paces away from the guards.

"I thought he was sweet," said Celéri. "I could think of several pleasant ways to keep him from talking."

And I could think of several not-so-pleasant ways, thought Umbrose.

As the three reluctant allies walked toward the makeshift capital of Valentia, they began to hear cacophonous booming noises, like rhythmic, distilled thunder from further up the path. When they grew closer, they saw a brown dragon of no inconsiderable size banging on the hollow trunk of an immense ancient cypress with two uprooted palm trees, each as thick as a man. The cypress looked like it must have fallen over in a storm a decade past. Its carved-out center produced the deep, resonant booms as the dragon smashed the palms clutched in his front claws down upon it. Dozens of sharp white teeth showed on the dragon's snout and to Umbrose's eye it seemed like the great beast was smiling.

Umbrose noticed dozens of familiar three-by-three grids were incised deeply into the dirt in the ground around the dragon—apparently by one of its long, sharp claws.

"Stop that racket!" shouted Sírénae, hoping to be heard over the din.

"Please," added Celéri, in a softer voice.

The dragon looked up, acknowledging the newcomers' arrival with a glance and reducing the volume of his pounding. "Eynon! It's good to see you again," he said. When Umbrose didn't respond immediately the brown dragon showed even more teeth in a larger smile. "Surely you haven't forgotten your old friend Brünedíxés already?" he said. "Don't you remember? I'm the dragon who escorted you to the western weyr and King Kârkingórēx."

"Of course I remember you," said Umbrose/Eynon, providing the response he knew the dragon wanted to hear. "Who could forget your magnificent brownness? It's just that I was distracted by your percussive prowess." Umbrose could guess the reason *this* dragon didn't lead the western weyr was that he had more teeth than wisdom in his skull, preferring mindless banging to considered contemplation.

As if to illustrate that point, Brünedíxés twirled the palm tree in his left claw then brought both his oversized drumsticks down on the hollow cypress in an intricate *boom-badada-boom-bada-BOOM* pattern.

Celéri and Sírénae covered their ears, but Umbrose clapped for the dragon's performance.

"Forgive my friends," said Umbrose. "They're not music lovers like I am."

Brünedíxés spread his wings and bowed to Umbrose, then dropped his improvised sticks and sprawled across the cypress like a cat on the arm of an overstuffed chair. "What brings you back to Valentia so soon?" asked the dragon once he had settled into what looked like a comfortable position—for a dragon.

"My friends Merry and Nyssia and I need to find Gwýnnett, Túathal, and Hibblig to ask them some questions," said Umbrose/Eynon. "We hoped to learn where they were exiled and visit them there to learn what we require."

Celéri/Nyssia added more. "We'd hope to find a tavern where legionnaires with loose lips might tell us where to find them."

"Why not ask Valentius and Aleña directly?" asked Brünedíxés, thereby raising Umbrose's assessment of his perspicacity by a few points.

"They're so busy we didn't want to bother them," said Sírénae/Merry.

"That makes sense," said Brünedíxés, thus restoring Umbrose's original assessment of the dragon's intellect. Brünedíxés picked up one of the discarded palm trees and used it to rub the scales on his back. A low thrumming came from deep in his throat.

"By any chance do *you* know where we might find Gwýnnett, Túathal, and Hibblig?" asked Umbrose.

"Indeed I do," said Brünedíxés. "It's fortunate you stopped to admire my impromptu concert."

Umbrose recognized a cue and clapped again. "Why, beyond beauty's own reward, is it fortunate we stopped, Your Brown Magnificence?"

"Because I'm the one who transported Gwýnnett, Túathal, and Hibblig into exile," said the dragon.

"Wonderful!" said Umbrose/Eynon. "Would you do us the favor of transporting us there as well?"

"Gladly," said Brünedíxés, "if you would do *me* a favor first."

"How may we assist Your Magnificence?" asked Umbrose.

Brünedíxés used one of his oversized drumsticks to point to the grids on the ground. "Would you play a game of Nine Squares with me? One of the legionnaires taught it to me and I need to improve my strategy?"

Celéri stifled a laugh and Sírénae, facing away from the dragon, gave Umbrose a look he interpreted as *Could the big beast possibly be that stupid?*

"I would be glad to," Umbrose replied. He hadn't played the game since he was half his current height, but his memory told him it was difficult to lose. Umbrose had originally learned *terni lapilli* or *three pebbles,* but from the incised grids it looked like the dragon was playing the legionnaires' variant of Rings and Crossed Swords, or Xs and Os.

Brünedíxés rubbed out half a dozen old diagrams and quickly sketched in four lines to make the grid. "You can go first, Eynon, since you're my guest."

"Thank you," said Umbrose. "If you want to improve your likelihood of winning, I'd recommend selecting who goes first by lot, since the whoever has the first move has a major advantage."

"I'll remember that," said Brünedíxés. "The legionnaires kept saying *humans first* because my great size was intimidating."

"They were taking advantage of you," said Umbrose. "Let me show you. The first one to move can always guarantee either a win or a draw." He used a stylus of solidified sound to place an X in the center square.

Brünedíxés countered with an O in the upper left and as play continued Umbrose caught the dragon in a position where he had *two* winning moves so Brünedíxés couldn't prevent the wizard's victory.

"Did you see what I did?" asked Umbrose.

"I think so," replied the dragon. Brünedíxés opened his toothy mouth wide as if to make more room for new information inside his skull.

"Now you go first, and I'll show you how I can force a draw every time," said Umbrose. He drew a new grid beside the first and watched Brünedíxés place an X in the center. Umbrose played to block the dragon, not to win, and quickly forced a draw. They played three more games, and all were draws.

It took the dragon a while to understand, but he eventually caught on. When he did Brünedíxés showed lots of teeth in his snout and smacked one of the palm trees against the hollow cypress, making a resounding boom. "I like it!" he said. "Maybe now I'll win a peccary instead of the legionnaires winning every time."

"I can see you playing for snacks, but what did the legionnaires get when *they* won?" asked Umbrose.

"Alas, they don't appreciate my drumming as much as you do," said Brünedíxés. "When they won, I would stop pounding on my tree for an hour."

"It's sad the legionnaires don't appreciate your percussive artistry," said Umbrose. "Still, they won't stop you moving forward."

"For which I'm exceedingly grateful," said Brünedíxés.

Umbrose considered his next words carefully but decided to proceed. "There is a variation on Nine Square that's more of a challenge," he said. He drew three grids in the dirt and labeled them A, B, and C. "Do you know about the *qua-qua* game the Roma wizards in Nova Eboracum?"

"No," said Brünedíxés. "But it sounds fascinating."

All dragons are intrigued by qua-qua, thought Umbrose. *Brünedíxés isn't sharp enough to wrap his brain around a four-by-four-by-four matrix, but he might be able to master a three-cubed one.*

"Imagine the three boards are stacked with A at the bottom, B in the middle, and C on the top," said the wizard. "The goal is to form three in a row on any single board or across all three boards, working in three dimensions, not just two. After all the squares are filled, you count the number of three-in-a-rows and the player with the most wins."

"I can picture that," said Brünedíxés. He rubbed the point of his snout with the back of a claw. "It seems to me that control of the center square on the B board is critical."

"It is," said Umbrose. "That's why it belongs to both rings *and* crossed swords." He drew a circle with an X inside it on the B board's center square.

"There are *so* many possibilities," said the dragon.

"Exactly," said Umbrose. "If you practice against yourself, I'm sure you'll be able to defeat the legionnaires more often than not."

"I'm sure you're right," said Brünedíxés. "Will you play a game of it with me?"

"We really have to be on our way," said Umbrose. Sírénae and Celéri, in their disguises, nodded.

"Of course," said Brünedíxés, clearly impatient to start playing practice games. He crouched to make it easier to step up to his back. "Climb aboard and I'll take you to them," he said. "Maybe we can play a game on our way?"

"I don't see why not," said Umbrose after the three humans were situated between the brown dragon's wings. "I'm glad to repay you for transporting us."

"You've amply repaid me for the trip by teaching me Nine Square strategy and a wonderfully complex *new* game as well," said Brünedíxés. He twisted his head to glance at his back and asked, "Is everyone secure?" Hearing acknowledgments from each of his passengers, Brünedíxés launched himself into the air and swung around to the south on a course for Caiman Island.

After a few minutes in flight, Umbrose generated an illusion of the three stacked grids ahead of them and invited Brünedíxés to go first. In his experience it never hurt to have a dragon in your debt.

Chapter 13

Laetícia's Study

Like a child on a long trip asking about when they'd arrive, Merry persisted in repeating her question for Eynon even as they lifted their flying disks up the many levels necessary to reach the top of the highest tower in the city. "*Why* do we have to talk to Laetícia? Why do *we* have to talk to Laetícia? Why do we have to *talk* to Laetícia?"

Chee and Ace tired of her annoying tactics after less than a hundred feet and swooped off with Chee on the back of Ace in his flying form, in search of more entertaining way to amuse themselves in Nova Eboracum.

"Patience, please," said Eynon when he couldn't stand one more repetition. He shifted from foot to foot on his flying disk and would have been displeased to learn his face looked like one of the cows back in Haywall who'd mistakenly eaten a bushel of nettles instead of good green grass. "I've got two reasons, but I'm not really comfortable talking about one of them, if you must know."

"I thought we could talk to each other about anything," said Merry.

"We can, but there are some matters I'd prefer to forget," Eynon replied.

"Such as?" asked Merry.

"Such as the way I screwed up the day I gated to the Tempest Isles when Sírénae's fleet was anchored there," said Eynon.

"Didn't you gate into a hurricane?" asked Merry.

"Close to one, anyway," said Eynon. "But I didn't *ad hoc* gate there, Laetícia did. And I think we'll have to go there again."

"To look for Celéri and Sírénae?" asked Merry. "I thought you could gate back to anyplace you'd already been?"

"I probably could have, if I'd had enough time to take in my surroundings and it hadn't been raining and lightning hadn't been flashing and..."

"Wait!" said Merry. She tugged on Eynon's arm, halting their ascent. Her eyes were wide, and she stared at Eynon in amazement. "You just *lied* to me. You *do* know how to *ad hoc* gate back to the Tempest Isles. You took Celéri's cloisonné tracking pins there and attached them to a sea turtle. I remember laughing about it."

"Blast," said Eynon. "I'm caught out already and I'd barely opened my mouth. I'm a terrible liar."

"I'll say," said Merry.

"How will I ever be able to lie to Laetícia?" asked Eynon.

"You *won't* be able to," said Merry. "Laetícia is the master mage of Occidens Province *and* its spymaster. She'll see through you like a pane of glass."

"I know you're right, and I don't want to be a pane," said Eynon.

"Too late for that," teased Merry. "Why would you ever want to lie to Laetícia anyway?"

"I'd like her to do me a big favor and one of my aunts used to say the best way to have someone do you a big favor is to start by asking them to do you a small one," said Eynon. "*Ad hoc* gating us to the Tempest Isles was what came to mind as a suitable small favor."

"I'd heard that notion, too," said Merry. "I've even used it on my parents a few times. What big favor do you want from Laetícia?"

"You'll see soon," said Eynon. "I've decided to just ask her outright and rely on her generosity."

"If I didn't know better, I'd think you're showing the first signs of wisdom," said Merry.

"Thank you, I think," said Eynon. The two resumed their upward motion.

"We're here," said Merry a few seconds later. It was hard to wait to hear what Eynon's big favor might be, but she knew she wouldn't have to wait long to hear it. Merry waved to the guards on the landing outside Laetícia's study. The guards—alerted by Antica at the main gate—were expecting them and let the two young wizards pass without challenge.

Laetícia met them in the entry hall leading to her study. "Welcome," she said. "The children told me about the *fun* you had with the glyppos on Valentia."

"It was fun only if you weren't the one being bashed about," said Eynon with a smile.

"It was fun," added Merry. She thought about Eynon's encounter with the huge beasts and the corners of her mouth rose slightly in a repressed smile.

"What brings the two of you here?" asked Laetícia. The beads in her braids clacked as she invited them into her study and directed them to comfortable chairs around a inlaid wood table.

"I thought we'd bring you a baker's dozen of dough rings," said Eynon. He handed a mesh bag of dough rings across the table to Laetícia.

"You're too kind," said Laetícia.

"It's our pleasure," said Eynon.

"No, really, you are too kind," said Laetícia, smiling at Eynon. "Primus, Seconda, and Tertia are the big dough ring eaters in the family. Quin and I are good for one or two apiece and they'll be stale before we can make much of a dent in a dozen."

"I expect the guards on the landing would be glad to help you out," said Merry.

"You're right about that," said Laetícia. "I'll see to it immediately after our meeting is over. Now what—beyond distributing dough rings—brings you here?"

"It's a lot like dealing with the glyppos," said Eynon. "Ever since I started my wander year I feel like I've been bashed and battered by one crisis after another, from Bifurlanders coming up the Brenavon to the recent invasion from across the Ocean."

"That's fair," said Laetícia. "Go on."

"I got very little training from Damon..." Eynon continued.

"And that was quite *unfair*," said Laetícia. "You were thrown into..."

Eynon put up his hand and Laetícia covered her mouth for a moment, then nodded for Eynon to continue.

"I know," said Eynon. "And thank you for saying that—but because of my lack of training I need a favor."

Merry put a supportive hand on his forearm.

"Name it," said Laetícia.

"I need master mage lessons," Eynon replied.

Laetícia sat back farther in her chair and sighed. "You're not asking for much, are you?"

"You're being ironic, right?" asked Merry.

"Correct," said Laetícia. "Roma wizards are trained for decades. Somehow I don't think Eynon is planning to spend that much time on his studies."

"I expect to spend a lifetime learning and improving my skills," said Eynon. "And I'll be glad to come back and learn more, but right now I'd like as much advice as you can give me in an hour— and maybe learn a useful new spell or two."

"Why only an hour?" asked Laetícia.

"Merry and I have to get to the Tempest Isles to look for Celéri, Sírénae, and Umbrose," said Eynon. "We can't put that off, but if you can give me an hour's worth of advice first, I'd be grateful."

"I'm tempted to say my first piece of advice is to stay and get more than an hour's worth of instruction," said Laetícia. "But you're right about that trio you think are on the Tempest Isles. The sooner we can find them and stop whatever malicious projects they have planned, the better. I'll do what I can to boil down my stock of wizards' wisdom and feed you a few tablespoons."

"Thank you," said Eynon.

"Do you mind if I stay for the lessons," said Merry.

"Mind?" said Laetícia. "Of course I don't mind. You're quite an impressive mage yourself—and it certainly wouldn't be worth the effort to stop you from listening even if I were so inclined, which I'm not."

"Great," said Merry. "Maybe I'll come back for spymaster lessons..."

"Does she always try to turn a dragonfly into a dragon?" Laetícia asked Eynon with a smile.

"Is that a rhetorical question?" Eynon replied.

"I suppose it is," said Laetícia. "Very well. Let's get started." She rose and collected glass goblets and a krater decorated with pyramids and sphinxes from a side table, then poured her guests generous servings of watered red wine. "Get comfortable and help yourselves to dough rings," Laetícia added.

"What variety of dough ring goes best with a red?" Eynon asked Merry.

"Probably the ones with all the different seeds," said Merry.

After spreading soft cheese on their dough rings, Eynon and Merry gave Laetícia their full attention.

"First," said the master mage of Occidens Province, "I'd advise talking to *all* the master mages, not just to me."

"I'm planning to," said Eynon. "Verro, Amber, and Magister Callidus are all on my list."

"Good," said Laetícia. "You should follow up with Ealdamon again as well. It may surprise you why he didn't teach you more."

"If I must," said Eynon.

"You've already learned a lot from Rōlin and Peregrína, even though they're not master mages," said Merry.

Eynon nodded.

"It's only common sense to seek wisdom from the wise," said Laetícia.

"And also sensible to find nuggets of wisdom in common folk with their heads seated firmly on their shoulders," said Eynon.

"Like your parents—and mine," said Merry.

"I was about to say that," said Laetícia with a smile. "Let me try another direction, one where you may not be as wise already." She sipped from her own goblet. "You've grown up around honest, well-meaning people."

"True," said Eynon.

"But you're at a disadvantage dealing with people like Gwýnnett, Túathal, and Sírénae," Laetícia continued.

"Don't forget Celéri," said Merry. "Even if we did get the better of her once."

"Or masters of deception like Magister Umbrose," said Laetícia. "He has no scruples."

"Is that connected to his role?" asked Merry. "No. It can't be. You're a spymaster and *you* have scruples."

"Fewer of them than you might think, when it comes to defending the people of my province," said Laetícia. She reached up to finger a bead in one of her braids. "I might torture a prisoner out of necessity if they withheld vital information, though I'd get no pleasure from it."

"While Umbrose would?" asked Merry.

Laetícia nodded.

"I believe you were trying to make a point," said Eynon after he wiped a dot of spreading cheese from his upper lip.

"I was," said Laetícia. "I'm trying to say that you must be careful not to expect everyone you encounter to be the same sort of honest, well-meaning folk you grew up with."

"I've been telling him that for..." Merry began. She stopped when Laetícia raised a finger and moved it side to side.

"From what I've seen, Eynon's open, trusting heart is part of who he is," said Laetícia. "He just needs to learn how to tell the difference between people who are worthy of his trust and people who are not."

"How can I do that?" asked Eynon. "It seems to me that many untrustworthy people present themselves as upright and honorable—though certainly Gwýnnett, Túathal, Sírénae, Celéri and Umbrose don't."

"Sírénae and Umbrose showed different faces as Western emperor and her spymaster across the Ocean," said Laetícia. "They wouldn't have risen so high or so fast if their unscrupulousness had been understood earlier. The Imperium has a School of Good Governance, after all. It was only people like Quintillius who could see Sírénae's actions close up who had reservations."

"It sounds like you're saying you can't tell if a person's inner self is foul or fair," said Merry.

"No," said Eynon. "I think Laetícia's saying it's sensible to *start* by trusting someone, so long as you're open to adjusting that evaluation as you learn more."

"My father used to say, 'When someone shows you who they are, believe them.'"

"Your father is a wise man," Laetícia told Merry.

"But what about people who make mistakes and regret them?" asked Eynon. "I've done things I haven't been proud of over the years."

Laetícia shook her head and smiled. "Why don't you answer your own question," she said. "How would you reconcile Merry's father's maxim with what you just said?"

Eynon paused and rubbed his chin, then spoke. "I suppose it's a matter of changing your behavior," he said. "If someone screws things up and then tries to make things better while not doing the same sort of thing in the future, then they've learned something. Demonstrating that you can do better is also a way of showing who you are."

"But what if they're just pretending to do better?" asked Merry.

"I won't live my life thinking everyone is trying to deceive me," said Eynon. "Though I expect when my nose has been rubbed in a dung pile often enough, I'm capable of changing my mind on that—at least for certain individuals."

"Thus ends the lesson," said Laetícia. "The only thing I'd add is the importance of listening to what others say about someone's character so you can benefit from their experience."

"So long as you also bear in mind that other people may have their own axes to sharpen," added Merry.

"This is making my head hurt," said Eynon. "I feel like a contortionist trying to bite my own nether cheeks. Can you teach me a useful new spell now?"

"Gladly," said Laetícia. "Wizardry grew out of Athican philosophy and there are still academies where philosophers and wizards ponder such matters, twisting themselves into knots in the process." She paused and set her shoulders. "I have a simple spell that should help you determine the truthfulness of others."

"Does it detect when people are lying?" asked Merry.

Laetícia laughed. "You'll still have to do that on your own," she said. "This spell will just give you more information to work with. It's one of my own and I haven't taught it to anyone because its usefulness would vanish if more people knew about it."

"Thank you for trusting us with it," said Eynon.

"I'm trusting *you* because you clearly *are* what you seem, an innocent with a good heart," she told Eynon. Laetícia waved toward Merry, "Your partner, however, is a different story—but I have confidence in her."

"So this is a spymaster's spell?" said Merry.

"Very much so," said Laetícia. She rose and went to a glass box near a window where she reached in and removed a tiny *something*. When

Laetícia returned, Eynon and Merry could see that it was a dull-brown beetle no bigger than thumbnail. The small six-legged creature was trying to climb up Laetícia's palm.

"What does this beetle have to do with the spell?" asked Merry.

"Have you ever wanted to know what was being said in a room you couldn't enter?" asked Laetícia.

"Like being a literal fly on the wall?" asked Eynon.

"Of course," said Merry, jumping in. "If I want to hear something like that, I can use the listening spell Doethan taught me."

"The same one you taught me on our trip down the Rhuthro," said Eynon.

"What if you want to see and hear what's happening far away?" asked Laetícia. "Or hear through walls or doors too thick for your listening spell to be effective?"

"I suppose this insect is going to help me do so?" asked Merry.

"Yes," said Laetícia. "My spell creates two small congruencies— one for sight, one for sound—on the beetle. You can leave it in a room and see and hear everything happening there."

"I can see how that would be useful," said Eynon. He and Merry watched as Laetícia showed them how to create and calibrate the small congruencies and the spell components needed to see and hear at the other end. Together they observed as the beetle flew around the room, providing different perspectives on the three wizards.

"This is great," said Merry. "How long does it last?"

"As long as the beetle lives," said Laetícia.

Eynon held out his hand and the beetle landed on his palm. "I have an idea that should make your spell even better," he told Laetícia. He concentrated for a moment, then looked up and smiled.

"What did you do?" asked Merry. Laetícia also looked at him, waiting for his answer.

"I created a tiny associated gate congruency, so the beetle can return to us when we've heard what we've needed," he said. "That way, we can bring the beetle back to use again, and I can make sure it gets something good to eat as a reward for its help."

"Further confirming your kind heart," said Laetícia. "I'd never thought of that. It makes good sense."

Eynon smiled and sipped his watered wine. "Thank you so much for the wisdom and the spell," he told Laetícia.

Occidens Province's master mage stood up and crossed to the glass box, then pulled out a drawer beneath it and removed a small glass vial. She reached back into the glass box and broke off a segment of leaf inside it, put the fragment into the vial, and handed the vial to Eynon. "You can transport the beetle in this," she said. "I gave you something for it to eat as well."

"Wonderful," said Eynon. "I was worried Chee might eat the beetle if I just let it hide in my hair."

"Glad to help," said Laetícia. "Safe travels."

"Thanks," said Eynon as he and Merry stood and boarded their flying disks, holding hands so Eynon could *ad hoc* gate them both.

"Is there a name for the spell you just taught us?" Merry asked Laetícia just before the young wizards gated out.

"Not a formal one," said Laetícia. "I just call it *bugging*."

Chapter 14

Uneasy Lies

Túathal stood alone on the shore of the Caiman Isle staring out across the bay, enjoying the sunshine, the breeze, and the cloud-dappled sky. He felt like a man who'd just woken up from a troubling sleep where his thoughts had been tormented by nightmares, fogged by Gwýnnett's potions, and—dare he say it—beset by his own mad obsessions. The fresh air, sun, and most likely the absence of Gwýnnett's compliance-inducing drugs seemed to reset his brain. His mind hadn't seemed so clear, nor his wits so sharp, since he'd engineered the death of Dâroth the Twenty-fourth, the Old King of Dâron, over two years ago.

Hibblig is off crafting a new magestone and artifact, mused Túathal. *Gwýnnett is looking for meat for tonight's dinner and mostly likely trying to replenish her pharmacopeia,* he considered. *I'll have to be extra-careful to avoid falling back under her control when she returns. In the meantime, what can I do to strengthen my own position in our little band?*

Túathal looked down and saw the tail spike from the horseshoe crab Hibblig had given him resting on the edge of a rock. He picked up the spike and slid it into the right sleeve of his tunic where it rested along his forearm. Túathal pushed the sleeve back and used a few plaits of sea grass to bind the spike loosely in place. Then he let the sleeve fall back, hiding the spike.

He brought his right fist to his chest in a Roma salute, then shot his arm out to full extension, catching the spike as it flew toward his fingers. *That will do as a poniard,* he thought. *Will it also work as a throwing dagger?* He took aim at the fronds atop a small palm tree, half the height of a man, and repeated his earlier maneuver, allowing the spike to fly free this time. It landed in the sand short of the palm. Túathal walked over, picked up the spike, and tried again, adjusting his aim and the intensity of his motion each time until he could reliably place the point of the spike in the center of any target closer than ten yards distant.

Invigorated by his target practice, Túathal set off along the beach, looking for the shell of a large sea turtle that could be used by Hibblig as a makeshift flying disk. The shell they'd been using to cook their dinners would fill that purpose in a pinch, but Túathal hoped to find an old empty shell on his walk that would be larger and better able to hold all three of them comfortably when the time came for them to leave their island exile.

Túathal held his hand above his eyes to shade them and looked north along the beach, away from the sun. The island was flat in that direction—it was flat in all directions, for that matter—with the only elevations breaking up his vision being hummocks of sand and clumps of trees back from the shore. He climbed on top of the nearest hummock, a large mound covered in sand and grass, hoping to see farther and identify a sea turtle shell along his intended path. Not for the first time he wished he had one of his wizards at hand to generate distance-seeing lenses.

Several hundred yards away, Túathal saw a crowd of sea birds gathered around an object that could have been the carcass of a large sea creature. It was too distant to confirm the precise identity of the expired animal, but Túathal resolved to move in that direction and inspect things for himself. Before he could take a step, the mound below him began to shudder and shift. The motion tossed Túathal off his feet and disturbed the sand on the mound enough to reveal the mottled green-brown shell of a giant shield-backed turtle.

Ah! thought Túathal. *The shell of this turtle should serve nicely.* He steadied himself and crawled along the creature's back until he was positioned leaning over the front edge of the shell, directly above the turtle's neck. He had to keep one hand on the shell's forward edge to stay in place as the large beast waddled toward the sea.

With careful and deliberate motions he positioned his spike at the base of the turtle's unprotected skull and slammed it home between vertebrae by thrusting against it with the base of his palm. Spinal cord severed, the turtle's motion immediately stopped as if it had hit a wall of limestone blocks. The deposed king saw the light leave the turtle's eyes as they closed and watched its massive head fall to the sand. Túathal smiled.

Carrion gulls circled closer overhead, noticing the turtle's new status. *You can't have him yet,* thought Túathal. *But you'll be welcome to the scraps afterward.* He took another look at the giant shield-backed turtle. Its shell was at least as long as Túathal's own height of six feet, four inches, and nearly that big from side to side. *There's a kitchen knife back at camp,* Túathal mused, *but I don't relish butchering an armored creature this size with a nine-inch blade. It's better to hope that Hibblig will return with a functioning magestone so he can dress the meat and clean the shell with magic.*

Túathal waved an opportunistic gull away from the turtle's head and bent down to claim the same delicacy the gull had been seeking. With a deft motion, Túathal inserted three fingers into the turtle's right eye socket and popped out an orb the size of a swan's egg. He used the edge of the spike to cut through the optic nerve's cable-like structure and brought the turtle's eyeball to his mouth to take a bite. *Delicious,* he confirmed.

Bending to the head again, Túathal cut a few three-inch lengths of optic nerve and tossed one in the air above him. A gull retrieved it and landed on the sand nearby to consume what it had acquired. It never finished doing so, however. Túathal's thrown spike pierced the gull's breast before the bird could swallow.

Too bad gulls are reputed to taste terrible, thought the former king of Tamloch. *Turtle meat, on the other hand, has the opposite reputation.* He leaned back against the shield-backed turtle's shell and took another bite from its eyeball, savoring the taste of the aqueous humor wetting his tongue and further whetting his appetite.

It doesn't much matter what Gwýnnett finds for us to eat on her foraging trip, Túathal considered after reclaiming his spike. *There's plenty of turtle meat for dinner—or for a week of dinners.* He finished the rest of the eyeball in a few bites and ruminated as he masticated. *What's next?* he mused. *Now that my mind is clear there's no reason why I can't reclaim my position as king of Tamloch.* He picked a bit of lens from between his teeth with the spike. *For that matter, I might as well add the crown of Dâron as well. I'd just have to eliminate Dârio and Nûd. Neither one has an heir and, in the confusion surrounding their deaths, I can position myself as the logical alternative.*

Túathal paused and shook his head, then smacked it back against the dead turtle's shell as if trying to knock sense into his brain. *Killing my son and my nephew isn't the best way to achieve my goals,* he thought. *That's my old megalomaniacal delusions returning, and I'll have to take care not to draw myself back into madness. Besides, killing them requires more resources than my spike and my will. I don't have as much as a wheelbarrow or a fire cloak to my name.*

He rubbed the back of his skull and reviewed his options. *I need more allies,* Túathal decided. *Hibblig and Gwýnnett have their talents, but it will take more than their assistance to restore me to my rightful station.* He heard footsteps crunching on the sand nearby accompanied by a screech from one of the gulls circling above. Túathal tossed another length of optic nerve into the air for the gull to claim and saw Hibblig striding confidently toward him. The wizard was grinning.

"You've made yourself an artifact for your new magestone, I see," said Túathal, noting that the iridescent pebble Hibblig had found earlier was now mounted in the center of a spiral shell hanging on a leather cord around the wizard's neck. "That's excellent news. You can see I've found us dinner—and something to serve as a flying disk until you can craft another."

"Well done!" Hibblig boomed. "I could eat that turtle shell and all. Making artifacts takes a lot of energy and a two-inch thick turtle steak will be a good start."

"Carve us several steaks," said Túathal. "I'm hungry, too. And I saved you an eyeball. You can snack on it while you butcher the turtle and clean the shell." Túathal knelt beside the turtle's head, extracted its remaining eyeball, cut the optic nerve, and tossed the orb to Hibblig.

The big wizard caught the offered orb and gestured behind Túathal. Gwýnnett was walking toward them from the direction of the camp. "I see you've been busy," she called as she grew nearer. "Looks like meat's back on the menu, boys. I found some fruit we can eat for dessert."

"Good," said Hibblig.

"Good, so long as *I* prepare it," added Túathal.

Gwýnnett sniffed. "If you must," she said.

Hibblig and Túathal both nodded.

Gwýnnett shaded her eyes and gazed northward, across the water. The others turned and did likewise. In the distance they could all see the unmistakable silhouette of a dragon against the blue, cloud-dappled sky. Not long afterward they could identify the dragon's rust-brown color.

"Hide your magestone," Túathal commanded Hibblig. "Be ready to shield us."

Hibblig closed the neck of his tunic, covering the spiral shell artifact that held his magestone. He moved into a defensive crouch awaiting the dragon's arrival.

Gwýnnett felt in a pocket of her gown for the leaves that wrapped one of the small golden apples. She didn't know how effective one of them would be against a dragon but was ready in case she had cause to find out. She moved closer to Hibblig and Túathal while spinning through reasons for the dragon's appearance in her head. It was far too soon for more supplies to be delivered. *Had Nûd and Dârio decided to execute them after all?* she wondered. *Highly unlikely.*

Blasts of wind from Brünedíxés' broad wings blew across them and droplets of salt spray peppered their faces as the dragon landed on the strand with a splash of sea and sand, half in and half out of the water. The smell of decaying seaweed, intensified by the disruption, assaulted their nostrils. Gwýnnett, Hibblig, and Túathal watched as Brünedíxés lowered his shoulder so his three passengers—Eynon, Merry, and Nyssia, a slim blonde woman known to Hibblig and Gwýnnett—could disembark.

"Here you are," said Brünedíxés. "Ask all the questions you want. They're not going anywhere." He scratched a trio of three-by-three grids in the sand. "I'm going to hunt up something for lunch," said the dragon, "but I hope we can play a few games before we fly back?"

"Of course," said Eynon. He drew an X and an O in the center square of the middle grid. "Good hunting."

When Brünedíxés was well out over the water, Gwýnnett glared at Eynon. "Here to gloat?" she asked. "Or here to kill us without any witnesses around to report the deed?"

"Nothing of the sort," said Eynon. He waved his hand and light flickered like reflected sunlight on the Ocean. The illusion disguising the identities of the three newcomers vanished.

"Celéri!" exclaimed Hibblig. The overly muscled wizard and the petite one briefly embraced, earning a disapproving glance from Gwýnnett.

Túathal nodded to Sírénae. "From one monarch to another, it's good to see you again," he said.

"Especially since you seem to now be *compos mentis,*" answered Sírénae. "Island life must agree with you."

"Only up to a point," said Túathal. "I find the scope of action here somewhat limited."

"I don't doubt it," said Sírénae. "We're here recruiting allies. Are you with us?"

"Yes," said Túathal, remembering he'd reached the same conclusion earlier.

"What next?" asked Gwýnnett.

"Gather 'round and I'll gate us to the Tempest Isles," said Umbrose.

When Brünedíxés returned, all he found waiting for him was the body of a blood-covered gull and the carcass of a dead, eyeless shield-backed sea turtle. With an unhappy sigh the dragon settled his hindquarters on the warm sand and used the tip of a claw to mark in Xs and Os on the three-by-three grids, playing against himself, and losing.

Chapter 15

Mégàrotáxus

It was late afternoon in the Tempest Isles when Eynon and Merry gated to a patch of beach on the southern edge of the Great Harbor. Chee and Ace immediately jumped off Eynon's shoulder and Merry's flying disk, respectively, and began searching for their preferred snacks of fresh fruit and small mammals.

"Don't go too far," shouted Merry at their familiars, even though she knew her instructions were unlikely to be obeyed.

"They'll be back once they've found something to eat," said Eynon. "I expect it's been a while since they've had a chance to hunt."

"Not that stalking wild grapes and berries is exactly hunting," teased Merry.

"Don't disparage my familiar," said Eynon. "Raconettes are omnivores and there may be ferocious beetles here on the Tempest Isles."

"I'll ask Ace to deal with any large insects that give Chee too much of a fight," said Merry.

"You're too kind," said Eynon with a grin.

He stepped closer to Merry and gave her a hug, then scanned up and down the beach, looking for signs that anyone had been there before them. Merry did likewise.

"I see footprints," said Eynon, pointing down. "Three sets of footprints."

"Two women and a man from the size of them," said Merry. "Celéri, Sírénae, and Umbrose, do you think?"

"That's a reasonable assumption," said Eynon. "We were right in guessing they'd come here. I wonder where they've gone?"

"It's probably too much to hope that they've built themselves a canoe and set off on the Great Warm Current for the White Isles, isn't it," said Merry.

"That doesn't seem like their style," said Eynon. "They're up to something, and we've got to stop them before they cause more trouble for Orluin."

A deep moan from farther down the beach prompted both young wizards to look up from the footprints in the sand and watch as what they'd taken for a pile of black rocks some distance away uncoiled itself into a black Roma dragon. Eynon and Merry immediately generated shields of solidified sound, climbed aboard their flying disks, and sought safety in altitude.

"Oooo-owwwww!" bellowed the dragon, who seemed to be simultaneously rubbing the top of her skull with a foreclaw and shading her eyes with one of her massive black wings before flopping back down on the sand with a *splat* as if all her bones had been transformed into jelly. "Ow-ow-ow-owwww!" the dragon continued, but now with more of a whimper than a bellow. "It *hurts!*"

"Is there anything we can do to help?" asked Eynon as he and Merry descended to stand beside the suffering dragon.

"What happened to you?" asked Merry. "For that matter, *who* are you?"

"I am Mégàrotáxus, second in command to Xaxidiánus," the dragon announced in soft tones. "Celéri gated me to a river in the west, and then gated me here before I had a chance to recover from the first round of disorientation sickness."

"Disorientation sickness?" asked Eynon.

"I read about it in one of my father's histories of the Imperium," said Merry. "Dragons always know where they are, unless a wizard gates them somewhere. It's very rare, since few wizards have the power to do such a thing and fewer still lack the judgment to try. It's said that dragons can *die* from disorientation sickness."

"Or just feel like they *want* to die," Mégàrotáxus declared. "Ooooowww!"

Merry generated an opaque mask to protect the dragon's eyes from the sun and Eynon disappeared, gating out temporarily. He returned moments later with a tree trunk as big around as the dragon's foreleg and twice as long floating in a field of solidified sound beside him. Remnants of thousands of thin, flexible branches were still attached to one end of the trunk.

"Chew on this, good dragon," said Eynon. "Willow bark helps reduce pain, at least for humans. It may do the same for you."

Mégàrotáxus wrapped her forelimbs around the trunk, pulled it close to her mouth, and proceeded to shred the bark and consume it in big gulps. A few minutes later her moans turned to sighs and she rested her head on the white wood of the stripped tree's surface.

"Thank you," said the dragon. "That helped."

"I'm glad," said Eynon.

"So am I," said Merry. "Do you, by any chance, know what happened to Celéri, Sírénae, and Umbrose?" she asked.

"They gated out," said Mégàrotáxus.

"Any idea where?" asked Merry.

"I heard them talking," said Mégàrotáxus. "They didn't know I could overhear them. Dragons have excellent hearing and mine is more acute than most."

Eynon smiled. The big Roma dragon must be recovering, since she was now bragging about her abilities.

"I'm pleased to learn of your exceptional hearing skills," said Merry. "You are truly a most excellent dragon."

Mégàrotáxus preened at the compliment, opening her mouth wide and showing off dozens of ivory scimitars lining her jaw.

Merry smiled back, showing fewer and much smaller teeth than the dragon. "What did they say?" she asked. "Did they mention their destination?"

"I heard all their conversations," said Mégàrotáxus. "Even though they didn't think I could. They said they were going to Valentia to find out where Túathal, Gwýnnett, and Hibblig were exiled." She sniffed. "You Orluinatics have odd names."

"The preferred demonym is Orluinians," said Eynon.

Merry gave Eynon a puzzled look. "It is?" she mouthed.

Eynon shrugged.

"Orluinians, not Orluinatics," said the dragon. "I'll make a note of it."

"Thank you," said Merry. "When did they gate out?"

"This morning, I think," said Mégàrotáxus. "At least I think it was morning. I didn't want to open my eyes."

"I'm glad you're feeling better now," said Eynon. "Would you like some help getting back to the rest of your wing?"

Mégàrotáxus covered her eyes with her wingtips then shifted to look at Eynon cautiously. "You're not going to *gate* me there, are you?"

"Of course not," said Eynon. "But I'd be glad to let Xaxidiánus know we've found you."

"He's been worried," said Merry.

"Xax is a good wing leader," said Mégàrotáxus. "I didn't mean to cause him concern."

"It's not your fault," said Eynon.

"It's Celéri's fault," said Merry. "She should have known better."

"I'll flame her if she ever comes near me again," said the dragon.

"And no one would blame you if you did," Merry responded.

"Once I'm feeling better," Mégàrotáxus clarified.

Eynon rubbed his chin then shook his head. He'd have to ensure Celéri and Mégàrotáxus didn't cross paths in the future.

Mégàrotáxus coughed and small jets of flame emerged from both ends of her anatomy. "Excuse me," she said. "Thinking about what Celéri did to me makes me *so* angry."

"I understand," said Merry.

Mégàrotáxus coughed again and instead of flames she emitted sparse clouds of water vapor that smelled not-so-vaguely of phosphorous sulfide. The dragon was clearly running out of steam and flopped back on the sand, resembling a pile of rocks once again and beginning to snore like a small sawmill.

She pulled Eynon aside for a quick conference, putting a privacy sphere around the two of them. "Any ideas on how to transport Mégàrotáxus to Valentia so she can rejoin her wing?" asked Merry.

"Viridáxés can carry her on his back, if another dragon can be convinced to guard Zûrafiérix," said Eynon.

"I hadn't considered that possibility, but it should work," said Merry. "Viridáxés is certainly big enough to carry Mégàrotáxus. Just don't let Kârkingórëx volunteer to stay with Zûra. Dáx would never go for that."

"I expect Xaxidiánus will want to pull that duty," said Eynon. "In fact, I'll suggest it when I ring up Valentius."

"Good," said Merry. "Where do *we* go next?"

"I'd like to talk to Verro," said Eynon.

"More master mage lessons?" asked Merry.

"Yes," said Eynon. "Something tells me I'm going to need all the advice I can get."

"I don't doubt that," said Merry. "Maybe Fercha will be with him and I'll have a chance to catch up with her."

"Sounds good," said Eynon. "Let's set things up for transporting Mégàrotáxus and be on our way."

After a few conversations via communications rings, Viridáxés agreed to carry Mégàrotáxus to Valentia a few days later. Zûrafiérix was more than glad to spend time with another dragon—any other dragon—since Viridáxés was not exactly a scintillating conversationalist. Beyond delivering the occasional large tuna, sea wolf, or humpback to their island home, Viridáxés' contributions to their clutch were minimal. Zûra would be pleased to have Xaxidiánus keep her company for a week.

Viridáxés was bored and ready for some sort of action, but was concerned about leaving Zûrafiérix with another dragon. Merry suggested asking Magister Callidus to chaperone, but Zûrafiérix said his presence wasn't necessary.

Before they could call for their familiars to join them, Eynon and Merry heard loud screeches from the edge of the forest above the beach. Ace came running out of the trees barking constantly with Chee on his back crying *Chee chee chee CHEEEE!* over and over again until Eynon was ready to throw them both into the harbor. Chee held a white feather in his right paw.

Merry took the feather and inspected it. "It looks like it's from the head of a snow gryphon," she said.

Eynon raised an eyebrow. "Thraxa?" he asked.

Merry nodded. "It must be," she said. "They'll be back for her, I'm sure. What do you want to do, capture her?"

Eynon took the bottle Laetícia had given him from his pouch and opened it. "No," he said. "If we're sure they're coming back, I think I'll just *bug* the place." The beetle flew out of the bottle and found a spot to rest in the fronds of a small palm just beyond the sandy beach.

"Smart," said Merry. "Now can we go find Verro?" she asked.

"Yes," said Eynon. "Next stop—Riyas."

"How do you know he's there?" asked Merry. "Can't you ring him up first to confirm that's where to find him?"

"I don't have a ring for Verro," said Eynon, shaking his head. "I should have, I know. All the master mages should be able to contact each other in case of an emergency."

"You can give him one of a pair of communications rings when we find him," said Merry. "I could use my ring for Fercha—she will likely know where to find Verro."

"No need to bother her unnecessarily," said Eynon. "We shouldn't assume married couples keep close tabs on each other's whereabouts."

"Good point," said Merry. She gave Eynon a sidelong glance and a small smile crossed her lips.

Eynon didn't notice. "All aboard, boys," he said to Chee and Ace. Once their familiars were in place, Eynon took Merry's hand and the two of them gated out for Tamloch's capital.

Two pairs of eyes focused on the spot they'd just vacated—one set hawk-like from the edge of the forest and the other huge and draconic, just poking above the surface of the harbor.

Mégàrotáxus slept on, oblivious to both observers.

Chapter 16

Roma in Bifurland

"My favorite drink is sorghum beer, but I have to say your mead is a close second," said Quintillius as the governor-general of Occidens Province took another swallow from the mug Signý had given him. He and Laetícia were with Bjarni, Signý, Amber, Flóki—the Nordland ambassador—and Flóki's wizard companion, Knútr. They were all seated comfortably on wooden chairs padded with thick fleeces from northern sheep in the common room of the guest house on Bjarni and Signý's farm near Bjarniston.

"I tried sorghum beer on a trip to Byzantium in my youth," said Flóki. "I can't say I found it that appealing, though it was better than drinking the turpentine that passed for wine the Athicans preferred."

"I agree with you there," said Laetícia. "The wines from grapes grown in the Western Empire are quite superior, though I'll hold up the wines from our vineyards along the Abbenoth as their equal." She took a sip of mead, smiled, and continued. "And the date palm wine from my home in the Southern Empire is only marginally better than drinking sap straight from sugar maple trees."

"I'm not familiar with sugar maple sap," said Flóki.

"The trees only grow in northern Orluin," said Bjarni. "We don't actually *drink* the sap. We boil it down to a syrup and pour it over griddle cakes."

"Sigrun and Rannveigr will tell you it's particularly delicious," said Signý, "though it's so sweet many adults find it cloying."

"Give me old fashioned sorghum molasses on my griddle cakes any day," declared Quintillius. "Just like my mother's servants used to make."

"You'd eat sorghum steaks if such a thing could be created," said Laetícia. She squeezed her husband's hand to let him know she was teasing him and to help Flóki and Knútr see them as a happily married couple rather than a pair of threatening Roma.

"Amber tells me you were already aware of Gertrude's plans against Nordland," said Knútr.

"Yes," said Laetícia. "Let's just say that Valens and Phraátēs, emperors of the southern and eastern empires, would prefer someone other than Gertrude of Mainz as emperor of the West. They have no interest in conquering Nordland and don't want to disrupt a balance with your quasi-independent realm that has served the Imperium well over the centuries."

"Quasi-independent?" said Flóki, looking like he'd just had a taste of Byzantine wine.

"She's right, and you know it," said Knútr. "Nordland only remains independent so long as the Imperium finds that status for us convenient."

"Sadly true," said Flóki. He took a large swallow of his mead, then licked his lips and smiled. "Under the circumstances, we don't have the luxury of deluding ourselves on that fact."

"However..." began Quintillius.

"...We all agree that Gertrude leading an effort to annex Nordland to the Western Empire would be contrary to our shared interests," continued Laetícia.

"For a great many reasons," said Quintillius. He put his arm around Laetícia's shoulder.

"Then what are we going to do about it?" asked Bjarni.

"And what resources does Gertrude have to draw on?" asked Signý.

"Fewer than she might desire," said Laetícia. "More than half of Gertrude's legions left with Sírénae for our shores—and the majority of *those* legionnaires are in the south on Valentia with Valentius and Callidus.

"Will Gertrude be able to entice many of them back into her service?" asked Flóki. "By promising them farms, perhaps? Our farms—in Nordland?"

"I'm sure there will be legionnaires interested in returning to the Western Empire," said Quintillius. "But I think they'd be more likely to serve with *my* legions than Gertrude's."

"Your legions?" asked Flóki.

"I'm glad Harald sent me with you," said Knútr. "Don't you get it? Phraátēs and Valens want Quin here as the next western emperor."

Flóki took a double swallow of mead, then smacked the heel of his free hand against the side of his head as if to pound sense into it. "I see," he said. "At least *now* I do." He looked closely at Quintillius and Laetícia. "I assume from your comments that you expect to be better neighbors to Nordland than Gertrude and Flavia Drusilla of the Northern Empire?"

"They couldn't be much worse," said Knútr before finishing a mug of mead.

"It's safe to say you'll find us more congenial neighbors," said Quintillius. "Starting with us returning the two provinces Gertrude took south of the Dane Mark."

"Such a gesture of friendship would be greatly appreciated," said Knútr.

"Can we be assured your warriors will stand with us against Gertrude and Flavia?" asked Laetícia.

"My brother will do whatever it takes to keep his *jarls* in line," said Flóki. "We'll fight side by side with you to retain our independence."

"What will you expect in return for your help?" asked Knútr.

Quintillius turned to Laetícia, who responded. "High salted cod quotas. More furs. Our choice of your best polished amber—and your firstborn children for our legions."

Flóki's eyes went wide until he saw Laetícia's smile.

"I was just kidding about that last part," she said.

"Maybe *you* were," said Signý, "but I can't speak for your sons Selr and Otr. If I know my daughter and niece, the boys may decide to stay in Bifurland to be close to Sigrun and Rannveigr."

"Or perhaps my sons will entice the girls—and their dragons— to come to Nordland to fight, or scout," said Flóki.

"We'll see about that," said Bjarni. He drained his mug of mead and put it on the floor and turned his head toward Quintillius. "Now we have to talk about important details like how we're going to get your legions from Orluin to the Western Empire."

"I have some ideas about that," said Amber. She nodded at Laetícia.

"You talk," said Signý. "I'm going out to the dragon barn to see what the young ones have gotten up to."

* * * * *

Sigrun took Selr's hand and tugged him toward the dragon barn while Otr allowed Rannveigr to steer him by the elbow in the same direction. The dragon barn was the largest building on Bjarni's steading. It was made from heavy stones, with a slate roof—wise design choices given that dragons can breathe fire.

"Do you have dragons in Nordland?" asked Rannveigr.

"What was it like crossing the Ocean?" asked Sigrun.

"Do you like my dress and apron?" asked Rannveigr. "I did the embroidery myself, though my father made my broaches."

"I did the embroidery on *my* dress, too," said Sigrun. "Do you like the dragons on our broaches? They're modeled on the dragons we fly."

"What's it like being a twin?" Rannveigr asked Otr.

"We're almost twins," said Sigrun, gesturing toward Rannveigr. "We were only born a week apart and we're always together. I'm a princess."

"And I'm a jarl's daughter," said Rannveigr. "Are you princes? You seem charming enough to be princes."

Selr and Otr exchanged a glance and began laughing.

"What?" asked Sigrun.

"Is it something we said?" asked Rannveigr.

"No, the Roma from the Western Empire took our eggs and dragons," said Otr.

"Crossing the Ocean was long and boring, though we did see whales and porpoises," said Selr.

"I like your dress *and* your embroidery," said Otr to Rannveigr. "Your broaches are lovely."

"Yes. You—and your dress—are lovely, too," Selr told Sigrun. "I like the dragons on your broaches, but I *really* want to see live dragons, not ones made from metal."

The girls' cheeks turned red, but they kept walking and continued to stay close to the boys.

"Being a twin is both great fun and a pain in the..." said Otr.

"As for that, it sounds like the two of you might as well be twins yourselves, if you're almost the same age and raised together," said Selr. "Otr and I got to spend at least some time apart when we were fostered out to different Western Empire noble families in the summer."

"Father said we needed to learn as much as we could about the Roma so we could understand how to play them off against each other," said Otr.

"We were really hostages for the king's good behavior, not fosterlings," said Selr. "But we did learn a lot about the Roma."

"And now we want to learn a lot about dragons," said Otr.

"And maybe other things," said Selr.

"Help us open the doors, please," said Sigrun when they reached the large wooden doors to the barn. The doors were lined with fire bricks, so it took a concerted effort to move them. With four strong young people helping, the doors were soon opened, then closed behind them as they entered the barn. The cavernous space was divided into sixteen stalls, each large enough for a dragon the size of a pair of warhorses, plus two much bigger stalls at the far end.

"Those are for a dragon queen and king," said Rannveigr, waving toward the bigger stalls. "We don't have any adult dragons now, but if we get any—"

"—or grow our own," added Sigrun.

"—we'll be ready," Rannveigr concluded.

"This is *my* dragon," said Sigrun, pointing to the first stall on the left. "Her name is Gylda."

"And this is *my* dragon," said Rannveigr. "She has a long, complicated name, but I just call her Nugget."

The dragons poked their heads out of their stalls and allowed the girls and, after a few tentative attempts, the boys to rub their brow ridges. The two couples were standing quite close together while they made the dragons croon with pleasure. It seemed perfectly natural for all concerned for Selr to embrace Sigrun and Otr to take Rannveigr in his arms. Both girls stood on their tiptoes, ready—and eager—to be kissed by their tall, handsome young visitors.

A small boy poked his head out of a neighboring stall. "What's going on?" he asked. He grinned and waggled his eyebrows as if he knew perfectly well what the girls had *hoped* would be happening. The two girls sprang apart from their young men, their cheeks as red as if they'd spent all morning outside in January without wearing scarves.

"Go *away*, Holgir!" said Sigrun.

"We're *busy!*" added Rannveigr.

"Who are they?" asked Holgir, pointing at Selr and Otr.

The two Nordland boys were grinning and shaking their heads. They had younger brothers and this wasn't the first time they'd been interrupted in their attempts at romance. Sigrun and Rannveigr weren't pleased by Holgir's sudden appearance. Both shot looks at the younger boy that would have pierced him dead if they'd been bolts from the crossbow Holgir usually carried.

"If you're not going to leave, go back in your stall and tend to your dragon," ordered Sigrun.

"And don't say a word," added Rannveigr. "Or else."

Holgir was wise enough not to say, "Or else what?" He retreated to the stall where he had been grooming his dragon and positioned himself so he could hear everything going on in the barn.

Sigrun turned to Selr and moved to stand directly in front of him. "Where were we before we were interrupted?" she asked.

Rannveigr shifted to a similar position with Otr. "Yes," she said. "Remind me, please." She tilted her head up for a kiss.

The osculations had barely commenced when the barn doors rattled open and Queen Signý stepped inside. "It seems I got here just in time," she said. "Take care, please. Don't frighten the dragons."

"Aunt Signý!" said Rannveigr.

"Mother!" said Sigrun.

Holgir popped his head above the door to his dragon's stall and flashed his best impish ten-year-old grin. "Hello, Aunt Siggý," he said, taking advantage of his favorite nephew status.

Signý shook her head, unsurprised by Holgir's presence. She tried, and failed, to hold back a smile. "Why don't you all go flying?" Signý suggested. "It's a beautiful day and I'm sure your guests would enjoy the view from a few thousand feet up on dragonback."

"That sounds great!" said Holgir. "I'll get the saddles."

"No," said Queen Signý. "Cook has a project for *you*. Something about two dozen dirty pots to wash."

"Yes, Aunt Siggý," said Holgir, resigned to his fate. He trudged toward the open doors, moving slowly so he could continue to hear what was said.

Sigrun stared at her mother and raised an eyebrow.

"Don't give me that look," said Signý. "I was young once, too." She motioned with her hands for the four of them to be on their way. "Have a nice flight, all of you," said the queen. "Find some thick clouds for your fun and be back in time to see to your dragons and get washed up for supper."

Chapter 17

Gertrude and Flavia Drusilla

Gertrude of Mainz stared out her window in the imperial palace at Nárbo but didn't really see the acres of lavender flowers lending color to the scenery before her. Her right hand absentmindedly played with the seven-tiered circular walnut and brass rack of communication rings on her desk, a work of art in itself commissioned by the disgraced and exiled former emperor of the West, Sírénae Accipiter. Gertrude knew it had been crafted by the famed Eastern empire artisan-wizard Lazí of Sûza and used tiny spheres of solidified sound to ensure the device turned smoothly and silently. None of the rings on the rack interested her, however. Gertrude was waiting to hear the three chimes of contact from one special ring—the lone one found on the third finger of her left hand.

Consciously slowing her breathing and her heartbeats, Gertrude tried to remain calm as she felt her life's goal of attaining imperial purple close to her grasp. She was the daughter of a retired legionnaire and a father who worked as an engraver in Mainz, the first of four children and by far the child who'd gone the furthest. Like her mother, she'd joined the legions as soon as she was old enough. Gertrude had seen the world, from commanding a cohort in the Caucasus mountains in the distant east to a stint as a diplomatic emissary to the court of the Jarl of the Smoking Isles in the middle of the Ocean to the west. It took her decades to return home and assume the position of governor of the Rhineland. Now she was serving as Western emperor in all but name.

Gertrude was so close to her goal that she could almost taste it but confirmed emperor and acting emperor were not the same titles, like the marked difference between the exquisite lavender honey Nárbo was famed for and the pedestrian clover honey consumed by the plebes. There were still obstacles to be surmounted, not least of which was getting back the legions Sírénae had enticed to accompany her to Orluin and Occidens Province. Her news from that distant outpost of the Imperium was incomplete and she trusted that her mentor would soon be in touch with more details about *her* legions' disposition. An emperor was not truly an emperor without a full-strength army to command.

A tall and solidly built Gothic woman in her forties, Gertrude had hair the color and cut of a lion's mane. She cultivated the look and was pleased that it intimidated many others, though not the woman she was expecting to hear from. She took deep breaths, lifted her shoulders, and felt the weight of her gold-washed *lorica segmentata* body armor rise and fall along with them. Matching gold-washed *manica*—arm guards—covered her forearms and a legionnaires' short skirt of red-dyed leather and gold-washed steel plates covered her legs to the knee. High red boots and greaves completed her ensemble, save for the helmet placed in easy reach on a corner of her desk.

She could still do a five-mile quick march in full kit and proved that fact to herself every morning at dawn. Save for the glint of cruelty in her eyes—or perhaps because of it—she felt herself to be the very model of a future Roma emperor.

Three familiar chimes sounded and Gertrude removed the ring from her left hand.

"I have two kinds of news," said Flavia Drusilla, emperor of the North, as her lined patrician face appeared in the expanded communication ring's interface.

"Good and bad?" answered Gertrude.

"Let us say good news and a collection of opportunities," Flavia Drusilla replied. She had risen to her current position through her administrative skills, not her martial ones, and her conversation had the subtlety of a slow poison rather than the bluntness of a blow from a gladius.

"I can't wait," said Gertrude. She wanted to hear the bad news first but knew Flavia Drusilla would dole out her information in the order she saw fit.

"Valens and Phraátēs want Quintillius to be Western Emperor," said Flavia Drusilla.

Gertrude grimaced. "Not unexpected, but disappointing." Quintillius was her age and barring accidents on the battlefield or of some *other* sort, her chance at the job after Quintillius was installed would be vanishingly small.

"There's still hope," said Flavia Drusilla. "Phraátēs is the key. He needs Nordland mercenaries to help him counter the waves of annoying steppes horse archer invasions and *I* will soon control Nordland."

"You expect to arrange a horse trade of sorts, then?" asked Gertrude. "You provide him with the warriors he needs, and he gives his support to me instead of Quintillius?"

"It's more complicated than that, but you have the general idea. I also control his access to northern furs and amber."

"And?" asked Gertrude.

Flavia Drusilla smiled. Gertrude was getting much better at understanding complex political negotiations. "And I promised Phraátēs you'd send him ten shiploads of Rhineland wine for his youngest daughter's wedding."

"And?" asked Gertrude, smiling herself this time.

"And we need to get your legions back from Orluin quickly. My sources tell me Valens is amassing troops in northwestern Mauretania, just south of the Pillars, and they're not there to practice desert maneuvers."

"I know about them," said Gertrude. "I've concentrated my remaining legions at the Pyrénées so Valens' forces will have to fight the mountain barbarians first. With luck, any victory Valens might gain will be a Pyrrhic one."

"Hah!" said Flavia Drusilla. "That's clever wordplay. A Pyrrhic victory in the Pyrénées. You're wise enough to know such a conflict would only delay Valens' occupation of Éberria, not prevent it—at least not without the return of your missing legions."

"Who are now under the control of Valentius," Gertrude grumbled.

"As my spies recently informed you," said Flavia Drusilla. "But there's more."

Gertrude exhaled and her shoulders slumped. "Tell me," she said.

"This is good news, of a sort," said Flavia Drusilla. "Word from Valens' court is that his wizards, assisted by mages in Orluin, have determined how to build reliable gates across the Ocean."

"*Good* news!" said Gertrude. "How is that *good* news? Quintillius could have his legions in Nárbo in hours if they could gate across the Ocean!"

"And *your* legions could return equally swiftly," said Flavia Drusilla, her voice as smooth as lavender honey. "We just need to eliminate certain *obstacles* first."

"Like Valentius," said Gertrude.

Flavia Drusilla nodded. "With Valentius out of the way, Quintillius becomes Valens' likely heir, and we can handle Quintillius."

"Only if we neutralize Laetícia first," said Gertrude. "That's no small task."

"But there are three small hostages we might take to guarantee her cooperation," said Flavia Drusilla. "Roma has a long tradition of fostering children at rivals' courts, after all."

"I assume you'll want the children held here in Nárbo?" asked Gertrude.

"I *want* them held in the lowest chamber of the deepest cheese cave you control but would settle for them being kept in the emperor's palace, so long as they can be held securely. This must be seen as your move on the board, not mine," said Flavia Drusilla. "Laetícia may suspect my involvement, but she won't be sure, and that will strengthen my hand when I recommend you for Western emperor over Quintillius. With Valentius out of the picture, her children as hostages, and Quin in line for Southern emperor, Laetícia won't fight *too* hard."

"We hope," said Gertrude. "I assume we will also need to obtain the secret of making trans-Ocean gates?"

"We will," said Flavia Drusilla. "My best mages have tried to duplicate that achievement, losing several junior wizards in the process, and we'll need to be able to build such gates to affect your legions' prompt return."

"More kidnappings, then?" asked Gertrude. "That's easier said than done where senior wizards are concerned."

"Ah," said Flavia Drusilla. "But two birds might fall with one stone. Laetícia is reputed to be one of the wizards skilled in building gates across the Ocean. With her chicks in your control, we can buy both your imperium and the prompt return of your legions using trans-Ocean gates."

"With only the small matter of an assassination and kidnapping three small children as impediments?" Gertrude observed.

"Yes," said Flavia Drusilla. "My sources in Orluin tell me Laetícia is in Nova Eboracum, but her children are with Valentius and his new wife on the southern island where they're building settlements. That should make it easy to accomplish two of the tasks with a single resource."

"Is Magister Callidus with Valentius?" asked Gertrude. She knew he was but wanted to confirm the quality of Flavia Drusilla's informants.

"He is," said the Northern emperor. "But he's not the mage he once was. Callidus shouldn't be able to mount much opposition to our plans."

"As you say," said Gertrude, giving a fractional nod. "Is there anything else?"

"There is one *minor* matter that is more my concern than yours," said Flavia Drusilla. "I must take steps to prevent Bifurland from allying with Nordland and standing in the way of my annexation of that annoying quasi-independent realm."

"You've wanted Nordland under your thumb since you became Northern emperor," said Gertrude. "They've been a useful foil as an independent kingdom for centuries. Why change things now?"

"Because Harald Magnússon is the most infuriating man on either side of the Ocean," said Flavia Drusilla. A muscle in the older woman's cheek twitched and Gertrude could see her mentor's face turn red beneath layers of artfully applied paints and powders. "I could, and probably should kill him."

"It's personal then?" said Gertrude, successfully hiding any indication of amusement.

"Yes!" said Flavia Drusilla. "There's always been an understanding between the kings of Nordland and the emperors of the North. Like a tame frog, when we said, 'Jump!' the Nordland monarchs would say, 'How many feet and in which direction?' I made this clear to King Harald on our first call."

"I take it the conversation didn't go well?" said Gertrude.

"I was never so insulted in my..." Flavia Drusilla paused and moved one hand to her collar as if to stop herself from completing the sentence. After a moment to compose herself, she continued. "I told Harald about the *tame frog* arrangement and he... I mean he..."

"What did he do?" asked Gertrude, trying to help Flavia Drusilla get past this obviously upsetting incident.

"He said he'd heard about the tame frog arrangement and disavowed it," said Flavia Drusilla. "Every time I asserted my traditional imperial privilege, he would drop a brass fastener into a steel bowl. It would ring and echo as he kept saying, 'Rivet. Rivet. Rivet.' He just grinned as he watched me grow more angry."

"That's terrible," said Gertrude. She hadn't heard this story and had to draw on all her soldier's discipline to keep from laughing, knowing that if she failed, she'd never be emperor of the West.

"I know," said Flavia Drusilla. "I cut the call and promptly gave you legions to take two of his provinces south of the Dane Mark. Harald stopped paying tribute and built a defensive wall just north of the lands we took. His merchants are circumventing established trading protocols with gates directly to cities in the other empires instead of using our factors. Now he's seeking to ally with Bifurland to resist me. It's intolerable."

"So *that's* why you loaned me those legions," said Gertrude. "I hadn't realized relations with Nordland were quite so strained and thought it was part of the usual give and take along the border. Half the time it seems to be just a matter of raiding for hams and cheese." She rubbed the side of her forehead and continued. "How do you intend to prevent a Bifurland alliance?"

"By dealing with King Bjarni the same way we will be handling Valentius, obviously," said Flavia Drusilla. "Queen Signý would be heart-broken and too busy dealing with domestic repercussions to mount any kind of fleet in support of Nordland, and their daughter is far too young to immediately step into any meaningful leadership role."

"Wouldn't some other relative just step in and take the throne?" asked Gertrude. "I'm not all that familiar with barbarian succession practices."

"Perhaps," said Flavia Drusilla. "But Queen Signý is formidable in her own right and may well fight to retain the throne for her daughter. However things work out, they'll be too busy to come to the aid of Nordland for at least a year, and by then it will be too late."

"Understood," said Gertrude. "So two assassinations and three kidnappings?"

"Bluntly put, but correct," said Flavia Drusilla.

"I don't have anyone particularly skilled in either art," said Gertrude. "Magister Umbrose and his associates took those talents with them when they sailed west with Sírénae."

"You'll be pleased to learn that I know three independent specialists with outstanding credentials who just happen to be available," said Flavia Drusilla. "Other than Umbrose, they're the best at their craft. You've probably heard of them. They're Athicans."

"Really?" asked Gertrude. "You don't mean you've been able to put Períkulōs, Perkússos, and Sikárias under contract? They have reputations as masters of disguise and superlative wizard assassins."

"No," said Flavia Drusilla. "I don't have them under contract— you do."

"And why am *I* the one to have made these contracts?" asked Gertrude, knowing full well the answer.

"Because it if ever comes out who hired them, *you'll* be blamed, not me," said Flavia Drusilla. "Consider it part of the price of the purple."

"I see," said Gertrude. She leaned her chin on her fist and stared into the interface of the communications ring. "When will they leave for Orluin?"

"They've already left," said Flavia Drusilla. "Three of your dragons are carrying them most of the way and they'll manage the rest of the trip on their flying disks."

"How did you arrange for three of *my* dragons to provide transport services without my personal approval?" asked Gertrude. She was curious about the answer and anxious to plug such a glaring hole in her security.

"Sikárias pretended to be you and gave the order," said Flavia Drusilla. "I understand her illusions can be very convincing."

"Undoubtedly," said Gertrude. "Thank you for planning ahead. I'm glad I could play some small role in your grand scheme."

"Don't be petulant," said Flavia Drusilla. "I had to move quickly, and it will be worth it to put you on an imperial throne."

"On that we agree," said Gertrude. She was willing to play the part of junior partner—for now—but that would change once she was confirmed as emperor of the West.

"Good," said Flavia Drusilla. "See to your southern defenses and keep me up to date on any news from Nárbo."

"Of course," said Gertrude.

Flavia Drusilla cut the connection and the circular communications interface contracted to a small gold ring, which Gertrude returned to the ring finger of her left hand. She admired the ring beside it on her middle finger. It was made from a dark metal and its inner surface was etched with a braided sucker-covered octopus-arms design. Magister Umbrose had given it to her as a gift when they'd worked together against the mountain tribes of Pyrénéans more than a decade ago. She extended her other hand and gave the rack of rings before her a spin, then stared again at the dark ring with the tentacle pattern. Perhaps the time would soon be ripe to reach out to her old colleague.

Chapter 18

Wizard Assassins

The wizard assassins Flavia Drusilla had hired through several layers of cutouts claimed their dragon mounts at the fortified garrison of Septéntriacastra near the border with the Kingdom of Nordland in the Western Empire. Of middling size and maximum ferocity, black-scaled Maniōdékles, Zágriostrax, and Grigórianōx had tremendous stamina. Under orders from Gertrude of Mainz and Sírénae Accipiter before her, the three dragons had crossed the length and breadth of the skies of Nordland many times, striking terror into that kingdom's inhabitants.

The trio of dragons had even flown the many empty miles to the Smoking Isle out in the northern Ocean and circled the jagged mountains and treeless plains of that isolated land. While there, they had seen calderas that belched hot lava like the volcanoes in Italia. When the dragons' fiery breath emulated the volcanoes destructive power and burned the tents of the annual gathering in the southwest of the island, they delivered a far from subtle message that all of Nordland only remained free so long as the kingdom continued to be useful to the Imperium.

For Flavia Drusilla, that usefulness was coming to an end.

The Northern emperor knew these dragons well. They often stopped for food and resupply at her administrative center of Nevaopolis, an outpost near eastern Nordland built on piles in the marshes at the mouth of the Neva River. Flavia Drusilla had no concern about the dragons' ability to transport their passengers all the way to Orluin, especially with strategic stops along the way. She didn't have much respect for their intelligence, but dragons grew wiser with age and these three were only in their twenties and largely isolated from mentors like Xaxidiánus, who'd been based in Nárbo before Sírénae took him and the six other dragons in the Western Empire's capital across the Ocean to Orluin.

Maybe the dragons would learn something of guile from their new riders? she considered.

A message came to her by ring, confirming her wizard assassins had departed. Flavia Drusilla had many agents inside the Western empire. She knew Sírénae kept dozens of informants inside the Northern empire to watch *her* actions but didn't know how many of those informants remained on Gertrude's payroll. It would be foolish to expect too few, and Flavia Drusilla was no fool.

Gertrude can live with me usurping her authority, thought Flavia Drusilla. *I had to act quickly. It's more important to have the wizard assassins in place on time than to stroke her ego. I know I'll have to take care she remains loyal to me once she's formally recognized as Emperor of the West, but I've arranged all the evidence to point to her being the one to send the assassins on* her *dragons, so that will be one more strand in the rope that binds her to me.*

Flavia Drusilla spared a moment to savor the mental image of Gertrude of Mainz bound before her, then she smiled and set her mind to other tasks. The trio of wizard assassins she'd set loose had never failed her before. She was confident they would eliminate their targets this time as well.

* * * * *

Períkulōs, Perkússos, and Sikárias were dressed as wealthy merchants under sets of warm flying leathers. Their magestones were well concealed by identical black silk scarves and their faces could be transformed to whatever appearances would be most useful at their destinations. They'd flown their dragons from Septéntriacastra across Gaul and Éberria with only a few stops in wild, unpopulated areas of the Western empire to avoid awkward questions from local officials.

Killing was the wizard assassins' business, but indiscriminate murders were wasteful and unprofessional. Their pay was exorbitant, and they knew they were worth every ounce of gold on deposit for them with banking houses in mountainous Helvetia that were famed for their discretion and confidentiality.

The three travelers didn't bother with disguises while flying across the Ocean. The two men resembled each other, and the woman shared their classic Athican features—dark hair, dark eyes, and skin bronzed by the sun. They could have been models for sculptures by Phidias in the time of Pericles, though their typical temperaments were more like cold, unfeeling stone than the warmly painted features carved from marble by true artists in ancient times.

The wizard assassins carried identical magestones, sharp daggers of obsidian smaller than a little finger obtained from a well-hidden quarry on the island of Melos in the Aegean Sea. Together, the trio had shaped shards of black volcanic glass into tiny knives then carefully mounted them in settings shaped like hilts made of silver from the mines of Laurion. Silver removed from those mines by slave labor more than two millennia earlier had paid for the two hundred triremes that defeated the Persian fleet at Salamis.

Now in their sixties, but still vigorous thanks to esoteric elixirs akin to healing potions but specifically designed to slow the aging process, they appeared to be in the prime of life. Only a close examination of the fine lines around their eyes, when they weren't transforming their appearances with illusions, revealed their decades of rigorous training and long years of practicing their deadly trade.

Their individual names were known to few, though their fearsome reputations as the *wizard assassins* brought terror to their potential targets. The fear was so great that rumors of a new assassination contract made nervous nobles double their strongholds' security and wary mages triple the wards on their towers.

Despite how the wider world knew them, when the three spoke to each other they could smile and joke like the old friends, colleagues, and more than colleagues they were.

After a dozen hours of flying from the coast of the mainland province of Éberria Lusitania, the three travelers and their mounts reached the westernmost of the Caprini Isles, volcanic peaks that poked their way up from the depths of the Ocean and were home to extensive unmanaged herds of sheep and goats left to multiply there centuries ago by the intrepid imperial sailors who'd first discovered the islands.

A few hours before dusk, the wizard assassins found a remote spot where they could rest—sleeping was possible, though not easy on dragonback—and sent their dragons off with instructions to consume no more than three of the island's hoofed inhabitants each. More would slow them down, so they'd be indolent for days. As it was, wizards and mounts alike would be resting for half a day before embarking on the longest leg of their journey that would take them to their next intermediate stop in the Tempest Isles. For now, the three wizards would enjoy a meal of their own before they slept.

"This wine is quite good," said Períkulōs after taking a sip from his artfully decorated brass goblet. He pointed to two matching goblets resting on a conveniently located flat rock. Períkulōs poured a generous portion of wine into the waiting vessels from a small cask made from Éberrian oak and diluted it with an equal portion of water from a similar, but larger cask.

"I'll taste it in a moment," said Sikárias. She pushed her long hair away from her eyes with a hand while expertly separating a roasted chicken into its component breasts, wings, legs, and thighs with sharp planes of solidified sound. She kept two physical daggers on her belt, one for cutting her food and one for cutting throats.

"The bread will be done soon," said Perkússos, who was warming sheets of wholewheat flatbread on a cooking stone.

"Don't burn it this time," said Períkulōs.

"I never burn flatbread," said Perkússos. "We just have different concepts of what it means to make well-toasted bread."

"A bit brown is good, but blackened is bad," said Sikárias. "You've liked playing with fire far too much since you were a child and don't know when enough is enough."

"Guilty as charged," said Perkússos. "I'll try to restrain myself."

"You should have restrained yourself when it came time to take this commission," said Períkulōs.

"Agreed," said Sikárias. "Why are we killing an emperor's heir and kidnapping children?" She arranged the pieces of chicken on an oval wooden platter and placed the platter on the flat rock beside the goblets.

"Because Gertrude is paying us an exceedingly large amount of money to do so," said Perkússos. "And after we succeed in our commission, we'll have the favor of the emperors of the West, North, *and* East."

"Along with the lasting enmity of the emperor of the South," said Períkulōs.

"Valens is an old man," said Perkússos. "He won't be our enemy for long."

"We need to be more careful about the enemies we make now that Sírénae is no longer able to support us," said Sikárias.

"That was—and is—a special relationship," said Períkulōs. He sat on one of the three upturned logs beside the flat rock they were using as a table and had another sip of wine before putting his goblet down and picking up a chicken breast, its skin crispy and flavored with lemon juice and oregano.

Perkússos delivered a stack of perfectly baked flatbread and sat on one of the other logs.

Sikárias moved the third log closer to Períkulōs, sat beside him, and stretched out a hand to take a piece of flatbread. She inspected it, smiled, and used it to pick up a chicken leg. "Nicely done," she told Perkússos. "Not burnt."

"I'm glad you approve," Perkússos replied. He muttered something like, "I burned the flatbread *once* a decade ago and she..." then let his words trail off as he used a round of flatbread like a pair of tongs to collect the second breast from the platter. After so many years the three of them were familiar with each other's preferences across many areas. *And,* Perkússos reflected, *we know exactly where to push each other to get our desired reactions.* He took a bite of chicken and nibbled a morsel of flatbread.

A loud flurry of *bleats* and *baas* in the distance, along with the *whoosh* of jets of flame, indicated the dragons were also savoring their meals and likely playing with their food.

"Tell me again why we're kidnapping the children," said Sikárias. "Wouldn't it be simpler to eliminate Quintillius and Laetícia?"

"An excellent question," said Períkulōs.

Perkússos took a moment to swallow before replying. "I think Flavia Drusilla is playing a long game."

"I thought Gertrude of Mainz was paying us?" said Sikárias. "That's why I took on her appearance to commandeer the dragons."

"And that's why I'm responsible for negotiating our assignments," said Perkússos. "I'm confident Flavia Drusilla *told* Gertrude to hire us."

"Which means?" said Períkulōs.

"Gertrude only thinks two or three steps ahead," said Perkússos. "She only sees the closest parts of the *shah-mat* board. Flavia Drusilla thinks a dozen steps ahead and not only sees the entire board but the hands that move the pieces."

"Interesting," said Sikárias. "What pieces would we be on a *shah-mat* board?" she asked the empty air.

Perkússos shook his head and considered ignoring the question, then decided to respond. "Pawns, but very capable ones," he told Sikárias. "Pawns with a talent for taking powerful pieces."

Sikárias nodded. The answer was accurate.

Perkússos continued. "I think Flavia Drusilla wants control of each of the other three emperors. Gertrude will owe Flavia Drusilla for her imperium. Phraátēs will need the Nordland mercenaries our true employer can provide to protect him from the steppes horse archers..."

"...and with Valentius dead, Quintillius is the logical option for Valens' heir as emperor of the South," said Períkulōs. Sikárias patted his knee.

"I expect we will end up delivering the children to the Northern imperial court at Byzantium," said Perkússos.

"Not Nárbo?" asked Períkulōs.

"Flavia Drusilla might tell Gertrude they'll be kept in Nárbo, but I can't see her giving up such important leverage," said Perkússos. "The children will end up in Byzantium."

"Where, I assume, they will be *fostered...*" said Sikárias.

"While serving as hostages to ensure the cooperation of Quintillius and Laetícia," said Períkulōs.

"It's good to know I didn't get *all* the brains in the family—just most of them," said Perkússos.

"Hold on to that delusion," said Períkulōs. "Can you exercise your mighty brain to determine which of us should handle each assignment?"

"We can decide that when we get to the Tempest Isles," said Perkússos. "I'll ring Flavia Drusilla's agent for the latest updates. There were rumors that the children were visiting Valentius and his new wife Aleña on Valentia."

"Send me to Bifurland then," said Sikárias. "I don't want to have anything to do with kidnapping children."

"You're not getting squeamish, are you?" asked Períkulōs.

"You know me too well to think that," she replied. "It's just that I find *most* children tiresome. Give me a straightforward royal assassination any day."

Now Períkulōs patted *her* knee. "You're a true artist at your craft, my dear."

"Thank you," said Sikárias.

"You can have assassination, not kidnapping then," said Perkússos. "King Bjarni is your assignment. Try to lay the blame on the Nordlanders."

"Not on Flavia Drusilla or Gertrude?" asked Sikárias with a falsely sweet tone that made Perkússos shake his head.

"Fine. Point made," said Perkússos. "I won't try to teach my grandmother how to spin."

"I'm only a year older than you," said Sikárias. "No need for insults— and I doubt I'll ever be a grandmother."

"There's still time," said Períkulōs.

"It's unlikely," Sikárias replied.

"We're also supposed to keep our ears open for details about new kinds of gates," said Perkússos. "There are stories circulating about gates built into communications rings and gates across the Ocean."

"Trans-Ocean gates would have saved us this trip," noted Períkulōs.

"But then we wouldn't have had a need for this lovely meal on a charming island," said Perkússos.

"Or hours of uncomfortable flight on dragonback," said Sikárias. She yawned, used the last bit of her flatbread to wipe her lips, and stood up. "I'm getting some rest," she said. Turning on her heel, she walked toward a pair of bedrolls atop thick fleeces twenty paces away.

"Be right with you," said Períkulōs. "I'll just help clean up."

"Go," said Perkússos. "I'll handle things and set the wards after I check on the dragons. I want to make sure they don't overeat."

"Thank you," said Períkulōs. "See you in the morning."

* * * * *

More than a day later the wizard assassins flew down through a bank of thick white clouds and saw the welcome sight of the Tempest Isles set amid sparkling blue waters below. They could see ships' masts to the east and sensed a familiar presence to the west beside the Great Harbor. Spotting the outline of a large black dragon, they landed their own exhausted dragons on the sand nearby and dismounted. Six figures came to greet them. Four were strangers. One was Sírénae, who nodded to them. The exiled emperor's spymaster was more animated in his greeting.

"Mother! Father! Uncle Kússos!" Umbrose exclaimed. "What are *you* doing here?"

Chapter 19

Riyas

Eynon and Merry gated into the skies above Riyas with Ace standing on Merry's flying disk and Chee perched on Eynon's shoulder. They floated at the approximate location where the two young wizards had engineered an illusion of that city to foil an attack by Viridáxés some months earlier. The weather was warm and skies to the west threatened rain, but for now it was a pleasant-enough day. Merry put her hand on Ace's head to prevent him from soaring off in search of small mammals—with wings, or without. Chee continued to cling to Eynon, making soft sounds as if he was tired of all the gating they'd been doing recently. Eynon stroked the fur on Chee's back and murmured wordless reassurances to his familiar. He nodded at Merry and the two of them began a gentle, curved descent toward the gates of Tamloch's capital.

Unlike their previous visit, when the gates of Riyas had been tightly closed, this time they were open, with creaking carts, heavy wagons, riders, and pedestrians passing through in both directions. A slack-jawed soldier leaning on a spear had a longsword hanging low on his hip, its point nearly touching the cobblestones. He was wearing an official green and gold Tamloch tabard and stood in a niche by the gate's entrance observing the varied traffic.

The expression on the guard's face made Eynon think the man resembled one of the cows he'd milked back in Haywall—and *not* one of the smarter ones. Eynon exchanged a glance with Merry and she raised an eyebrow. Clearly, the guard's function was simply to be there as a symbol of royal authority, but he was failing at even that small task. Merry made a mental note to advise Jenet that such a public post might be better filled by a soldier a few inches up from the bottom of the barrel. Eynon and Merry approached the soldier together, their expectations set at or slightly below ground level.

"We're looking for Verro," said Eynon.

"He's not here," replied the guard as he continued to lean on his spear, now tilted toward Eynon. He scratched at his nose and shook his head, obviously regarding the young wizard as a temporary annoyance that kept him from returning to whatever passed for thoughts behind his somewhat glazed eyes.

"How about Doethan?" asked Merry.

"Who?" asked the guard after a yawn.

"Princess Rúth's new husband," Merry answered.

"I can't be bothered with all the goings on in the palace," said the guard, tilting his spear toward Merry. "Least of all who might have married who. Things there was better when Túathal was on the throne. He gave us extra rations of beer."

"I see," said Eynon.

"So do I," said Merry. They both realized that the guard had been one of Túathal's soldiers, selected more for obedience than initiative.

"I don't care *what* you see," said the guard, who exerted a small amount of effort to thrust his jaw forward. "Do your seein' elsewhere. Now you and your scruffy lookin' beasts can move along."

"Gladly," said Eynon. He took Merry's hand and the pair walked into the city side by side.

As they went, Merry leaned down and rubbed the fur on her rockhound's head. "Who's he calling scruffy looking?" she said. "I think you're a handsome boy."

Chee clapped at this, then turned to look back toward the gate. He made a face in the direction of the guard, not that his gesture was noticed.

"You're handsome, too," Eynon told Chee. He turned to Merry. "How are we going to find Verro now?"

Merry pointed at the tall building made from thick gray blocks with a tinge of green directly ahead of them. "I think that's the mayor's office—City Hall. We can ask Mayor Cáinta. I expect she'll know something about Verro's whereabouts. Failing that, you can always ring Dârio."

"I could, couldn't I," said Eynon. "Nothing like going to the top to get answers."

"If you want answers, it would be better to ask Jenet," teased Merry.

"We're here, so let's start with Cáinta," said Eynon.

There weren't guards with spears and swords at City Hall, but there was a solidly built older woman with her hair hidden under a green and gold tartan scarf. She was enthroned in a well-padded chair behind a massive desk covered with carvings of acanthus vines and stylized clovers. The desk was so wide it blocked half the hall just inside the entrance to the building. A thick book the size of a tipped-over tombstone rested on the desk before her.

"Please state your business," said the woman in a matter-of-fact tone as if she repeated the phrase a thousand times a day, which she likely did. Eynon had the sense that the *please* part had only been added after Dârio had replaced Túathal as Tamloch's ruler.

"We're here to see Cáinta," said Merry.

"Do you have an appointment?" asked the woman at the desk. She ran her finger down a page in her book. "No, I see that you don't. No appointments for any young Dâron wizards listed here. I have the head of the Company of Mercers, a delegation of worsted wool weavers from the western quarter of the city, and a banker-academician-mathematician from Bhaile Pónaire hoping to buy a lot to build a lending office on the list, but no Dâron wizards." She looked up at Eynon and Merry and sniffed. "I can fit you in for a quarter hour just before noon a week from today. Would that do?"

"It most certainly would *not*," said Merry. Ace made a low growling noise in the back of his throat and Merry tapped him on the top of his head to indicate he should stop.

"We need to see Cáinta as soon as possible," said Eynon after taking a slow, calming breath.

"As soon as possible will be just before noon a week from today, as I've told you," said the woman.

"But we need to see her now," said Eynon. He was disappointed that his voice was getting both higher and louder as he spoke to Cáinta's appointments secretary. He took another breath and spoke in a more moderate tone. "It won't take long. I only have one question for her."

"One question often has a way of transforming into three and then ten," said the woman.

Merry nearly laughed because the woman sounded so like her own mother, Mabli. She suppressed her laugh but correctly guessed the woman's next sentence.

"Poor planning on your part does not constitute an emergency on the mayor's part."

"Do you know who you're talking to?" asked Merry.

"Two young wandering blue wizards, I assume," said the woman. "The old stories say such wizards are easily lost."

"My companion is Eynon of Haywall, Master Mage of Dâron," said Merry. "The two of us created the illusions that distracted the great green dragon Viridáxés and prevented him from burning Riyas to the ground."

"I didn't see any such illusion—or dragon," said the woman. "Like a sensible person, I was taking shelter in the tunnels beneath the city during the siege."

"You *must* have heard about the illusions and dragon from others who saw them?" declared Merry.

"I'm not likely to believe nonsense when someone tries to cover my head with a woolsack of fabrications," said the woman, who then stood up behind her desk, revealing herself to be a few inches taller than Merry. "And don't you go trying to impress me with any absurd tales about someone your age being Master Mage of Dâron. My daughter is betrothed to the *king* of Dâron, and my future son-in-law will put you in your place with a crossbow bolt if you're lying to me."

"*You're* Bonnie's mother?" asked Eynon.

"I am," said the woman. "My name is Sórcha. How do you know my daughter?"

"Nûd is my friend," Eynon began.

"You mean His Majesty King Dârianûd, Dârioth the Twenty-fifth of Dâron," Sórcha corrected.

"He was just Nûd when Eynon met him, Sórcha," said Merry. "He was working as a servant for Master Mage Ealdamon—and it hasn't yet been determined if he's Dârioth the Twenty-fifth or Twenty-sixth."

"Unstop your ears and listen more closely," said the woman. "My name is said *Súr-kah*—and I won't put up with any disrespect for the ruler of Dâron, no matter what his dynastic designation."

"Yes, Sórcha," said Merry, using the woman's preferred pronunciation.

"I mean no disrespect for my friend Nûd," said Eynon, "but we really need to find Verro. I need his help."

"Well, why didn't you say so in the first place?" asked Sórcha. "You didn't need to bother the mayor with such a request."

"We didn't?" asked Merry.

"Of course not," said Sórcha. "I'm here to see no one wastes the mayor's time, but I'd be pleased to tell you where to find Verro at present."

Eynon exhaled slowly. "And where would that be?" he asked after four heartbeats.

"At the Great Falls, with Fercha and Princess Rúth and Doethan and Their Majesties of Tamloch and Dâron," said Sórcha. "I should be there as well as the mother of one of the brides, but given my important duties for the mayor, I had to remain here."

"I... see..." said Eynon.

There was a sudden clacking of footsteps from the hall behind Sórcha and Mayor Cáinta appeared, standing in the space beside her appointments secretary's desk. She stood taller than Eynon remembered, and her hair was now a deep brown, not the gray it had been a few months earlier. It was as if Túathal's departure had taken a great weight from her shoulders and given her space to grow into the woman she wanted to be.

"Eynon, Merry!" exclaimed the mayor. "It's *so* nice to see you. What brings the Master Mage of Dâron and his talented partner to Riyas?"

"He *is* the Master Mage of Dâron?" said Sórcha, her jaw several inches lower than it had been a moment before.

"Of course he is," affirmed Sórcha. "These two young wizards' illusions saved us from the great green dragon. They're heroes of the city."

"Sórcha said she could fit us in to see you for fifteen minutes a week from today," said Merry.

"Nonsense," said Cáinta. "Eynon and Merry don't need an appointment to see me. They've earned the right to see me whenever it's convenient—for *them*."

"Thank you," said Eynon. He smiled at Sórcha, then at the mayor. "Sórcha has already answered the question I'd come to City Hall to ask."

"Which is?" asked Cáinta.

"Where we can find Verro," said Merry. "We understand he's at the Great Falls helping plan two royal weddings."

"Yes," said Cáinta. She stepped over and hugged the two young wizards before continuing. "And at a very romantic location between Tamloch and Dâron."

"Cheeeeee...." sighed Eynon's familiar as he crouched on Eynon's shoulder and clasped his front paws over his heart, as if he'd understood Cáinta's words.

Eynon reached up and stroked Chee's back. "Then it's time for us to be going," said Eynon, nodding to Merry. "We have to fly west to connect with Verro—and it will be a pleasure to see the others there as well. Unfortunately, it will take us hours to get to the Great Falls from here."

"Even with my line-of-sight gating," said Merry.

"I think I can save you some time on your journey," said Mayor Cáinta. "There's a fixed gate to the Great Falls from the Royal Palace. Túathal had Verro construct it for him so he could visit the Inn at the Falls more easily."

"Excellent," said Merry.

"Can you take us to the gate?" asked Eynon.

"Of course," Cáinta replied.

"May I join you?" asked Sórcha. "I've always wanted to see the Great Falls but didn't want to take the long overland journey."

"You'll see it at the weddings," said Cáinta. "I'll escort these young wizards and their familiars, while you..."

"Let all the people with scheduled appointments know you've been temporarily delayed," said Sórcha.

She sighed as the young wizards and the mayor waved to her and disappeared out the entrance to City Hall, ascending into the sky to fly toward the royal palace. Sórcha shook her head and rubbed her temples. *There was something I was supposed to tell the Master Mage of Dâron,* she realized. *It was a message from the warden at the royal prison, so it can't be that important.* "It's no matter, I'm sure," she said aloud. Whatever the warden had told her was permanently banished from her mind as she got on with the much more critical task of examining her schedule book while wishing she had a goblet of winter wine.

"Now what am I going to tell the head of the Company of Mercers?" she wondered.

Chapter 20

Admiral Pixo

Admiral Pixo shifted his stance on the bare stone of the rocky promontory, his body still more comfortable with the ever-moving deck of a ship than more stable dry land. His fleet of forty vessels bobbing in the harbor before him was less than a tenth the size of the original invasion fleet he'd commanded when his emperor, Sírénae Accipiter, had led an invasion force from the Western Empire to its province in Orluin.

Deposed emperor is more accurate, Pixo thought. *Or perhaps twice defeated emperor after the Orluin Alliance and Valentius had convinced Sírénae's legions to defect and gate south to an unsettled island larger than the Green Isle. I should have joined them,* Pixo mused, *but my niece convinced me to follow her and Sírénae to the Tempest Isles instead.*

The harbor's waters were crystal clear and so transparent Pixo could see coral-covered rocks not far below. He'd initially planned to anchor in the Great Harbor to the west, a vast expanse of deep water protected by a thin fishhook of land, but he'd changed his mind. It had seemed much more prudent to shift to the eastern anchorage at the other end of the Tempest Isles after losing two ships to attacks by a leviathan—or perhaps by a pair of them, it was difficult to tell. The beasts were so huge they needed deeper water than the relatively shallow harbor before him. So far, they'd only been bothered by opportunistic sharks and barracudas.

Supplies hadn't been a problem. His crews had been able to catch and roast wild pigs and cattle scratching out a living from the scraggly vegetation of the Tempest Isles, their ancestors released there by previous generations of sailors. Pixo was also fond of the large red onions that had developed from *allium* plants originally grown on the Isle of Dogs. There was something in the soil here that changed the onions' color and gave them a mild, pleasant flavor.

Unfortunately, his stomach had been tied in knots of late—no surprise, given all that had happened—and all he could keep down was ship's biscuits dipped in honey.

This wouldn't be a bad place to retire, thought Pixo, *if I didn't have to worry about the local inhabitants.*

He considered that this end of the isles appeared to be lightly populated with the locals wisely staying a respectful distance away from the ten centuries of legionnaires in the Emperor's Own. He was glad most of Sírénae's Praetorians had remained loyal. There were still quite a few locals elsewhere on the Tempest Isles, however. His sailors were still traveling in large parties on foraging expeditions farther west on the islands ever since three of them failed to return from a trip to the Great Harbor. He'd see to it that at least a dozen legionnaires would accompany his sailors on such trips in the future.

If only all the wind wizards hadn't deserted with Magister Callidus and gone to Valentia, as that previously unsettled southern island was called, thought Pixo. *I could have had one fly over to the Great Harbor to see if my niece, the emperor, and her unsettling spymaster, Magister Umbrose, were waiting at the rendezvous point Celéri had specified.*

Admiral Pixo smiled to himself at the foolishness of one of his ideas to alert Celéri to his presence. Setting large smoky fires, using precious firewood, didn't transmit any sort of message to the Great Harbor because the prevailing westerlies sent all the smoke drifting east, not west. There was always enough wind to prevent any substantial height of smoke plume from forming.

If only I hadn't lost my communications ring with Celéri, thought Pixo. All of his communication rings had been on a fine chain he kept in a sea chest in his cabin on the *Menodorus Maximus,* his flagship. Unfortunately, that noble vessel was one of the two lost to the leviathans. Pixo had been lucky to be consulting one of his senior captains aboard the *Aquitainia* when the great beasts attacked. Crews from several ships rescued the sailors and legionnaires aboard the flagship, but his communication rings—and his beloved books—were now at the bottom of the Great Harbor alongside the shattered hull of the second ship lost, the *Gallia Lugdunensis*.

Pixo turned his head from side to side and sighed. *I should have worn the rings on my fingers,* he reminded himself, *but they caused me pain when I had to write reports.* He rubbed his fingers together and grimaced. *If only I hadn't run out of the potion that dulled the ache months ago.*

Perhaps Celéri could make me more, thought Pixo. Then, upon further reflection, he reconsidered. *Celéri never specialized in healing. She was always more interested in spying and destruction than preserving. Given my deployments at sea and her own commitments studying magic, we haven't spent much time together. She was an adorable toddler, though. From what I've heard, she still acts like someone toddler-aged more often than not. She even claims that* she *is an emperor, which is ridiculous and contrary to every Roma tradition.*

He gave a slight sigh and then a longer, deeper one. *Maybe if I'd been a better influence in her life,* Pixo mused. *No, she is who she is, and I'm getting too old for second thoughts and self-recrimination.* He looked down at his gnarled hands, worn from too many years of tying knots and writing reports to superiors. *Skip all that,* he thought. *It doesn't matter why. I'm just getting old. The days when I could wield a sword and lead a boarding party are long past, though I expect I could still hold my own in dire need.*

Pixo considered the land and water around him and decided it wasn't a place where he wanted to retire after all. His old friend Callidus often talked about retiring to a tower in the Pyrénéan mountains between Gaul and Éberria, once all the rebels had been dealt with. A villa in a seaside village in southern Italia, on the Calabrian coast perhaps, was more to Pixo's preference, though after following a deposed emperor he doubted he'd ever have an opportunity to buy one. Exile was now his lot, or execution should he ever recross the Ocean to the Imperium.

Valentia, where most of Sírénae's legions had gone after the so-called Battle of the Abbenoth, was reputed to have both high mountains and scenic coasts. Perhaps he could build his villa there and Magister Callidus could *ad hoc* gate in to visit and enjoy games of *shah-mat* and glasses of wine from a terrace with a view of the water. *That would be a good life,* thought Pixo. *Provided Sírénae— or Celéri—didn't kill him first, one as a calculated act, the other as a whim. Or vice versa.*

His mind went back to his rapid exit from Nova Eboracum. It stabbed his heart to leave hundreds of vessels, each one known to him by name, bobbing at anchor in the harbor. The forty-two ships they'd sailed for the Tempest Isles were ones that could carry the troops of the Emperor's Own legion and the small proportion of his sailors who remained loyal to Sírénae. That loyalty was sorely tested on the trip here, however. Attempts to forage along the north shore of Isla Longa met with failure and starving soldiers and sailors were desperate for food. Later, when they tried to approach an island listed on his charts as Bucket Island at nightfall, the roar of a great beast—probably a dragon—larger than Pixo had ever heard before, discourage him and his fleet from anchoring nearby. If not for the fish they'd managed to catch *en route,* he'd have surely faced a general mutiny.

Thank goodness the powdered oranges had held out, preventing the Sailor's Disease, thought Pixo. He smiled as he remembered the familiar tang of the powder doled out daily to every man, woman, and child aboard a Roma ship. Pixo ran his tongue around his gums, remembering how much they'd ached on a voyage from Nárbo through the Pillars and south along the west coast of Afarika to the Southern Empire outpost at Table Bay. They'd taken on water in a storm and the barrels of powered oranges, knocked against a bulkhead as the ship tossed, had lost their structural integrity and gotten wet, their contents spilled and spoiled. Only the crocks of pickled cabbage the cook from Gothland had brought along for his personal use had saved the crew from lost teeth or worse.

I wonder how Sírénae plans to recover from this latest set of reversals, thought Pixo. *It's one thing to thumb her nose at the other three emperors and sail west to carve out a new empire, but quite another to be left with a mere thousand legionnaires and forty ships.* As far as Pixo knew, all of her dragons had gone over to Valentius as well. He'd miss the emperor's dragons. Xaxidiánus was a skilled *shah-mat* opponent in his own right, even if they did have to use duplicate boards of vastly different sizes when they played each other.

Celéri added the chaos of a Wizard Queen to the situation, mimicking the play of that style of *shah-mat* where the queen could gate to any open square, not just move horizontally and vertically. Wizard Queen games tended to be fast and quite costly to other pieces. Pixo hoped Celéri's ego and impulsiveness wouldn't lead to too much carnage. He shook his head. His niece was hot-blooded, Sírénae was cold-blooded, and Umbrose was effectively bloodless, caring not a single drop of whatever noxious ichor-like fluid flowed through his veins for anyone other than himself and Sírénae.

Maybe Wizard Queen chess was what gave Celéri the idea she could be a wizard and *an emperor,* he considered. *In any competition between my niece and the team of Sírénae and Umbrose, I'd bet against Celéri, though sometimes youth and energetic unpredictability* did *win out over age and treachery.*

Pixo squared his shoulders and prepared to walk back down the path to the harbor. He promised himself to put an expeditionary force of sailors and legionnaires together in the morning to forge overland to the Great Harbor to see if Celéri, Sírénae, and Umbrose were waiting for him at the prearranged rendezvous point on the shore of the Great Harbor. It wouldn't be good for his health to keep any of them waiting. Shouts from ships and shore below made Pixo pause. He saw more than a dozen sailors' and legionnaires' arms pointing to the skies in the east and looked up to see what had caught their attention.

Dragons!

Chapter 21

The Great Falls

Cáinta wished the young wizards and their familiars well, then pointed at a fresco of The Great Falls painted on the plaster in what had been Túathal's royal bedroom. "Just step through and you'll be at the Inn of the Falls," she said.

"Isn't there a passphrase?" asked Merry.

"There must be *some* sort of security on this gate," added Eynon.

"Oh dear," said Cáinta. "What *was* that phrase?" The mayor rubbed her forehead, then smiled. "I remember," she said. "Verro was explaining it to Fercha while I was watching. He told her Túathal had given him the phrase to use. It was supposed to remind him about Zeno's Dichotomy Paradox."

"That's the one where—" Eynon began.

"—Zeno demonstrated you can't get there from here," Merry finished, adding a short laugh at the end.

"In a manner of speaking," said Cáinta. "When I was a girl I learned it as you can never actually get *anywhere* because first you have to go half the distance, then half the remaining distance, then half of what's left, without ever arriving."

"But after several iterations," said Eynon, "the remaining distance is so small you really *are* there."

Merry touched Cáinta's arm. "Paradoxes aside, good mayor, we have to be on our way. Do you remember the passphrase now?"

"I do," said Cáinta. She faced the fresco and spoke. "Inch by inch. Step by step." Slowly, she turned toward the young wizards. Behind her, a rectangular shape the size of a door on the right side of the painted plaster wall began to shimmer. "The gate is activated," said the mayor. "Enter it quickly, and good luck. Say hello to everyone for me."

"Of course," said Eynon as he and Chee entered the gate and disappeared.

"We'll be glad to," said Merry before she and Ace did likewise.

"Someday, *I'd* like to visit the Inn at the Falls," said Cáinta to the empty air. "Perhaps I'll be invited to the weddings." She sighed and noticed the dust on the furniture in the room, resolving to tell one of her friends on the palace staff to tidy up the old king's bedroom from time to time. She understood why Dârio and Jenet had no interest in sleeping in Túathal's bed, but that was no excuse not to keep things clean. Squaring her shoulders, Cáinta left the room and headed for the stairs and the long walk to her office. The sooner she got back to City Hall the fewer complaints Sórcha and the worsted wool weavers of the city's western quarter would have for her.

* * * * *

Eynon, Merry, and their familiars found themselves in a narrow corridor that seemed to be carved into gray limestone. The only illumination was a series of widely spaced wizard lamps attached to the ceiling and leading away from the featureless wall behind them. A sound like a strong wind blowing through the leaves of millions of trees surrounded them. It seemed to resonate in the solid stone and they could feel a thrumming vibration through their boots.

Ace hopped off Merry's flying disk and started running along the corridor. Chee jumped from Eynon's shoulder and gave chase, catching up and climbing on Ace's back after a few dozen of the rockhound's steps. Soon they disappeared into the distance with a chorus of echoing barks and calls of *Chee! Chee!*

"What's that *sound?*" asked Eynon.

"Think about it," said Merry. "Where are we?"

"At the Great Falls..." Eynon responded. Then he smacked the heel of his palm against his forehead, removed it, and said, "Oh."

"Oh indeed," said Merry. "That must be the sound of falling water. A *lot* of falling water."

"Suddenly I need to..." Eynon began.

Merry raised her hand. "Don't think about it," she said. "There are sure to be garderobes at the inn."

"I hope so," said Eynon. "I have to say this isn't the most welcoming entrance to an inn I've ever seen." He squeezed his legs together and took a deep breath, then put his flying disk on his back and took Merry's hand.

"Not that you've been in that many inns," Merry teased.

"True," said Eynon. "Just the inns I've visited with you on our travels. Before that, I didn't have much opportunity. There are only two inns in all the Coombe. One on the upper Rhuthro River at the baronial seat in Caercadel and one by the big spring in Wherrel, not far from the northwestern entrance to the valley."

"That's near the quarry where we found Viridáxés," said Merry.

"Right," said Eynon. "And where we fought Verro's wizards and soldiers trying to steal magestones."

"And where we *also* fought those Southern Clan Lander wizards from the Falcon Clan not so long ago," said Merry. "Brùtha, their leader, really had it in for you."

Eynon rubbed the back of his head where he could still feel where Brùtha's falcon familiar had struck him with its talons. "Can we talk about something more pleasant, please?" he asked Merry.

She leaned over and gave Eynon a kiss on the cheek. "You don't want to take advantage of the two of us being alone in the almost dark then?" she asked, squeezing Eynon's hand.

"Not when I don't know if a cave bear or a spherical boulder might be headed our way down the corridor," said Eynon.

"I can understand such concerns interfering with your amorous instincts," said Merry. "I guess we should follow Ace and Chee and see what lies ahead." She tugged at Eynon and the two of them set off to follow the lights along the corridor.

The main passage hewn out of the limestone continued for several hundred paces. Many dark, narrow side passages opened off the main one, but Eynon and Merry kept moving and didn't stop to investigate them. After walking for long enough to wonder if they'd ever get anywhere, they reached a well-lit intersection. A corridor led up at a steep angle to their right and opposite it one also led upward, though it wasn't as steep. The path ahead continued with what seemed to be a gentle downward slope. There were four wizard lamps where the corridors crossed, so at least they would be in good light while they sought illumination as to which way to go. The vibration of the Great Falls seemed even stronger as they stopped to debate.

"Which way do we go?" asked Eynon.

"Why would you expect me to know any more than you do?" replied Merry, using the traditional wizards' tactic of answering a question with a question. She shifted her gaze from one side to the other and sighed. "I have no idea," she said.

"Which way would Ace and Chee go?" Eynon wondered.

"Probably straight," said Merry. "Downhill is easier."

"Unless Ace is flying," said Eynon. He grinned at Merry, and she gave him a mock frown.

"Oh, come *on*," said Merry. "Let's explore!" She let out a slow breath, then took Eynon by the elbow and steered him along the downward-sloping corridor. Ten-score paces on they noticed the walls were growing damp and the rushing sound was growing so loud it was almost deafening. Finally, the corridor came to an end in a high-ceilinged chamber twenty feet or so wide. Before them was a thick curtain of water, backlit by what they assumed must be the sun. They noticed Ace and Chee off to one side of the chamber, staring at the flowing display as if entranced. Their familiars didn't even acknowledge their presence.

Eynon stepped close to the curtain of water and reached out his hand to touch the flow. "Amazing!" he said as he pulled back his cold wet hand and pressed it against Merry's forehead.

"Hey, stop that!" Merry protested. Then she lifted one of her hands to keep Eynon's hand where it was. "On second thought, don't stop. It feels nice. Let me return the favor."

Eynon bent his head down so Merry could put her chilled hand on his forehead. "You're right. It feels delightful after a long walk."

For a few seconds they took turns flicking water at each other's faces. Ace and Chee finally noticed them and started doing the same to each other. When Ace put the front half of his body into the flow then pulled back and began to shake, Eynon erected a shield of solidified sound to protect him and Merry from the flying droplets.

The two young wizards laughed, then Merry looked at the flowing curtain again and tilted her head. "We must be behind the falls," she said.

Eynon nodded. "Agreed," he said. "That's a lot of water."

Merry noticed that Eynon was shifting from one foot to another in an odd dance. His face was scrunched up like he'd just taken a bite from a sour apple.

"What's wrong?" she asked.

"All this flowing water is affecting me," said Eynon.

"What do you mean?" asked Merry.

"Could you turn your back, please?" he asked.

"Why?" asked Merry. Then she saw Eynon's wide eyes and pained expression, connecting it with his movements. "Ah," she said. "Can I watch?"

"I'd really prefer it if you didn't," said Eynon.

"It's not like it's something I've never seen before," said Merry. Sunlight filtering through the curtain of liquid reflected off her eyes, making them look even more mischievous than usual.

Eynon's cheeks were the color of cherries. "Just turn around," he said.

Merry did. Eynon stood close to the wall of falling water, added his own small contribution, and sighed.

"Feeling better now?" asked Merry.

"Much better," said Eynon. He stared at the flowing curtain. "I wish we could see what's on the other side."

"You can take the farm boy out of the Coombe, but you can't take the Coombe out of the farm boy," teased Merry.

"What's that supposed to mean?" Eynon protested.

"I would think a master mage could figure out *several* ways to see through a wall of water," she replied.

"Oh, right," said Eynon. He rubbed his chin and muttered softly. "I could freeze a section of the curtain and... no, that wouldn't work. And there's too much of it to turn it to steam..."

Merry stuck a finger in Eynon's ribs. "You're overthinking it," she said. "Be yourself, not Aristotélēs."

"I'll try," Eynon replied. He splashed cold water on his face, emulated Ace by shaking it off, and promptly formed a cylinder of transparent solidified sound three feet in diameter, inserting it into the liquid wall. Water parted around the cylinder and Eynon extended the tube until it was long enough to emerge on the other side. Merry leaned close and together they could dimly see a river valley far below them, shrouded in mist.

"It's beautiful," said Merry.

"It certainly is," said Eynon. "My sister Braith would love to see it. I should ring her and see if she wants an invitation to the royal weddings."

"As if you have any doubt about her answer," teased Merry. After a few more minutes, she stepped away and Eynon dissolved his cylinder.

"I could look at that for hours," said Eynon. He splashed more cold water on his face.

Merry did the same and stepped back from the curtain. "This is a lovely view, but we've *got* to see the Great Falls from the other side," she said.

Eynon nodded. "Time to backtrack and try one of those ascending corridors?" he asked.

"Yes," said Merry. She crossed to Ace, scooped up the rockhound, and hugged him, remembering too late that he was still quite damp. She temporarily held her familiar away from her body, channeling heat toward Ace and her damp clothing through a congruency to dry both of them off. Merry hugged Ace again. The rockhound reveled in her warm embrace and no longer seemed quite so captivated by the water. Jumping down to the stone floor, he trotted beside Merry as the young wizards walked up the corridor along the way they'd come originally, with Chee in his usual spot on Eynon's shoulder.

"Which one should we take?" asked Eynon when they reached the crossing.

"The steeper one," said Merry. "I want to get to the surface and have a better view and I expect the steeper path is the best way to get there."

She was proved correct when they'd followed the corridor in a broad upward arc, eventually reaching a landing furnished with comfortable chairs and a wizard lamp chandelier. A wide, polished marble stairway flanked with ornate balustrades decorated in a trefoil motif led up to the left. Sunlight filtered into the stairwell from above.

"We must be in Tamloch territory," said Eynon as they climbed the marble stairs.

Merry moved to a step above Eynon and put a finger to his lips. "Shhhh," she whispered. "I think I hear voices. Listen!"

Eynon leaned forward and followed Merry's imperative instruction. He didn't just listen, however. He also recognized several of the speakers. Eynon grinned at Merry, took her hand, and led her up the wide stairs at a quickstep. As they ascended, Merry could make out familiar voices as well, including her mentor Fercha's.

"We'll form shields of solidified sound in case it rains," Fercha was saying.

Princess Rúth's voice replied in a firm tone. "That's all well and good, but I want you wizards to be able to focus on the ceremony, not on working magic. Tamloch will supply pavilions on the island."

"And I'm sure Dâron will supply more to set up near the Inn to protect all the food and drink," they heard Doethan say.

"It's kind of you to make that offer on behalf of my kingdom," teased Nûd's voice.

"Stop it!" came Bonnie's response. "Of *course* we'll provide pavilions. Both kingdoms should have them at each location."

"Kennig and I will handle the decorations," they heard Inthíra say.

"I don't mind being volunteered in a good cause," came Kennig's amused response.

Eynon and Merry grinned at each other and climbed the last steps on the broad marble staircase to emerge into a bright, spacious room worthy of a royal palace. It had a domed, white marble ceiling and tall walls with three-story windows.

"We wouldn't mind being volunteered ourselves," said Merry as they emerged.

All conversations in the room stopped momentarily, as if cut off with an axe, then resumed at a much higher volume with a dozen people speaking at once. The hubbub and rounds of hugs continued until Eynon had a chance to catch his breath and speak. "Congratulations on your upcoming nuptials," he said to Nûd, Bonnie, Dârio, and Jenet.

The couples were each holding hands, seeming somewhat overwhelmed. Given what Eynon knew about their capacities— particularly Jenet's—that was saying something. The royals stood in front of windows with views of both falls, the horseshoe-shaped one on the Tamloch side and the straight one on the side belonging to Dâron. When Eynon and Merry saw the spectacular view before them, they lost all connection to their immediate surroundings, involuntarily walking past the kings and future queens of two kingdoms to press their noses against the window glass and stare.

Smiles flashed on the faces of everyone else in the welcoming hall of the Inn at the Falls. They'd each done the same when they'd first seen the wonder and power of the flowing water. Chee and Ace were the first to break nature's spell once they noticed the fruit, sliced meat, and bread rolls spread out on a nearby table for the guests. The two familiars, captivated more by the food than the distant views which entranced them far less than a wall of water they could touch, rushed toward the table. Princess Rúth intercepted the eager familiars before they could wreak havoc on the food, tossing Chee a ripe pear and Ace a morsel of ham. In a corner of the hall, Bonnie's owlberron familiar, Béryl, opened one eye, yawned, and returned to her nap.

After giving Eynon and Merry a few minutes to soak in the impressive scenery, Verro and Fercha approached them.

"It's a good spot for a wedding, don't you think?" said Verro.

"It's lovely," said Eynon, not turning away from the window.

"Wild mammoths are knocking over the walls of the palace in Brendinas," said Fercha.

"That's nice," said Merry.

Fercha and Verro exchanged a glance, nodded at each other, and simultaneously cast opaque planes of solidified sound in front of the young wizards, blocking their view.

"Hey!" said Eynon, turning rapidly.

"Wait! What did you say about mammoths?" said Merry as she turned as well.

"I was just trying to get your attention," said Fercha.

"Unsuccessfully," said Verro. "What brings you here, by the way? Not that we're not glad to see you."

"Eynon wanted to talk to you," said Merry. "He wants to talk to all the master mages in Orluin."

"A potentially worthwhile endeavor," said Verro.

Eynon was about to reply when he heard a buzzing sound and felt his right hand vibrate. He held the hand out in front of him, identified the ring responsible, and removed it. A three-note chime sounded and Eynon expanded the ring until it was three feet in diameter. He saw his sister in an unusual position, more than half buried under mounds of hay in what must be Haywall's hay barn.

"Braith," he said. "So nice to hear from you. I was just about to ring you to see if you want me to get you an invitation to the double royal wedding."

"Of course I would, you idiot," Braith replied. "But there's no time for that now. The Southern Clan Landers are invading the Coombe!"

Chapter 22

Braith's News

"What?" said Eynon.

"You heard me, brother," Braith answered. "Don't be a bigger dimwit than you were when you—"

"No need to go into that," said Eynon. "I was only eleven at the time." He made a beckoning gesture to his sister with his free hand. "Tell me more," he said.

"I don't *know* much more," said Braith after she brushed bits of hay out of a corner of her mouth. "I was in the hay barn getting some hay to restuff my mattress..."

"Alone?" asked Eynon using a tone reserved for brothers talking to their younger sisters.

"No, if you must know," said Braith. "But that's none of your business and stop teasing. This is serious."

"Sorry, force of habit," said Eynon. "You're right."

Braith continued in an urgent whisper. "As I was saying, I was in the hay barn and then I heard screaming from the direction of our favorite neighbor's cottage."

"Aunt Glynneth?" asked Eynon.

"Yes," said Braith. "I pushed open the bottom of the door to the hayloft and looked out to see three falcons circling Glynneth and pecking at her head. Then I saw three Southern Clan Lander wizards and a large contingent of their warriors with huge two-handed swords and long spears were rousting everyone in Haywall out of their homes."

"Brùtha of the Falcon Clan practically *told* us they were scouting for an invasion," said Merry. "We should have..."

"Warned the Coombe," said Eynon. He smacked the center of his forehead with his free hand. "This is all my fault. What about our parents? Are they safe?"

"I don't know," said Braith. "They're away visiting cousins in Liamston."

"Thank goodness for that," said Eynon. He glanced at Merry. "Liamston is in the far northeastern corner of the Coombe. It's the farthest point from the Southern Clan Lands."

"Right," said Merry. "I've seen maps of the Coombe. Let me talk to your sister." She moved close to Eynon so she could see Braith clearly through the communication ring's circular interface.

"Hello, Merry," said Braith.

"Hi Braith," said Merry. "Could you count how many warriors you saw in Haywall?"

Braith paused for a moment, then replied. "Two dozen," she said. "Maybe as many as thirty. Only the three wizards, though. Two women and a man. Each with a falcon familiar."

"Got it," said Merry. Through the open channel of the ring she and Eynon could hear shouts and screams close to where Braith was hiding.

"I'm going to get my sister," said Eynon, handing the ring to Merry.

"Wait," said Merry. "Think, then act."

"I *am* thinking," said Eynon. "I'm going to *ad hoc* gate to Haywall, rescue Braith and bring her here, then pop back to the Coombe and reconnoiter." He looked at the others in the great hall of the Inn at the Falls. "Verro, take Fercha, Inthíra and Kennig with you and *ad hoc* gate to the green magestone quarry near Wherrel. Inthíra can keep you all hidden."

Verro nodded, as did the others Eynon had named.

"Doethan, can you get to the Rhuthro valley quickly?"

"Yes," the older wizard replied. "My emergency gate is near my tower."

"Good," said Eynon. "Take Merry with you. She can raise troops from the barons along the Rhuthro and organize them to march west into the Coombe. I'm sure her father Derry will pull his people together quickly. You can help speed their progress."

"Gladly," said Doethan.

"Plant your end of our matched gate rings where the baronial troops will be needed," said Merry. "I'll set my end and they can pass through to the Coombe immediately."

"That sounds like a good plan," said Eynon.

"I'm coming with you," said Dârio. He put his hand on the hilt of his sword.

"No," said Eynon.

"No," echoed Jenet.

"No," said Nûd. "The Coombe is part of Dâron. I'm responsible for its defense."

"We're allies," Dârio protested. "I want to help."

"You can help by using your head, my love," said Jenet. "What if this attack is a distraction and Sírénae decides to strike at Riyas?"

"Sírénae *and* Celéri have been beaten," said Dârio. "Who could attack us?"

"Don't count Sírénae and Celéri out," said Eynon. "But they're not the only threat."

"Bonnie and I will take the fixed gate from the Inn to the royal palace in Brendinas," said Nûd. "I'll collect the royal guard and use another pair of gate rings if you have them to get my forces to the Coombe within the hour."

"Here," said Merry, handing a ring to Nûd and its mate to Eynon. She gave her partner a second ring and passed *its* mate to Jenet. "Now both Dâron *and* Tamloch can send troops and help defend the Coombe."

"We'll have to act quickly," said Kennig, who had spent several years in self-exile in the Southern Clan Lands. "I know Brùtha. She can be ruthless and is not above torturing and enslaving prisoners."

"She was certainly not all that fond of me after I captured her," said Eynon.

"The fact that she's personally attacking Haywall confirms that," said Merry.

"What can I do to help?" asked Princess Rúth.

"Collect supplies of healing potions," said Eynon. "You can also serve as a central point for communications since you're the prime coordinator for the Alliance."

"Caches of healing potions are already in place in Riyas and Brendinas," said Princess Rúth. "Wizards had plenty of time to make them when we were underground. I'll also alert Laetícia and

Amber, so they can have Occidens Province and Bifurland ready to assist."

"Thank you," said Eynon. "I should have thought of that."

Braith's voice came across the interface. "You don't need to take time to get me," she said. "I'm safe enough here in the hay barn."

"Unless one of the Southern Clan Landers puts a match to it," said Fercha.

"Why would they want to burn the hay they'll need for the cattle they capture?" asked Doethan. "It doesn't make sense."

"Brùtha isn't known for being sensible," said Kennig. "Behind her back we called her Brutal Brùtha."

"How large a force do you think the Southern Clan Landers could have put together?" Eynon asked Kennig.

"Several thousand, at least," said Kennig. "The Falcon Clan is influential, and the farmland in the Coombe is a lot better than the thin soil on the southern mountainsides. It's a tempting prize."

"That they've been *trying* to take on and off for years," said Eynon. "Unfortunately, the baron of the Coombe in Caercadel only has a few knights. We've relied on local levies to defend ourselves against small Southern Clan Lander raids in the past, but they've never sent in thousands of warriors before."

"Then it's a good thing you're organizing such a strong response," said Verro. He grinned at Fercha. "I'm looking forward to a battle where I won't have to moderate my magical attacks because I'm fighting someone I love."

Fercha grinned back. "All married couples quarrel," she said, blowing Verro a kiss.

"Not with fireballs and lightning bolts," said Verro.

"True enough," said Fercha. "Shouldn't we all be on our way."

"We should," said Eynon. "All things considered, I'm going to gate you out of Haywall, little sister."

"I *told* you I'm safe here," said Braith.

A familiar head attached to a tall, lanky body rose out of the hay beside Braith. Eynon's sister tried to shove the head back down, but its owner resisted. He pulled bits of hay out of his tightly curled black hair.

"Go ahead, reconnoiter and find out the extent of the invasion," said Felix, a young Roma wizard from Occidens Province. "I'll keep Braith safe."

Eynon looked at Merry and the two of them grinned. Shouts and screams came across the interface at a higher volume.

"Thank you," said Eynon. "I'll be on my way. It's time to defend the Coombe!"

"Scout things out first and update us, please," said Nûd.

Jenet nodded her agreement.

Eynon returned her gesture with a grim smile then immediately gated away, his departure punctuated with a small pop of in-rushing air.

Chapter 23

Scouting the Coombe

Eynon gated into the air fifty feet above the flagstone courtyard connecting his family's home to the cottages surrounding it. He smiled as he remembered the reactions from his neighbors when Rocky the wyvern had landed on those smooth gray stones several months earlier near the start of his adventures. Dark clouds were roiling around him as if a thunderstorm would soon roll through to add its violence to the valley Eynon called home. He could feel energies build in the skies around him but it hadn't yet started to rain.

After a deep breath to center himself, Eynon shoved his memory of Rocky into the back of his mind and focused on taking in the tactical aspects of the scene below him. Chee sensed Eynon's intensity and held on to his shoulder, staying quiet even after a peal of thunder boomed in the darker parts of the clouds above him.

Eynon and Chee watched as a dozen Southern Clan Lands warriors, some in mottled kilts, some in dark leggings bound with thin strips of leather, herded several of Eynon's friends and neighbors into a circle in the center of the courtyard. Most of the invaders carried six-foot spears tipped with sharp steel points that they used to prod their captives. Two of the warriors held crossbows and were on alert for threats.

Concerned by the crossbows, Eynon created a plane of solidified sound the same slate color as the sky between himself and the observers on the ground, disguising his presence. Then he generated distance lenses and watched as a familiar Falcon Clan mage wearing a small brown jasper magestone in a leather headband stepped out of "aunt" Glynneth's cottage holding what must be one of his neighbor's famous sweet cakes in his hand. The wizard took a bite from the sweet cake, smiled, and began barking orders. Eynon invoked the listening spell Merry had first taught him on their trip down the Rhuthro and focused his augmented ears on hearing what was said. He took careful note of the large, dun-colored gyrfalcon perched on the invading wizard's shoulder, promising himself not to be taken by surprise again.

"Lock them in the hay barn for now," said the Southern Clan Lands' mage. "Truss them up and make sure they can't get free. We need them as hostages and will put them to work shortly."

"Who made *you* boss?" asked a short woman in gray leggings and a homespun brown shirt. She had a long pheasant tailfeather in her black felt hat and carried a spear a foot taller than she was.

"Shut your face and do what Máclaesh tells you," said a woman with two long braids who was carrying a crossbow. She shifted her body for a moment, so her weapon pointed at the short woman then returned it to its original position. "The Coombe isn't ours yet."

"It will be soon enough," said the woman with the spear. "Are there more of those sweet cakes to be had, wizard?"

"Yes," said Máclaesh. "I'll share them out *after* you see to the prisoners."

"Whatever," said the woman with the spear. "We'll tie them up but will just have to untie them again so they can do the milking. I wouldn't mind a nice mug of warm milk laced with a few ounces of applejack tonight." She poked at Glynneth with the tip of her spear and the white-haired woman took a step back into the already tight circle of her fellow villagers. "You'll find me some applejack, won't you, old crone?"

Glynneth didn't reply but set her jaw and glared at the spear woman. Eynon had seen that expression before. He smiled. His mother had always said his neighbor could teach stubborn to a mule.

"Enough," said Máclaesh. "No one is drinking anything stronger than apple juice until we've consolidated our conquest."

The short woman with the tall spear pulled her weapon back and planted its butt end on the ground. With her free hand she removed a leather bottle from a belt on her waist, popped the cork with her teeth, and took a long drink. From her expression it was clear she wasn't drinking water. "That's what I think of your commands, wizard," she said. "You and your kind have been too frightened of the Blue Tabards and *their* wizards to take the Coombe earlier. We should have claimed it as ours in my mother's day."

"You're a fool," said the woman with the crossbow. "One of the blue-robed wizards brought down half a mountain on us. The only reason we've got a chance to hold the Coombe is because the Dâron wizards are still dealing with an invasion of Roma from across the Ocean."

"That's old news," said Máclaesh.

"Not according to Merrillōn," said the spear woman.

Máclaesh held up his left hand, silencing both his critics. He removed a ring from his middle finger and expanded it as three tones sounded. Eynon shifted his position so he could see who the wizard with the jasper magestone was talking to. He wasn't surprised to recognize a familiar face.

"We've taken Wherrel and the green magestone quarry," Eynon heard Brùtha tell her fellow Falcon Clan wizard. "Brynhill is ours as well, and we have a contingent of wizards and warriors heading south to intercept any forces the baron in Caercadel sends in our direction. Tell me good news, Máclaesh. Is Haywall secure?"

"Yes," Máclaesh replied. He took another bite from the sweet cake, swallowed, and wiped crumbs from his lips. "We took it without resistance. My team is binding our hostages and locking them in the village hay barn until we can put them to proper work. They're our bargaining chips in case the king of Dâron tries to force us out."

"Excellent," said Brùtha. "No sign of that blasted young wizard with the red magestone?"

Máclaesh waved the remaining half of the sweet cake in front of the interface. "The only thing out of the ordinary I've found in this village is the quality of their baking," he said. "I'll save a few of these delicious cakes for you to have for dessert tonight."

Brùtha nodded, then frowned. "Don't get complacent, Máclaesh. I don't want you hurt. I have plans for you tonight and need you healthy."

"Far be it from me to interfere with your plans, my dear," said Máclaesh. He licked his lips and smiled at Brùtha. "I'll be careful if you will. What have you heard from Liamston?"

Eynon listened closely, since Braith had said their parents were visiting relatives in that village in the far northeastern corner of the Coombe.

"We've captured the wharf and the gristmill," Brùtha replied. "But all the locals left before we arrived. They must have been warned."

"Fewer mouths to feed," said Máclaesh.

"Fewer hostages and fewer captives to put to work," said Brùtha. "I don't like it."

"I told you we should have built more wide gates," said Máclaesh. "Merrillōn recommended…"

"Merrillōn can fall back in the river," said Brùtha. "He's not the one who had to build gates in enemy territory. If we'd constructed gates *in* the Coombe, we would have completely lost the element of surprise."

"Yes, I know," said Máclaesh. "We all agreed that one wide gate outside the Wherrel Gap would be best, but don't second guess yourself if word got to Liamston early. I saw a rock dove leaving Haywall as we arrived. In hindsight, it could have been carrying a message."

"You could have sent Falshia after the dove," said Brùtha.

Máclaesh swallowed the last bit of sweet cake and stretched his free hand up to stroke his gyrfalcon. "Hindsight has raptor's vision," he said. "Our attention was focused elsewhere."

"Keeping attention focused is essential to our program of distraction," said Brùtha. "Especially. Right. Now!"

The wizard known as Máclaesh pointed his upraised hand directly at Eynon's disguised position and sent five beams of tight light from his fingertips, outlining Eynon's exact location.

Without warning, three fireballs shot out from nearby clouds and bracketed Eynon's position overhead. Their bright light temporarily blinded him and the blast of the fireballs' detonations so close to him simultaneously deafened Eynon and gave him a headache that felt like his brain was an iron bar being beaten flat by the hammers of a dozen blacksmiths.

Disoriented, he lost control of his flying disk and began to plummet to the ground. Halfway to the courtyard he was struck by three lightning bolts, leaving his hair standing on end and every nerve cell in his body tingling. Eynon fell toward the flagstones.

At least it wasn't falcons this time, he thought, before unconsciousness claimed him.

Chapter 24

In Brùtha's Hands

Eynon opened his eyes then promptly closed them again. He could feel his head pounding like a glyppo was using it for stomping practice. His stomach was close to rebellion, ready to demonstrate reverse peristalsis, and his torso ached with what felt like deep internal burns. He fought to pull his thoughts together into some coherent form and barely succeeded.

How would I be feeling if I hadn't had my shields up? he asked himself. *Worse,* he concluded. *At least the fall didn't kill me—though if it had, I wouldn't be in so much pain.*

Eynon didn't know whether or not he could trust his eyes, since from his single glimpse, the world seemed upside down. Every muscle in his body was tingling from the shock of all the lightning bolts. Adding to his disorientation, he could no longer sense the familiar weight of his red magestone in its gold artifact setting on its chain around his neck.

He tried to move his legs but couldn't and realized his ankles were bound—and his knees. His inner ears told him his body was shifting, tracing pendulum tracks in the air.

In the air? thought Eynon. *I'm hanging head down?*

He briefly opened his eyes again, cautious of potential vertigo, and saw familiar brown robes with red-ochre trim which he knew belonged to Brùtha of Bald Peak, a Southern Clan Lands' wizard of the Falcon Clan. The agate magestone on a leather bracer on her forearm glinted with magical energy. She was the person on the other end of the communications ring conversation he'd all too recently overheard, before being struck by fireballs and lightning. He realized he was suspended by his feet from the tripod frame his fellow villagers in Haywall used to drain and dress deer and beef cattle. That realization wasn't cheering.

"Hah!" said Brùtha. "The sleeper wakes. You're smart, but not smart enough to avoid the trap we set for you, murderer.

Soon, you'll join all the Southern Clan Landers who died when you brought down a mountainside on top of them."

The wizard with the jasper magestone on a headband spoke. "Your little beast ran off toward the hay barn," he said. "We'll get it soon enough so the creature can dance for us as we deal with you."

Eynon was glad Chee had escaped, then far from pleased when his body rotated half a turn and he suddenly saw more stars than he'd ever counted on a dark night. The tip of a heavy boot had connected with the back of his skull, imparting enough force to make his head reverberate like a gong struck by a war hammer. His body swayed through more degrees of arc and he sensed himself spinning as well. Eynon felt the sour contents of his stomach exit his mouth as he swung back toward Brùtha, glad to be hanging upside down.

Brùtha laughed and Eynon could hear others laughing with her—Máclaesh and the other Southern Clan Landers occupying Haywall, he assumed. Losing the contents of his stomach gave Eynon one less thing to think about. He was no longer queasy, but his mouth tasted sour, and he saw a few drops of blood, likely from the back of his head, joining the smelly mess on the ground below him.

Ground, not flagstones, thought Eynon. He wasn't in the village proper and remembered the tripod frame was five hundred paces away where the smells of slaughter wouldn't disturb his neighbors' dinners. Eynon breathed through his mouth and fought to reclaim his equilibrium. *You haven't felt this bad since you almost drowned on the Rhuthro on your trip with Merry* his memory asserted. With that observation granting him perspective, Eynon had attention to devote to someone talking.

"Why kill him?" Eynon heard Máclaesh say. "Why not make him a slave and put him to work?"

"Mages make poor slaves," said Brùtha. "Would you make *me* a slave if you held me captive?"

"Point taken, my dear," said Máclaesh. "If you were my enemy instead of my wife, I'd slit your throat and see you buried under heavy stones if I ever had you as my captive. You're not someone I'd let live if you were truly against me. You're as dangerous as a rattletail."

"Then realize that I consider this boy more dangerous than an entire den of vipers," said Brùtha. "He's only alive until the rest of the Falcon Clan wizards can arrive to witness my victory and celebrate his execution."

"Why wait if he's such a threat?" asked Máclaesh. "Why not kill him now?"

Brùtha pointed to the gold artifact with a red stone that dangled from her carved brown leather belt. "He's not much of a threat without his magestone," she said. Eynon swung back toward her and she jabbed one of her claw-like fingernails into the center of his forehead, twisting it to nearly free a circular patch of skin and sending more blood unto the ground.

The pain of Brùtha's new attack focused Eynon's mind. He inhaled and sensed the blue magestone in a silver setting—Fercha's artifact—that he'd found on the day he'd first set out on his wander year. It was against his skin, under his tunic and beneath his sky-blue robes. His gloating captor had missed it, though she'd have no reason to look for it. As far as Eynon knew he was the only mage to have two magestones. He remembered the first day of his wander year when finding Fercha's original artifact had set him on the path of wizardry. He could use it to show Brùtha he wasn't defenseless.

The Falcon Clan wizard waited with her finger extended for Eynon's forehead to swing back into range to leave another wound. Her fingernail gouged out another circle of skin and Eynon heard her chuckle with a malice that made him shiver. He smelled the coppery tang of blood mingled with the stink of his own fear sweat. Then he heard the familiar three chimes of a communications ring and saw Máclaesh opening a connection. Eynon couldn't see who Máclaesh was talking to, but he could hear the conversation well enough. Brùtha stopped disfiguring Eynon's forehead to listen, leaving the young mage literally hanging.

While gathering his strength, Eynon bided his time, waiting to see what he might learn.

"We've taken the castle at Caercadel?" said Máclaesh, replying to some distant speaker. "That's great news!"

Eynon remembered his trips to Caercadel in previous years to deliver his family's share of Haywall's grains, fruits, and vegetables. He'd been too young to enjoy the inns' beer then and hoped he hadn't lost his chance to sample their brews forever. *You have more important things to worry about,* he reminded himself.

"Tell them to be sure everything is secure before they sack the seven inns," said Brùtha. "That beer is for all of us, not just for them."

"Did you hear that?" asked Máclaesh. He nodded to Brùtha. "He said they've only tapped the barrels at one of the inns and are saving the rest to share out."

"They'd better not be drunk when I fly down there," said Brùtha.

"He says they won't be," said Máclaesh. "They're holding the baron and his knights in their own dungeon."

"Good," said Brùtha. "Make sure they're ready to repel any forces coming into the Coombe up the Rhuthro. Chain citizens of Caercadel to the poles of the wharfs along the river as hostages."

"He says he knows the plan," said Máclaesh. He angled the ring's interface toward Brùtha so she could see the scarred face of a wizard in robes covered in so many patches it was difficult to ascertain their original color. His magestone glinted like fools' gold from a wooden artifact the shape of a Roma scutum suspended from his left ear. "Stick to your own business and let me do my job."

"I'll stick you with a dagger if you screw this up," said Brùtha. "Call back if you spot any forces coming up the Rhuthro." She motioned to Máclaesh. "Cancel the connection and find out what's happening in Wherrel."

Máclaesh didn't answer—he just did as he was instructed, contracting one ring and opening another. Eynon couldn't see the interface this time, since Máclaesh had turned it toward Brùtha.

"You've rounded up all the residents?" Eynon heard Brùtha say. "Have them collect more magestone dust from the quarry. We'll need to get more wide gates built quickly to move more of our people in to occupy all the surrounding farms. The Blue Tabards won't fight us if it puts the farmers and villagers at risk."

Eynon spit blood out of his mouth. "I wouldn't be so sure about that," he said.

"Shut up," said Brùtha. She leaned closer and shoved Eynon's chin none too gently with the heel of her hand, setting him swaying faster. "Have we heard anything from Liamston?" she asked Máclaesh.

"I'll try to raise them," said the wizard, closing his current ring and selecting another. He tried to expand the new ring, but it wouldn't open. "No response," he said.

"They're probably busy capturing the town," said Brùtha.

"Or maybe they're still on their way," said Máclaesh.

"If they were still marching northeast, they'd answer," said Brùtha. "Check back in a few minutes."

Máclaesh nodded and returned the new ring to his hand. Brùtha turned her focus back to Eynon, sticking out one of her talons to intercept his forehead a third time.

Eynon, however, was ready for her. He'd spent his time while the two Southern Clan Lands' wizards were diverted by checking the status of their varied invading parties to map out a plan of attack. When Brùtha's nail was about to carve him again, Eynon trapped Brùtha's hand with a circle of solidified sound. The band of energy around her wrist clamped her in place and contracted until it just broke the skin, leaving a thin line of red. Five planes of solidified sound separated Brùtha's long fingernails from the ends of her fingers, leaving them to fall soundlessly on the damp ground. A sphere of force around Brùtha's head cut off her air supply before she could shout for help. Another sphere around the head of Máclaesh prevented the second wizard from responding.

Eynon sensed his flying disk a dozen feet away and pulled it toward him with a tendril of force, bringing it below him to support his chest and torso. With three deft strokes of solidified sound he released the bases of the tripod frame—eight-foot lengths of tree trunks as wide as Eynon's calves—and carried them as well as his own body upward.

Brùtha, Máclaesh, and half a dozen other nearby Southern Clan Landers started to react, but Eynon was faster. He cut the rope connecting him to the tripod frame while keeping the lengths of braided hemp binding the tree trunks together intact. Using forces moderated by his blue magestone he set the trunks in motion like giant scythes. Where they struck, Southern Clan Landers went to the ground and stayed there. Eynon was particularly pleased to see that Brùtha had fallen into the puddle of mingled blood and vomit. He released the sphere of solidified sound around her head for a few seconds so she could have a face full of both. Before Brùtha could respond, Eynon used a thin sliver of solidified sound to slit the leather of her bracer and carry her agate magestone up to him.

Another tentacle of force removed the headband with his jasper magestone from Máclaesh's head, dropping it on the ground, and a third reclaimed Eynon's red magestone from Brùtha's belt. He felt restored when the chain of his artifact slipped back over his neck.

Most of the invaders he been caught off guard by the spinning tripod frame while Eynon was collecting magestones, but one woman with a crossbow got off a shot at Eynon. The point of her bolt pierced his robes and lodged in his tibia where his leg extended out beyond his flying disk. Too late, he shielded his body where it was vulnerable and sent a fireball off in the direction of the archer to discourage her from additional attacks. The quarrel in his leg didn't hurt—much—since there were few nerves affected, but it felt like the worst shin splint imaginable whenever he flexed his leg. Eynon made the tree trunks spin faster then cut the ropes binding them with a sharp plane of solidified sound. They flew out in three directions, bowling over all the Southern Clan Lands' warriors still standing.

At least Chee is safe, thought Eynon. *With luck he's with Braith and Felix. I hope they're safe, too.* He rubbed his forehead and saw his hand come away looking as red as the magestone he'd found at great risk in Melyncárreg. *I'm going to need more than one healing potion and soon,* he considered. *And not one of mine.*

A spear thrown by another Southern Clan Lander got past the spinning tree trunks and clanged off the bottom of Eynon's flying disk.

Merry would tell me it's time to retreat and return to fight another day, thought Eynon. *I think I agree with her—but where should I go? I know,* he considered. *I need a first-rate healer.*

Air popped into the space where Eynon had been as he *ad hoc* gated to Riyas.

An angry falcon racing to strike Eynon's head screeched in frustration in the suddenly empty air.

Chapter 25

Eynon and Uirsé

Eynon barely had the strength to land outside City Hall in Riyas after he'd appeared in the sky above Tamloch's capital. Door guards found him unconscious on the cobblestones and alerted Sórcha, who promptly sent for her niece Uirsé, an excellent healer. When he woke, Eynon found himself comfortably tucked into a warm bed in a small, pleasant room, with tall windows letting in sunlight. Uirsé was spooning sips of an odd-flavored broth into his mouth. Eynon coughed and sat up.

No, it's not broth, Eynon realized as his mind became less muddled. *It's healing potion.* "Thank you," he said to the young, brown-haired wizard caring for him.

"Rest," said Uirsé. She tilted the bowl of potion to his lips. "And drink. Now that you're awake that's a much faster way of getting the potion inside you than using a spoon."

"Gladly," said Eynon. He took the edges of the bowl in both hands and consumed its contents in three swallows.

"That will take care of the cuts on your forehead and your other superficial injuries," said Uirsé. "But you'll need to stay in bed, rest quietly, and recuperate for a week. You've got quite a bit of internal damage."

Eynon shook his head and tried to get out of bed, but Uirsé put a hand on his shoulder and pushed him back into the mattress.

"How does a person get their insides cooked and electrocuted simultaneously?" she asked.

Uirsé produced a second bowl, real broth this time. As he spooned up the nourishing liquid, Eynon shared the story of the attack on the Coombe and his capture by the Southern Clan Lands wizards. When he'd finished, Uirsé shook her head slowly and gave him a *you idiot* look. "You walked into an ambush," she said.

Eynon nodded and tried to get out of bed again. Uirsé gently pushed him down into the goosefeather pillows.

"Rest," she said. "Healer's orders."

"I can't rest," said Eynon. "I have to get back and help the Coombe. Braith and my parents and Chee and all the people there are in danger."

"You're in danger of dying from internal injuries if you don't stay quiet," said Uirsé.

"That doesn't matter," said Eynon. "There's more, and worse."

"Worse than an invasion from the Southern Clans and all your friends in danger?" asked Uirsé.

"Yes," said Eynon. "Brùtha—the leader of the Southern Clan Lands' wizards—has my magestone."

"You mean this?" she said, pointing to the red magestone in a gold setting resting on Eynon's chest. "You were carrying it—and an agate magestone in a carved leather bracer when the door guards found you in front of City Hall. I put your magestone back around your neck after we got you into bed. In my experience, wizards heal better when they're in contact with their magestones." Uirsé took the bowl of broth from Eynon's hands temporarily.

With a grateful glance, Eynon put his fingers around his red magestone, held it tightly, and sighed.

"Feels good, doesn't it?" said Uirsé.

Eynon was about to answer but Uirsé put a finger to her lips and motioned that he should finish his broth before continuing. He nodded, took the bowl back, set its lip to his lips, and drained it in a series of slow gulps.

"Better," said Uirsé.

"I've still got to get back to the Coombe," Eynon protested.

Uirsé pointed to a gold communications ring on her finger. "Salder says he's with Merry and their father," she reported. "Derry's levies and more well-trained folk from the other baronies along the Rhuthro valley are in the Coombe now and fighting the invaders."

"And I need to help them," said Eynon. He smiled, remembering Merry's reaction when she'd first learned her older brother Salder was still alive and spying on Tamloch for Dâron.

"I thought you might say that," said Uirsé. "Even though Verro, Fercha, Doethan, Inthíra, Kennig, Bonnie, and royal forces from both Tamloch and Dâron are defending the Coombe?"

"It's *my* home," said Eynon.

Uirsé sighed. "Understood. I'd probably do the same. I have a very special potion that should restore you quickly—though there's one chance in ten it will put you to sleep for a week."

"Only one chance in ten?" asked Eynon. "You're not just saying that so you can make me sleep?"

"I'm not," said Uirsé. "And I was so sure of your answer that I already requested the potion. It's on its way."

As if on cue a young man in green robes not much older than Eynon appeared at the door to the room. His hair was very curly and stood out from his skull like a dandelion in seed. He was nearly out of breath and called out when he saw Uirsé. "Master Healer, Master Healer," he said, pausing to refill his lungs between repetitions. "I brought the bottle you asked for! It's a strange one."

"Apprentice Clýne, I asked you to *fetch* the bottle, not comment on its appearance, but thank you for returning so quickly," said Uirsé.

"I'm glad to serve, Master Healer," said Clýne. He gave a small bow and handed the bottle to Uirsé. Clýne stared at Eynon and his red magestone while Eynon focused *his* attention on the bottle.

"I agree, it *is* strange," Eynon remarked after a good look. The bottle was made from clear glass with a mostly spherical base and a very long narrow neck that curved like a swan's. The neck went through the side of the bottle and connected to the bottom of the rounded base in one smooth, continuous surface. It was filled with a fluid the color of deep red roses and Eynon could see gold and silver glints from within it as sunlight struck the contents. "What is it?" Eynon asked.

"A congruent bottle," said Uirsé.

"Do you mean it's connected to some remote source of red fluid through a congruency, so it constantly refills itself?" asked Eynon. "That would be useful."

"I agree," said Uirsé. "But this bottle is different. Its inside is the same as its outside."

"Then why does it look like the red liquid is only on the inside?" asked Eynon.

"The mathematics behind that are complicated," Uirsé answered.

"I still want to know," said Eynon. He put the bowl that had once held broth on a small table beside his bed and tried to make a shape like the bottle out of solidified sound in the air in front of him.

"No magic!" said Uirsé. "You're supposed to be resting."

"Yes, Master Healer," said Eynon in a tone that copied Clýne's. He smiled at the apprentice.

Uirsé turned her head and motioned Clýne closer. "If you're going to listen in, you might as well help—and learn something."

"Yes, Master Healer," said Clýne.

Eynon laughed and so did Clýne and Uirsé because Eynon's earlier words had captured the apprentice's inflection perfectly. Eynon grimaced—the laugh had caused him pain. Uirsé wagged a finger at him and mouthed the words, "Stay still."

Eynon nodded and tried to comply.

Uirsé addressed her apprentice. "You have some skill with solidified sound," she said. "Make a ribbon as long as your forearm and connect the ends to form a hoop."

"Any particular color?" asked Clýne.

"Whatever you'd like," said Uirsé.

Seconds later, a hoop of ribbon two fingers wide and a cubit in circumference appeared above Eynon's bed. It's color was the same red as Eynon's magestone and it was constructed from illusionist-caliber solidified sound, with the grain on the ribbon clearly visible.

"Nicely done," said Eynon. "I need to introduce you to my friend Inthíra. She can help you make your illusions even better."

"I saw the copy of Riyas you made to fool the huge green dragon," said Clýne. "That was awesome."

"Back to the matter at hand," said Uirsé. "Can you both see that the hoop has an inside and an outside?"

"Yes," said Eynon and Clýne in near unison.

"Very good," said Uirsé. "Now break the hoop, give the ribbon a single twist, and reconnect the ends."

"Like this?" asked Clýne, following her instructions.

"Exactly like that," said Uirsé. "Now does the hoop have an inside and an outside?"

Eynon stared at the construct and frowned.

Clýne made a copy of the hoop of ribbon without the twist, in yellow this time, and held the two floating side by side for comparison. "I don't think so," said the apprentice.

"Neither do I, but I'm not sure why," said Eynon.

"Watch," said Uirsé. "Make an ant on the ribbon and have it start walking," she told Clýne.

"Yes, Master..."

"Just do it," said Uirsé.

Clýne did more than requested, generating a red ant on the yellow ribbon and a yellow ant on the red one. They both started marching. The red ant simply circled the inside of the yellow ribbon, but the yellow ant traversed what seemed like both sides of the red ribbon to return to its starting point.

"Do you understand now?" asked Uirsé. "The bottle is like a plane rolled into a tube and given a twist, then connected to itself using a congruency."

"Hmmmm..." said Clýne, who had sent the yellow ant marching again.

"I don't, really," said Eynon. "But my brain still feels funny."

"You *were* blasted by lightning bolts not long ago," said Uirsé. "Drink the potion and if it doesn't make you sleep for a month, it may clear your head." She handed the unusual bottle to Eynon. He tilted it, trying to figure out how to drink from it.

"How do I...?" Eynon began.

Clýne waved a hand and the ants and ribbons disappeared. "You make a hole in the bottle with a congruency, I expect," he said.

Uirsé looked at the apprentice and shook her head. "I've told you a thousand times to let patients figure such things out for themselves."

"But he's in a hurry to save his home," said Clýne.

"Thank you," said Eynon. He held the bottle close to his mouth and used a small bit of magic to create a congruency near the bottom. Sparkling red liquid gushed out and into Eynon's waiting mouth. He glanced at Uirsé and she nodded, so he drank the entire contents of the bottle, then dispelled the congruency. He could feel the potion working immediately, healing the damage done to his internal organs by the energies of the fireballs and lightning blasts that had slipped past his shields.

Clýne took the empty bottle from Eynon's hands and Uirsé put her fingers on Eynon's wrist to sense his pulse.

Eynon winked at Clýne, yawned, closed his eyes, and feigned falling asleep, complete with theatrically exaggerated snores.

"Nice try," said Uirsé, "but your heartbeat gives you away. The potion is working. You should be strong enough to return to the Coombe in a few minutes."

Close by, Clýne stared at the congruent bottle as it began to refill itself with the same red liquid.

Eynon noticed it too, and decided he'd return and examine the bottle's function in more detail later. For now, he twisted his wrist away from Uirsé's fingers and gripped her hand.

"I'm in your debt," he said. "I can feel my mind get shaper, as if it's a blade being honed by a whetstone."

"There's no debt," said Uirsé. "Healing is a gift freely given—and I'm glad your head isn't fuzzy now. You'll need your wits about you when you return to the Coombe."

"Accept my gratitude then," said Eynon. He smiled at Uirsé. "While we wait until it's safe for me to leave, could you help me with my quest?"

"What sort of quest are you talking about?" asked Uirsé. Clýne leaned closer to listen.

"I'm trying to learn how to be a good Master Mage," said Eynon. "I decided I'd ask every master mage I knew for advice, and for a helpful spell. You're a Master Mage of a sort..."

"A Master Healer," noted Clýne.

"...so *you* count, too," Eynon completed. "What advice would you offer me? And what spell, if you're willing to share one?"

"As far as advice goes, I'd tell you not to push yourself too hard, though I know that would go unheeded," teased Uirsé. "From what I've heard, you don't need to be told to value life. You always seem to find solutions that don't involve killing."

"I wish that was always true," said Eynon, "but Brùtha reminded me I killed many of her kinfolk when I blasted off the top of one of their mountains with a fireball and caused an avalanche."

"What were her kinfolk doing at the time?" asked Uirsé.

"Invading Dâron to fight in the battle of the Brenavon," said Eynon.

"So they were soldiers trying to kill the people of Dâron," said Uirsé.

"You blasted off the top of a mountain?" exclaimed Clýne.

Uirsé silenced her apprentice with a look and watched Eynon nod slowly. "Would you have done the same if you could do it over?" she asked.

"I'd try to find a way to stop the Southern Clan Landers without killing any of them," Eynon replied.

"Then I don't have advice to give you," said Uirsé. "You seem to have learned what I would have taught you on your own." She paused and rubbed her chin, then fingered the gold ring on one hand. "Maybe there is some advice I can offer after all," she said. "Learn to forgive the people you love—like I finally forgave Salder. He was a spy for Dâron, and I was a loyal Tamloch healer, but that didn't change how he loves me or how I love him."

"Merry and I were so pleased when the two of you got back together," said Eynon.

"Salder and I were rather pleased ourselves," said Uirsé. She gave Eynon a smile that embodied pleasant memories.

Eynon frowned, remembering the destruction his fireball on the mountaintop had caused.

As if reading his thoughts, Uirsé said, "Learn to forgive yourself, my friend. You didn't intend to kill Southern Clan Landers. You were learning the extent of your own magical strength."

"They're still dead, though," said Eynon.

Clýne was tilting the now full congruent bottle this way and that, watching its contents slosh this way and that, still sparkling in the sunshine. Eynon and Uirsé ignored him.

Uirsé gripped Eynon's hand tightly, squeezing hard enough to temporarily break the cycle of sadness stemming from contemplating the deaths he'd caused. She stared at him and said, "I'm going to teach you the secret of healing."

"I'm listening," said Eynon. "I can't think of anything more important to learn."

"That's an essential first step," said Uirsé. She put her thumb and forefinger very close together. "Our bodies are made of tiny bits, each one specialized to do its part, like ants in a nest or bees in a hive."

"Of course," said Eynon. "Skin, hair, eyes, lungs, heart..."

"They all work together," said Uirsé, "and all follow a pattern inscribed inside them."

"The pattern that tells skin to be skin and the liver to be the liver," chimed in Clýne.

"It's good to know you were listening to *your* lessons," said Uirsé. "Now I'm helping Eynon."

"Yes, Master Healer," said Clýne.

"The patterns are writ small, but with research, study, and specialized healing spells they can be read," said Uirsé. "Healing is understanding the patterns and helping our bodies restore themselves *to* those patterns."

"I see," said Eynon. "That explains why my healing potions are often less effective. I think my magic was trying to force healing instead of allowing people drinking them to find their bodies' own patterns and heal themselves."

"It's a common apprentice mistake," said Uirsé. She smiled at Clýne, and he looked at the floor for a moment before returning her smile.

"It took me months of practice to make a *good* healing potion," said Clýne.

"Show Eynon," said Uirsé.

Clýne projected the steps in the air above Eynon's bed using constructs of solidified sound. Eynon saw corkscrews unravel and flatten out into interlocking ribbons that split and reformed as the truly effective healing potion formulation lesson proceeded. He could finally see the complex, yet simple patterns at work with the potential for creating endless forms most beautiful and most wonderful.

When Clýne's visual lesson was complete, Eynon nodded. "I think I understand now," he said.

"There's more," said Uirsé. She put one of her hands on Eynon's red magestone and the other on the heart-shaped green magestone embedded in a small gold disk hanging on a chain around her neck.

Eynon could sense something transferring from Uirsé's magestone to his own. It felt like the spells inside Fercha's original magestone that helped him control and moderate the power of his red magestone.

"When you need it, you should now be able to sense the patterns inside you and heal yourself, at least to some degree," said Uirsé. "You can explore these new capabilities when you have some free time, which I expect will be in six or seven years, given how busy you keep yourself."

"Thank you *so* much!" said Eynon. He squeezed Uirsé's hand and nodded to Clýne for his help as well. "You truly are a master healer."

"I think enough time has passed for you to leave if you wish," said Uirsé. She stepped back and Eynon swung himself around on the bed and got to his feet. Clýne helped him back into his sky-blue wizard's robes and Eynon shifted his shoulders and adjusted his belt until the folds of his robes felt right.

"Before you gate back to the Coombe, I should warn you," said Uirsé.

"About what?" asked Eynon.

Clýne was grinning, which made Eynon wary.

"The potion in the congruent bottle is powerful stuff," said Uirsé. "You're clearly not going to sleep for a month, but you may well sleep for two or three days straight soon."

"How soon?" asked Eynon.

"A week, if you're lucky," said Uirsé.

"Five days," mouthed Clýne.

"Duly noted," said Eynon.

"One more thing," said Uirsé. "It doesn't take a sage to predict you'll be risking your life in the near future."

Clýne nodded, agreeing with his mentor's statement.

Uirsé shook her head slowly, lifted her eyes toward the ceiling, and waved her apprentice toward the room's door. "Fetch a bundle of healing potions for Eynon," she instructed. "One of the sort we carry on the battlefield. I expect our guest might find them useful. They're faster and require less focused magic than encouraging self-healing."

"Yes, Master Healer," said Clýne. He smiled at Uirsé, then at Eynon, and departed on his errand.

When Clýne was gone, Uirsé gave Eynon more advice. "The first sign of the congruent bottle potion's debt coming due is an inescapable desire to yawn," she said. "Given the dose you took, you should be able to make it through the royal wedding without yawning, but not much past it. I'll be there to assist you to a bed if Merry doesn't have that job covered."

"Thank you," said Eynon. "I'll warn Merry so we won't have to bother you."

The room's door swung open hard enough to bang against the wall. Clýne held a canvas sash with loops for six leather-wrapped healing potion vials out to Uirsé. She rolled up the vials and handed them to Eynon, who put them in his pack.

"I'm sure these will be very useful," said Eynon. "I really appreciate your gift."

"Just don't act recklessly because you have them," said Uirsé. "Or perhaps I should say *more recklessly than usual.*"

Clýne snickered.

Eynon laughed, knowing he deserved the apprentice's reaction. He bowed to Uirsé. The pop of air as he gated out provided punctuation for his departure.

"I'm impressed," Uirsé told Clýne after giving him a stern glance for his snicker. "The way you taught Eynon really helped me see the point of your power of illusion as an aid to instruction."

"I'm glad it proved helpful," said Clýne. "Perhaps I can store the sequence of illusions in a receptacle of some sort and play them back later for other apprentices?"

"An excellent idea," said Uirsé. "Now let's gather a few more healers and supplies so we can be ready for Verro to *ad hoc* gate us to the Coombe to help the wounded."

"Yes, Master Healer," said Clýne. He set off at a trot to do as Uirsé instructed.

Chapter 26

Defending the Coombe

"I need to get back to Brendinas to ready the royal guard," said King Nûd from the welcoming hall at the Inn of the Falls.

Bonnie took Nûd's hand and nodded while Béryl woke up from her nap and padded over to join them, flexing the wings of her owl-like front half and clacking the claws of her ursine hindquarters on the stone floor.

"I should get back to Riyas for the same reason," said King Dârio. "We can worry about wedding planning later."

"I'll alert Quintillius and Laetícia and request their help under the terms of the Alliance," said Jenet. "Occidens Province always has a full legion prepared for immediate action."

Merry nodded to Nûd. "With your permission, I'll go to the Rhuthro valley and notify my father about the Southern Clan Landers' invasion. He can organize the Rhuthro militias and lead them across the mountains into the Coombe."

"An excellent idea," Nûd replied.

Jenet stepped to one side and opened a communications ring to contact Laetícia, speaking in soft, but urgent tones once the connection was established. Bonnie did the same, using a communications ring to alert her cousin Uirsé in Riyas that healers might be needed.

Merry handed Nûd one of a pair of gate rings, then did the same for Dârio, handing him half of another set. "I'll let you know when I'm in the Coombe and you can use these gate rings to get your forces in place faster," she said. Both kings gave small bows of thanks.

"I'll drop you off at Applegarth as an intermediate destination when I *ad hoc* gate to the Coombe to help Eynon with scouting," said Verro.

"Thank goodness there are already gates in place between the Inn at the Falls and three of the four Alliance capitals," said Princess Rúth. "We won't lose too much time in transit."

Kennig stepped forward and used his skills with illusion to make himself seem ten feet tall for a moment, capturing everyone's attention. Returning to his normal size, he spoke. "We should take five minutes to consider our strategy before simply throwing Alliance troops into the Coombe. I spent many years in the Southern Clan Lands, and I know how their leaders think. Brùtha, her fellow wizards and the Clan chiefs will have contingencies in place to stop any counterattacks."

"Like what?" asked Jenet. She'd finished her remote conversation, closed her communications ring, and was running through dozens of possibilities in her head like moves on a *shah-mat* board.

"Like holding the people of the Coombe hostage," said Kennig. "They'll threaten to kill innocent people if we try to reclaim the territory they've taken."

"What can be done to prevent such a thing?" said Nûd. "We have to keep the folk of the Coombe—loyal citizens of Dâron—from harm."

"Besides not sending troops in," said Jenet.

"I have some ideas," said Kennig. "Here's what I'm thinking..."

* * * * *

There were only three gaps in the mountains surrounding the Coombe, which usually helped make the territory easier to defend. In the northwest, the Wherrel Gap was marked by the limestone quarry just outside it where green magestones could also be found. In the southeast, near the baron's castle and the town of Caercadel, a small river had cut an opening in the mountains before it made a sharp turn north to flow along the lands of the larger baronies of the Rhuthro valley to the east. Finally, in the far northeast, the narrow Liamston Gap opened to provide an alternative route to the Rhuthro for farmers and merchants in that far corner of the Coombe.

Networks of kinship and trade crisscrossed the Coombe like furrows on farmers' fields intersecting with cow paths, tying the orchards of Brynhill, the wheat fields near Caercadel, the dairy farms of Haywall, the stonecutters of Wherrel and the weavers of Liamston together into a beautiful tapestry of lives and landscape.

After the dislocation caused by the evacuation to escape Sírénae's massive invasion, the Coombe was slowly returning to the comfort of its former quiet customs, with a few more people from *outside* now wed into Coombe families after romantic connections made during their underground exile, and a few Coombe-folk following their new partners to settle in other parts of Dâron, or even Tamloch and Occidens Province.

For generations, only small, sporadic raiding parties of Southern Clan Landers had crossed the Coombe's boundaries from the west, and they were usually repulsed without much loss of life by the baron's knights and hastily assembled local levies. This time was different. Thousands of well-armed Southern Clan Landers had left their mountain homes in the southwest and entered the Coombe through a wide gate constructed near the Wherrel Gap. A similar armed force had marched more than fifty miles from Southern Clan Lands' territory to the Caercadel Gap and invaded from that direction. Part of both groups had split off to head for Liamston to hold off armies trying to retake the Coombe from the northeast.

Nûd, Dârio, and Quintillius—via communications ring—promptly agreed that Dârio would lead Tamloch troops to the Liamston Gap, Quintillius would send a legion to the Caercadel Gap, and Nûd would muster Dâron's forces at the Wherrel Gap. Merry's father, Baron Derry, would lead the Rhuthro valley militias over the mountains and into the Coombe from a fourth direction.

Verro and Laetícia, as master mages able to *ad hoc* gate, were essential to the success of Kennig's plan. Laetícia reached out to Magister Callidus to enlist his services and Merry promised to keep trying to contact Eynon, so he could help as well. Merry projected a calm exterior, but everyone around her could see her inner tension and worry over why Eynon hadn't answered. To distract her, Fercha took her through gates from the Inn at the Falls to Brendinas to Fercha's tower so Merry could line-of-sight gate to help her father.

* * * * *

Verro was busy *ad hoc* gating, transporting Kennig, Inthíra, Doethan, and Callidus to their required destinations. It was therefore more than an hour before he was able to disguise himself as a cloud and scud along as if blown by the wind from the quarry at Wherrel to arrive over Eynon's home village of Haywall. He checked above and around him for hidden wizards but could find none. Turning his attention below, Verro could see Southern Clan Land warriors tying a gray-haired woman to a heavy wooden beam that held the doors of what looked like a hay barn tightly closed. Stacks of hay were piled around the walls outside the barn and many of the warriors held lit torches as well as spears and crossbows at their stations around the building.

Closer to the center of the village, a wizard with a jasper magestone and a falcon on his left shoulder was conversing with someone through a communications ring. A woman looking over the man's right shoulder didn't seem happy. Verro triggered a listening spell and positioned his cloud illusion so he could see the ring's interface using magnifying lenses of solidified sound. A voice so loud it almost didn't need his listening spell's amplification came through the ring's gold circle.

"I'm telling you Brùtha, there's an entire Roma *legion* marching up the road beside the river," said a man wearing a flat brown cap sporting a pheasant feather. "My people here in Caercadel are ready to turn and run."

"Hold fast," said Brùtha over the shoulder of the wizard with the jasper magestone. "We have to maintain control of the baronial seat. You've got the hostages in place, don't you? Follow the plan."

"Of course we do," said the man. "They're tied to tall posts set every six feet around the castle, as you instructed, and my best warriors are behind them, ready to slit their throats."

"Good," said Brùtha. "Remind your fellow clan-folk they don't have anything to worry about. The legionnaires won't attack if it means civilians will be killed."

"I don't know about that," said the man with the cap. "I've heard stories about how the Roma deal with their own captives."

"Maybe if these were the invading emperor's forces," said Brùtha. "Sírénae has a particular reputation for ruthlessness, but Quintillius isn't that sort. He formed an alliance with the blue-tabards, after all."

"But there are so many of them," said the man.

"Tell them you'll cut off a prisoner's head if they get too close," said Brùtha. "Then *do* it if necessary. That should slow them down."

"It should, I expect," said the man. "Or at least I hope it will. How are things going at your end, Máclaesh?"

"We've got all our prisoners in the village hay barn," said the wizard with the jasper magestone. "Still no opposing forces in sight, but we're ready to burn the barn—or threaten to, at least—if and when they appear."

"Keep an eye out for a Roma wizard with beaded braids," Brùtha told the man in Caercadel. "Her name is Laetícia—she's a master mage and reputed to be *very* capable. Don't drop your guard for the beat of a hummingbird's wings."

"How long will we have to maintain this standoff?" asked the man with the flat cap and feather.

"Not too long, I hope," said Brùtha. "I'm cultivating friends in high places."

"Higher than the master mage of the Roma on this side of the Ocean?" asked the man.

"As a matter of fact, yes," said Brùtha. "But that's my worry, not yours. Just keep your people's swords at their captives' throats and stay strong."

"I guess we should all hang together or..." said the man.

"Don't complete that statement," said Brùtha. "You know the Roma don't go in for hanging. Just follow the plan." She nodded to Máclaesh and the wizard with the jasper magestone cut the connection.

"Perhaps the Roma don't hang their opponents," Máclaesh told Brùtha, "but the blue-tabards do, and so do the green-tabards. I don't even want to think about what the Bifurlanders are reputed to do to *their* captives."

"Get your feet out of a cold stream, Máclaesh," said Brùtha. "We all agreed on this course of action. We *need* the Coombe's farmland. Our children are starving. The mountain soil just isn't productive enough for our clans' growing population."

"I know, my dear, I know," said Máclaesh. "I just wish we don't have to break quite so many eggs to make this omelet."

"Falcons have no qualms about breaking eggs, Máclaesh," said Brùtha. "At least when they're not their own." She rubbed her head. "Blast that young wizard!" she said. "It's going to take me days I don't have to find a new magestone and craft a new setting."

"Maybe it's time for another wizard to take charge," said Máclaesh.

A slim dagger materialized from Brùtha's sleeve. Its point pierced three layers of clothing covering her fellow wizard's ribs.

"Then again," Máclaesh noted with a small shake of his head. "Maybe not."

"You're living proof of an old saying," said Brùtha.

"And which old saying would that be, my dear?" asked Máclaesh.

"Too soon old, too late smart," Brùtha replied.

"I'm not the one who had her prisoner escape and her magestone taken," said Máclaesh. He grunted when Brùtha gave her dagger a small twist, gouging out a bit of his flesh. "Fine, fine, you're in command, dear wife. What was I thinking?"

"Not much, obviously, my lomg-suffering and misguided husband," said Brùtha.

"Long-suffering at your hand," Máclaesh protested.

"True enough," said Brùtha. "Now call up the clan chief in Wherrel."

* * * * *

Verro heard a familiar voice whispering beside him as he hid in a cloud illusion above Haywall.

"She's quite ruthless, isn't she?"

"Eynon?" Verro whispered back.

"Yes—and this time I had the good sense to check the clouds around me for wizards waiting in ambush."

"Is *that* what happened to you?" asked Verro. Eynon nodded while Verro continued. "I always check my surroundings, as a matter of course. And I put up detection spells and strong shields. I'm surprised you could circumvent my wards."

"I don't know how I managed that," said Eynon. "I saw you and must have just *slipped* past them, somehow."

"We can figure that out later," said Verro. "In the meantime, were did you go? I thought you were supposed to be scouting for us."

"It's a long story," Eynon replied. "And I'm not proud of it. For now, I heard most of what Brùtha said. How can I help?"

"In quite a few ways," said Verro. "Are *you* the reason Brùtha doesn't have her magestone?"

Eynon displayed a leather bracer holding an agate magestone. "I might be."

Verro smiled and added a cloak of solidified sound around them so they could talk without whispering. "I'm glad you're back," he said. "We can really use your help." He explained Kennig's plan and Eynon rubbed his chin.

"That could work," said Eynon. He stared down at his flying disk and frowned.

"What is it?" asked Verro.

"Some of the Southern Clan Lands' children are orphans because of me."

"That may be true, from what I heard about you blowing the top off a mountain," said Verro, "but if all goes well, your efforts may prevent a good number of children in the Coombe from *also* becoming orphaned."

Eynon squared his shoulders and straightened his back. He could see he was almost as tall as Verro, though not nearly as well-muscled as the older wizard. "When we've dealt with the Southern Clan Landers, will you give me a piece of advice, one master mage to another, and teach me a spell you've found particularly useful? That's why I was looking for you at Great Falls. I'm trying to get Master Mage lessons."

"Certainly," said Verro. "My father-in-law was always one to advocate experience as the best teacher, but I don't think there's any problem with helping new wizards along."

"Thank you," said Eynon.

Verro looked Eynon up and down, noting the younger man's hopeful expression. "My first piece of advice is to contact Merry and let her know you're safe," he said. "Partners worry about each other and last time I saw her she was trying to hold far too much anger and concern inside her."

"Anger?" asked Eynon.

"Yes," said Verro. "I could see she was angry at you for whatever dumb thing she expected you had done. I think she was also far from happy that you weren't responding to her attempts to ring you."

Eynon looked down at his fingers. All his communications rings were gone. "Brùtha must have taken my rings!"

Verro pointed at the leather bracer in Eynon's hand. "Then you'll just have to trade Brùtha for them. But first find Merry in Applegarth."

* * * * *

Two hours later, Nûd sat on Rocky's back a hundred paces away from the Wherrel gap. Bonnie hovered beside him, riding Béryl, her owlberron familiar. A thousand members of the Dâron royal guard, some on foot, some astride, were arrayed behind them, their banners streaming. Ahead of them, blocking the gap, were sixty thick posts arrayed in five rows, each holding a Coombe hostage. Southern Clan Lander warriors in tartan kilts or braies—pants bound tight with strips of leather—stood beside them with spears pointed at their captives' throats.

A tall Clan Lander with a brown kilt and a saffron-colored linen shirt stepped forward and gave a defiant ululating shout that was echoed by all the warriors behind him. Nûd thought he must be a clan chief. He turned to Bonnie and gestured, making a cone with his hands. Understanding, she generated a spell to amplify his voice.

"What do you want?" Nûd asked.

"We want you to go back to Brendinas, King of the Blue-Tabards. We want you to leave us alone to enjoy our new lands and new slaves without interference."

"These are not *your* lands," said Nûd. "They belong to the kingdom of Dâron. And the people you hold are not *your* slaves. They are free citizens of the kingdom."

"They don't look free to me," said the clan chief. As if on cue some of the warriors behind him poked or jabbed their captives, making them moan and scream.

"I don't want to kill you," said Nûd.

"And I don't want to die—though I wouldn't mind killing you if I had the opportunity," said the clan chief. He spat on a tuft of grass three feet ahead of him. "Take your great black beast and your clanking knights and your concubine riding a misshapen gryffon away from here. If you don't, I'll gift you with the head of one of our new slaves for every ten minutes you remain."

"That's not much of a bargain," said Nûd. "I get something I have no use for, and you lose the future services of what you call a slave. That's muddled thinking, my friend."

"I'm *not* your friend, King Blue-Tabard," said the clan chief. "And don't go trying to confuse me with sophistry. I've read the Athican and Roma sages."

"I'm glad to know I'm dealing with an educated man," said Nûd. "As such, you'll understand that it is a much better bargain if both sides receive something they value in any negotiation."

"This isn't a negotiation, Blue-Tabard. It's an ultimatum. Leave, or we start lopping off heads."

"I was thinking you might be more interested in exchanging your hostages for ours," said Nûd. He raised his head and Kennig dropped the illusion that had been hiding him and the sixty Southern Clan Lands' children tied together by their wrists around him. "We haven't harmed any of them," said Nûd. "And we won't—but we will take these children and foster them to families in Dâron, Tamloch, and Occidens Province if you don't release your captives and leave the Coombe."

A flying disk with two riders flew in from the east and landed beside the clan chief. Brùtha and Máclaesh stepped off and stood beside him. "Kill them," Brùtha ordered, pointing at the bound Coombe-folk.

"Shut your mouth, wizard," said the clan chief. "Two of my own children are over there."

"We need the land," Brùtha protested. "All our children will starve without better land."

Eynon and Merry dropped their own illusions and appeared beside Kennig.

"There's plenty of good farmland to the west," said Merry. "I'm sure King Nûd would grant you some of it."

"Bah!" said Brùtha. "The western lands are flat. We're mountain clans. *This* land has good farms *and* mountains. It's perfect for us."

"I may be able to help you with that concern," said Eynon.

"Why should we care about the words of a murderer and a thief?" asked Brùtha. "You killed our clan-folk and stole my magestone."

"Only after you took mine while torturing me," said Eynon.

"I want to hear what he has to say," said the clan chief.

"So do I," said Máclaesh. He looked at Brùtha then turned away.

"Here," said Eynon, holding up Brùtha's leather bracer. "Let's do an exchange of our own to show our mutual good faith. Your magestone for my rings."

Brùtha stared at the bracer as if willing it to float across the distance between them on its own. Reading her intent, Eynon lifted the bracer on a tendril of solidified sound and extended it half the distance toward Brùtha.

"Now my rings," said Eynon.

Brùtha glared at Eynon with a hatred as powerful as one of Eynon's own fireballs, but Máclaesh nodded and removed most of the rings from Brùtha's fingers, holding her arms and body in place with his own bands of solidified sound.

"You'll regret this," Brùtha muttered.

"Maybe. Maybe not, my dear," said Máclaesh. The falcon on his shoulder screeched as he sent the rings he'd taken out to join Brùtha's bracer.

"Switch," said Eynon. He took control of the rings and pulled them toward himself while Máclaesh captured the bracer and snapped it into his waiting hands.

"Give it to me husband," Brùtha commanded. She reached for the bracer.

Máclaesh held it away from her. "We're going to listen to the young wizard first, before I return this," he said.

"That seems wise," said the clan chief. "Speak," he told Eynon.

"I'll be glad to," said Eynon.

"We both will," said Merry. "Eynon created a new kind of gate—a ring gate. They're like fixed gates, except they're portable. They're matched pairs of rings, like communication rings, but they can expand to a much larger size so a cart and a team of oxen can fit through them. You could put one ring in the mountains and another on good farmland to the west."

"Having the best of both worlds," said Eynon. "We'd make you all the rings you need."

"And show us how to make them?" asked Máclaesh.

"If any of your mages have the skill to craft them, certainly," said Merry.

"It's not easy," said Eynon. "You have to balance the congruencies and ensure the two rings are..."

"Save the details for another day," said Merry, putting her arm around Eynon's waist. "What do you think of our proposal?"

"We get good farmland, and we don't have to leave our mountains?" asked the clan chief.

"And we don't have to fight blue-tabards, green-tabards, and legionnaires?" asked Máclaesh.

"We can't trust him," said Brùtha, pointing at Eynon. "He brought the side of a mountain down on us."

"We *were* invading Dâron at the time," said the clan chief. "It's not like we're blameless." He looked longingly at his children. "And I don't want to see more of our clan-folk die needlessly."

"A valid point," said Máclaesh.

The clan chief stepped a dozen paces forward and spoke directly to Nûd. "I assume you've put the same proposal to my counterparts in Caercadel and Liamston?" he asked. "What was their response?"

"They've both accepted," Nûd replied.

The clan chief turned back to Máclaesh. "Confirm that, please."

Máclaesh secured Brùtha's bracer under his robes. A few moments later, after two quick conversations by communications rings, Máclaesh nodded. "He's correct," said the wizard.

"Then I agree as well," said the clan chief. "I assume clan chiefs will have access to prime farmland?"

"We can work all that out," said Nûd. "Release the children."

Kennig waved a hand and the ropes binding the young Southern Clan Landers, who proved to be more of Kennig's illusions, disappeared.

The clan chief shouted an order to his warriors, and they started cutting the ropes that bound the Coombe folk to the poles where they'd been held captive. It was a noisy process, with cries of joy from the children and Coombe folk as well.

Amid the happy confusion came a man's scream. It was Máclaesh. Brùtha had poked him in the ribs with her dagger, before reclaiming her leather bracer and agate magestone from inside his robes. Before anyone could react, she was gone, the sound of in-rushing air from her absence lost amid the general din.

"Healer!" shouted the clan chief.

"I'm here," came a pleasant voice quite familiar to Eynon. Uirsé and Clýne had just *ad hoc* gated in on the back of Verro's flying disk. "Stand back and let us work," said Uirsé and she and her apprentice hurried to Máclaesh. A thin trickle of the wizard's blood was dripping out onto the grass. Máclaesh held his side and groaned. "She's always had quite a temper," he said through a clenched jaw.

"Can Brùtha *ad hoc* gate?" Merry asked Kennig.

"Yes," said the illusionist.

Merry put her arms around Eynon and hugged her back. "I now know there's a good reason why you didn't answer when I tried to ring you," she told him. "But please do what you can to *not* give me such scares in the future."

"I'll do my best," said Eynon, "but no promises."

"Of course not," said Merry. "And now you have a powerful Southern Clan Lands wizard who wants to kill you."

"She's wanted to kill me since we first met her at the green magestone quarry," said Eynon. "Now she just has more reasons to want to kill me."

Ace sniffed around Merry's feet and barked. "Who's a good boy?" said Merry, reaching down to pat her familiar's head.

"Blast!" Eynon exclaimed. "I've got to get Chee."

"Don't forget your little sister," teased Merry.

"I expect Felix is taking good care of her," said Eynon.

"I'm sure he is," said Merry. She grinned at Eynon. "Your parents are fine, by the way. Last I heard they were visiting with Dârio and Jenet after their local militia joined up with Tamloch's royal guard."

"That's good to hear," said Eynon. "Any news about Aunt Glynneth?"

"She didn't enjoy being bound to the hay barn's door, but Felix says she told him that a new batch of sweet cakes will be coming out of the oven within the hour."

After brief goodbyes, and a quick check with Uirsé to confirm Máclaesh would recover from the *gentle* minstrations of Brùtha's dagger, Eynon, Merry, and Ace flew east toward Haywall, Chee and sweet cakes.

Chapter 27

Haywall

Three things caught Eynon's attention before he and Merry even landed in Haywall. The first was the smell of smoke, the second was Baron Derry, Merry's father, who was leading a contingent of his knights holding two dozen disarmed Southern Clan Landers at spear point in the village courtyard, and the third was Felix, the young wizard from Occidens Province, standing with his arm over the shoulder of Braith, Eynon's sister. Felix and Braith both looked like cats who'd knocked over pitchers of cream—a not-uncommon occurrence in a village famed for its dairy products. They both had bits of straw in their hair and their clothes contributed to the smell of smoke without being the sole source of it.

"It's good to see you, daughter," called Derry. He turned to send a contingent of his knights off to escort their Southern Clan Lands prisoners to the wide gate outside Wherrel and return them to their own lands. Given the angry looks from Haywall's villagers he thought it wise to remove the invaders expeditiously. That important task accomplished, Derry stepped over to the descending wizards.

Eynon thought Merry's father looked much more impressive in his armor—steel plates riveted to a brown leather coat—than he had in the rustic clothing and broad-brimmed straw hat he'd worn when Eynon first met him. Derry now wore what looked like a bowl on his head, but made of steel, not straw. It seemed more sensible than a full barrel helm if you were traveling by shank's mare rather than on horseback. Derry didn't wear a tabard over his armor, but had the Applegarth flag, a wavy vertical blue line between two red apples, on shield-shaped pieces of white cloth attached to his shoulders to mark his rank.

Derry moved closer, his arms and his smile wide as he approached Eynon and his daughter. "I haven't seen you in..."

"Three hours since I told you to head west to help the Coombe-folk," teased Merry. At her feet, Ace barked to add emphasis.

"Well, yes," said Derry. "It's very convenient having a wizard in the family. That ring gate of yours saved us quite a lot of time and effort having to hike over the mountains."

"I'm glad you approve," said Merry. She gave her father a hug. "We need to march *all* these Southern Clan Landers to Wherrel and send them through the wide gate connecting back to their lands."

"I think we can manage that," said Derry. "Especially since that young man of yours has figured out how to stop the Southern Clan Landers from raiding us whenever they please." He turned to Eynon. "How are you doing, lad? Set fire to any more trees lately?"

"Not in the last week or two," said Eynon. "Though I did bog down invading legions in mud."

"So I'd heard," said Derry. "Nicely done." He sniffed the air. "What happened here? It smells like smoke, but I don't see any fires burning."

Felix spoke up. "The Southern Clan Landers were going to burn the hay barn with most of the people of Haywall locked inside it, once they'd heard about forces from Dâron, Tamloch, and Occidens Province coming to retake the Coombe."

"They'd put hay all around the barn and set fire to it," said Braith, "but Felix put the fires out with magic before the flames could set the barn alight. He said he used solidified sound to keep the air away and starve the fires. He's a very talented wizard."

Eynon smiled as he watched Braith stare up to give Felix a look that reminded him of the expression she'd previously reserved for eating Aunt Glynneth's sweet cakes hot from the oven. He debated not teasing his sister, but decided, as her older brother, that he must. "What were you and Felix *doing* in the hay barn, by the way? I know you were there before the rest of the villagers were forced inside."

Braith put her hand over her heart and feigned shock. "What is any young couple doing in a hay barn, brother? We were looking for needles, of course."

Merry grinned at Eynon and clapped her hands to acknowledge Braith's response. Eynon's face turned red and Merry tugged on his neck, so he was close enough to kiss him on the forehead. "Never ask a question when you don't really want to know the answer," she told him.

"That's good advice for dealing with children, not just siblings," said Derry.

"Plenty of time yet for that," said Merry. "And you can start working on Salder and Uirsé first."

"Your mother has that effort well underway," said Derry.

"Of course she has," said Merry, her grin growing wider.

"As I understand it, your brother and Uirsé are planning to marry quite soon," said Derry.

"Are they expecting?" asked Merry.

"There *are* other reasons for a couple to wed," said her father.

"Quite true," said Merry. "Though come to think of it, I wouldn't mind being an aunt."

"Nor I a grandfather," said Derry, "however, the timing of that status is a matter for your brother and Uirsé to decide."

"Is there much damage to the hay barn?" Eynon asked Felix, hoping to change the subject.

"Very little," the tall young Occidens Province wizard replied.

"Nothing that can't be fixed with a new coat of buttermilk and brick dust," said Braith as Felix paused to take a breath. "I can recruit my friends to help repaint." She pulled Felix closer to her and continued. "We won't even need ladders if Felix stays for a few days. We can paint the second floor as I ride with him on his flying disk."

Eynon looked at Felix to see how his friend from Nova Eboracum felt about his sister's suggestion and noticed a tilt of Felix's head, raised eyebrows, and a big smile. *I'll have to get him alone sometime and warn him about all my sister's bad habits,* he thought. Then he reconsidered. *It's probably wiser for him to get to know Braith better and draw his own conclusions.*

"I'm glad to stay for a few days and help Haywall recover from the aftereffects of the invasion," said Felix. "I've painted boats, but I've never painted a barn before."

"If you enjoy it, there are enough barns in the Coombe to provide you with lifetime employment," said Eynon.

"I don't think there's any danger of that," said Felix. "Mafuta has other plans for me."

Eynon saw an expression on his sister's face that was easy to interpret. Braith had plans for Felix, too.

"You can stay with us," Braith told Felix.

"He can stay with Aunt Glynneth," said Eynon. "After her recent traumatic experiences, I'm sure she'd appreciate the company."

Braith made a small frown and stuck her tongue out at Eynon. He kept a straight face and didn't laugh, then was startled when Merry cried out and pointed up toward the east. A familiar wizard with two equally familiar passengers was approaching from that direction. It was Doethan, with Eynon and Braith's parents.

"Welcome back!" said Eynon when the flying disk landed. "How did things go in Liamston?"

"Well enough," said Eynon's father, Daffyd. "We had enough warning of the Southern Clan Landers invasion to get everyone out of town and up into the mountains."

"When King Dârio and Jenet and the Tamloch royal guards came through the Liamston Gap, they didn't have to worry about the Clan Landers threatening hostages," added Glenys, Eynon's mother.

"Your parents organized the Liamston folk into a militia and were ready to attack them from one side while the royal guard attacked from the other," said Doethan, who wiped drops of sweat from his bald head and smiled. "I was headed here to find you and brought them with me. They wanted to be sure you and Braith were safe."

Glenys noticed how Braith and Felix were standing. "I can see that *you* were safe, at least, daughter."

"Nice to see you again, Felix," said Daffyd. He took in the bits of hay in Felix and Braith's hair and on their clothes. "Did you find any needles?"

"Father!" Braith protested.

"I'm glad neither of you was hurt," said Glenys to her children.

"Not for lack of trying," said Merry, soft enough so only Eynon could hear her.

"What did you need to find me for?" Eynon asked Doethan.

"I need a pair of ring gates so I can help move the Southern Clan Landers under guard in Liamston back to their own territory," Doethan replied. "I figure that I can put one ring in Liamston and the other at the Southern Clan Landers' own wide gate near the quarry in Wherrel and get that process started."

Eynon turned to Merry. "Do we have any more gate rings?"

"Two more pairs," said Merry. "But that's all." She handed one of the connected pairs to Doethan who nodded his thanks.

"We'll have to get busy making more gate ring pairs," said Eynon. "Especially to help the Southern Clan Landers get to their new farmland."

"You can teach me how to make them and I can see to it," said Doethan. "I'm good at making communications rings and I understand gate rings are just a refinement of that process."

"Gladly," said Eynon.

"Speaking of farmland for Southern Clan Landers," said Merry. "Why didn't you encourage them to resettle near Three Mountains Valley, where they'd have good land close to high mountains?"

"Southern Clan Landers can be quarrelsome," said Eynon. "I didn't want to give Rōlin and Peregrína the aggravation."

"Oh," said Merry. "That was good thinking."

"And I'd imagine, over time, some of the Southern Clan Landers might resettle at their new farms along the river bottoms just west of *their* mountains," said Doethan.

"Putting them a good deal farther away from the Coombe," said Daffyd.

"Which would be very good indeed," said Glenys.

"With more gate rings in use, I don't think anywhere will be far away from anywhere else," said Felix. "There are even gates across the Ocean now. I may get to visit the part of the Southern Empire where my parents and grandparents came from someday."

"I'd like to see the Southern Empire," said Braith.

"Plenty of time for such things later," said Glenys.

Much later, thought Eynon, interpreting his mother's tone of voice. Braith's wander year was still many months away.

Braith's eyes went wide, and she pointed to the western skies. "Two flying disks!" she shouted. "Green robes and blue."

Eynon saw Felix shade his eyes and could sense his fellow wizard generating distance-seeing lenses of solidified sound.

"It's Verro and Fercha," said the tall Occidens Province wizard.

"Just who I wanted to talk to," said Eynon.

Before the new arrivals could land, Aunt Glynneth came out of her cottage carrying a tray heaped high with something that smelled delicious.

"Who wants a sweet cake?" she asked.

Chee came running into the courtyard from the direction of the hay barn, jumped high in the air, snatched up a sweet cake and, after a graceful landing, launched himself from the cobblestones to Eynon's shoulder. He gobbled up what he'd taken in four bites, spilling crumbs down Eynon's robes and trying to say *chee-chee-chee* even though his mouth was full.

"Nice to see you too," said Eynon. "Why didn't you also get a sweet cake for *me*?"

Chapter 28

Eynon and Verro

Without any assistance from Chee, Eynon kissed his honorary Aunt Glynneth on the cheek and claimed three sweet cakes.

"Only one, you young rascal," scolded Glynneth.

"Two are for Fercha and Verro," said Eynon. "I know better than to be greedy."

"Your parents raised you properly, I'd say," Glynneth grumbled.

"With plenty of help from you, auntie," said Braith, claiming three sweet cakes herself and avoiding Glynneth's wrath by promptly delivering two of them to Daffyd and Glenys.

Merry gave Glynneth a small bow and waited for a nod before taking a cake. She broke off a corner of the sweet cake and tossed it high. Ace caught it in the air and swallowed it whole. Merry rubbed his head when he nudged her leg. "No more for now," she told her familiar. "You can catch some unwary bats tonight."

Braith and Felix were alternating bites on a sweet cake, with Eynon's sister taking a delicate nibble then holding it high for Felix to consume a more substantial portion without removing his arm from around Braith's shoulders.

"Were we that cute?" Merry asked Eynon softly.

"You were," said Daffyd, Glenys, and Glynneth simultaneously.

"Some would say you still are," said Doethan who hadn't joined in with the others' reply because his mouth was full.

Eynon was spared further embarrassment by Fercha and Verro's arrival. He greeted his fellow wizards and offered them the sweet cakes he'd reserved for them, giving credit to his aunt for her baking skills.

After thanking Glynneth for her treats and eating his sweet cake, Verro took Eynon by the elbow, pulled him a dozen steps away from the others. The older wizard cast a sphere of silence around them. Eynon noticed that Fercha had taken Merry off in a different direction.

"I've just seen to getting the Southern Clan Landers on their way back to their mountains," said Verro. "Kennig has been immensely helpful, since he lived with them, and Inthíra has been a calming influence when tempers start to flare. Say what you will about the Southern Clans, they love their children and didn't want to see them threatened."

"Not that we would have hurt them," said Eynon.

"The clan chiefs didn't know that," said Verro. "They would have been ruthless had the situations been reversed. In fact, they did take Coombe children as hostages."

"That's probably why Kennig's plan worked as well as it did," said Eynon.

"We'll need your help to identify good farmland along the western rivers and set up ring gates from the mountain settlements," said Verro.

"You may need me less than you think, after Merry and I train Doethan how to make ring gates," said Eynon. "I still need to learn from all the master mages in Orluin."

"That's why I came to find you in Haywall," said Verro. "You'd made it seem important we talk, and I thought it would be wise for us to do so soon, before some new crisis materializes." He looked Eynon up and down and from his expression Verro was pleased with what he saw. "You said you wanted advice, from one master mage to another, and also a spell?"

"Yes, please," said Eynon. "I'd welcome whatever advice you think a new master mage should be given and would value your help teaching me a spell you've found particularly useful."

Verro wiped cake crumbs from his lips and held out one hand. Tiny sparks of lightning snapped from fingertip to fingertip. He extended his other hand and cupped a small fireball in his palm. Then he canceled those spells and dropped his hands to his sides. "I don't think you need much assistance with offensive magic," said Verro. He rubbed his chin. "However, Brùtha wants to kill you and she's by no means your most dangerous enemy. I think you might find defensive magic more useful."

"Merry and Uirsé and my parents would agree with you, I'm sure."

"We'd best find somewhere more isolated for the defensive training I have in mind," said Verro. He waved for Chee to jump off Eynon's shoulder. After the familiar scampered over to Ace, Verro put his hand on Eynon's forearm and *ad hoc* gated them away.

* * * * *

Eynon found himself standing on a broad, slightly domed expanse of exposed limestone surrounded by thickly forested mountains much taller than the ones that enclosed the Coombe. The air smelled of spruce and pine and the tang of smoke from back in Haywall had vanished completely. Far to the left a forlorn double row of marble columns stood, looking like the ruins of an Athican civic building. It was cold, not far above freezing, and Eynon summoned heat from a small congruency to keep himself warm. He looked to his right and saw a particularly tall mountain, topped in white like the peaks bordering Three Mountains Valley, and turned to Verro.

"We're a bit more than two hundred miles north of Riyas in the White Mountains of northern Tamloch, not far from our border with Bifurland," said Verro, answering Eynon's unspoken question. He pointed at the tallest mountain. "That's the White King," Verro continued. "Various other peaks are his queen, counselors, knights, and castles."

"Not literal castles, I assume," said Eynon. "They're named for pieces on a *shah-mat* board?"

"Correct," said Verro. "Though in this case, it's the king that's mad, not the queen."

"I don't understand," said Eynon.

"Ah," said Verro. "You've never heard of the Mad Queen game?"

"I've only played *shah-mat*," Eynon replied. "I don't know much about its history."

"Scholars say we got the game from far to the east," said Verro. "Originally, the queen could only move one square diagonally. The Roma in Éberria wanted a faster game, however, and opted for allowing queens to move as many squares as desired, horizontally, vertically, *and* diagonally. For a generation, that version was called the Mad Queen game."

"Interesting," said Eynon. "I didn't want to say anything about a mad king, in case you might think I was talking about your brother."

"Don't worry about that," said Verro. "Túathal was and likely *is* truly mad. I'm not ashamed to admit it." He waved a hand toward the tallest mountain. "However, the White King has been considered mad since our ancestors first explored this territory, long before my brother lost his sanity. The weather on top can change faster than a sailor's luck in a dice game and the winds there can be worse than a hurricane."

"Sounds dangerous," said Eynon.

"Believe me, it is," said Verro. "When the weather is clear you can see for a hundred miles in all directions from the summit, but five minutes later a snow-squall might suddenly appear and make it hard to see the tip of your nose."

Eynon shook his head, acknowledging Verro's words and pointed toward the distant row of marble pillars. "What are those? Remnants of a royal palace?"

"No, they're what's left of an inn built several centuries ago by Duke Bretton, a man who was once one of Tamloch's senior nobles. He had the inn constructed as a summer retreat and a place where he could invite his friends to enjoy the scenery and the cooler temperatures," said Verro. He motioned to the trees stretching off into the distance. "These were once the duke's woods."

"What happened to the rest of the building?" asked Eynon.

Verro laughed. "Wizards happened," he said. "As I was told, one of the kings of Tamloch decided to hold a conference here to improve trade amongst the people of Orluin—sort of an earlier version of the Orluin Alliance I suppose but to encourage buying and selling, not mutual military support."

"I take it things didn't go well?"

"You might say that," said Verro. "The Bifurlanders objected to the valuations placed on their seal furs and walrus ivory, while the Dâron representatives thought their grain and wrought iron should be worth more. None of the parties, particularly the Roma, approved of establishing a common trading currency for the continent. The committee in charge of that supposedly wanted to call the new units of exchange *Luinees,* after Or*luin.* Can you imagine? Tempers grew heated, with one thing leading to another and soon wizards from three kingdoms and Occidens Province were throwing massive fireballs *inside* the inn. The noise of the detonations brought rocks and snow down off the mountains and crushed half the structure, along with a large percentage of the conference participants."

"Ouch!" said Eynon, thinking about his own fireball that brought down half a mountain on the Southern Clan Landers. "Does that have anything to do with all the bare rock around us?"

"It does," said Verro. "The master mages of Dâron, Tamloch, Bifurland, and Occidens Province had put up their shields in time and emerged from the wreckage of the inn. There's a painting in the royal palace in Riyas showing them standing at four corners of a grassy field and throwing fireballs so huge they vaporized all the dirt and vegetation in between them, leaving only bare rock behind."

"That explains why the rock here looks a lot like Roma cement," said Eynon after he'd looked at the ground. "It's been baked in place."

"I'd never thought about it," said Verro, "but you're right. Three monarchs and a governor-general died in the avalanche, and so did Duke Bretton and his heir, so the land reverted to the crown of Tamloch. It's been kept undisturbed as a memorial to the people who lost their lives, and to human folly, I expect. I *ad hoc* gate here when I want solitude to think, or peace and quiet to develop new spells."

"It's beautiful," said Eynon as his eyes took in the impressive scenery. He took a deep breath and turned to Verro. "You talked about teaching me a new sort of defensive magic?"

"That's right," said Verro. "Do you know about the Platonic solids?"

"Tetrahedron, hexahedron, octahedron, dodecahedron, icosahedron," Eynon recited.

"What are some other shapes you learned when you studied geometry?" asked Verro.

"Like spheroids, ellipsoids, and cones?" said Eynon.

"Exactly," said Verro. "They're all standard forms a great many wizards can construct from solidified sound, largely used for defensive magic, since very few mages have your creativity." The older wizard paused for a moment, using the fingers of one hand to rub his temples. "What did Damon teach you about making shields?" asked Verro when it appeared he'd determined an approach for teaching Eynon.

"Mostly hemispheres, to block direct attacks, or full spheres to protect all sides," said Eynon. "I've also used combinations of hemispheres and cones—teardrops—to fly faster. I love the name for them I read about in one of the books in the library at Melyncárreg, *lachrymiforms*."

"Which is just the Athican way of saying teardrop shaped," said Verro.

Eynon smiled and Verro asked another question. "Do you know the trick about making lenticular shields—two conjoined convex shields like a lens—to take in energy thrown at you, store it, and release it back at your attackers?"

"Yes," said Eynon. "I figured that shape out on my own and used it against Brùtha and the other Falcon Clan wizards when Merry and I first met them at the quarry near Wherrel. It seemed like quite a useful offensive trick and a great way to turn enemies' spells against them."

"I'm not surprised," said Verro. "You're good at coming up with things like that on your own." He put a hand on Eynon's shoulder to make sure he had the younger wizard's full attention. The green mage-stone in the gold cuff on Verro's wrist sparkled with an internal light. "What I want to teach you now is how to make shields that are tightly fitted to your body, so you can leave them in place without them getting in the way of most interactions."

"That would be wonderful," said Eynon. "I can't keep spherical shields in place if I want to be around people and hemispherical shields leave me vulnerable. Where do we start?"

"Let me think," said Verro. He paused for a moment then stepped back and snapped his fingers. "I know," he announced. "Thinking about Kennig changing his appearance when he collected the Southern Clan Lands' children gave me inspiration."

"Oh," said Eynon. "Are tightly-fitted personal shields like illusions?"

"Indeed they are," said Verro. "Have you ever truly thought about *how* you use solidified sound to make illusions?"

"Not really," Eynon replied. "I mostly just think about what I want them to look like and they just snap into place, somehow."

Verro used a tendril of solidified sound to fetch a fragment of stone pillar from the old inn. He dropped the piece of marble on the ground in front of Eynon. It was a flat circular section from the middle of a column with fluting around its circumference. "Use your illusion magic to make a copy," Verro instructed.

Eynon complied, generating a near-perfect imitation of the fragment a foot to one side.

"Good," said Verro. "Now look at the illusion you've generated. Really *look* at it."

Eynon stared at the fragment he'd constructed, inadvertently letting the tip of his tongue extend from his mouth as he focused.

Verro watched Eynon make lenses of solidified sound that allowed the younger wizard to magnify his vision.

"It's *triangles!*" said Eynon. "Thousands and thousands of triangles."

"Correct," said Verro. "I'm not much of an illusionist, but the books I've read on that subject told me that triangles are a very effective way to mimic complex shapes, like that slice of pillar."

"How does that help me with tight personal shields?" said Eynon.

Verro didn't answer. He gave Eynon a few moments to consider the matter for himself and was rewarded when he saw Eynon transform his sky-blue robes into what looked like a second skin of polished steel formed from a multitude of three-sided shapes.

"Of course," said Eynon. "It's rigidity and resistance to magic." The steel morphed into silver, then gold, then a series of jewel tones, and finally seemed to disappear.

"Good for you," said Verro. "You've realized something it took me quite a while to understand myself. Your new shields don't have to be visible to be effective."

Eynon made a face like he'd just bitten into a sour apple. "How will I know if my tight personal shield *is* truly effective?" he asked.

Verro flicked his fingers and a small fireball flew from his hand and struck the center of Eynon's chest, where it flared briefly and disappeared. "That's how," said the older wizard. "I'll help you figure out how to refine your tight shield so it will keep you safe from most physical and magical attacks."

"Thank you," said Eynon.

"Don't thank me until after we determine how good your tight shield is," said Verro. Tamloch's master mage boarded his flying disk and flew a dozen feet in the air. Eynon did likewise so the two of them were floating within arm's reach of each other.

"How will you help me refine my tight shield?" Eynon asked.

"By attacking you and seeing how well they protect you," said Verro. He accelerated away from Eynon and gained altitude.

"Now you're sounding like Damon," Eynon called. He could feel his jaw muscles tighten as he worked to improve the protection his thousands of triangles provided. A lightning bolt cast by Verro interfered with his concentration. Eynon was pleased when the lightning's charge didn't hurt him but dissipated in a corona of electric sparks inches from his body.

"That was just a small bolt," shouted Verro from high above. "I didn't want to fry you if your shield wasn't effective."

"Do your worst," said Eynon. "I mean best, I mean…"

A fireball as hot as a dragon's flaming breath and the size of a fully-grown wyvern smashed into Eynon. He screamed and immediately opened a congruency to a region of intense cold, keeping it open until his teeth started chattering.

"Did I mention that it can be wise to overlap your triangles?" asked Verro.

"No. You. Did. Not," said Eynon, biting off each word to keep himself from sending a fireball of his own back at Verro. He adjusted the shapes forming his tight shield and asked Verro to try again.

"I'm going to try something different," said Verro. "Prepare yourself."

Eynon stood firmly in place, waiting to see what Verro had up the voluminous sleeves of his robes. He didn't have long to wait. A cylindrical hole appeared in the air above Eynon and tens of thousands of gallons of water began to pour through it. Eynon's flying disk was forced down to the exposed limestone and Eynon, who remained upright for a few seconds as the water flowed, finally took two steps, clutched his throat, and collapsed, unmoving, to the bare ground.

Verro closed the congruency linked to the Great Falls and descended to confirm that Eynon was unhurt. When he reached the younger wizard, Eynon's eyes were open. Verro extended his hand and helped Eynon get back to his feet. "I should have warned you not to make your tight shield completely airtight," he said.

"Or to open a congruency... to let me breathe... if I did seal it completely," said Eynon, pausing between phrases to fill his lungs.

"All things considered, you did quite well," said Verro. "I'm impressed."

After several more deep breaths, Eynon asked a question. "Tell me, why don't all wizards keep up tight shields all the time? It would make them practically invulnerable."

"I can think of three reasons," said Verro. "First, only highly skilled wizards or illusionists can generate tight shields."

"Like master mages or wizards like Kennig, Inthíra, and Merry?"

"Correct," said Verro. "Second, it takes a great deal of concentration to maintain tight shields. I'm confident you can keep yours in place for quite a while, especially with the incentive of having so many people at large who'd like to kill you, but at some point your focus will slip."

"Or I'll need to sleep," said Eynon.

"Also correct," said Verro.

"And third?" asked Eynon.

"Third, you'll need to eat and perhaps do some intimate activity that would require you to drop your tight shield."

"That makes sense," said Eynon. "I expect Merry would prefer to kiss lips rather than triangles."

"Of that I have no doubt," said Verro. "If you plan ahead, other sorts of wards can protect you when you drop your tight shield, like a traditional sphere or a hexahedron."

"I'm not sure I like the idea of living in a bubble, even a tightly-fitting one," said Eynon.

"None of us do," said Verro. "For myself, I only generate a tight shield when I put myself in situations of heightened danger."

"Ummm," said Eynon.

"Right," said Verro. "You seem to jump out of the frying pan and into the fireball. Perhaps you'd best practice maintaining your tight shield whenever you're awake."

"Do I have any other options?" asked Eynon.

"You could work on getting faster at generating your tight shield when necessary and learn how to construct sensitive detection spells around you to sense danger," said Verro. "Detection isn't my magical specialty, but Amber, Bifurland's master mage, is known for extensive expertise in that area. Perhaps Amber can help you."

"Thank you," said Eynon. "I'll have to fly to Bjarniston next, then."

"I'll *ad hoc* gate you there," said Verro. The older wizard's eyes caught movement in the trees in the direction of the White King. Verro tugged Eynon's arm and put a finger to his lips to signal Eynon to keep silent. Then he pointed.

A giant creature, larger than the biggest bull wisent Eynon had seen in the large herds near Melyncárreg, was emerging from the forest. Its body was covered in thick, gray-white hair and its solid legs looked more like an elephant's than the legs of any sort of cattle. The beast's most remarkable feature, however, was a huge horn that curved up from its nose, covering half as much of an arc as a mammoth's tusks and coming to a point just as sharp.

"Is that a unicorn?" asked Eynon softly. Something about the creature seemed familiar.

"Some say so," said Verro. "I'm reserving judgment on the matter. Sometimes one will approach me when I come here to think."

"It's beautiful—and terrifying," said Eynon.

"An apt description," said Verro. "The beast is curious. I've gathered that much, at least."

"In that, we're alike," said Eynon. He brought his palm to his forehead but didn't slap it to avoid startling the unicorn. "I remember now. The unicorn reminds me of Maddox."

"Maddox?" asked Verro.

"An animal *friend* of Rōlin and Peregrína's," said Eynon. "Sort of a giant shaggy battle unicorn. They think he's the last of his kind, but now I'm sure he's not."

"He may still be," said Verro. "We have no idea whether or not this unicorn is male or female."

"True," said Eynon, with a sigh. "I'm not going to approach close enough to check, that's for sure." Eynon grinned, then shook his head quickly, as if to dislodge cobwebs in his brain. "I almost forgot," he said softly. "Do you have any special words of advice for me, one master mage to another?"

"Advice," mused Verro, frowning. Then he smiled. "Here's my advice," he said quietly. "Play *shah-mat* with Jenet. She's one of the best players I know."

"I'm not a good *shah-mat* player," said Eynon. "I won't be a worthy opponent. What good would it do me to play her?"

"You'll know the answer to that question when you've played her enough to know the difference between a *shah-mat* novice and a master," said Verro.

"Thank you," said Eynon. "I'll talk to Jenet at her wedding and set up a date and time for a game."

"I'd recommend talking to her after her wedding and after her honeymoon, for that matter," said Verro. "I think her attention will be focused elsewhere before then."

"That sounds wise," said Eynon.

"One more thing," said Verro.

"Yes?" said Eynon.

"Here's some advice from a man who almost killed the woman he loved in a wizards' duel," said Verro.

Eynon leaned closer to Verro to make sure he didn't miss anything the older wizard said and Verro didn't keep him waiting.

"Make the people you love a priority," said Verro. He closed his eyes as if he was playing streams of memories on the backs of his eyelids. When he opened his eyes a few moments later his face held a wistful expression. "For decades Fercha and I loved each other but circumstances wouldn't allow us to live together or raise our son together."

Verro put a hand on Eynon's shoulder. "Don't let an opportunity pass to tell the people you love that you love them," the older wizard continued. "It felt like a vulture was tearing out my liver whenever kingdom politics forced me to work against Fercha."

"That's a graphic and gory image," said Eynon.

"It's from an old Athican story," said Verro.

"I've read it," said Eynon. "It's the tale of how the first philosopher-mage brought the secret of fireballs to the other members of his academy. I was always more intrigued by the woman who discovered how to use magic to chill wine. That was really cool."

"Literally," said Verro. "Just don't let old stories get in the way of sharing your feelings. Follow the path of fire, not ice, in your relationships."

"I'm sixteen," said Eynon with a smile.

"And fire is easier at that age?" asked Verro. "While someone as ancient as I am would find ice a more familiar?"

"You're not ancient," said Eynon. "If that's what you mean, Ealdamon is far older than you are and last I'd heard he and Astrí have been on an extended second honeymoon for weeks. I expect there's certainly more fire than ice in their rekindled relationship."

"May we *both* have the same fire in our relationships when we're their ages," said Verro.

Eynon nodded his agreement.

The two wizards boarded their flying disks, grasped hands, and *ad hoc* gated away.

Back on the expanse of exposed limestone, the great horned beast crossed to where the wizards had been standing where it nosed the fragment of pillar and the duplicate Eynon had created. The illusion disappeared when touched by the unicorn's horn and the great beast shook its head, sniffed the air, and returned to the forest.

Chapter 29

Merry and Fercha

"Your skills at wizardry have greatly improved," said Fercha.

Merry didn't reply at first. Her attention was focused on Verro, and more particularly on Eynon. When the pair of them *ad hoc* gated out, she realized Fercha had been speaking to her. "Errr, what?" she asked.

"I didn't ask a question," said Fercha. "I just remarked on your skills increasing. It seems like years since you first broke into my tower, but it's only been a few months. You've come a long way since your first lessons in magic."

"I suppose I have," said Merry. "I was surprised my talents for working with tight light, generating illusions, or line-of-site gating developed so quickly."

"You likely have potential for other skills as well," said Fercha. "There's a lot we don't understand about magic and what each wizard can do with it."

Merry shook her head slowly. "True enough," she said. "I have no idea what else I can do."

Fercha smiled. "Challenging times can develop our untapped potential quickly," she said. "There have surely been enough challenges, with invasions from Tamloch, Bifurland, an overwhelming number of exiled Roma showing up to establish a new empire, *and* the Southern Clan Landers trying to take over the Coombe. You've been at the center of all of them."

"It's not like you've been far from the center of any of that yourself," said Merry. "And your son is now on the throne of Dâron."

"I'd hoped to spare Nûd that burden," said Fercha. "Growing up with Damon in Melyncárreg as the child and grandchild of powerful wizards I kept expecting him to become a mage and thereby avoid the burden of wearing a crown."

"Nûd is doing a fine job as king," said Merry. "He doesn't have a swelled head and cares about his people, not his privileges."

"Sadly, that's not thanks to anything I contributed to raising him," said Fercha. "Nor much to my father and mother's attentions."

"My sense of things was that Nûd raised himself, with help from the library at Melyncárreg and loving guidance from Rōlin and Peregrína," said Merry.

"Along with the positive influence of his friendship with you and Eynon," Fercha added.

"And Rocky and Bonnie," said Merry.

"I hardly think Bonnie would appreciate being mentioned in the same phrase as a wyvern," teased Fercha.

Merry laughed. "She'd understand what I meant, and she's *very* good for Nûd."

"Just as you're very good for Eynon..." said Fercha.

"...and he's very good for me," said Merry.

The two women nodded at each other and shook their heads, speaking hundreds of unsaid words in a shared glance.

"Eynon is off learning spells for defensive magic from Verro," said Fercha. "Would you like to learn more magic from me back at my tower?"

"Gladly," said Merry. "I thought you'd never ask."

The two wizards boarded their flying disks and rose twenty feet into the air. Ace barked and was ready to shift to his winged form and join them, but Merry waved for him to stop. "Stay with Chee, Braith, and Felix," she called down. "Eat some Coombe bats. I'll be back for you when Fercha and I finish my lessons."

Ace gave a bark of comprehension and stepped over to Braith, who rubbed the top of his head.

"Ready to fly?" asked Fercha.

"Take my hand," said Merry. "We can get there faster with my line-of-sight gating."

"This should be interesting," said Fercha. "It looks like I'll be a student as well as a teacher."

"And teaching something is often the best way to learn it," said Merry.

She took Fercha's hand and the two of them line-of-sight gated toward the distant mountains.

* * * * *

Merry and Fercha floated beside Fercha's blue spiral tower as the waters of the Rhuthro flowed peacefully below them. A wide, leaded-glass window near the top of the tower was directly before them.

"That was impressive," said Fercha. "It only took you ten jumps to get here. Do you think line-of-sight gating is something that can be taught?"

"I don't really know," said Merry. "I figured out how to do it on my own, though Doethan helped me refine my skills."

"He's a good teacher," said Fercha.

"So are you," said Merry. She looked through the window's glass, noting the configuration of the room visible through it.

Fercha smiled. "You're kind to say so. See how you feel after your next set of lessons."

"I doubt my opinion will change," said Merry.

Fercha waved toward the flat top of her tower. "Shall we land and enter through the trap door?" she asked.

"I'd like to try something first," said Merry. "Especially since you're here to help me if something goes wrong."

"What are you considering?"

"I want to gate *through* the window to the room beyond," said Merry. "I *think* I simply jump from one point in space to another when I line-of-sight gate, but it could be that I'm just crossing the distance so quickly it just seems that way."

The corners of Fercha's mouth turned down. "You want me to catch you if you smash into the window like an inattentive bird?"

"I don't think that will happen, but it if does, then yes. Please."

"Go ahead," said Fercha.

Merry seemed to flicker. Fercha saw her inside the tower, then outside again. Merry touched Fercha's forearm and in a heartbeat both wizards were inside the tower. The circular space they now occupied was the familiar workroom where Merry had crafted her artifact.

"Fascinating," said Fercha. "I've never seen or heard of any such magic before. This is bad."

"Did I do something wrong?" asked Merry.

"No, you're fine," said Fercha with a small shake of her head. "I was just considering the implications of your new talent for personal security. I hope you *can't* teach me how to line-of-sight gate, since it would be nearly impossible to protect someone from an assassin with such abilities."

"You could keep people you want to protect in rooms without windows," said Merry.

"That's not practical for leaders like Nûd and Dârio," said Fercha.

"Or Eynon," said Merry.

Fercha sighed. "We can consider the ramifications of your new talent later," she said. "Would you like something to drink before we start your lesson? I don't have anything to eat here in my tower, but I do have some aged applejack."

"From Applegarth?" asked Merry.

"Of course," said Fercha. "I only drink the best and have loved your family's strong cider since Doethan first poured me a mug when I came to the Rhuthro to build my tower."

"Only a small one," said Merry. "I want to keep my wits about me so I prove an attentive student."

Fercha tilted a glazed earthenware jug and filled two mugs with an amber liquid. The room quickly filled with the scent of apples. "You may find the cider will help with your lesson," said Fercha.

Merry took her mug and gave Fercha a quizzical look.

"I want you to give up your preconceptions," said Fercha. She took a sip of her cider and indicated Merry should do likewise. "You see," she said, "I'm going to teach you to *ad hoc* gate."

"What!" Merry exclaimed, glad she hadn't had a mouthful of cider before she'd heard Fercha's words. "You can teach me how to *ad hoc* gate? Then why does that skill seem restricted to master mages?"

Fercha took two slow sips as if she enjoyed making Merry wait for an answer. "Every mage can *ad hoc* gate," she said at last. "But only under limited circumstances."

"Oh!" said Merry. "You're talking about *emergency* gates. I know they exist, but never figured out where to put my sanctum, and never had anyone help me learn how they work."

"We'll do that today," said Fercha. "It's usually part of any new wizard's training, but yours was, shall we say, an accelerated course. In our haste some things fell out of the basket. Have you given any thought to where you might want to locate your bolt hole?"

"I'd thought about choosing Applegarth, but..."

"You don't want to select anywhere obvious," said Fercha. "The point is to be safe in case anything truly threatening happens to you. I had to use my emergency gate after a wizard's duel made me lose my artifact. It saved my life." *And Verro's emergency gate saved him as well,* she thought.

"There is one spot I'd considered," said Merry. "It's..."

"Don't tell me," said Fercha. "Wizards' sanctums should only be known to themselves. It defeats the point if you share the location."

"Verro told me—and Eynon—about *his* sanctum," said Merry. "He took us there when Eynon was hurt."

"One of the *many* times Eynon was hurt," said Fercha. "I hope Verro can help him improve his defense. Verro had to set up a new emergency refuge after he showed the two of you his old one. Of course, it's less of a problem to do that when you can *ad hoc* gate."

"I'm not sure I understand," said Merry. "Is emergency gating truly *ad hoc* gating and can all mages truly do it? That suggests all wizards should be able to *ad hoc* gate whenever they need to." She swallowed some applejack and waited for Fercha to answer. Her mentor paused, clearly ordering her thoughts.

"Have you read any books on the history of magic?" asked Fercha.

"A little," Merry replied. "But they weren't very helpful—mostly commentaries on Aristotélēs and the ancient Athican mages, or abstruse books on magical theory from the Imperium. It was hard to make sense of them."

"I'll give you some background then," said Fercha. "*Ad hoc* gates were discovered before emergency gates."

"I'd heard that story," said Merry. "Eilmer, a scholar-mage in Londinium was in a tearoom and made a small gate by accident so he could pet his cat Snowball, who was at his home a mile away. The cat walked through the gate and sat on Eilmer's lap. Then Eilmer made a bigger gate he could walk through so he could take her back to his apartments. I thought the Roma mages of Eilmer's day determined only a very small number of mages could *ad hoc* gate. Where do emergency gates fit in?"

"Eilmer made his discovery over eight centuries ago," said Fercha. "Scholars of magic learned to build fixed gates using frames to hold congruencies and the wizards who could create gates themselves— *ad hoc* gates—without frames became known as master mages or magisters, as the Roma call them. Over time, the magisters learned how to gate themselves without even generating interfaces."

"Now they just *pop*," said Merry.

"That they do," said Fercha.

"What about emergency gates?" asked Merry. She moved her hands in an encouraging circular motion.

"I'm getting to them," said Fercha. "It was all because of a goose."

"Huh?" said Merry.

"Patience," said Fercha. "This all happened near Eboracum..."

"Nova Eboracum?" asked Merry.

"No, the original Eboracum, in the northern part of the White Isle," Fercha corrected. "As I was saying, an older mage..."

Merry looked at Fercha and grinned.

"Quite a bit older than me," Fercha continued, "was flying home from a knitter's guild meeting..."

Merry interrupted. "Mages knit?"

"Many do," said Fercha. "These mages were known to knit with strands of solidified sound, not yarn, but that's peripheral to the story."

"Sorry," said Merry. "Go on."

"As I was saying, the older mage was flying home. She'd had several glasses of wine at the meeting and her brain must have been fuzzy as she tried to graph out complex knitting patterns in her head. That meant she didn't see the lone migrating goose who smacked into her, knocked her off her flying disk, and sent her plummeting hundreds of feet toward the ground."

"Did the feathers fly?" asked Merry.

"In a way," said Fercha. "The goose and the wizard didn't fly, however. They fell."

Merry leaned forward. "Then what happened?"

"We have to rely on reports from a shepherd boy on a nearby hillside," said Fercha. "But the Moon was full, and he said he saw things clearly. Before the older mage's body could strike the earth, a shimmering circle of *something* opened up beneath her and she disappeared."

"Fascinating," said Merry. "That's quite a yarn."

"Enough about yarn," teased Fercha. "I told you they were knitting with solidified sound."

"I'll have to try that myself, though I'll have to learn to knit first," said Merry.

"Something else I can teach you," said Fercha. "Doethan knits nets of solidified sound to catch fish. He could also teach you."

"Later," said Merry. "What happened to the older mage?"

"She woke up the next morning in her own bed wearing the robes she'd had on the night before," said Fercha. "And her favorite flying disk was nowhere to be found."

"How long did it take her to work out what had happened?"

"Not that long," said Fercha. "First, she had a cup of willowbark tea to ease her aching head. Then she rummaged around until she found a battered old flying disk she'd made as an apprentice decades earlier. It wasn't more than a few hours before she was retracing her path in the sky from the night before."

"Did she find her favorite flying disk?" asked Merry.

"She did," said Fercha. "The shepherd boy had propped it up on sticks to keep the sun off his back and was licking goose drippings off his fingers when she found him."

"Better than goose droppings," said Merry.

Fercha shook her head. "If your mother heard you talk..."

"She'd say, 'There you are, sounding like your father,'" said Merry.

"Likely so," said Fercha. Both women laughed and Fercha continued. "The older mage heard the shepherd boy's tale about the shimmering disk and recognized it as a congruency. She took back her favorite flying disk and promised to replace it with a light-weight awning of colorful woven solidified sound within the week. He gratefully accepted and gave her a drumstick. Eating the goose was fine with the older mage, especially since the bird had almost caused her death. Now, as she chewed, the older mage considered the opportunity her collision with the goose presented."

They both had another sip of applejack. Merry made impatient circles with her hands again.

"The older mage told her fellow knitters her strange story and they started to experiment," said Fercha. "They made up lots of healing potions and took turns knocking each other off their flying disks. Several broken limbs and a broken neck later, they were able to reliably replicate her extraordinary gating."

"What was the secret?" asked Merry.

"The threat of death or serious injury," said Fercha. "Risks of that sort must trigger something in wizards' minds to allow them a special sort of *ad hoc* gating."

"Sounds like a way to ensure a mage's survival *in extremis,*" said Merry.

"And that, sadly, is the crux of it," said Fercha. "Wizards *do* have some control over where they come out when they emergency gate, however. It's a matter of fixing a location—your sanctum or bolt hole or refuge, call it what you will—strongly enough in one's mind that it becomes the default destination for such gates."

"How do I fix a location?" asked Merry.

"By setting an anchor," said Fercha.

"Like on a ship?"

"A metaphorical anchor," Fercha replied. "It's really a circle—part symbolic, part physical. I'll show you the steps and you can perform them at the place you decide to use as your sanctum."

"Thank you," said Merry. "What are these metaphorical anchors made from?"

"Almost anything that can be used to mark them out," said Fercha. "Sand, powered magestones, iron filings, pebbles, even flour or salt if you have to. I'd recommend small stones from a river, the kind that are well-polished and smooth."

"Why so?" asked Merry.

"I used fine sand at my refuge and some of it washed into a nearby lake, so my emergency gate dropped me into the water," said Fercha. "Which reminds me, I need to go back and correct that—and update my emergency kit."

"What's in an emergency kit?" asked Merry.

"Food that keeps well, spare robes, blankets, bedding, an extra flying disk, since losing your disk in flight is a common reason emergency gates are triggered," said Fercha. "You probably saw a lot of Verro's kit at his sanctum."

"I did," said Merry. "And that makes sense. Healing potions might be smart, too."

"Of course," said Fercha. "I forgot to mention them. And if your sanctum is dark, preset light spells would be helpful as well."

"I think I get the idea," said Merry.

Fercha stepped to a bookshelf and pulled down a volume bound in calfskin. "There's a checklist of recommended items to include in an emergency kit here," she told Merry, opening the book to a particular page. "The spell to set your anchor is on the previous page. Would you like to copy them?"

A moment later, a simulacrum of the page with the checklist appeared in the air in front of Merry. Fercha smiled, flipped back a page, and watched as Merry generated a version of that page as an illusion to join the other.

"That should do it," said Merry. "I've memorized the pages and can call them up again when I need to reference them. I'll head off to my planned sanctum and set up my anchors."

"Be sure to ward it to prevent unwanted visitors," said Fercha. "You don't want to emergency gate on top of an angry cave bear."

"That's good advice," said Merry. "I already ran into one in caverns connected to Verro's refuge."

"While you're gone, I'll see to maintaining my own sanctum," said Fercha. "I don't want to land in a cold lake again. I expect Verro and Eynon will be returning to Haywall. I'll head there when I'm done, and you can do the same. If all goes well, I'll see you again soon."

"Sounds good," said Merry. "I appreciate your help. Having an emergency gate in place may save my life."

"It saved mine," said Fercha. "Safe travels."

"And you as well," said Merry.

A moment later, Merry was on her flying disk outside the tower, waving to Fercha before disappearing into a dot in the distance.

"I've got to get her to teach me how to do that," said Fercha.

"Hoo!" said an owl who suddenly flapped his wings and flew from a stool in a shadowed corner to perch on Fercha's shoulder.

"There you are, Tuto!" said Fercha. "I thought you were sleeping." She smoothed her familiar's feathers. "As for who, I mean Merry, of course."

"Hoo-wheet?" asked Tuto.

"Yes, I'll read you a page from Pliny the Elder's bestiary before I go," said Fercha. "And I can't wait to introduce you to my son's fiancée, Bonnie. She has an owlberron familiar. I'm sure you'll love her!"

"Hoo..." said Tuto, sounding far from convinced.

Chapter 30

Eynon and Amber

The master mages of Tamloch and Dâron appeared in the skies far to the north of their previous location. They were several hundred feet in the air, descending over a prosperous-looking steading with a large dairy barn. The collection of buildings reminded Eynon of Haywall.

"Is this Bjarniston?" Eynon asked Verro.

"No, it's King Bjarni's farm," Verro answered. "He spends most of his time here and Amber is usually close by."

"Oh," said Eynon. "Thank you. You've saved me a lot of time."

"Wait and see," said Verro. "Amber goes where Amber wishes. There's no guarantee Bifurland's master mage is with Bjarni—or even that the king is at his farm. It's just the best place to start looking."

Eynon nodded. "Amber is difficult to get to know. All three of the gold-robed Bifurland wizards seem enigmatic to me."

"It's an image they cultivate," said Verro. "Amber most of all," said Verro. "The previous master mage of Bifurland was also self-contained and mysterious."

"It seems odd to me, what with King Bjarni and Queen Signý being so open and friendly," said Eynon.

"You haven't spent much time around Bifurlanders, have you?"

"No," said Eynon. "Am I missing something?"

"You're missing a great deal," said Verro as they neared the ground. "I'd explain it to you, but I'd have to start more than a thousand years ago and we don't have the time. Suffice it to say that the Bifurlanders are a lot like the sunlight and darkness of their northern clime."

"What do you mean?" asked Eynon.

"In the summer, the sun in Bifurland is above the horizon until midnight," said Verro. "Often, Bifurlanders have similar sunny dispositions."

"Does that mean the sun hardly shines during the winter?" asked Eynon.

"It does," said Verro. "Bifurlanders' temperaments can be equally variable."

"I have a lot to learn," said Eynon.

"See," said Verro as they stepped onto a gravel road. "You're already growing wiser."

"If you say so," said Eynon. He looked up and saw three familiar small gold dragons doing acrobatic maneuvers overhead. "Look," said Eynon, pointing at the dragons. "I wonder if Sigrun and Rannveigr are riding them?"

"I expect we'll find out soon enough, if they've noticed *our* appearance," said Verro. "Let's go to Bjarni's guest house. That's the most likely place to find him—and Amber."

Some distance closer to the king's hall a woman wearing traditional Bifurland knotwork broaches at her shoulders and carrying a large wheel of cheese in her arms saw the two wizards approach. Her eyes went wide, and she ran off to disappear behind the guest house.

"I think our arrival will soon be announced," said Eynon.

"I agree," said Verro. "Are your new tight shields up?"

"I've had them up since you taught me how to make them," said Eynon. "Maintaining them is a challenge, but I can manage it."

"Good," said Verro. "King Bjarni and Queen Signý are friends, but we're here without warning and there's no telling whether we'll get a summer or winter welcome."

"What about Amber?" asked Eynon.

"With Amber you can never tell," said Verro, "though Bifurland's master mage has warmed to me over the past few months since the signing of the Orluin Alliance."

"If that's warm, I wouldn't like to see cold," said Eynon.

"Amber is likely to surprise you then," said Verro.

"I hope so," said Eynon.

Before the two wizards could reach the door to the guest house, King Bjarni stepped out to welcome them with Queen Signý only a pace behind.

"What brings two eminent master mages to my humble steading?" asked Bjarni with a grin.

"Your steading is as humble as the governor-general's palace in Nova Eboracum," teased Verro.

"Without the hypocausts and mosaic tile floors," added Signý.

Eynon, who was very fond of the Roma's heated floors, tried his own hand at teasing. "How do you keep your feet warm then?" he asked, assuming an air of innocence that required very little acting ability.

"We're hearty folk in Bifurland," King Bjarni replied.

"And we have saunas," said Queen Signý. "We heat large rocks in special rooms, then douse the rocks with water, take off all our clothes, and bathe in the steam."

"Everyone at the same time?" asked Eynon. He could feel his face turning as red as he imagined the hot rocks would be.

"Of course," said Signý. "King and thrall, tottering grandsire and toddling babe. We'll heat the stones up and have a sauna tonight if you can stay."

"I'm... I'm... here to find Amber," said Eynon.

Verro held back a smile and waved to the golden-robed wizard stepping out of the guest house. Amber was followed by two unfamiliar individuals. One was a tall, robust, and middle-aged man with reddish-blond hair, a long, neatly trimmed beard, and an elaborately waxed and curled mustache. His ice-blue tunic covered in exquisite embroidery marked him as a nobleman. The other person was thin, beardless wizard dressed in gold robes that matched Amber's own.

"You both know Amber," said King Bjarni. He extended his arm and indicated the nobleman. "This is Prince Flóki Magnússon, brother of the king of Nordland, Harald Magnússon." Bjarni motioned toward the wizard next to Flóki. "This is Knútr, a mage from Harald's court." Bjarni nodded to the two new arrivals, then extended both his hands to call their attention to Verro and Eynon. "These good wizards," he told the Nordlanders, "are Verro and Eynon, the master mages of Tamloch and Dâron, respectively."

"Your fame has reached us even across the Ocean," said Flóki. "Which one of you froze Bjarni's longships in the Brenavon?"

Eynon tentatively raised his hand.

Flóki slapped Bjarni on the back, smiled at Eynon, and laughed. "That must have been quite a surprise, eh cousin?"

Bjarni was about to offer a heated reply but saw Signý's warning expression and simply said, "True enough."

"Verro's a powerful mage as well," said Signý. "What brings you here? If Eynon wanted to find Amber, that mission is clearly accomplished."

Eynon stepped close to Amber and whispered something. Amber nodded and turned to Signý. "Dâron's master mage wants to speak with me privately," the Bifurland wizard told the queen. "We'll return when we return."

King Bjarni smiled at Amber. "You could give a sphinx lessons in inscrutability, my friend."

Amber put a hand on Eynon's forearm and the two of them *ad hoc* gated away with a paired *pop-pop* of in-rushing air.

Bjarni turned to Verro. "I'm glad you're here. Quintillius and Laetícia just left, and I have a lot of important news for Nûd and Dârio."

"And Jenet and Duke Háiddon," added Signý.

"Can I hear this news over a horn of mead?" asked Verro.

"I don't see why not," said Bjarni as he escorted everyone back inside his guest house.

* * * * *

Eynon's hair blew around his head and the folds of his sky-blue robes rattled against his body with a sound like their bedsheets when he and Braith had hung them out to dry on a windy day. He and Amber were standing on a high rocky promontory overlooking a dark sea tossed by whitecaps.

"Where are we?" he asked.

"A thousand miles north and east of Bjarniston," said Amber.

"Why did you take me *here?*"

"Laetícia told me of your quest to learn from every master mage in Orluin," said Amber. "I'm pleased I was next on your list. We're here because I assumed you'd like me to teach you the art of detection."

"I'd like you to share whatever wisdom you think is best," said Eynon, "though Verro told me you're very skilled at spells for sensing danger."

"In that he's correct," said Amber. "I thought we'd start here at Orluin's End so you could learn how to listen."

"Orluin's End?" asked Eynon.

"Yes," said Amber. "This rock is the easternmost point of Orluin. The Smoking Isle lies far to the north and east. If you could find a dragon to fly you several thousand miles due east across the Ocean, you'd eventually reach the shores of Éberria, or more specifically, the province the Roma call Lusitania."

"I see," said Eynon. He peered to the east as if he could glimpse that distant land. Then he tilted his head, pushed locks of his hair out of his eyes, and gave Amber a puzzled smile. "If I'm supposed to learn how to listen, why take me to a place where the wind is forever howling, and the waves are constantly pounding?"

"Do you always ask so many questions?" said Amber. "No, wait, don't bother to answer. Of course you do. It would be easier to expect the sun to stop shining."

"I'm sorry," said Eynon.

"Nothing to be sorry about," said Amber. "Asking questions is one way to learn—it's just not the *only* way. Close your eyes and listen, really listen, and tell me what you sense other than the wind and surf."

Eynon did as Amber instructed and closed his eyes. At first, he focused on the wind and the different sounds it made when it blew straight, or when it spun in eddies, or when it struck the Ocean and the bare face of the rocky promontory where they stood. Then he listened to the waves, taking in their rhythms and the random dance of their curved foaming tops. When he'd reached the limits of his unaided ears, he triggered the listening spell Merry had taught him on the second day of their trip down the Rhuthro. General patterns of sounds resolved themselves into collections of sonic details, how the way he turned his head made the noise of the wind vary and how waves differed if they struck the cliff face directly or if they first had to break around boulders before reaching the massive outcrop of rock.

After several minutes, he opened his eyes and nodded at Amber.

"Good," said Bifurland's master mage. "I sensed you trigger a basic listening spell—let me teach you a more sophisticated one."

Eynon wisely said nothing, but made it clear his attention was completely on Amber as the Bifurland mage took him step by step through generating the spell.

"Have you heard of parabolas?" asked the gold-robed master mage.

"Like the paths of rocks thrown from catapults?" asked Eynon.

"Yes, but turn the path upside down and spin it to make it three dimensional, like clay being formed on a potter's wheel."

"Forming a sort of bowl or wide cup?"

"Exactly," said Amber. "It's a lot like holding your hand to your ear to hear better."

Eynon nodded. "One of the old men in Haywall has a brass ear trumpet. It's shaped like a flower. He never polishes it, though."

"Some flowers have petals that form paraboloids," said Amber, ignoring Eynon's digression.

"Parabo*loids*?" asked Eynon.

"Mathematicians call them parabolas when they're graphed in two dimensions," said Amber. "Mathematicians and mathemagician scholar mages call the three-dimensional versions paraboloids."

"That seems sensible enough. Unfortunately, I don't think I'll ever be a mathemagician. I can't remember the equations to graph even simple parabolas," said Eynon. "I can picture them, but I don't remember how to describe them with formulas."

"That's unimportant right now," said Amber. "We're less worried about theory than practice." Amber gestured and a golden paraboloid of solidified sound formed in the air between them. "Observe," said Bifurland's master mage. "Constructs of solidified sound in the shape of paraboloids are quite good at taking in vibrations, like noises in your vicinity. With the right supporting constructs to amplify what the paraboloids gather in, you can hear sounds as soft as the clack of a spider's legs and mandibles as she weaves her web."

"Really?" said Eynon, more as an expression of surprise than as a question. "That's impressive. How does the paraboloid spell differ from the simple version I cast earlier?"

"Your listening spell doesn't collect sounds," said Amber. "It opens a congruency between two points, like a limited form of communications ring, so what you want to listen to is effectively closer. It won't help you hear the soft footsteps of someone coming to slide a knife between your ribs unless you're specifically listening for them."

Eynon rubbed his chin. "I see—or at least I *think* I see," he said. "The paraboloid-listening spell can pull in sounds from as far away as you want to push the construct?"

"Accurate, as far as it goes," said Amber. "But to truly detect threats coming from any direction, you need to push out six paraboloids at the same time."

"I'm not sure I understand," said Eynon. "How do I generate six at once?"

"This from the man who projected an illusion of the entire city of Riyas to fool a dragon?" teased Amber.

"Not that Viridáxés was all that hard to fool," said Eynon.

"Even so," said Amber. "Picture a cube in your head—then project it in the air in front of us."

"Gladly," said Eynon. A heartbeat later a white cube floated at eye level a few feet away. Small black circles like pips on a die appeared.

Amber gave Eynon a sharp look and the pips promptly vanished.

"Sorry," said Eynon softly.

"Back to the lesson," said Amber. "Project paraboloids out from each of the six faces of the cube. Put each construct's vertex at the center of the cube."

"Even the side facing down?" asked Eynon.

"What do you think?" asked Amber.

"I guess that side is important, too," Eynon admitted. "What if I'm flying—or I'm on the ground and someone is in a tunnel underneath me?"

"Very good," said Amber. "It's essential to listen and try to detect threats from all directions."

"That makes sense," said Eynon. "Once I'm pulling in all these tiny sounds, like the flap of a butterfly's wings, how do I make them loud enough to truly *hear* them?"

"By creating another set of constructs at the center of your cube to amplify small sounds and make them larger," said Amber. The gold-robed wizard showed him how to craft the hundreds of miniature gates that transformed whispers into shouts. Eynon followed Amber's instructions and added them to his paraboloid cube.

"Now I understand why there was so much math in most of the books of magic at the library in Melyncárreg," said Eynon.

"A thorough understanding of mathematical concepts is essential for a mage—especially a master mage—if you really want to know what you're doing," said Amber. "But you seem to be doing well by instinct without a strong grounding in theory. To remedy that lack, you should spend time with Bonnie and her teachers at the institute in Bhaile Pónaire or Dâron's own Valley of the Towers. They can help you improve your knowledge of the underlying mathematics."

"Sounds like a major project," said Eynon. "At least I *like* math, even if I haven't learned much of it beyond Euclid and Pythagoras."

"Liking a subject is a good start," said Amber, "and you're still quite young. You'll have plenty of time to learn." Amber inspected the paraboloids and tiny amplifiers Eynon had generated, then nodded to him. "Shift your cube to put yourself at its center and *listen*. Then tell me what you hear."

Eynon turned his constructs transparent and shifted the paraboloids' shared vertices to converge near his ears. Then he expanded the parabolas out for hundreds of yards and triggered the amplifying spells to take in every sound the paraboloids collected.

Amber watched him closely and silently counted seconds: one, two, *three*.

Eynon screamed, dispelled his constructs, and put his hands over his ears. He glared at Amber, showing uncharacteristic anger. "Why didn't you warn me?" he asked.

"Because all wizards have to learn that lesson for themselves," said Amber. "It was probably worse for you because you could expand your paraboloids farther than most mages."

"How can you *function* when you're detecting so many sounds?" asked Eynon. "The sheer cacophony would drive you mad."

"I assure you, I am as sane as any wizard in Orluin," said Amber.

"Is that a high bar?" asked Eynon.

"Probably not," said Amber, sharing a small smile. "But you *don't* have to constantly cope with all those noises at once. The *next* thing I'm going to teach you is how to automatically evaluate the relevance of the sounds around you."

"I should hope so," said Eynon. "I think I heard two moles arguing over a worm three feet under the soles of my boots!"

"The key is pattern," said Amber, extending an arm to point at the Ocean below. "Look. What do you see?"

"Waves," said Eynon. "They hit the rocks and cliff at regular intervals." He tilted his head. "Is that what you mean by patterns?"

"Yes," said Amber. "Whenever you gate into a new environment, find the patterns of background sound and lay it over the sounds your detection spell captures."

Eynon smiled. "I get it," he said. "I can concentrate my focus on the sounds that *differ* from that underlying pattern."

"I knew you had good instincts," said his gold-robed mentor. "Try again. Sample sounds, but don't amplify them *too* much. Form a pattern and then pay attention to what doesn't match."

Eynon shook his head, as if trying to dislodge webs in his brain spun there by his first use of the detection spell. Then he walked through the steps Amber had described for him.

Amber watched him as he did so. When Eynon's detection spells were complete, Amber spoke. "Close your eyes."

Eynon did. Not being able to see made it simultaneously easier and more difficult to manage what he'd just learned. He heard a clatter behind him to his left. "Did you just toss a pebble?" Eynon asked.

"I did," said Amber.

Eynon pushed his tongue against his lower teeth as he tried to process and filter all the sounds his augmented ears received. He wondered if the new technique Amber had taught him might work on other senses and instead of paraboloids generated a set of cones from solidified sound to funnel air toward his nose, helped along by congruencies producing gentle wafts of wind.

Amplifying sound is one thing, but how do I amplify scents? he wondered. He squeezed his hands together as he considered the matter, then realized he'd come up with the answer. *Compressing the air into a smaller volume should concentrated scents.* He tried his new technique, taking a deep breath through his nose. This time, Eynon wasn't overwhelmed as he'd been with concentrated sounds. He discovered a deeper appreciation for the salty tang of the Ocean and the hint of pine resin carried by the crisp air sweeping over the promontory.

Eynon rubbed his nose. Amber noticed.

"What is it?" she asked.

Eynon explained his new technique. "I can augment my sense of smell as well."

"Let me try," said Amber, generating the necessary structures of solidified sound immediately after speaking. The gold-robed mage bowed to Eynon. "I'm clearly not just a teacher but a student. You're quite a creative wizard."

Eynon bowed in return. "You taught me the concept—I just adapted it."

"We can worry about credit for amplifying scents later," said Amber. "In the meantime, both enhanced senses will give you additional ways to detect threats—and opportunities. You've got the basics of cone and paraboloid detection down. Now it's time for your final examination. Keep your eyes closed."

"Wait! What?" said Eynon.

Amber touched his arm and the two of them *ad hoc* gated away from Orluin's End.

* * * * *

Eynon knew they were now inside a large building. Familiar scents, more than sounds, told him they were in a hay barn—but not the one in Haywall. There wasn't any lingering smell of smoke. He gathered new ambient sounds from around him and formed a new pattern so he could attend to anything that differed from his baseline. He tried to do the same with scent patterns, but with less success.

"Where are we?" asked Amber.

Eynon inhaled and smelled dragons. *Young* dragons, not too far off. He smelled cows, drying grain, fresh manure, and brewing ale.

He smiled as he detected the sweet, spicy odor of mead. Switching to evaluate what his ears were collecting, he heard familiar voices near at hand, coming from somewhere above him. *In a hay loft?*

"That feels nice," came Sigrun's young soprano. "Kiss me again, Selr."

"Stop that, Otr," said Rannveigr. "It tickles."

Eynon stifled a laugh and leaned down to whisper in Amber's ear. "We're in the hay barn at Bjarni and Signý's steading."

"Congratulations," said Amber softly. "You passed."

Bifurland's master mage *ad hoc* gated them out into a flower garden not far from the main hall at the steading. For the moment, they were alone.

Eynon opened his eyes and inhaled the now intoxicating scents of the blossoms around him. He turned to Amber. "Thank you," he said. "You haven't just taught me a detection spell; you've opened me up to a new world of sensory experiences."

"I'm glad you've found it helpful," Amber replied. "It will take you months and years to hone your detection skills—and be careful. Loud noises and intense scents can stun those senses as much as a bright lights can blind your eyes. Opponents may use them against you, and you need to practice maintaining your vigilance."

"That's good advice," said Eynon. "Speaking of advice, I've asked other master mages for special words of wisdom. Do you have any to offer me, master mage to master mage?"

"I do," said Amber, pulling him over to a bush covered in red blooms and directing him to sniff them. "Always stop to smell the roses."

Chapter 31

Three Trios

Nine people sat on stones arrayed around a fire on a pink-sand beach on the Tempest Isles' Grand Harbor. A pig was roasting over the glowing coals, its rotation controlled by magic. Four black dragons were sleeping farther down the strand, accompanied by a snow-gryffon. A thick stand of trees formed a line of green a hundred yards up from the beach.

The individuals present were grouped in three trios: the Orluin exiles Gwýnnett, Túathal, and Hibblig, the Roma exiles Celéri, Sírénae, and Umbrose, and the wizard assassins, Períkulōs, Perkússos, and Sikárias. Celéri was not-so-subtly flirting with Hibblig by licking her lips and touching his forearm as they talked, feeding his already oversized ego. Umbrose was leaning close to his father, Períkulōs, in a conversation the others wisely chose not to overhear. Túathal stared out at the harbor as if he could see what swam beneath its placid blue surface. Gwýnnett sat quietly, observing the others, and calculating ways to manipulate them to her own advantage. Sikárias, Umbrose's mother, had her eyes closed but wasn't sleeping. Sírénae tried to project an air of authority and was somewhat successful.

"When will the meat be ready?" asked the one-time emperor.

"In an hour," answered Perkússos.

"So soon?" asked Sírénae.

"I'm cooking it from the inside with heat magic," Perkússos replied. "The smoke from the fire is only to add flavor."

"And *I'm* pleased you're using wizardry to direct the smoke upward and keep it out of our faces," said Sírénae. "When I was with my legions in the field, campfire smoke had no respect for my imperial rank."

"Wizards give emperors certain advantages," said Perkússos.

"For a price. And wizards with your unique skills," said Sírénae, taking in Umbrose, his parents, and his uncle with one wave of her hand, "are well worth it." She rested her chin on her fist and tilted her head as if considering her next words carefully. "Would there be any chance of hiring your services to advance *my* aims, instead of the aims of Gertrude and Flavia Drusilla?"

Perkússos answered her. "What sort of wizards would we be if our missions could be changed, and our services redirected in response to a higher bidder?"

"Very wealthy ones," said Sírénae.

"We're already rich," said Perkússos.

"And you're hardly in a position to pay us more than Gertrude of Mainz," added Períkulōs.

Túathal shifted his gaze from the harbor to the wizard assassins. "She may not be," he said, indicating Sírénae with a flick of his fingers. "But I can top Gertrude's payment if you add in two more targets."

Sírénae, Celéri, Gwýnnett, and Hibblig couldn't disguise their surprise at this revelation.

"Really?" said Perkússos.

"Quite a bit of the wealth of Tamloch is hidden in places only I know," said Túathal. "It's a very prosperous kingdom and I was its king for decades."

Sírénae, in particular, looked at Túathal with new respect. She caught his eye and they both nodded. "I can sweeten any arrangement further," she said.

"In what way?" asked Perkússos.

"How would you like to have *three* emperors beholden to you, not just two?" said Sírénae.

"By reneging on a contract with Gertrude and Flavia Drusilla?" said Perkússos. "I don't see how that would work."

"You wouldn't be repudiating your contract exactly," said Sírénae. "Simply adjusting its goals."

"I'll say again," said Perkússos. "In what way?"

"By assisting me in becoming the new *Southern* emperor," said Sírénae.

Túathal cleared his throat.

"And then using the might of three empires to establish Túathal as king of all Orluin," Sírénae continued.

"Emperor of Orluin," said Túathal quietly.

Gwýnnett's attention sharpened at his remark. The prospect of becoming an emperor's "consort," even if only in name, was appealing. She was the mother of Túathal's heir, after all. *I seduced Túathal once, I can do it again,* she considered, thus demonstrating far more hubris than Hibblig.

"Interesting," said Perkússos. "But if three of the four empires are controlled by our *friends,* what would that do for our prospects for future commissions?"

Most of the people around the fire laughed.

"If you believe there would be no further call for your services, there's a bridge over the Tiber I want to sell you," said Sírénae.

Perkússos nodded and addressed Túathal. "Just how large a payment do you contemplate to *adjust* our goals? And who are the additional targets?"

Before Túathal could answer, Sikárias opened her eyes and spoke. "I can hear swords crossing not more than a mile east of here—perhaps sailors from the ships we saw anchored at the other end of the island clashing with the local population."

"What?" said Celéri.

"I believe another band of locals has just arrived at the edge of the forest behind us," said Sikárias. "I'm hearing lots of snapping twigs and heavy footsteps, at least. I suggest we prepare to be attacked."

"I'll help the sailors," said Celéri. She boarded her flying disk and set off toward the east without another word.

Hibblig stood and flexed his muscles. "I'm ready to defend us," he said.

Umbrose looked at his family members and all four of them disappeared, hidden by spells of concealment.

"What do *we* do?" Gwýnnett asked Túathal, batting her eyes and earning a shake of the head from the former king of Tamloch.

"I doubt *we* need to do anything," Túathal answered.

"It's always a pleasure to watch professionals at work," said Sírénae. "Blast," she said as the pig on the spit stopped turning and smoke blew into her face. "Make yourself useful," she told Gwýnnett.

"Turn the crank so the meat doesn't burn. I expect we'll have more mouths to feed soon."

Gwýnnett, unused to such treatment, sat like a statue for so long that Túathal moved from beside her and crossed to the fire to work the crank that turned the spit. He inhaled deeply. "The pig should be done soon," he said. Then he turned to Sírénae. "A word of advice— or caution for you, emperor. Don't let Gwýnnett anywhere near your food."

"Duly noted," said Sírénae.

Gwýnnett pointedly did *not* reach for any of the small yellow *apples* she had hidden in the folds of her underskirts. She gave Sírénae a small smile that acknowledged the wisdom of Túathal's words.

* * * * *

Celéri only had to follow her ears to find the battle to the east. From her vantage point twenty feet up, she could hear swords ring as blows were struck. In a clearing in the forest below she could see flashes of sunlight reflecting off blades. She generated distance-seeing lenses and saw a dozen Roma sailors *and her Uncle Pixo* fighting with twice that number of what she took for locals, long-haired inhabitants of the Tempest Isles who mostly kept their distance when Roma ships came to their harbors. The local warriors wore motley leather armor that blended into the colors of the forest and carried circular wicker shields that looked like flattened baskets. They carried swords and spears, many of which seemed to be of Roma manufacture.

The sailors were loosely gathered in a circle, their backs to each other. At least two locals, usually one with sword and shield and one with a long spear, engaged with each sailor. Her uncle was holding his own, swinging a wide blade and fending off spear attacks with a steel buckler in his left hand. The two sides in the conflict were too close together for Celéri to take effective action against the locals without harming the sailors.

I need a distraction, she thought. Celéri opened a congruency, adjusted potentials, and sent a bolt of lightning down, aiming at a spot close to the fighting. It snapped and cracked, working as she'd hoped when the fighting paused briefly as the attackers stopped to identify the new threat. Celéri followed her bolt with a fireball that burst just above the clearing. She'd configured it to deliver more light than heat, trying to temporarily blind the combatants and give her time to pick off the locals individually.

While Celéri's eyes were closed to prevent her bright fireball from blinding *her*, a spear thrown by a local warrior pierced her flying disk *and* the instep of her right foot. She cried out, removed her injured foot from its stirrup, and gripped it tightly. Her efforts momentarily staunched the flow of blood from the wound but standing on one foot overbalanced her and caused her flying disk to tip precariously. The spear, which was still connected to her disk, increased her disk's wobble. Celéri quickly lost altitude. When her flying disk tipped further, she fell. It wasn't far—only four or five feet— her back and buttocks crashing onto yielding vegetation of the clearing instead of hard stone. Her inelegant and undignified landing knocked the air from her lungs and simultaneously removed all her restraint as she considered how best to deal with her attackers.

From her position on her back, she used a focused beam of hot tight light to cauterize her wound. Celéri attempted to stand and found she could put weight on her injured appendage if she stepped on the ball of that foot. Moving was awkward and painful, but not impossible. Her quick action was fortuitous, since seconds later three spear-wielding warriors with wicker shields came close and surrounded her, ready to do her more damage. Fueled by her anger, Celéri created a sphere of solidified sound around her body then expanded it so rapidly and with such force that her attackers were knocked back and dropped their weapons.

Spotting her flying disk close at hand, Celéri removed the spear from it and put her arm through its straps, transforming the disk into a shield. She took out her dagger and using a spell she had researched, but never tried before, she generated a long, narrow congruency to the same plane wizards used to create fireballs and attached it to her weapon's hilt. She now held a flaming sword. It crackled with heat and seemed eager to burn whatever it touched. Celéri felt her own face radiate with a rising battle fury.

In three strides she crossed the distance between herself and one of the locals who'd attacked her. The man was on the ground, still stunned by Celéri's expanding sphere of solidified sound. Her heart pounding and her foot still in pain, Celéri raised her flaming sword, raging and ready to immolate the man where he cowered. Her cheeks seemed as hot as her blade. Before she could strike, Celéri felt a hand on her shoulder. She turned, ready to strike down a new attacker, but paused with her weapon inches from a familiar face.

"*Uncle Pixo!*" she shouted. "I almost killed you."

"You almost killed that man as well," said her uncle. "Your fireball earlier did the trick. After your lightning bolt distracted the locals, I told my sailors to close their eyes. We recovered quickly and were able to disarm the rest of the locals, save for the three you stunned somehow."

"I used an expanding sphere of solidified sound to push them back," said Celéri. She observed, with some relief, as the local warriors she'd stunned got to their feet and ran into the surrounding forest, leaving their swords, spears, and shields behind.

"You didn't learn *that* trick at your combat wizards' school in Nárbo," said Pixo.

"I tend to be more creative with my magic," said Celéri.

"I *see*," said her uncle, nodding toward Celéri's flaming sword. "I don't think you need that now." He gave her a gentle, avuncular look.

"You're probably right." Celéri dispelled her blade and felt the heat seep out of her cheeks as the flames vanished. She put her dagger back in its sheath on her belt. With a small sigh, Celéri removed her flying-disk shield and inspected it for damage. There was only a thin, red-tinged hole where the spear point had pierced its surface. It was still functional. She winced when she put weight on her injured foot.

"You're hurt!" her uncle exclaimed. "One of my sailors knows something about tending wounds. I'll call her over."

"No," said Celéri. "It's an annoyance, not life-threatening. Nothing a healing potion won't cure." She looked at her uncle and smiled. "You wouldn't happen to have one of those with you, would you?"

"Sadly, no," Pixo replied. "I was going to ask you for more of that medicine that helps my stiff fingers."

Celéri took her uncle's hands in hers, feeling their strength and warmth despite their enlarged joints. "Do you really need that medicine?" Celéri teased. "You seemed quite proficient defending yourself with a blade against the local warriors."

"Old sea-dogs can still bite," said Pixo, "but I'll pay the price in pain for today's swordplay."

"I have some new friends who may have potions to help us both then," said Celéri. She pointed to her flying disk. "Climb aboard and I'll take you to our camp on the Grand Harbor. It's only a mile to the west. You were nearly there."

"I wouldn't mind a trip by air," said Pixo. "Only a mile to the west, you say? Let me tell my sailors. I expect the local warriors will give us a wide berth now that they know we have a wizard to defend us."

"Not just one wizard," said Celéri. "Five of us."

* * * * *

The first indication of the local warriors' attack on the campsite by the Grand Harbor was a spear thrown from the tree line that landed in the sand at Hibblig's feet. The big wizard shook his fist, picked up the spear, took five steps forward, and threw it back in the direction it had come from. He added kinetic energy to the shaft as it flew and guided its path, so it struck the trunk of a tree so hard most of its point was embedded in the wood.

More spears were launched from the forest, some aimed at Túathal, Sírénae, and Gwýnnett. All fell short. Túathal stopped turning the spit and picked up two of the weapons, handing one to Sírénae. Then he returned to rotating the pig, keeping his eyes more on the threatening forest than the roasting meat.

"Hibblig," said Sírénae. "I realize you want to deal with our attackers yourself, but I think the others will have them well in hand.

May I suggest you concentrate on defending those of us who are *not* wizards until the threat is neutralized?"

Hibblig turned, saw the commanding expression on the former emperor's face, and thought better of his planned reply. "If I must," he said with a shrug. The big wizard returned to the others by the fire and constructed a thick hemisphere of solidified sound to protect them. He stood beside Sírénae and watched as she rhythmically went through the steps of a Roma legionnaire's spear drill. He turned away from her so she wouldn't see the uncertainty in his face as he realized she could easily take him in a fight if he didn't use magic.

Gwýnnett got up from her stone seat and approached Túathal. The deposed king of Tamloch warned her off with his eyes, even though he could sense she was afraid and seeking reassurance. It wouldn't do to have Gwýnnett too close to the spit. He took a moment to contemplate the thought of substituting Gwýnnett for the pig turning above the coals and allowed himself a smile.

"What?" said Gwýnnett.

"Nothing," said Túathal. "I was just thinking about how our new arrivals will likely handle the locals."

"They'll slaughter them all, won't they?" asked Gwýnnett.

"Perhaps," said Túathal. "We'll know soon enough. At least now that Hibblig understands his proper role we're less likely to be skewered ourselves."

"Like you skewered me all those years ago?"

"Don't remind me," said Túathal. "I've been trying to forget that night for nearly two decades. Unfortunately, there wasn't any other way to produce an heir, and a cuckoo's egg."

"That's an odd way to refer to our son," said Gwýnnett. "And your plan to rule in Tamloch *and* Dâron didn't work so well, did it? Dârio and Nûd saw to that."

"That remains to be seen," said Túathal. He gestured toward Sírénae with his hand that held the spear. "I'm a patient man."

"An emperor needs a consort, if only for form's sake," said Gwýnnett quietly.

"I'd rather have a snow-gryffon as a consort than you," said Túathal.

As if on cue, Thraxa chose that moment to prowl into the camp, her wings held tightly against her body. She eyed the roasting pig and growled. Sírénae smiled at her former pet, now Celéri's familiar, and attempted to stroke her feathers. Thraxa snapped her beak, clearly indicating that such a touch would be unwelcome.

"There will probably be plenty for you to eat soon," Sírénae told Thraxa. "Patience, my pretty."

The snow-gryffon turned her raptor's gaze away from her former mistress and toward the tree line. Seconds later, the beast and the humans in the clearing heard screaming. The screams grew louder, then diminished and finally ended.

Four wizards walked out from the trees. As they approached the campfire, Celéri descended to join them, with Admiral Pixo riding with her on her flying disk.

"We heard the screaming," said Celéri, addressing Umbrose and his family. "Did you kill them all?"

"We didn't kill any of them," said Umbrose.

"Why not?" asked Gwýnnett.

"Because no one paid us to," said Perkússos as he took Túathal's place, turning the spit with a tendril of solidified sound.

"We made ourselves look like creatures out of nightmares and roamed the forest," said Sikárias. "Giant, carnivorous, red-eyed bats, dire wolves, cave bears, long-toothed tigers…"

"None of those were ever on the Tempest Isles, were they?" asked Gwýnnett.

"Does it matter?" asked Períkulōs. "Fear is fear."

"And we may have helped that fear along with membranes of solidified sound that generate unconscious anxiety-producing vibrations," said Sikárias.

"Well done," said Sírénae. "And economical."

Thraxa rubbed her head against Celéri's thigh, and the young wizard stroked her familiar's furred flanks and feathers. "Are you hungry, dear one? I'll get you a nice big fish from the harbor soon." Celéri nodded to Sikárias. "Would you teach me how to do that vibration spell?"

"For a fee," Sikárias replied.

"How about for information," said Celéri. She motioned for her uncle to step forward. "Tell them, Uncle Pixo."

"About what?" asked her uncle.

"About, umm, you know," said Celéri.

Umbrose and Sírénae's body language shifted. Pixo had their full attention. The same was true for all the others on the beach.

"Oh, yes, right," said the Roma admiral. "I got this from some of Magister Umbrose's spies who caught our last ships. There's a big celebration planned."

Túathal prodded Pixo's back with the butt of his spear. "Get on with it. Details. What *sort* of celebration?"

"I was getting there," said Pixo. "The spies say..." He paused, in part to build suspense and more to emphasize that Túathal's words hadn't influenced him. "They say there's going to be a double royal wedding— the kings of Dâron and Tamloch will wed, not to each other but to their fiancées, mind you, at the Great Falls on Midsummer's Day."

"Interesting," said Sírénae.

"Everyone who is anyone in Orluin and Valentia will be there," Pixo continued. "I was told there's an island in the river just above the Great Falls that belongs to both Tamloch and Dâron..."

"I know it well," said Túathal.

"And they're having a huge feast..." said Pixo.

Gwýnnett rubbed her hands together. "Really?" she said.

"That's what Magister Umbrose's spies reported," said Pixo.

Períkulōs turned to Perkússos. "Are you thinking what I'm thinking, brother?"

"It sounds like quite an opportunity," Perkússos replied. "We wouldn't have to split up to do what needs to be done then, would we?"

"We could kill more than two birds with one stone," said Sikárias.

"Kill?" said Celéri.

"Yes, kill," said Sikárias. She nodded at Sírénae, then Túathal, and received their nods in return. "It's what we're being paid for, after all."

Not knowing quite how she felt about assassinations at a wedding, Celéri took a step forward and winced, forgetting for a moment about her injured foot. "By the way," she said to everyone in general and the wizard assassins in particular. "Does anyone have a healing potion?"

Chapter 32

Merry's Sanctum

Merry left Fercha's tower flying southeast, bearing in mind her mentor's advice to keep the location of her sanctum secret from everyone. *Except Eynon,* thought Merry. *I'll tell him, of course.* She remembered the bearskin rug she'd shared with Eynon at Verro's sanctum and decided she'd find something similar for *her* emergency refuge when she established it. For now, once she was out of Fercha's sight, Merry circled back to head north along the river to the cave in the mountains between the Coombe and the Rhuthro she remembered spotting on a hike a two years ago.

The scenery below her was achingly beautiful. After traveling with Eynon to the jagged peaks of Melyncárreg and Three Mountains Valley, her home territory's more gently rolling mountains covered in a mix of conifers and hardwoods felt welcoming and familiar. She imagined Eynon would have similar feelings when he returned to the sheltered, undulating fields of the Coombe. Merry still remembered how much her mother, Mabli, had yelled at her for staying away from home on her hike, which had lasted for close to a week. Derry, her father, had kept his face stern but winked at Merry as she listened.

Later, she heard her father tell her mother, "She's close to her wander year and has to stretch her legs and her capabilities."

"What if she'd been bitten by a rattletail? Or mauled by a bear? Or eaten by a wolf?" Mabli protested.

"*Our* daughter?" said Derry. Merry still remembered overhearing her father's tone of pride. "I think she'd be more likely to roast the rattletail for dinner, ask the bear to share its honey, and turn the wolf into a pet."

"Well…" said Mabli, who wasn't blind to Merry's skills and sensibilities, knowing that her daughter was more fond of longbows and books than the domestic arts.

At least I'm learning a bit about cooking from Eynon, thought Merry. *That should make my mother happy.*

She continued to follow the course of the Rhuthro until a tributary joined it from the northwest, then proceeded along that stream until she reached the village of Hunter's Home. It was a collection of a few small stone cottages with thatched roofs and none of the inhabitants looked up to notice her in the sky overhead. Sheep grazed on nearby hillsides and goats pranced around a communal enclosure.

Hunter's Home was one of the last outposts in that part of western Dâron. It had been where she'd followed a game trail and hiked uphill for several miles before coming across the cave. Merry hoped she'd recognize its location from the air, but it was too difficult to make out details on the ground, given all the trees. She landed, put her flying disk on her back, and began pacing along a narrow track that seemed at least somewhat familiar.

A quarter mile along, Merry smiled when she crossed a well-constructed single-arched stone bridge over a swift-running stream feeding the tributary. A faded sign, now illegible, bore some sort of message in what had been red letters. She remembered the sign and hadn't been able to read it on her previous trip either. The bridge was particularly memorable because it was like the carefully crafted bridges her father's folk had built over similar streams flowing into the Rhuthro on the road south from Applegarth to her father's baronial seat.

She kept walking. To her left the ground fell away to a wide flat area covered in wildflowers near the tributary while to her right the land rose steeply and featured frequent outcrops of gray limestone covered in moss and lichen. They emerged from wooded ground like downed trees sticking up from sandbars on the Rhuthro. A hundred paces farther up the path she saw a stack of flat rocks someone had assembled next to a pair of huge boulders. They reminded Merry of a rattletail's tail, and she carefully checked the ground around her for any signs of snakes, noticing only a blacksnake slithering away into a crack between the boulders. She expected to find the entrance to *her* cave not far from here.

If memory serves, she thought, *it was just a bit upslope. Ace would have found it for me in seconds.*

It took Merry a bit longer, but eventually she reached an extensive outcrop of weathered limestone and spotted a gap on its exposed surface ten feet high and a few feet wide leading into the mountain. She could smell cool clean air breathing out from the cave and smiled, fondly recalling her initial explorations nearly two years ago when she was so much younger. It had seemed like such an adventure then and, to be fair, it was still an adventure now. She generated a flexible shield of solidified sound in front of her. Holding her hand out, palm upward, she spoke a single word: "Llachar!" A globe of bright light floated above her palm. She directed it into the gap and followed.

The first hundred feet were much as she'd remembered exploring by torchlight earlier—a narrow passageway hemmed in by rough stone walls. After a few more paces Merry stepped into an open space whose size she hadn't been able to determine with a torch. Now she increased the luminosity of her globe of light and generated a dozen more similar balls of illumination, sending them off in all directions to reveal the chamber's full dimensions.

Merry was pleased and surprised to see a generally elliptical space as big as the milking barn back in Haywall. Its walls were embellished with pillars, icicles, and columns of stone reflecting dozens of colors from orchid to ochre. Here and there, bright yellow flows of stone drizzled along darker rock like honey dripping down from a dipping stick. Everything had a light sheen of water that made the rock surfaces sparkle in her *llachar* lights as if they'd been lacquered.

The colorful walls captured her attention so completely that she nearly tripped over a glittering nodule the size of a turkey's egg as she moved farther into the open space. From what she could tell, it seemed like it must have recently worn its way out from a seam of clay higher up on a nearby wall. The nodule was made from some sort of translucent, faceted mineral that Merry thought might be quartz, though something about it reminded her of the rocks she'd seen at the green and blue magestone quarries. She thought it worth further study, squeezed it into her pouch, and continued her subterranean investigations.

The chamber she now occupied was cool and moist and, as far as Merry could tell, unoccupied. She didn't spot any nesting materials or piles of bones, at any rate. Still, it was too close to the cavern's entrance to be an effective sanctum. Merry felt air flowing from an opening ahead of her, summoned her multiple glow balls around her, and pressed on deeper into the cave system. Five minutes of walking along what seemed to be an ancient underground watercourse, or the cylindrical path of a giant worm tracing brought Merry to another, far larger chamber. She heard water running. *A stream must be nearby.*

A loud noise engaged on her attention. It was regular, rhythmic, and rasping, like a crosscut saw going through trunks of ironwood trees and seemed to be coming from ahead. Merry continued toward the noise and saw a gently arched natural stone bridge crossing a crevasse directly in front of her. The volume of the rasping increased as she paced onward and so did the sound of running water.

All her senses alert, Merry took two steps onto the bridge. The rhythmic noise abruptly stopped, replaced by an odd spluttering exhalation like the sound of a woolly mammoth yawning. The change left Merry off balance. She looked left and right but should have been looking down, because a huge hairy hand much larger than her own suddenly reached up from below the bridge and wrapped around her right boot. It held her so tightly she felt like she had been rooted there for sixteen summers.

"WHO. ARE. YOU!" came a bellow from below the bridge. It was so deep and resonant it could have come from an owl the size of a dragon.

Merry involuntarily squeaked, feeling like a mouse in the grasp of a giant. Mastering her fear, she squared her shoulders, remembering her skills and lineage. "I'm Merry of Applegarth, daughter of Derry and Mabli, the Baron and Baroness of the Southern Rhuthro, and a wizard of Dâron. Who are *you?*"

An upper torso rose from below the bridge to join the hand holding Merry's boot. The skin on his face and the exposed portions of his fur-covered body were the same gray as the stone dust on the floor of the cave. She could see unkempt hair, a shaggy beard, a protruding brow, and a nose like an overstuffed sausage casing. He wore a necklace of wolf's teeth alternating with small, rounded pebbles—garnets and amethysts from their colors—strung together on a leather cord. For all his savage appearance, the eyes beneath his brow ridge were black orbs that sparkled with intelligence, reminding Merry of Roma wizards' obsidian magestones.

"I am Berrt," said Merry's captor. He paused for a moment, cupped his chin with his free hand, and added, "Of the Seven Mile Cave and the Short-faced Bear Clan."

"Pleased to meet you, Berrt," said Merry. "Now that we've been introduced, you can release your grip on my boot. I'd hate to have to blast you with a thunderbolt."

Berrt snatched away the hand holding Merry with a speed that belied his bulk. "Wizards," he muttered, shaking his head. "How far do I have to go to be rid of them?"

"Did wizards wrong you?" asked Merry. She looked down and saw Berrt was standing on a ledge beside the bridge. He was half a foot shorter than Eynon but three times as broad across the shoulders.

"Wizards," said Berrt. "Fierce-faced warriors with swords and spears. Farmers with axes who cut down forests—they all wronged us."

"Us?" asked Merry.

"My people," said Berrt. "We crossed the Ocean on boats of ice long ago to get away from *your* people, but you followed us."

"Sorry?" said Merry, unsure of how to respond to such a statement. She thought she now knew just what Berrt was, but had always believed his people were just stories told to frighten children into behaving.

"I doubt you personally persecuted my people, young wizard," said Berrt, smiling at Merry. Then his smile turned into a glare. "Are you here to attack me?"

"Not at all," said Merry, smiling. "I'm here to find a safe place to escape to in case I'm in danger."

"I'd thought Seven Mile Cave was safe," said Berrt. "If you're not here to kill me, it's probably safe enough for you—unless I get hungry." Berrt opened his mouth showing big teeth, then closed his jaws and smiled again. "Don't worry—I don't eat your people, though I wouldn't turn down a tasty haunch of venison or wild boar."

"Neither would I," said Merry. "Do deer ever wander into this cave? And is it really seven miles deep?"

"No," said Berrt of the Short-face Bear Clan. "Deer don't enter here, but I often go out at night to hunt. I usually just catch unwary squirrels and hares, but sometimes I can take down a buck or doe with a thrown rock. Once or twice a year I might surprise a sleeping boar." He shrugged his massive shoulders. "I'm good at throwing rocks. As for this cave, I'm not really sure if it's deeper. I've measured out at least seven miles during my own explorations and it's as good a name as any."

"I suppose so," said Merry. "Are there any chambers farther into the cave that might fit my purposes?"

"Snug, dry, with a defensible entrance and a source of water?" asked Berrt.

"You've named most of my requirements," said Merry. "I'll also need room for supplies and a comfortable bed," she added.

"I know just the place," said Berrt. "If you promise to provide me with a fat ewe or nanny goat, I'll gladly escort you there. I enjoy a nice leg of mutton, but fresh goat is my favorite."

"I'm more partial to lamb than mutton, when I can get it," said Merry. "My mother fixes it with mint sauce. Why are you so fond of goat?"

"Because of the billy goats," said Berrt. "That was when I lived under a bridge *outside* this cave."

"If it's nearby, I think I crossed it," said Merry. "It's a well-made bridge."

"It was my home," said Berrt. "Until they came."

"Humans?" asked Merry.

"Billy goats," said Berrt. "We had a *difference of opinion* and I left."

"What sort of difference?" asked Merry.

"I wanted to eat them, and they didn't want to be eaten," said Berrt. "The biggest one butted me so hard..." He put one of his massive hands over his eyes and sighed.

"The biggest one..." Merry said, encouraging Berrt to continue.

Berrt didn't move his hand. "He knocked me off the bridge. My bridge. I fell in the water and was halfway to the junction with the Rhuthro before I could get my feet under me and climb out. My people aren't good swimmers."

"You're so solidly built I expect you don't float," said Merry. "That makes it a lot harder to swim."

"Perhaps," said Berrt. "Those billies were gruff and rude, bleating for me to get out of their way."

"You *did* want to eat them," said Merry.

"Goats are *for* eating," said Berrt. "The ancient sages tell us that is their reason for existing."

"Don't forget their hair for spinning, their milk for cheese making, and their hides for leather," said Merry. She paused and tilted her head. "You've read the Athican philosophers?"

"No," said Berrt. "I've heard the wisdom of the ancient sages of my people. For all I know your Athicans may have learned their wisdom from us."

"That might be," said Merry. "I've heard your people are far older than mine. Be that as it may, I assume eating fresh goat meat is your way of getting back at your tormentors?"

"Precisely," said Berrt. "I'll admit it's petty, but they shamed me. I retreated into this cave complex and took up residence beneath *this* bridge. Billy goats don't bother me here and I have plenty of time to consider our sages' wisdom."

"Such as?" asked Merry.

"Such as various problems of philosophy," said Berrt. "For example, if I stood at a fork in the road with a single individual on one fork and a dozen of children on the other..."

"I've heard this sort of problem," said Merry. Her words came out faster than the flow of the stream below the bridge. "There's a tree at the fork and you've got an axe."

"Yes, and a team of runaway horses pulling a heavy wagon is approaching," said Berrt.

"You can drop the tree across one fork to save the ten children or across the other to save the individual," said Merry.

"Indeed," said Berrt. "Which way do you push the tree?"

"You've got to save the ten children," said Merry.

"What if the individual is a wizard about to develop a spell to end hunger forever?" asked Berrt. "Ten lives lost versus better lives for hundreds of thousands?"

"Uhh..." said Merry. She squinted and rubbed her chin.

"What if one of the children will grow up to slaughter multitudes on the battlefield?" said Berrt. "What if I throw my axe and slay the lead horse but I end up as the only one trampled?"

"All these troll-ey problems you present are complicated," said Merry. "They make my head hurt. I'm not sure if people are duty-bound to sacrifice themselves in such circumstances."

"Ah, you've identified my people," said Berrt. "We call ourselves the First Ones, but you call us trolls, the fearsome monsters who frighten human children. Given how you treat us, is it any wonder that I spend my lonely days in a cave contemplating complex moral calculations?" Berrt held his arms out with his palms turned up. "Are the lives of a hundred members of a troll clan worth more or less than the life of a single human? I know how *your* people have answered that question over the centuries."

"I'm... sorry..." said Merry. She opened her pouch and pulled out the glittering nodule she'd found earlier. "Here's a present for you. I'll still bring you a goat, but I thought giving you something beautiful might provide you with a clearer understanding of my own intentions." She handed Berrt the egg-shaped piece of quartz.

The troll's eyes grew wide as he took what Merry offered. His lower jaw fell, and his breath came quicker. One of Merry's glow balls left her control and began to orbit around Berrt's head, sparking like true lightning bugs, fireflies far rarer cousins.

"I feel strange," said Berrt. "What have you *given* me?"

"From your reaction, a magestone," said Merry.

"The gems that give wizards their power?" asked the troll.

"That allow wizards to channel and focus their power," said Merry. "I didn't *know* it was a magestone until I saw you perform magic."

"I'm making magic?"

"Look above your head," Merry replied.

Berrt glanced up and saw the glow ball circling above him. "You're not doing that?"

"No," said Merry. "You are. It's not that surprising to me. The first Athican wizards were philosophers who used their powers to stay warm and chill wine."

"It would be nice to be warmer," said Berrt. "It's always cool in this cave, even in summer. Will you teach me wizardry?"

"I'm still a student myself," said Merry. "But I'll find you a good teacher. I promise." *Doethan would have been ideal, since his tower isn't far, but he's living with Princess Rúth in Riyas these days,* thought Merry. *Eynon still has to meet with Magister Callidus. Perhaps the magister can take on a new, and somewhat unusual apprentice?*

Berrt inserted the nodule into his beard immediately below his chin. His hair was so thick and bushy the nodule stayed in place while the troll rubbed his hands together. Seconds later, small flames floated above his palms.

"Oh!" said Merry. "That's marvelous!" *He's like Eynon,* she considered. *A natural wizard. Who'd have thought it possible?* "With such untutored talent there's no time to waste in finding you a mentor. Please take me to the chamber you recommend as my refuge, and I can be on my way to get you one."

"And a nanny goat," said Berrt.

"Of course," said Merry.

Berrt pulled himself onto the bridge and led Merry along a maze of twisty little passages, that seemed all alike. She kept a careful count of her steps and each turn, noting the few distinctive features she could discern as they traveled. Now that he was standing and his face was well lit, she realized Berrt was handsome in his own way. With his hair and beard trimmed and a decent tunic instead of old furs, he wouldn't look that different from some of her father's larger knights.

After half an hour, Merry judged they were at least a mile into Seven Mile Cave. Berrt made the sphere of light circling his head glow brighter and Merry saw they'd reached a chamber that reminded her of Verro's sanctum where she and Eynon had once enjoyed cavorting on a bearskin rug.

"This is perfect," she told her new friend. "Give me a moment to mark it as my sanctum and we can retrace our path. The sooner I find you a mentor, the better. You're able to work simple spells with your magestone in its current state, but you'll want to cut and polish it, then craft a proper setting for it promptly."

"I can't wait," said Berrt. "May I stay and watch? I suddenly find myself far more interested in the mechanics of magic than I was in moral calculus."

Merry nodded and traced the outline of an apple in the floor of the chamber with the point of her eating dagger. She then inscribed a circle a bit larger than her flying disk around the apple and sent magic from her magestone into the tracings, making them shine with blue light.

Berrt clapped his hands in wonder. "How impressive," he said. "Does this mark your sanctum?"

"If I did it correctly, it will anchor my emergency gate," said Merry. "I'll be able to gate here instantaneously if my life is ever threatened."

"I'll have to learn that magic," said Berrt. "It would have been useful."

"For dealing with billy goats?" asked Merry.

"Exactly," said the troll. He waved her to the chamber's exit and guided her back to the cave's entrance, his steps as light and fast as an eager child's. At times, Merry had to run to keep up. "Here we are," said Berrt.

"I'll buy a goat at Hunter's Home and bring it here," said Merry.

"Forget the goat, bring me a tutor," said Berrt. He moved his hands to flick his fingers outward as if speeding her on her way.

"I appreciate your new priorities," said Merry as she stepped on her flying disk. "I'll be back as soon as I can."

"It can't be soon enough," said Berrt. "Stay away from teams of runaway horses."

"I'll do my best to avoid them," said Merry. She waved to Berrt, rose above the nearby trees, and line-of-sight gated a few miles southeast toward the Rhuthro. *I'll have to ring Eynon,* she thought. *He won't believe this—or maybe he will. We can meet at Fercha's tower.*

High in the air behind her bursts of colored light were exploding like fireworks. Berrt was teaching himself how to be a wizard.

Chapter 33

Magister Callidus

Eynon was waiting on top of Fercha's tower when Merry's line-of-sight gating jump brought her beside him. The two young wizards embraced and brought each other up to date on their latest activities in a volley of rapid sentences.

"You've got to teach me tight shield and extra-sensitive detection techniques," said Merry, her face only a few inches from Eynon's.

"You met a *troll* wizard?" said Eynon. "I'd heard about trolls, but I never thought they were real."

"Berrt is real enough," said Merry. "But he's not a wizard yet—just someone with great natural talent. Like another one-time apprentice I know." She tapped Eynon on the sternum and kissed him.

"That was nice," said Eynon. "I've missed you."

"We've only been apart for a few hours," teased Merry. "I'd take you to my new sanctum so we can start fixing it up, but I promised Berrt I'd find him a mentor as fast as possible."

"Don't look at me," said Eynon. "I'm still learning myself."

"I was thinking Magister Callidus," said Merry. "He's a master mage and you still have to talk to *him*, don't you?"

"That's right," said Eynon. "I've met with Laetícia, Verro, Amber, and Uirsé so far."

"Why Uirsé?" asked Merry.

"She's a master healer."

"That makes sense. You've also had the dubious benefit of instruction from Ealdamon, so Magister Callidus is the remaining master mage on this side of the Ocean for you to consult."

"No," said Eynon. "There is another."

Merry thought for a moment, took a step back from Eynon and glared at him. "There's nothing that woman can teach you."

"Celéri isn't all bad," said Eynon. "She had a creative strategy with her 'chariots' at the Battle of the Abbenoth."

"Hah!" said Merry. "She's foolish—and she tried to seduce you when we were collecting honey."

"You tried to seduce me," said Eynon, keeping his face expressionless.

"I didn't just try," said Merry. She stepped closer and hugged Eynon again. She kissed him behind his ear and felt him start to blush, which made her smile.

"I'm very glad you seduced me," said Eynon. "Though I don't recall putting up much of a fight. As for being foolish, Celéri doesn't have a monopoly on that." He shook his head.

"We've both been fools from time to time," said Merry. She kissed him on the nose and they both laughed, breaking the pattern of thoughts about their own misguided actions that Merry could sense risked leading them down a rabbit hole. "There's one more master mage besides Celéri, by the way."

"I have *no* interest in hearing anything—spells or advice—from Magister Umbrose," said Eynon. "The man makes me feel like worms are crawling under my skin."

"I feel the same way," said Merry, "but for me, it's dung beetles, not worms. I can see you wanting to talk to Celéri. There's still good in her, I think. But Umbrose is irredeemably evil."

"No one is evil in their own eyes," said Eynon.

"One of Ealdamon's epigrams," said Merry. "I understand the point, but Umbrose seems evil enough to me."

"And to me," said Eynon. "Shall we stop off in Haywall and collect Chee and Ace, or gate directly to Valentia?"

"Gate directly," said Merry. "I promised Berrt I'd try to get him a mentor as quickly as possible."

"Hold me close," said Eynon.

"You can gate me if we're just touching fingertips," teased Merry.

"I know but hold me close anyway."

Merry did, and the two *ad hoc* gated away with the sound of an extra-loud pop echoing across the nearby waters of the Rhuthro.

* * * * *

Eynon and Merry appeared in the air above the clearing in Valentia where Eynon had first encountered the glyppos. This time, he wisely adjusted his altitude to be out of range of the great beasts' mace-like tails. The glyppos didn't notice the two young wizards, which suited Eynon completely. Once was one time too many to be battered and batted about by the elephantine armored animals. With Merry by his side he guided his flying disk and followed a path through the tropical trees toward Portus Aleña, the island's largest settlement.

Soon, they saw a large, fortified enclosure filled with rows of white canvas tents. It was exactly like the drawings of Roma camps Eynon had read about in one of his uncle's books. Ditches had been dug around all four sides of the camp and the excavated dirt was mounded beside them. Hundreds of frond-trees had been cut down and turned into stockade walls atop the mounds. Still more frond-tree trunks had been sharped and turned into stakes facing outward to discourage attackers.

"All that defensive effort seems a excessive on an unpopulated island," said Merry, who was flying close enough to Eynon to be easily heard.

"From what I've read, legionnaires make such camps every time they stop for the night," Eynon replied. "I expect they're used to being threatened and simply built their fortifications the way they always have."

"I can think of another possibility," said Merry.

"What's that?" asked Eynon.

"Maybe they want to discourage glyppos."

"Could be," said Eynon. "And where those big plant eaters go, the meat-eating megatheres will likely be prowling about looking for their next meals."

"True enough," said Merry, examining the camp more closely. "There are a few concrete and wood buildings inside the fortifications. It's not just tents."

"Probably administrative centers," said Eynon.

An unfamiliar voice from above them answered Eynon. "One of them is the governor-general's palace," said a pleasant soprano belonging to a wizard flying close behind them. She had wind-tousled hair and appeared to be not much older than Eynon and Merry.

"Another is our wizards' hall," said the new arrival, giving them a welcoming smile.

"Is that where we'll find Magister Callidus?" asked Merry.

"It is," said the wizard. "He sent me to welcome you to Portus Aleña and prevent our sentries from challenging you, not that they would. You're the famed Eynon and Merry and friends of Valentius and Aleña. I'm to escort you to the palace."

Eynon smiled awkwardly and nodded. "You know our names, but who might you be?"

"Elianora," said the wizard, "but please, call me Nora. Everyone does."

"Much as we'd like to visit with Valentius and Aleña," said Merry, "we're here to see Magister Callidus."

"In that case," said Nora, "I'll take you directly to the wizards' hall." She descended and brought her flying disk even with Eynon and Merry's. "I've heard so much about you both," Nora exclaimed. "You're the ones who outsmarted Celéri."

"Do you know her?" asked Merry.

"I lived on her hall in the palace at Nova Eboracum," said Nora. "But none of us student wizards knew her that well. She always seemed to have something to prove, though I'd heard she's an orphan and that can make anyone seek validation." Nora shook her head. "Now she's a magister who can *ad hoc* gate, has the emperor's snow-gryffon as her familiar, and hasn't been seen in weeks."

"You heard about Celéri and us making honey?" asked Eynon. "Is that what you meant about us outsmarting her?"

"I know Celéri brought honey for the emperor," said Nora. "I didn't know you had anything to do with that. I was talking about the Battle of the Abbenoth and your trick with freezing our legions in sodden ground. I was a scout wizard above the battlefield and had a good view of what happened. Magister Callidus told us you were responsible for that trick."

"On the winning side, we call it a tactic, not a trick," said Merry, smiling at Nora.

"I didn't mean to offend," said Nora.

"You didn't," said Merry. "I was just teasing you."

"Oh! That's fine then," said Nora, smiling back. "I'm used to being teased. Everyone says my hair looks like a frightened wild animal." She tried to smooth her chaotic brown locks and failed. Soon, Nora was waving at two sentry wizards floating near one of the four gates to the fortified camp as they passed over the wall around Portus Aleña and descended toward to the second-largest building. "Here we are," she said.

"And here's Magister Callidus," said Eynon as he saw the tall master mage stepping out of the door of the building. "Thanks for your help, Nora."

"Will you tell me the story of Celéri and the honey someday?" asked Nora.

"If time permits, we'd be glad to," Eynon replied.

Nora gave Eynon and Merry a shy smile, bowed toward Magister Callidus, and flew off.

"Welcome!" said Magister Callidus. "To what do I owe the pleasure of your company?"

"We've come to ask for favors," said Eynon. He stepped off his flying disk and slipped his arms through its straps, so it rested on his back. Merry did the same.

Merry was about to launch into a detailed explanation of her meeting with Berrt but thought better of it. "We'd greatly appreciate your help," she said instead.

"It sounds like we have long conversations ahead," said Callidus.

Eynon looked at Merry, then at Callidus. "Before we start," he said, "Nora told us Celéri is an orphan."

Merry put an arm around Eynon's waist.

"That's true," said Callidus. "They were both wizards. I told her they died in battle."

"They didn't?" asked Merry.

Magister Callidus shook his head slowly. "They died—at the hands of wizard assassins hired by Flavia Drusilla as part of her ongoing feud with Sírénae. They were two of my best."

"How sad," said Eynon.

"Wizard assassins," said Merry. She exchanged a glance with Eynon and looked like she'd just taken a bite of an unripe apple.

"Enough about that," said Callidus. "It sounds like we have a lot to talk about and that can be thirsty work. Come inside and I'll treat you to something special to drink that should make you smile. There's a fruit native to Valentia we're calling pinkfruit because its flesh is a sort of salmon pink. I've got chilled pinkfruit juice and libum cakes flavored with pinkfruit purée instead of honey. I expect you'll find both delicious."

"Lead on," said Merry.

"I can't wait to try them," said Eynon.

* * * * *

The magister's office was more comfortable than Eynon and Merry had expected. The building's thick walls made it cooler inside, even though Eynon noticed a pair of congruencies allowing chilled air to circulate in the office keeping the room at a perfect temperature.

Their chairs had comfortable, overstuffed cushions and the refreshments their host provided proved every bit as tasty as promised. Eynon had already asked for recipes. Their drinks were served in fired clay cups and the libum cakes rested on glazed plates decorated with a border pattern of stylized Ocean waves.

"My father would love to grow pinkfruit," said Merry after she wiped libum-cake crumbs from a corner of her mouth.

"I don't think it will grow in your part of Orluin," said Callidus, "but your father is welcome to try."

Eynon was alternately sipping juice and nibbling on a libum cake, which he learned was a rather dense Roma version of cheesecake. From his expression, he was clearly delighted.

"I'm glad you're enjoying what I've offered," said Magister Callidus after a few sips of his own juice. "So tell me, what sort of favors would you like me to do for you?"

Merry and Eynon exchanged a glance and Eynon shrugged. "I'll start," said Merry. "I just met a troll in a cave near the Rhuthro—that's a river in western Dâron."

"I'm familiar with the geography of Orluin," said Callidus. He inspected Merry's face but found nothing but eagerness. "You don't seem to be damaged by the encounter."

"Oh, no," she said. "He tried to scare me at first, or actually he *did* scare me, but I later found him to be more of a philosopher than a monster."

"Not that it's always easy to tell the difference," said Callidus.

Eynon and Merry exchanged another glance and offered brief smiles.

"I gave Berrt—that's the troll's name..."

Callidus nodded.

"... a piece of simple quartz that was actually a magestone."

Callidus leaned toward Merry.

"And Berrt turned out to be a promising wizard. He was creating light bursts with his unpolished magestone as I gated away."

"Fascinating," said Callidus. "A troll wizard. There were rumors of others in Nordland in ancient days, but I never put much stock in them. Trolls are formidable enough *without* wizardry."

"I expect they are, when they want to be," said Merry. "I promised Berrt I'd find him a teacher."

"And I was the first person who came to mind?" said Callidus.

"The second, or maybe the third," said Merry. "Doethan, my mentor before I met Fercha, was my first choice, but he's living in Riyas with his new wife, Princess Rúth, and I can't see Berrt being happy living in a city."

"But you think he'd live in a *castra* like Portus Aleña?" asked Callidus. "We're still not much more than a military camp."

"I thought he could live somewhere outside the camp, where you could tutor him privately," said Merry. "He doesn't trust many humans and says we've been persecuting his people for centuries."

"More like millennia," replied Callidus. He rubbed his chin. "That's quite a favor, but I expect something along those lines could be arranged. I must admit, the prospect of training a troll-mage is intriguing. Especially one also interested in philosophy."

"So you'll help him?" asked Merry. "That's wonderful, thank you. I really appreciate it."

"Thank *you*, young wizard," said Callidus. "I've trained thousands of human apprentices over the years, but never a troll. Tell me, how old is Berrt, do you think?"

"It's hard to tell, since he seems to have lived a difficult life," Merry replied. "He could be positively ancient, over forty, but I can't be sure."

Eynon's face lit up in a wide grin. He knew Merry was teasing Callidus. So, apparently, did the magister.

"Over forty," said Callidus, rubbing his chin again and tilting his head to regard Merry closely. "Positively ancient, you say?"

"At least three toes of a foot in the..." Merry began, then she grinned.

"You don't need to complete that sentence," said Callidus. "I know the phrase. It's like the early emperor stabbed by his so-called friends in the Senate—literally stabbed—who told his physician to call on him tomorrow, when he'd find him a grave man."

Callidus, Eynon, and Merry all smiled.

"I didn't mean to offend you," said Merry.

"No offense taken," said Callidus. "From the vantage point of fifteen, everyone older seems ancient."

"Sixteen," said Merry.

Eynon's face made it clear he was trying to hold back laughter. Merry elbowed him and he released a risible response. Merry and Callidus joined him, sharing unrestrained laughter.

"*Sixteen,* then," said Callidus after catching his breath. "Well, I've always said you never know if you've mastered any sort of magic until you try to teach it. Goodness knows I've been teaching students long enough. How will we get Berrt the Troll Mage to Valentia?"

Eynon finally had a chance to contribute to the conversation. "I can *ad hoc* gate you and Merry close to the cave where she found Berrt," he offered. "Merry can guide us the rest of the way. Then you can *ad hoc* gate yourself and Berrt back here."

"And you'd be able to take Berrt home easily," said Merry.

"Or Berrt could simply stay in his familiar surroundings, and I could gate in to give him lessons," said Callidus. "Given the legionnaires' likely reactions to a troll, that might be better than finding him somewhere to live nearby."

"I hadn't thought of that option," said Merry. "You're a wise man."

"An *ancient* wise man," said Callidus.

"They say wisdom grows with age," said Eynon.

"No need to stroke my ego," said Callidus. "That's only true for some. Many fools stay fools forever."

"You, at least, are no fool," said Eynon.

"You'd be surprised," said Callidus. He took another sip of juice and swallowed. "That was one favor, but you said you were going to ask for *favors*. In what other way or ways may I assist you?"

"I'm trying to learn how to be a better master mage," said Eynon.

"Proving that the young can also be wise," said Callidus with an approving nod.

"I've already talked to Laetícia and Verro and Amber," said Eynon.

"The master mages of Occidens Province, Tamloch, and Bifurland," Merry added.

Callidus smiled and Merry's cheeks turned red when she realized she was explaining something the magister already knew well.

Eynon squeezed Merry's hand and continued. "I asked each master mage to teach me a useful piece of magic and to share words of wisdom. Laetícia taught me a special listening spell to *bug* people. Verro showed me how to generate shields that would fit close to my body, and Amber explained how to detect potential threats by heightening my senses."

"Those are all valuable spells," said Callidus. "They all seem focused on defense, however. What about spells for attack?"

Eynon looked down, lacing and unlacing his fingers.

"He's naturally quite offensive," Merry replied.

Eynon turned to glare at Merry until he realized she was teasing. This time, she squeezed one of his hands and told Magister Callidus about the power of Eynon's fireballs and how he froze a stretch of the Brenavon solid, trapping hundreds of Bifurland dragonships.

"Not every form of magical attack is quite so flashy," said Callidus. "Perhaps you'd like to learn more subtle offensive magic?"

"If you can teach Eynon to be subtle, you *are* wise," said Merry.

"I'll try my best," said Callidus. He stroked his chin and appeared lost in thought.

Eynon and Merry felt somewhat uneasy, as if hungry wolves were creeping up behind them. They held hands and looked over their shoulders, trying to understand their suddenly increased wariness.

Eynon's back teeth felt odd, as if they were resonating to some unheard tune.

"Are you doing that?" Eynon asked Callidus.

"And if so, *what* are you doing?" added Merry.

"Demonstrating subtle auditory magic," said Magister Callidus. He'd stopped rubbing his chin and regarded Eynon and Merry.

"Some sort of solidified sound?" asked Eynon.

"Sound, yes, but not *solidified* sound," said the magister. "Solidified sound isn't really sound, by the way. It's built on vibrations, like sounds, but it doesn't register on our ears. I'm talking about sound itself, what we hear—or perhaps what we don't *quite* hear."

"I don't understand," said Merry.

"I'll try to explain," said Callidus. "Are you familiar with tight light?"

"Merry's really good at generating it," said Eynon.

"Excellent," said Callidus. He focused on Merry. "You're familiar with the spectrum, then?"

"Of course," said Merry. "The colors of the rainbow."

"Do you know that there are colors below red and above violet?"

Merry tilted her head. "I hadn't considered it until you told me, but it makes sense." Her eyebrows rose and Eynon imagined a *llachar* light had materialized above her head. "Of course," she said. "We use colors below red to see using night-vision lenses."

"Very good," said the magister. "At the other end, many insects see using colors above violet. Flowers look quite different through insect-vision lenses."

"I'll have to try that," said Merry.

"Are you saying sound works like light?" asked Eynon.

"Of course it does," said Merry. "Think of a man's deep voice compared to the voice of a small child."

"Or a dragon's bellow to Chee's screeching," said Eynon.

"You've got it," said Callidus. "Our ears can only perceive a certain range of sounds, much like our eyes can only see certain colors. When you were worried earlier, I was generating sounds low enough to be just below what your ears could hear. Sounds like that put us on edge, without really knowing why."

"I'll say," said Merry. "I kept worrying some predator was about to pounce."

"It's a subtle magic," said the magister. "Sub-sonic vibrations can disconcert your enemies and affect their judgment at a level below conscious thought."

"Fascinating," said Eynon. He thought for a few seconds. "You must generate such sounds using vibrating membranes of solidified sound, like huge drums!"

"Precisely," said Callidus. He glanced left and right, slapping at his bare wrists. Eynon did the same.

Merry smiled. "I made sounds just *above* what our ears can hear."

"Or rather, what we can barely perceive, but not interpret properly," said Callidus.

"Like mosquitoes flying nearby," said Eynon, realizing why he'd been slapping and stopping.

"I think you've both got it," said the magister.

"Thank you for the lesson," said Eynon.

"You're welcome," said Callidus. "Ready for another?"

"Of course," said Eynon.

"I'm all ears," said Merry. She generated an illusion that gave her ears like a mammoth's for a moment.

Callidus smiled and used an illusion to give himself rabbit ears, making Merry and Eynon smile in return. "This is a different way to use sound—provoking calm, not fear," he said. "Listen."

The young wizards leaned back, their flying disks pressing against their padded chairs, and did so. They could make out soft sounds, just at the threshold of audibility.

"What am I hearing?" asked Eynon. He stretched and covered his mouth to stifle a yawn.

"Waves," said Merry. "Like the Rhuthro lapping against its banks." She yawned without any attempt to disguise it and could feel tension flowing out of the muscles in her neck and shoulders.

"Close," said Magister Callidus. "I modeled them on Ocean waves I heard on a beach in southwestern Britannia when I was inspecting tin mines for the emperor. I found them very soothing."

"I'll say," Merry replied. "The sound of them is making me want to take a nap."

Eynon's eyes were closing and his chin was heading for his chest. He shook his head to stay awake. "That's very effective, and very subtle," he said. "More vibrating membranes of solidified sound?"

"Yes," said Callidus. "The repetition is key, though it helps to add a bit of randomness."

"So listeners continue to focus on the pattern?" said Eynon.

"Correct," said Callidus. "When Umbrose wasn't around, I used this technique to calm Sírénae and discourage her from particularly rash decisions. It worked well on Thraxa, too."

"Good to know," said Eynon. "I suppose bird songs or insect noises would work as well?"

"So long as they're calming, not threatening," said Callidus. He stood and paced around his office, pausing behind Eynon and Merry, resting a hand on the top edge of each of their flying disks before returning to his chair. "I have one last piece of subtle magic to teach you," said the magister.

"That's very generous of you," said Merry. She rubbed her eyes and took another swallow of pinkfruit juice.

"I owe quite a lot to you and your friends," Callidus replied. "If not for your success at the Battle of the Abbenoth, Sírénae would have likely had me killed." He shook his head. "To think I once loved her."

"I'm sorry," said Eynon.

"What's the last lesson?" asked Merry.

"For that we'll need to go outside," said Callidus. He stood again and led them out of his office and the wizards' hall to a square of bare ground fifty feet on a side packed hard by legionnaires' boots just outside the main doors to hall. The square was empty, but rows of white canvas tents stretched off before them.

Nora appeared from around a corner of the wizards' hall, her hair still looking like she'd been struck by a lightning bolt moments before. "Is there anything you need, magister?" she asked.

"Have you improved your aim throwing balls of solidified sound?" asked Callidus.

"I've been practicing every day," said Nora. "I can hit what I'm aiming at three times out of four."

"Keep at it until you can hit ninety-nine out of a hundred," said Callidus.

"Yes, magister," said Nora.

"Prepare yourself," said Callidus. "You'll soon be attacking our guests."

Nora's mouth fell open. "Magister?"

"It's all for a good cause," said Callidus. He turned his attention to Eynon and Merry. "Fly up twenty or thirty feet and try to dodge the balls of solidified sound Nora will throw at you. If one of them hits you, it will hurt but it won't kill you. I've got healing potions if she manages to do any real damage."

Eynon and Merry looked at each other, shrugged their flying disks off their shoulders, and boarded them. When they were twenty-five feet up, Nora rose on her own flying disk, generated a pair of spheres of solidified sound as big as her head, and launched them at Eynon and Merry.

Dipping and banking, Eynon avoided the sphere aimed at him. He felt it pass a few feet from his torso. Merry wasn't as lucky. She rose to avoid the ball of solidified sound targeting her and the construct clanged off the bottom of her flying disk, causing Merry to wobble in the air. Eynon swooped closer to help Merry but his flying disk didn't seem as responsive as usual to the guidance of his feet as he tried to shift his position. It felt like there was a short delay between when he tilted his body and when his disk changed course.

Nora's second pair of spheres struck home, hitting Eynon between his hip bones and Merry below her ribcage. Eynon's tight shield reacted and prevented any major damage, but Merry's breath was knocked out of her and she doubled over. Fighting his recalcitrant flying disk, Eynon moved close to Merry and put his arm around her, throwing up a thick hemispherical shield to protect them both.

"That's enough," Callidus told Nora. "Your aim *is* improving. Fetch a chair for Merry, please."

"Yes, magister," said Nora. She hurried off into the wizards' hall.

Eynon and Merry descended to land beside Callidus. Merry was rubbing her belly and shaking her head.

"What did you do to our flying disks?" asked Eynon.

"What do you *think* I did?" asked the magister.

"You. Made. Them. Delay. Responding," said Merry, pausing to draw in air between each word. "That's. Tricky."

"Indeed," said Callidus. "I exaggerated the effect for instructional purposes, but you can see how a small delay can disrupt an enemy wizard's timing and maneuverability."

"How?" asked Eynon. Then he answered his own question. "When you stood behind us."

"That's right," said Callidus. "Enchanting their flying disk is one of the first spells wizards learn. It's done by rote, and few truly understand its nuances. I simply made a few *adjustments* after the fact."

Nora arrived with a chair and placed it behind Merry, who gratefully sat.

"Lesson—painfully—learned," said Merry.

"Please show us how you made the adjustments," said Eynon. He and Merry and Nora listened carefully as Callidus explained, then demonstrated by removing the delays from Eynon and Merry's flying disks. Eynon flew up and confirmed his disk was now working properly and descended again.

"I'll test mine later," said Merry. She continued to sit but was no longer short of breath.

"This has been truly educational," Eynon told Callidus. "All these new subtle spells will be useful. Before we leave for western Dâron, do you have any particular words of master mage wisdom to share? I'd greatly appreciate any advice you have to offer."

Nora smiled at Callidus as he paused to consider Eynon's request.

"What?" said the magister.

"You're always quick to give *us* words of wisdom," said the wild-haired wizard.

"Very well," said Callidus. He turned to Eynon. "Here's my contribution—you never really understand something until you have to teach it."

"Thank you," said Eynon. "I'll remember."

Merry stood up and stretched. She rubbed her belly again and stepped aboard her flying disk. "Time to head north and meet a troll mage," she said.

"Troll mage?" said Nora.

"Nothing for you to worry about," said Callidus.

"When that's accomplished, I can talk to the last master mage on my list," said Eynon.

"Who might that be?" asked the magister.

Merry made a sucking on a persimmon face. "Celéri," she said.

"Celéri," said Callidus, keeping his voice flat.

"Celéri?" echoed Nora.

"Uh huh," said Eynon. "She can *ad hoc* gate, so she's a master mage."

"How will you even know how to find her?" asked Callidus.

"I bugged the clearing on the Tempest Isles where she and Sírénae and Umbrose were staying," Eynon answered.

"You *what?*" said Callidus. He gave Eynon a stern look, shook his head, and addressed Nora. "Bring that chair inside again. We're all going back to my office. We've got a *lot* more to talk about."

"Yes, magister," said Nora.

Eynon and Merry followed Callidus into the wizards' hall with Nora and her chair trailing behind.

Chapter 34

The Bug

"You've known where to find Celéri, Sírénae, and Umbrose and never thought to *tell* me?" said Magister Callidus once they'd returned to their seats in his office.

Nora sat behind Callidus, hoping not to be noticed and dismissed.

"Sorry," said Eynon. "I didn't think of it."

Merry held back a smile because Eynon's face temporarily resembled a bewildered ewe's.

"They're still dangerous," thundered Callidus. "Celéri may still be redeemable, but we're well past that for Sírénae, blast it, and as for Umbrose..." His hands formed fists.

"I told Laetícia I thought they were on the Tempest Isles," said Eynon. He paused for a moment, then smiled, looking like a *llachar* light had just appeared above him. "Didn't she tell you about Celéri, Sírénae, and Umbrose likely being on the Tempest Isles?"

"No," said Callidus. "She didn't."

"Yet," said Merry.

"Maybe she plans to ring you soon and tell you," said Eynon. "As I'd mentioned, she *is* partly responsible for helping me find them." He tilted his head and his eyes unfocused briefly. "I remember leaving one of Laetícia's *bugs* near the spot where we thought they camped so I could listen in on their discussions."

"You *what?*" said Callidus, his voice rising. The magister's hands tightly gripped the arms of his chair and slowly relaxed as he mastered himself during a pause to take three long, deep breaths.

Eynon fidgeted and looked down at his boots while Merry alternated her attention between him and Magister Callidus, continuing to hold back her amusement—and concern. Nora closely followed all that was happening without drawing any attention to herself.

Callidus closed his eyes for a moment and pressed his lips together. After taking another deep breath he opened his eyes and spoke to

Eynon in a calm, measured tone. "I'm glad you decided to monitor that trio," he said. "Amidst all your travels seeking master mage lessons, did you ever manage to access your bug and listen in on any conversations?"

Eynon shook his head. "I'm sorry, Magister," he replied. "I didn't." He sat up straighter and added, "I guess I forgot."

"Hmmm..." said Callidus. "No sense sighing over spilled cream after the cat's already lapped it up." He gave Eynon a small smile and asked, "You're sure you used one of Laetícia's bugs?"

"Yes, Magister."

"Good," said Callidus. "Her bugs usually have long memories."

"Memories?" said Merry. "What do you mean?"

"Spymasters seldom have time to listen in on bugs all the time," said the magister. "Laetícia's bugs, and my own, can store and replay several days' worth of conversations."

"How so?" asked Merry out of her personal curiosity about the art of being a spymaster.

"The waves of light and the vibrations in the air from speaking are stored on a twisted strip of solidified sound accessed through a congruency," Callidus answered. "The longer the strip, the more scenes and conversations can be captured before writing over what came before. I expect Laetícia used a strip long enough to hold a week's worth of sight and speech. That's what I do, and I expect the standards in the Southern Empire are similar to the ones taught where I learned in the west."

"So we can hear everything said near my bug?" asked Eynon. "It hasn't been a week since I placed it."

"That's correct," said Callidus. "Or perhaps what I hope. Even better, Laetícia's bugs probably have filters so they only store information when people are talking, not background noise or silence."

"Providing greater storage capacity!" said Merry.

Callidus nodded at Merry then rubbed his chin. As if just thinking of something, he gave Eynon a hard look. "You didn't modify Laetícia's spells on the bug, did you?"

"Just a little," said Eynon. "I set up a congruency so I could retrieve it when necessary and ensure that it got a good meal."

Callidus smiled. "You've made things easier with your kind heart then," he said. "Fetch back the bug and we'll determime what it's recorded."

"Gladly," said Eynon. A small dun-brown beetle no bigger than his thumbnail appeared in his cupped palm. He handed the bewildered six-legged creature to the magister.

"Just a moment," said Callidus. He placed the insect on a side table and issued a command. "Nora, fetch some tasty leaves. We should reward this creature for its efforts on our behalf."

"Yes, magister!" said Nora. She ran from the office like a hare pursued by a hungry fox.

"Ah, yes," said Callidus. "Laetícia did use a long memory strip and a filter for conversations. I'll play it back with sight and sound."

Nora returned with an assortment of leaves. Callidus gestured for her to put them on the side table near the beetle, which promptly began to sample them.

"Bring your chair around in front," Callidus told her. "You might as well have the same view as the rest of us and further your education. Remember to say nothing to the other student wizards about what you learn, however."

"I'd never..." began Nora.

"See that you don't," said Callidus, softening his tone with a smile.

Merry gestured for Nora to place the chair she carried next to hers and the three young wizards watched as Magister Callidus projected what the bug had captured into the air in front of them.

In the projection they saw an older man dressed as a Roma admiral speaking. *"They say there's going to be a double royal wedding—the kings of Dâron and Tamloch will wed, not to each other but to their fiancées, mind you, at the Great Falls on Midsummer's Day."*

"That's Admiral Pixo, Celéri's uncle," said Nora.

"Just watch and listen," Magister Callidus admonished.

"Sorry," said Nora.

Back in the projection Sírénae was speaking. *"Interesting,"* she said.

"Everyone who is anyone in Orluin and Valentia will be there," Admiral Pixo continued. *"I was told there's an island in the river just above the Great Falls that belongs to both Tamloch and Dâron..."*

"*I know it well,*" said Túathal.

Merry nudged Nora. "He's the former king of Tamloch. Last time I'd seen him he was a madman."

"*And they're having a huge feast...*" Pixo continued.

They watched an older woman with blonde hair rub her hands together and say, "*Really?*"

"That's Gwýnnett, the new king of Tamloch's mother," Eynon whispered to Nora. "She's not a nice person," he added.

Magister Umbrose put a finger to his lips.

Admiral Pixo was still talking. "*That's what Magister Umbrose's spies reported,*" he said.

The bug's vantage shifted, revealing two men and a woman. The three looked close enough in appearance to be siblings with dark hair, dark eyes, and sun-bronzed skins. It was clear Eynon, Merry, and Nora didn't recognize them and equally apparent, given the shocked expression on the face of Magister Callidus, that he did.

One man turned to the other. "*Are you thinking what I'm thinking, brother?*"

"*It sounds like quite an opportunity,*" the other man replied. "*We wouldn't have to split up to do what needs to be done then, would we?*"

"*We could kill more than two birds with one stone,*" said the woman with similar coloring to the two men.

Celéri spoke, sounding tentative. "*Kill?*" she asked.

"*Yes, kill,*" said the woman who they watched nod at Sírénae, then Túathal, receiving acknowledging nods in return. "*It's what we're being paid for, after all.*"

Magister Callidus waved his hand, freezing the projection. His face resembled that of parents who'd just been informed of the death of their child. "This is bad," he said. "This is *very* bad."

"Who *are* those people?" asked Merry. "Do you know them?"

"Only by reputation," said Callidus. "Their names are Períkulōs, Perkússos, and Sikárias. They're the most dangerous wizard-assassins in the Imperium."

"Oh," said Eynon. "The ones who killed Celéri's parents?"

"Most likely," said Callidus.

"We have to stop them," said Merry.

"I've only heard them spoken of in whispers," said Nora. "They never fail."

"There's always a first time," said Eynon.

The ashen face worn by the magister as he stared at the frozen projection told them Callidus didn't share Eynon's optimism.

Silence followed, broken only by the distant bellows of a pair of massive glyppos fighting for dominance.

Chapter 35

Royal Couples

Two kings—and cousins—sat opposite each other at a modest square table in the private dining room of the Dâron royal palace in Brendinas. Their respective fiancées occupied the remaining sides of the square.

"Nothing like thwarting an invasion to work up an appetite," said King Dârio as he chewed on a morsel of roast lamb dipped in garlic sauce. He smiled at Jenet, seated to his left, and winked at her.

The Earl Marshal of Tamloch slowly waved her upraised eating knife from side to side while rolling her eyes. "If by that you mean you'd like us to amuse ourselves horizontally this evening," said Jenet, "I'd be glad to. Just don't fill up too much on lamb and pass *me* the garlic sauce. Your breath won't be a problem if we both reek of garlic."

"Yes, dear Marshal," said Dârio. He nodded at King Nûd of Dâron, and that worthy monarch extended a long arm to slide the bowl of sauce previously mentioned closer to Jenet.

Bonnie elbowed Nûd and pointed to the cube of roast lamb impaled on the tip of her own eating knife. "Now *I* can't reach the garlic sauce," she protested.

"That's easily remedied," said Nûd. He pushed his chair back, stood up, and crossed to a sideboard covered in bowls and platters. He rubbed the feathers on the back of Béryl's head as he passed the spot on the stone floor where Bonnie's owlberron familiar was contentedly gnawing on the remains of a plucked and cooked duck. Nûd smiled, remembering how members of the palace staff had requested any of the fowl intended for the owlberron be *sans* feathers, to make their post-dining cleanup easier. He selected another bowl of garlic sauce from the sideboard and returned, placing it between himself and his fiancée.

"Thank you, my love," said Bonnie. She dipped her cube of lamb with her left hand and squeezed Nûd's thigh out of sight under the table with her right.

Nûd blushed while Dârio and Jenet tried to keep their expressions neutral.

Jenet nudged a shallow platter of baked and salted chickpeas toward Nûd. "Here," she said. "You know what they say about chickpeas, don't you?"

After seeing Nûd's puzzled expression, Dârio explained. "According to the ancients, they're the ultimate aphrodisiac. And like the lamb, they also go well with garlic sauce."

"I'd never heard about that for chickpeas," said Nûd. "Asparagus, yes, given the shape of the spears, but never chickpeas."

"Asparagus makes your urine smell funny," said Dârio.

Nûd nodded.

"I'd heard about chickpeas as aphrodisiacs," said Bonnie. "It was common knowledge at the Institute. One of my teachers used to expound on them after he'd had a few cups of wine." Bonnie unfocused her eyes, dropped the pitch of her voice an octave, and recited her teacher's words from memory. "Pay attention young scholars. Three types of food particularly encourage production of the male seed: highly nourishing foods, foods which promote wind from the buttocks, and foods which are warm and moist. Only one perfect foodstuff found in nature combines all three essential properties: the chickpea. Be sure to keep that in mind as you set out to perpetuate the next generation of scholar mages."

"That was marvelous!" said Jenet as she clapped her hands and laughed along with Nûd and Dârio.

"Pass the chickpeas," said Nûd.

"Don't worry, I'll serve you," said Dârio. He reached with a long-handled serving spoon and heaped a tall mound of baked chickpeas on Nûd's trencher. Bonnie took the spoon from Dârio and added more to Nûd's pile.

Nûd smiled between bites as he chewed his way through the crunchy legumes. "Satisfied?" he asked Bonnie when he'd finished them all.

"I expect she will be later," said Dârio.

It was Bonnie's turn to blush. Jenet smacked the back of Dârio's hand with the silver ladle she'd just used to transfer a serving of sautéed green peas and white scallion bulbs to her trencher.

Dârio feigned shock like a wizard's lightning bolt had landed in his lap and the four of them laughed.

"I expect we're all nervous about the upcoming ceremonies," Nûd admitted.

Dârio slapped his chest. "Not me. Jenet has everything mapped out with the precision of a military campaign."

"I hope it's better than that," said Nûd. "Most of the histories I've read indicate military campaigns often end in disaster."

"I just want a nice, sweet ceremony with all of our friends there to celebrate with us," said Bonnie.

"I'm trying my best," said Jenet. "Royal weddings are complicated. Weddings for two royal couples on an island between *both* kingdoms can be even more so."

"At least we've dealt with the Southern Clan Landers," said Dârio.

"For now," said Jenet. "We've been fighting off their incursions since my grandfather's great-grandfather's days."

"This time their threat might really be over," said Nûd. "At least for a few generations as they clear farmland far to the west of Dâron."

"Yes, but Eynon's ring-gates will change everything," said Bonnie. "How long before they use such gates to attack us again?"

"Thanks for referring to Dâron as *us,* my love," said Nûd. "My hope is to build ties of trade with the Southern Clan Landers, providing them with steel for plows and markets for their excess grain."

Bonnie leaned over and kissed Nûd. "I love your optimism."

Nûd put an arm around Bonnie's shoulders. "If we don't try to make friends of our enemies it will be war forever."

Bonnie kissed him again and cuddled into his embrace.

"We seem to have achieved some sort of friendship with the Northern Clan Landers," said Dârio.

"On the basis of *the enemy of my enemy is my friend,*" added Jenet. "So long as we leave them alone."

"And the Bifurlanders don't stir them up," said Dârio.

Jenet spoke to Bonnie. "Speaking of Bifurlanders, what do you think of asking Sigrun and Rannveigr to strew flower petals on our path as we walk between our assembled guests to the site of the ceremonies?"

"That sounds nice," said Bonnie. "If they're not doing it by flying overhead dropping petals from the backs of their dragons."

"I'll square that with Queen Signý," said Jenet.

Nûd and Dârio nodded. Signý, like Jenet, knew how to get things done.

Bonnie laughed and changed the subject. "I wanted to tell you I talked to Kennig," she told Jenet. "He assured me he and Inthíra can moderate the roar of the falls so everyone at the ceremony will be able to hear our pledges clearly."

"Good," said Jenet. "Doethan says he will keep mist from the falls off the food for the feast."

"Because there's nothing worse than damp cake," teased Dârio. His face looked like he was a small boy who'd just dropped a frog into his sister's mug of milk while her back was turned.

"Keep that up and I'll let Linette have you," said Jenet.

"Your younger sister does have certain charms," said Dârio.

"Keep *that* up and you may find yourself tossed in the river and going over the falls," said Nûd.

"With so many powerful wizards in attendance at the ceremonies, I'm sure someone would rescue me before that happened," said Dârio.

"I hope so," said Nûd. "I have *no* interest in being king of both Dâron *and* Tamloch."

"You're busy enough as it is," said Bonnie. "And Jenet will make an excellent queen. I'm counting on her advice on how to fill that role myself."

"You'll be a wonderful queen," said Nûd.

"I'll be the first wizard as a royal consort," said Bonnie.

"Yes, but the prohibition is against wizards as rulers, not as consorts," said Nûd. "Everyone loves you."

"Because they can see how much *you* love me," said Bonnie.

"My father tells me you *are* quite popular with the people of Dâron," said Jenet.

"Just have lots of children to ensure the succession," said Dârio. "That way, if a few of them decide to be wizards it won't be a problem, like it was for Princess Seren."

Bonnie's cheeks went pink. "We'll do our best," she said.

"Thank you, my love," said Nûd. "Speaking of Princess Seren, have Damon and Astrí responded to our invitation?"

"They didn't, but Laetícia let me know the invitation was delivered," said Jenet. "The two of them have been literally undercover—or under the covers—as guests of Quintillius and Laetícia at the governor-general's palace in Nova Eboracum."

"Huh," said Nûd. "That explains why they weren't still at the Inn at the Falls. I expect Damon is trying to give Eynon lots of room."

"There can only be one master mage per kingdom?" asked Bonnie.

"It's not that," Nûd replied. "I think it's more a matter of giving Eynon a chance to shape his role himself instead of trying to fit into something set for him. For that matter, Damon hasn't really served as the master mage of Dâron in decades. I think he stayed away in Melyncárreg in part to keep *me* under wraps. That's probably why he wrote his *Epigrams*. It was a way of sharing his wisdom with the kingdom without being physically present very often."

"The senior wizards of the kingdom had to step up with Ealdamon absent," said Dârio. "Fercha in particular, though Doethan could be counted on to help when we needed him, even if he did prefer to hide in his tower on the Rhuthro."

"Inthíra too," said Jenet. "She was always there for my father when he needed a wizard."

"I expect illusion magic can be particularly valuable for an Earl Marshal," said Nûd.

"By making our forces seem larger than expected, for one," said Dârio.

Jenet nodded. "Do you think Ealdamon knew Astrí was Seren?" she asked.

"I'm not sure," said Nûd. "I *do* know Damon wasn't fond of Gwýnnett. He'd told me *that woman* was one of the major reasons he hated to come to court."

"I sympathize and concur with that sentiment," said Dârio. He touched Jenet's hand. "I was much happier with you and your sister when I visited your father's estates than when I was forced to spend time with my mother."

"And *my sister.* Right," said Jenet. She grinned at Dârio, then shifted to a more serious expression. "Since you've mentioned Gwýnnett, I want to update you on security for the weddings."

The others leaned closer to listen.

"All the cooks and bakers will be watched and guarded," Jenet continued. "And I've arranged for tasters to sample every dish before it is served to guests. Merry's brother Salder is inspecting our suppliers."

Bonnie nodded. "My cousin Uirsé promised to be there with a contingent of her healers and quite a few doses of healing potions in case any of the tasters fall ill."

"Or any of the guests go over the falls," said Dârio.

Jenet ignored his comment. "My father and Duke Néillen are coordinating physical security," she continued after a pause to wipe a jot of garlic sauce off her chin. "Roma legionnaires provided by Quintillius are supplementing their forces and King Bjarni has promised Bifurland warriors to make security for our weddings an all-Orluin effort."

"Excellent," said Nûd.

"There's nothing better to build bonds of friendship than celebrating together," said Dârio.

"What about magical security?" asked Bonnie. "I told you about the volunteers from the Institute at Bhaile Pónaire. Any scholar mage who welcomes seeing one of their own become a queen will be there, and even more planned to attend once I told them about the free feast."

"Good," said Jenet. "Inthíra has done the same for the scholar mages in our Valley of the Towers. I used two of the gate ring pairs Merry gave me to ensure the scholar mages can get to the Great Falls easily."

"Are easily distracted scholar mages good options for protection against attacks from hostile wizards?" asked Nûd.

"The scholar mages aren't our primary shields," said Jenet. "Laetícia promised she would assemble a group of her best Roma resources—both spy wizards and martial mages—as our first line of defense from inimical wizardry."

"I'm pleased to hear that," said Dârio. "The Roma have been thwarting plots and conspiracies a lot longer than we have in Dâron and Tamloch."

"Yes, but look at how much intrigue still remains in the Imperium," said Nûd.

"One of my teachers at the Institute used to say, 'Humans are intriguing animals,'" said Bonnie. "She didn't mean that people were fascinating to study—though we are. She meant that *intrigue* is an essential part of human nature."

"I can't disagree," said Jenet. "All we can do is our best to ensure our weddings go smoothly."

Dârio kissed her cheek. "Thank you for all your efforts on our behalf, dear lady," he said.

Nûd and Bonnie clapped softly, adding their agreement. Pointing to a small cask on the sideboard, Nûd asked, "More Applegarth cider, anyone? I'm thirsty, and the cider may counteract some of the strength of the garlic sauce." Seeing three nods, he got up to deliver the cask to the table.

"Bring that small, bowl with the green fabric cover with you, please," said Bonnie. "I made something special for us to share."

"Of course, my love," said Nûd. He tucked the cask under one arm like he was transporting a suckling pig and handed the covered bowl to Bonnie.

As he filled their mugs with cider, Bonnie removed the cover on the bowl, displaying a collection of several dozen light green and blue spheres the size of small grapes. "I made these for us," she said. "They're almond paste flavored with mint and covered in hardened sugar syrup. The green ones are wintergreen, and the blue ones are spearmint. I know wintergreen is from berries, not mint leaves, but I like the taste."

"Are the colors for Tamloch and Dâron?" asked Nûd.

"They are," said Bonnie. "I thought we might want to serve them between courses at our wedding feast."

Jenet took the bowl from Bonnie and shook it gently, hearing to small candies rattle. "They look really interesting," she said. "How do you make them?"

"With wizardry," said Bonnie. "I watched Uirsé make pills filled with medicine using the same technique. It doesn't take much sugar, which is good because sugar is so expensive."

"We have to trade for it with the Roma," said Dârio. "Occidens Province imports loaves of sugar from the Isles of Dogs. Valentius had some aboard his ship, I'd heard."

"That's my understanding as well," said Bonnie. "I used some of Uirsé's. You don't need a lot." She passed the bowl around the table and each person took a green and a blue candy. "I made the flavored almond paste first," Bonnie continued. "Then I captured bits of flavored paste in tiny globes of solidified sound and dipped them in hot sugar syrup. Once they were coated, I held the globes up out of the syrup until they hardened. The color comes from crushed mint leaves and blueberry skins boiled with the sugar and water."

"I can't wait to taste them," said Nûd. "Dâron first, of course." He popped a blue sphere into his mouth. Bonnie was pleased to see him smile. "It's delicious," he said. "The wintergreen is very refreshing." The green sphere was next and Nûd continued to smile. "The spearmint is excellent as well. I can feel it counteracting the garlic sauce, too."

"Let me confirm that," said Bonnie. She bit into a blue sphere, chewed, swallowed, and leaned over to give Nûd a kiss on the lips that continued for several seconds. "Yes," she said. "Definitely confirmed." Nûd just nodded.

Jenet and Dârio exchanged smiles, popped spheres into their own mouths, and kissed.

"I think they're marvelous," said Jenet. "Everyone will love them—especially once they taste them at our wedding feast."

"Perhaps we can use them to boost revenue for the kingdom," said Nûd. "You could call them *Queen's Favors*."

"Or I could share the recipe widely, building good will across Orluin," offered Bonnie with a smile. "Producing the small spheres of solidified sound needed to make them would also be good training for young wizards and give *them* a chance to make a few coins, or a few new friends."

"That sounds even better," said Nûd.

Dârio stretched and yawned theatrically, ending up with his arm around Jenet. "Now that my breath is fresh, I think it's time for a *nap*."

"A nap or a *nap?*" asked Jenet.

"What do *you* think?" Dârio answered.

Holding hands, both couples left the room, leaving Béryl sleeping soundly on the floor.

Chapter 36

Laetícia and Callidus

"Períkulōs, Perkússos, and Sikárias?" whispered Laetícia.

At the other end of the communications ring linkage, Magister Callidus nodded once, then moved his head slowly from side to side as if he'd just felt the weight of the Great Pyramid descending upon his shoulders. "I'm afraid so," he said. "Eynon used the bug you gave him to listen in on Sírénae, Umbrose, and Celéri at their camp on the Tempest Isles. They were joined by the three wizard assassins. I saw them and heard them discussing their plans to attack at the wedding."

"Did you learn anything about their assignment?"

"They've been hired to kill Valentius, kill King Bjarni…" Callidus began, trailing off before finishing.

"And?" said Laetícia. "Is there more?"

"Yes," Callidus responded. "They intend to kidnap your children."

Laetícia shook her head. The sound of the beads in her braids clattered like fist-sized hail on a tile roof. "The thrice-blasted she-wolf!" she exclaimed.

"Sírénae?" asked Callidus.

"No, Flavia Drusilla," said Laetícia. "This is part of her long game. With Valentius dead, Quin is Valens' likely choice as his heir to the Southern Empire and Flavia Drusilla can install Gertrude of Mainz as emperor of the West instead of him. If she holds our children hostage, we'll be forced to support Flavia Drusilla's agenda moving forward."

Callidus nodded. "Leaving only Phraátēs, emperor of the East, to vote against her," he said.

"Until she can manage to replace *him* with one of her puppets as well," said Laetícia. "I think I even know who she's grooming for that role—a Persian who claims descent from Alexander."

"That doesn't exactly narrow the number of candidates," said Callidus. He flashed a small smile and so did Laetícia.

"True enough. It doesn't really matter who she intends to install as Phraátēs' heir, only that she is the width of a few hairs away from establishing herself as Dictator over the entire Imperium."

"And here I thought *Sírénae* was devious," said Callidus.

"Sírénae was groomed and mentored by Flavia Drusilla," said Laetícia.

"But Flavia Drusilla underestimated Sírénae's ambition."

"I don't think so," said Laetícia. "Would such a safe and unimaginative person as Gertrude be considered for the purple without Sírénae as a counterexample?" Laetícia put one palm on her forehead and slowly removed it. "I think Flavia Drusilla's only miscalculation was that Sírénae was able to convince so many of her legions to follow her to Orluin. Flavia Drusilla will need Gertrude to regain most of those legions to assert her control over the West."

"From what I've learned listening in the shadows at legionnaires' campfires and bugging taverns here in Portus Aleña, a great many legionnaires would be more than glad to return to their homes in the Western Empire," said Callidus.

"Quintillius and I thought that likely as well," said Laetícia. She leaned closer to the communication ring's circular interface. "Valens and Phraátēs are backing Quin for western emperor, assuming most of the legionnaires here in Orluin would follow him back to Nárbo."

"I expect more than eighty percent of them would," said Callidus.

"Good," said Laetícia. "When the time is right, they can use the fixed gates between Portus Aleña and Nova Eboracum and board the transport ships still floating in our harbor."

"Will you have enough skilled sailors to recross the Ocean?" asked Callidus.

"If we don't, we can recruit experienced sea captains from the Imperium," said Laetícia. "We have a working trans-Oceanic gate so they could get here quickly."

"I expect Admiral Pixo might be interested in assisting," said Callidus.

"Can he be trusted? He's Celéri's uncle."

"And none-too-pleased by his niece," said Callidus. "I think he can."

"Where might I find him?"

"On the Tempest Isles."

"Interesting," said Laetícia. "We wondered where he and his small flotilla ended up."

"If I know Pixo, and I do, I'd bet all his best sailors are with him. They'd give you a big head start on recruiting crews for your crossing."

"That's good to know," said Laetícia. "If and *only* if we can stop the three assassins from killing Valens and King Bjarni..."

"And from kidnapping your children," said Callidus. "It was delightful seeing them here on Valentia, by the way. Aleña loved spending time with them. She's pregnant, you know."

"I do," said Laetícia. "Tertia couldn't stop talking about glyppos."

"They are amazing creatures," said Callidus.

"Amazingly huge and aggressive, for plant-eaters."

"Eating plants doesn't imply passivity," said Callidus. "Witness Orluin's wisents."

"And mammoths," added Laetícia. "Dragons, on the other hand..."

"Are carnivores," said Callidus. "But not all dragons are bad-tempered and aggressive."

"Speaking of dragons, how are those wild dragons from western Orluin managing on Valentia?"

"Quite well," said Callidus. "They're mostly staying away from Portus Aleña, and the legionnaires are fine with that. Apparently there are lots of large and tasty fish in the waters surrounding this island."

"Good to know," said Laetícia. "I'm hoping they'll be willing to breed with our Imperial dragons. We've been cultivating traits like obedience to orders for too many generations. Our war dragons could use more aggression."

"So long as they don't literally bite the hands that feed them," said Callidus. "Some of the western dragons aren't well socialized."

"The same can be said for a lot of legionnaires," said Laetícia. "If Eynon's there, can he talk sense into them? He brought them east, after all."

"Eynon and Merry are gone," said Callidus. "She was unhappy because I couldn't immediately return with her to start teaching wizardry to a new apprentice near her home along the Rhuthro.

She was also none too pleased by Eynon's insistence on meeting with Celéri to 'finish' his master mage lessons and refused to accompany him."

"Merry has more common sense than Eynon," said Laetícia.

"I don't know about that," said Callidus. "My impression is that Eynon is simply more trusting. He seems to think Celéri isn't evil, just headstrong, and I agree with him. Perhaps the lad can persuade Celéri to switch sides."

"Hah!" said Laetícia. "The only side Celéri is on is her own."

"Perhaps," said Callidus. "However, I think you underestimate her capacity for growth. She was one of *my* students, not yours, and I bear some of the blame for not stressing the importance of demonstrating responsibility, rather than seeking personal power. She's young enough life could still teach her that lesson, even if I could not."

"Given the twin examples of Sírénae and Umbrose, is it any wonder she took the path she did?"

"I carry some of the blame for Sírénae as well," said Callidus. "I should have brought her ruthless excesses to the attention of the preceptors at the Imperial School of Good Governance years ago."

"If you had, those toothless old lions would have done nothing," said Laetícia. "Their mission is training honest bureaucrats, not reining in candidates for the purple. Sírénae's successes in battle and in pacifying local uprisings by any means necessary served only to improve her standing as a potential future emperor. Don't waste time flogging yourself with your own scourge."

"Thank you for saying so," said Callidus. "You're right about not crying over spilled wine. Sírénae is a city whose walls have already fallen. The whole matter is more painful because I once loved her, and perhaps still do. But that's no matter. I hold out hope that Celéri can still change her path and return to the *Via Appia Magica,* the true road of a virtuous Roma master mage."

"All magical roads lead to Roma?" said Laetícia. "Fair enough. But some mages cross the Rubicon when they do so, while others follow the laws of the Senate and People of Roma. Celéri doesn't seem like a woman who follows anyone's laws but her own."

"She's young," said Callidus. "She's a new master mage. And she's ambitious. Both of us were all three once."

"Neither of us ever defied all laws and customs and thought to proclaim ourselves as an emperor," said Laetícia. "There are witnesses to Celéri making exactly that declaration."

"So she's a fool as well," said Callidus. "Which one of us has never been foolish?"

"There's foolish and *foolish*," said Laetícia. "Celéri hasn't merely piled Pelion on Ossa, she's stacked Etna atop Vesuvius."

"With explosive results, I get your meaning," said Callidus.

"What do you intend to do about her?" asked Laetícia.

"Do?" replied Callidus. "I'm not sure what I *can* do. At present my hope is that a younger man may prove more persuasive in teaching her wisdom, since my attempts as a more seasoned mage have obviously failed."

"You mean Eynon," said Laetícia.

"Yes," said Callidus. "He intends to find her and ask her the same things he asked of the two of us, and Verro and Amber and Uirsé."

"The healer from Tamloch?" asked Laetícia. "Bonnie's cousin. I suppose she *is* a master healer."

"Celéri is the remaining master mage to consult on this side of the Ocean," said Callidus.

"Aside from Umbrose."

"True, but Eynon is wise enough not to seek *his* advice. I hope."

"I can admire the skills Umbrose demonstrates as a spymaster, without admiring the swamp of a mind that guides his actions," said Laetícia. "The man's psyche is so twisted it would make a pit of writhing vipers look straight."

"Be glad you didn't have to work with him close at hand for decades," said Callidus. He leaned closer to the interface and whispered. "I learned something more about Umbrose from Eynon's bug."

"Do tell," said Laetícia, leaning closer herself.

"Períkulōs and Sikárias are his parents," said Callidus. "Perkússos is his uncle."

Laetícia sat back and took a deep breath. The beads on her braids clacked again as she shook her head. "That explains a lot," she said after a longer pause to fully comprehend the news. "He's carved from the same wood."

"Of a diseased family tree," said Callidus.

"That's rotting at the root," said Laetícia. "Now that I've ground that metaphor to sawdust, you know what we have to do."

Callidus sighed.

"Don't be like that," said Laetícia. "They plan to kill my friends and kidnap my children. What *else* am I going to do?"

"The question isn't what are we going to do," said Callidus. "It's whether any of us will live through it. You know their reputations."

"Períkulōs, Perkússos, and Sikárias still have to breathe air to live," said Laetícia. "Their hearts have to pump blood. Their brains have to guide their actions. Garrotes, swords, and nerve toxins will work as well for us as for them. So will strangling spheres of solidified sound, fireballs, and lightning blasts."

"Yes, but..."

"They plan to *kidnap my children!*" said Laetícia. "Their lives are forfeit."

"How many of us will die in the attempt?" asked Callidus.

"I don't intend to do this alone," said Laetícia. "Mafuta will join me, and Felix. Verro and Amber as well, they're not squeamish. If Verro comes, Fercha will join him. Damon has been enjoying my hospitality—I'll insist he come along to pay me back for his room and board. From the way I've heard he trains apprentices, he has the proper attitude. Perhaps Kennig, too. He can be hard when he needs to be, and we could use a skilled illusionist. With you, that makes five master mages and several other strong wizards against Umbrose and the wizard assassins."

"Each assassin is likely of master mage caliber," said Callidus. "With Umbrose and Celéri it would be five master mages versus five. Unfortunately, our opponents have much more experience with killing than we do."

Laetícia moved her hand, opening it up to show her empty palm, acknowledging the words Callidus spoke. "What choice do we have?" she said. Callidus could see one of her hands ball into a fist and a tear begin to form in one of her eyes. "I can't stand by and do nothing. We have to stop them. We have to *end* them."

"I don't disagree in principle," said Callidus. "The question is how to accomplish that goal without turning your children into orphans and killing every master mage in Orluin in the attempt."

Laetícia's free hand covered her eyes as she hid her tears.

"I learned more about the others on the Tempest Isles with Celéri, Sírénae, Umbrose, and the wizard assassins," said Callidus. "Túathal, the former king of Tamloch, Gwýnnett, the princess of Dâron, and Hibblig, a wizard who was one of Gwýnnett's playthings, are also with them."

"Túathal is mad, Hibblig thinks with his groin, and Gwýnnett is ineffectual without her stock of poisons," said Laetícia. "We don't need to worry about them."

"You're out of date," said Callidus. "From what I observed through the bug, Túathal is thinking clearly again now that he is out from under the influence of Gwýnnett's potions. The same is true for Hibblig. He's a talented wizard, though nowhere near master mage level. And Gwýnnett may have access to whatever pharmacopeia the wizard assassins brought with them or that she gathered on her own. All three of them are dangerous."

"I stand corrected. We need to include neutralizing them in our plans as well," said Laetícia.

"Whatever we plan, it won't be successful without the element of surprise," said Callidus. "Given how long the wizard assassins have been at their trade, I expect it will prove quite difficult to catch them off guard."

"Granted," said Laetícia. She had mastered her face and now sat like she'd been carved from marble.

"The wedding isn't until noon on the summer solstice. That's two days from now," said Callidus. "We have time, though not much of it."

"And?" asked Laetícia.

"We can use that time, short as it is, to plan something truly surprising," he said. "Perhaps the others can offer insights as well."

"This is a Roma problem," said Laetícia. "*We* should provide the solution."

"Remember, they intend to kill King Bjarni as well," said Callidus. "This is a problem for the Orluin Alliance, not just us Roma. I wasn't present when the charter for the alliance was signed, but I do support it. We should get as much advice as we can, in keeping with operational security and expedience."

"Gather a small team and talk through our strategy immediately, you mean."

"I thought that's what I said."

"Yes, thank you, you did," said Laetícia. "Forgive me. I was thinking like a mother, not a spymaster. I'll contact the key participants as soon as we end this call. How soon can you be here?"

"Within the hour," said Callidus. "I just have a few things to set in motion here before I leave—like warning Valentius and Aleña."

"That *is* important," said Laetícia. "Assuming it will take the others a bit longer, I will schedule our meeting for two hours from now. We can meet in my study."

"Are you confident of your own security?" asked Callidus.

"As much as anyone can be," said Laetícia. "With the proper shields, I can at least guarantee we won't be overheard. I can tell everyone we're planning a big surprise for the royal weddings."

"That's as good as can be expected given the short notice," said Callidus. "I'll end this call so you can contact the others."

"Right," said Laetícia. She sighed and moved to cut the communication ring's connection.

Callidus waved a hand. "Wait," he said. "There's one more thing you need to know."

"What's that?" asked Laetícia. Her expression indicated she was clearly ready to get on with the next steps on her mental to-do list.

"It's about Eynon, Merry, and Celéri."

"What?"

"Eynon *ad hoc* gated Merry away a few minutes ago," said Callidus. "When he returned, he told me he took her to Fercha's tower because it was close to the new apprentice Merry wanted me to teach. He did so even though she wasn't speaking to him. I expect that made her even more angry."

"Merry's frustrated that she can't *ad hoc* gate," said Laetícia.

"And understandably so, given all her other exceptional talents," said Callidus. "But I think she was even more upset about Eynon wanting master mage lessons from Celéri."

"A lover's quarrel?" asked Laetícia. "Or Merry wanting to hit Eynon over the head with a rock for being an idiot?"

"Some of both, but more of the latter, I think," said Callidus.

Laetícia lowered her head before raising it and speaking. "Then what happened?"

"Eynon rounded up two glyppos using solidified sound and *ad hoc* gated himself and the two beasts away with pop that made my ears hurt," said Callidus. "I expect he wants them as a distraction."

"How many guesses do I get about where he was going?" asked Laetícia. Her expression shifted from anger to concern then back to anger.

"You should only need one," said Callidus.

"Celéri," said Laetícia.

Callidus nodded slowly.

"So much for the element of surprise," said Laetícia.

"From what I've learned, Eynon is often surprising," said Callidus. "I'll follow what I can using the bug he sent back to the Tempest Isles. It can provide us with updates."

"Good," said Laetícia. "It will be difficult to plan our operation against the wizard assassins without them."

"Eynon knows we're planning to attack the wizard assassins," said Callidus. "If he's captured and questioned..."

"They'll know we're coming," said Laetícia. "They'd be fools not to expect that already."

"And they're not fools," said Callidus. "See you in two hours then."

"Two hours," Laetícia repeated. She sighed, frowned, and cut the connection.

Chapter 37

In the Guest House

"Wizard assassins have been hired to *kill* me?" said King Bjarni from a comfortable chair in his farm's guest house.

"That is the warning shared by Laetícia," said Amber.

"Who hired them?" asked Queen Signý from a chair near where her husband was sitting.

"There's some confusion on that issue," Amber replied. "From what Laetícia has been able to determine, Gertrude of Mainz hired them, but did so with instructions from Flavia Drusilla."

"I warned you," said Prince Flóki Magnússon. He was pacing beside the unlit hearth in the guest house and his hand went to his sword hilt. "Flavia Drusilla wants Nordland."

"Flavia Drusilla wants control of the entire Imperium, according to Laetícia," said Amber.

"When will the assassination attempt occur?" asked Signý.

"It was supposed to be at the royal weddings in two days," said Amber. "Valentius is also to be killed, and the children of Quintillius and Laetícia are to be kidnapped and held hostage."

"Convenient," said Bjarni. "All their victims would be in the same place."

"Correct," said Amber. "Laetícia has called all the master mages of Orluin together in Nova Eboracum to plan our attack and eliminate the threat..."

"...of Períkulōs, Perkússos, and Sikárias," said Flóki. He spat into the hearth. "Given their reputations..."

"Yes," said Amber. "They *are* formidable, but so are the master mages of Orluin."

"Indeed," said Signý. "Please keep us informed."

"Of course," said Amber. "In the meantime, more wizards will be guarding your farm."

"Why bother, if the assassins aren't planning to strike until the wedding?" asked Bjarni.

"Laetícia's information may be out of date," said Amber. "Better safe..."

"...than sorry," Signý completed.

"Err in haste, repent at leisure," said Bjarni, providing a similar maxim. "You're not one to make mistakes, Amber. Thank you."

Knútr, the slender, gold-robed, and unbearded Nordland wizard who'd accompanied Prince Flóki across the ocean raised an arm, causing the gray raven perched on Knútr's shoulder to caw and relocate to the mantle of the hearth. "Would the services of another master mage be of assistance?" he asked Amber.

"Certainly," Amber replied. "If Flóki can spare you."

"Given that thwarting Flavia Drusilla's plans in Orluin would help Nordland, I'm sure I could be spared—right, my prince?" said Knútr.

"So long as you don't get yourself killed," said Flóki. "My brother would never forgive me."

"I'm sure Harald would find it in his heart to do so if it ended the threat to Nordland from Flavia Drusilla and Gertrude," said Signý.

"For all my queen's appreciation of political realities, I hope you *both* remain among the living," said Bjarni.

Knútr's raven familiar said, "Caw! Caw! Caw!" in support of Bjarni's statement.

For the space of a breath, everything was quiet. Then the silence was broken by a boom like a massive tree trunk smashing into the gates of a fortress as the door to the guest house crashed open and five young people entered, chattering faster than squirrels.

"There's a mammoth in the orchard!" shouted Rannveigr. Her blonde braids swayed as she looked left and right around the room.

"He's eating the pippins!" said Otr.

"And stripping leaves from all the trees he can reach," said Selr.

"May we herd him away with our dragons?" asked Sigrun, addressing her mother.

"I want to *flame* the mammoth!" said Holgir. He was a head shorter than Selr and Otr but shouted even louder than the others.

"No one is flaming mammoths today," said Signý, her eyes focused on Holgir. She shifted her attention to Sigrun. "Yes, you may herd the mammoth away from the orchard. Try to move him toward the oaks at the far northwest corner of the farm. They're due to be coppiced this fall and having them lose their leaves won't matter."

"Yes, Mother," said Sigrun. The girl kept her expression neutral until Rannveigr grinned at her and she laughed. "I *told* you I could get permission!"

"Yay!" said Holgir. "Mammoth herding!" He mimed holding the reins of his dragon and banking from side to side.

"No flaming!" Signý commanded. "Your dragons are far too young to breathe fire."

"Yes, Mother," Sigrun repeated.

"And be careful," Bjarni added.

"We will be," said Rannveigr. The grin on her face made her statement less likely, but Bjarni smiled at her and the other young people anyway. He'd been their age once himself and had once tried to wrestle a cave bear—unsuccessfully.

Sigrun took Selr's hand and tugged him back toward the open door. Rannveigr did the same to Otr. Holgir skipped around the room 'flying his dragon' and made a face at Knútr's raven. The bird shook its head and seemed to shrug. Knútr returned the familiar's gesture, adding a smile.

When the five children left the room, Knútr stepped over to Amber and summoned the raven to return to its usual shoulder perch. When the gray raven flew over and landed securely, the two wizards climbed aboard their flying disks and popped out using an *ad hoc* gate Amber created.

Bjarni smiled at Signý and Flóki. "Shall we watch the mammoth herding?" he asked. "I could use some amusement."

"And I would like to see more of your small gold dragons in action," said Flóki. "Perhaps we could even have a few eggs to take back to Nordland?"

"Not for another dozen years or more," said Signý. "None of ours are mature enough to clutch."

"I can be patient, when I have to," said Flóki.

"Living on the northern edge of the Imperium, I expect that's a necessity," said Bjarni. "Come along, then. We'll see how the young people manage their self-assigned project."

As the three of them stepped out of the guest house, Flóki asked, "Are you often bothered by mammoths here?"

"No, thank goodness," said Signý. "The largest herds are north of the Whale River and usually the smaller herds stay far away from our garths and farms."

"This one is probably a lone male roaming about," said Bjarni.

"A mammoth version of that *wander year* custom I've heard about in books about Dâron?" asked Flóki. "There are dozens of romances popular in the Imperium featuring Orluin young people wandering through wild, uncivilized lands."

"Of course, to the people of the Imperium all of Orluin is considered uncivilized," said Signý.

"Almost by definition," said Flóki. "Along with Nordland. They keep wanting to civilize us."

"But enjoy their fantasies by romanticizing you as northern barbarians," said Bjarni. "I think everyone in Orluin from Tamloch south does the same for us Bifurlanders."

"*Bifurland barbarians* sounds better than Nordland barbarians," said Flóki. "I'll have to try using that phrase in a poem."

"Happy composing," said Bjarni. "I'd appreciate a copy of whatever you write."

"Gladly," said Flóki. "Once I write it. And assuming Amber and Knútr and their master mage colleagues are successful."

"If they're not, I'll likely be decomposing," said Bjarni.

"You're too stubborn to decompose," Signý told her husband. "They'll dig you up five centuries later looking like you've just been taking a nap, like those corpses excavated from berry bogs."

"What a cheering thought," said Bjarni.

* * * * *

The young people were already flying toward the orchard on dragon-back when Signý, Bjarni, and Flóki reached the top of a small rise with a good view of the trees and the invading mammoth. As expected, it was a young male wandering far from his herd, though it was unusual for mammoths—even young males—to be on their own instead of in small groups.

Signý noticed the mammoth had particularly handsome curving tusks that encompassed an arc of almost three-quarters of a circle from where they erupted from the massive beast's jaws. His long stringy fur was reddish brown and was falling out in places as the mammoth transitioned from his winter coat to his summer one. The great beast's eyes had a wild look, as if he wasn't sure what to make of gold dragons the size of warhorses winging toward him. *I hope the children don't frighten him,* thought Signý. *The last thing we need is a mammoth rampaging through our barley fields and knocking down barn walls.*

The mammoth was using its trunk to pluck small, ripening apples from a tree in the northwest of the orchard when the dragons arrived. Sigrun, with Selr behind her, hovered above the mammoth on Gylda, while Rannveigr and Otr, aboard Nugget, circled nearby. Holgir, riding his mount, a sweet-tempered dragon the boy had named Killer, flew above them. Signý, with Bjarni and Flóki beside her, watched as Sigrun shouted to Rannveigr and Holgir to map out their strategy.

A few seconds later, Holgir and Killer descended to literally get in the mammoth's face, hovering only a few feet in front of the beast's curved tusks. At the same time, Sigrun and Rannveigr brought their dragons in close from the south. At a prearranged signal, all three dragons bellowed. Unfortunately, they sounded more like the honks of *basso* geese than the rolling tympanic thunder of a deafening roar from immense dragons like Viridáxés or Zûrafiérix.

The mammoth lifted his head, briefly regarded the gold dragons, then returned to plucking pippins from branches.

"What do you think they'll try now?" Bjarni asked Signý.

"I'm not sure," Signý replied. "It will depend on how much they planned ahead."

"I have a prediction," said Flóki. "My sons have ram's horns. If they blow them they'll make as much noise as those dragons' attempts at bellowing."

Prince Flóki's prediction was accurate. Gylda and Nugget moved closer to the beast, allowing Selr and Otr to blow their horns only inches from the mammoth's nearer ear. Sigrun and Rannveigr immediately directed their dragons to rise, which was a good thing because their actions *did* prompt a reaction this time as the mammoth turned rapidly and attempted to smack the annoying noisemakers with his trunk. When he realized he'd failed, he trumpeted his frustration and shook the tip of his trunk in defiance.

Signý laughed at what happened next. While the mammoth was distracted, Holgir—on Killer—flew in beside the beast's hindquarters with a flaming torch and set the tip of his tail alight.

"You told them no fire," said Bjarni to Signý.

"She said their dragons couldn't breathe fire," noted Flóki.

"The prince is correct," said Signý, "though Holgir doesn't need much of an excuse to play with flames."

"I know," said Bjarni. "It took him a year of running errands for Amber to earn a fire stone."

"Someday he's going to set his bed straw on fire," said Signý.

"At present, his actions seem to be effective," said Flóki.

The mammoth was decidedly unhappy to have a flaming tail. He started to move northwest, rumbling along the ground moving uphill away from the orchard and two gold dragons who had swooped in to discourage movement in any other direction. This particular mammoth proved smarter than the average cave bear, however. After realizing that moving quickly merely fanned the flames burning the tuft of hair on the tip of his tail, he tried a different tactic and simply sat, quenching his burning tail in the grass and dirt. Steam, and a bit of smoke rose up from beneath the mammoth. The great beast returned to his feet and glared at his tormentors.

"It's a good thing we had a wet spring," said Bjarni.

"Agreed," said Signý. "If the ground hadn't been damp Holgir's stunt could have set the grass on fire."

The royal trio didn't have to wait long to see what happened next. Sigrun and Rannveigr instructed their dragons to hover over the mammoth and handed ropes to their companions. The Nordlanders carefully positioned loops of rope near the points of the great beast's tusks. Once in place, the girls guided their dragons forward so the loops slid along the tusks until the mammoth could be pulled by the strength of two dragons. Holgir and Killer added another loop of rope around the mammoth's singed tail. All three dragons pulled, but the mammoth resisted, its mass much greater than the sum of all three dragons. In the end, Selr, Otr, and Holgir had to drop their ropes or risk their dragons being tossed about in the air like three gold kites in a storm.

"Will they give up?" asked Flóki.

"I don't think so," said Signý.

"But they're flying away," said Flóki.

Signý smiled.

"They're flying back to the grain barn," said Bjarni. "Didn't the barn cat there..."

"Yes, she injured her leg," said Signý.

"While the cat's away..." said Bjarni.

"Oh," said Flóki. "Clever!"

The mammoth did not immediately return to the orchard. Instead, he watched the dragons carefully as they left to land near a large building. He saw their riders climbed down and enter the building, disappearing from view. When the annoying humans were no longer in sight, the mammoth began to move back toward the trees holding tasty maturing apples. He stopped when he saw the humans emerge from the building carrying small wicker baskets. His wariness increased when the dragons and their riders returned.

Signý and Bjarni laughed when they saw Sigrun and Rannveigr empty baskets full of mice around the mammoth's feet. Flóki applauded when Holgir dumped his basket top of the mammoth's head, causing some of the mice to run up into the thick fur of the beast's forehead and others to scrabble down along the sensitive skin of the mammoth's trunk.

Finally, the mammoth had enough. He shook his massive body, trying to dislodge the tiny boarders, and flipped his truck back and forth faster than a dog wagging its tail. Then he trumpeted his displeasure and stepped carefully, moving away from the orchard and toward the stand of oaks he could see in the northwest. Their green leaves would be tasty, even if they wouldn't be as delicious as pippin apples.

The young people and their dragons landed beside Signý, Bjarni, and Flóki on the small rise where they stood.

"Nicely done," said Bjarni as he observed the smiles on the dragonriders' faces.

"You didn't give up and kept trying new approaches," said Flóki as he put his arms around his sons.

"I just hope the master mages prove equally resourceful dealing with their challenges," said Signý.

"They will," said Holgir. "Even if it will be less of a mammoth undertaking."

Selr and Otr had to pull Sigrun and Rannveigr off their cousin before some semblance of peace was restored and they all returned to the guest house for lunch.

Chapter 38

Roast Pork and Glyppos

Gwýnnett was far from pleased by her present circumstances. She missed her well-appointed suite of rooms and her fawning servants at the royal palace in Brendinas. She missed hot baths, fine clothes, and excellent meals from the palace kitchens. From time to time, she even missed the attentions of men, like Hibblig, who she'd wrapped around her finger with her potions—but most of all, she missed her private apothecary's workshop where she prepared the potions and other items that gave her power and control.

Here on the Tempest Isles she was treated as an afterthought, largely ignored by the wizard assassins, Umbrose, and Sírénae. Túathal and Hibblig acknowledged her existence, but kept her at polearm's length, which was understandable, given what she'd done to them. Still, she missed being treated like a princess.

Celéri, although warned about the dangers of leviathans, was sitting on a rock at the edge of the surf, bathing her injured foot in salt water. Her uncle was beside her, complaining about his digestion and lamenting the fact that all his stomach would tolerate at present was ship's biscuits dipped in honey. He'd sent his sailors back with instructions to transport tents and supplies to this side of the island.

As Perkússos continued to rotate the roasting pig over hot coals, Gwýnnett paced along the pink sand beach until she found what she was looking for—a large empty conch shell pushed up out of the surf by a high tide. She held the shell to her ear and could hear the sound of the ocean. Back near the others, Hibblig was grinding red onions, salt, and juice from a native succulent into a sauce for the roast pork using a deep cylindrical mortar and a long, club-like pestle he'd carved from blocks of pale coral using constructs of solidified sound.

Facing away from the others, a small smile flashed across Gwýnnett's face. She turned and brought the conch shell to Hibblig. He put his hand up to warn her not to come too close. Gwýnnett gave Hibblig a much bigger smile. "I not looking for trouble," she said. "I'd just like your help cutting the tip off this shell to make it a trumpet. I had one when I was a girl and thought it might be entertaining to see if I still remember how to sound one."

Hibblig frowned, then nodded and rested his pestle in the mortar, freeing his hands. "Very well," he said, clearly not trusting her but having no specific reason to deny her request. "Just don't try to play it near me. I'm enjoying the relative peace here and consider the lapping waves sufficient accompaniment for my life at present."

"Of course," said Gwýnnett. She approached close enough to hand the conch to Hibblig and directed his attention to the pointed tip of the shell, indicating with one hand where she wanted him to cut it. Her other hand surreptitiously plucked the toxic yellow 'apples' from a fold of her dress, holding them by their stems to avoid their caustic skins and dropping them into the pulped mass of red onion sauce in the coral mortar beside Hibblig. For good measure, she poured in the sap from the *yellow apple* tree she'd kept in a clamshell as well.

The overly muscled wizard sliced the tip of the conch shell off with a plane of solidified sound and polished the opening into a proper mouthpiece using a cone of similar construction. He indicated that Gwýnnett should back up and tossed her the shell, waving her off with one hand and taking up the pestle again with another. "That should do," he said. "Now go away."

Gwýnnett could see why he'd carved a physical mortar and pestle rather than mixing the ingredients in his sauce using constructs of solidified sound. The pestle seemed to attack the mortar and its contents as Hibblig dug in and ground the onions into a smooth sauce. After ten minutes, Hibblig carried the mortar over to Perkússos.

"Use this to baste the pig," said Hibblig. "It should add a nice flavor to the meat."

Perkússos bent and sniffed the contents of the mortar. "I think you're right," he said. The wizard assassin did something with his hands while staring at the sauce. Hibblig couldn't follow it precisely, but it looked like the wizard assassin had created some sort of special lenses from solidified sound. "Good for you," Perkússos told Hibblig. "I don't detect any known poisons in your concoction and it smells good enough." The wizard assassin generated a ladle from solidified sound and used it to coat the crackled outer skin of the roasting pig with sauce. Soon, the odor changed from simply meaty to savory and both men smiled. "Thank you," said Perkússos.

"I'm glad to pitch in," said Hibblig. He stepped away and looking around, trying to find Gwýnnett but couldn't spot her. *Perhaps she's gone off to play her conch trumpet,* Hibblig considered. Behind him, Túathal approached Perkússos and beckoned him farther down the beach. Períkulōs replaced his brother in tending to the spit while Túathal and Perkússos paced a hundred yards farther around the arc of the Grand Harbor.

Túathal spoke first. "About my offer," he said.

"I wondered when you'd get to that," said Perkússos. "Just how much more do you intend to offer?"

"What are Gertrude and Flavia Drusilla paying you?"

Perkússos drew a number in the sand with a small, pointed shell, then erased it with the toe of his boot.

"That's quite a large sum," said Túathal. He looked at the wizard assassin as if measuring his worth then continued. "I can double your fee," he said.

"You'd mentioned two more targets," said Perkússos. "Would they be included in your proposal?"

"I'll pay extra for them," said Túathal. "Their deaths are particularly essential to my plans."

"Who else do you want us to kill?"

"Two men who will also be at the wedding," said Túathal. "The kings of Dâron and Tamloch."

"Interesting," said Perkússos. "Of course they'll be at the ceremonies, considering they're the ones being joined to their brides. We should be able to make that happen."

"Good," said Túathal. The former king of Tamloch named a large sum that proved to the wizard assassin just how much Túathal wanted a clear path to his domination of Orluin.

The two men nodded, turned, and walked back to the others, following the enticing odor of roast pork with red onion sauce.

* * * * *

Gwýnnett lowered shell trumpet from her ear. She'd walked into the trees above the beach and had found a spot to listen in on Perkússos and Túathal. She sighed, disappointed that Túathal wanted their son dead—and his brother Verro's son killed as well, all to clear his own path to power.

I won't warn Túathal not to eat the pork, thought Gwýnnett. *Or Hibblig. Pixo can get me off this wretched place and back to civilization on one side of the Ocean or another.*

She shifted her position and continued to watch from the trees as Hibblig, Túathal, Umbrose, Sírénae, and the three wizard assassins ate slices of roast pork with apparent pleasure. It seemed like Pixo offered to fetch a plate of meat for Celéri, but the young wizard shook her head, glad to keep her feet in the cool water and converse with her uncle.

Then a pair of huge beasts covered in some sort of armored plates appeared on the beach next to the spit where most of the pig continued to roast. They bellowed angrily and swung their tail clubs widely, knocking over the spit and sending pork parts and embers flying. The swinging tails didn't hit any humans, however. Everyone who'd eaten the pork was collapsed on the sand. Gwýnnett smiled.

Your spells could check for every poison known to the Imperium, she thought. *But the yellow 'apples' I found are native to an obscure island in the sea south of Orluin and unknown to your magic. I don't know if its poisons are deadly, but they seem to be at least debilitating.*

Gwýnnett put her shell trumpet down and rubbed her palms together, then looked toward the shore to check on Celéri. To her surprise, only Pixo was present. The young wizard was gone.

Chapter 39

Eynon and Celéri

Eynon *ad hoc* gated himself and the two glyppos onto the beach at the Tempest Isles' Grand Harbor where Laetícia's bug had shown him the wizard assassins and the others were congregated. In the seconds before the glyppos reacted in anger and in terror, Eynon saw that almost everyone present was flat on the ground, unmoving, so he used tendrils of solidified sound to prod the glyppos away to the west along the arc of the hook-shaped harbor instead of risking them staying in their current positions and trampling anyone.

Turning his head, Eynon spotted Celéri not far away. She had her flying disk strapped to her back and was sitting on a rock near her uncle. With a small *ad hoc* gate jump, Eynon appeared behind Celéri, leaned down to put his arms around her waist, and performed a much longer *ad hoc* gating jump, transporting them to a familiar place he thought would provide plenty of privacy for conversation.

More by luck than by planning, the interior of Farnam's cabin on the Rhuthro was unoccupied. Eynon shifted Celéri's surprised form so she could sit in the center of a long bench placed along one side of the table where Eynon had shared spirals of baked dough with Merry months earlier. He watched Celéri wince as she put weight on her right foot. He extended his hand, and she took it as she slowly lowered herself down to the bench.

"You're hurt," said Eynon. "What happened? How can I help?"

Celéri squeezed Eynon's hand and looked up at him, trying to appear seductive but failing because pain distracted her. "The point of a spear pierced my foot," she said, extending her right leg toward Eynon. "It hurts like it's been stung by a nest of scorpions. As for what you can do to help, you can find me a healing potion, or at least kiss my injury to make it better. Then you can kiss a few other places."

"I have a healing potion," said Eynon. "I made it myself."

"Are you any good at making them?" asked Celéri. "I don't want to drink one of yours and suddenly sprout an extra arm, even though that might have certain advantages."

"The worst my potions have done is cause someone to grow an eye in the middle of their forehead," said Eynon. He leaned his flying disk against the bench, took off his pack, and started to search inside it.

Celéri shrugged her flying disk off her back and put it in the center of the table. She ran her fingers over the narrow strip of damage where the spear had gone through the disk before piercing her foot. While Celéri watched Eynon dig through the contents of his pack she generated a small sphere of transparent solidified sound to serve as a stool and help her keep her foot elevated.

"Here it is!" Eynon announced, pulling a small glass vial wrapped in leather out of his pack and holding it up to show Celéri. It was part of the bundle of six vials Uirsé had given him. "You're in luck. It's *not* one of mine."

Celéri took Eynon's wrist and pulled him down to sit on the bench beside her. She popped the cork on the vial and swallowed its contents. She smiled gratefully at Eynon then put a hand behind his head, drew him closer, and kissed him.

Eynon could taste the healing potion on Celéri's lips. Part of his mind was noticing Uirsé's potions tasted much better than the ones he'd made while the remainder of his mind was spinning from the kiss and all the thoughts it sent careening around his skull like balls in a *qua-qua* game. He moved away from Celéri on the bench.

"Didn't you like the kiss?" asked Celéri. "That *is* why you grabbed me, isn't it? Especially without Merry around?" She stretched and put weight on her right foot, pleased that the healing potion was already working its magic. "Now that I'm feeling better, we can use one of the beds in this cabin to have some fun. I'll even remove my charm that prevents conception. Imagine the children two master mages could produce!"

Eynon notice Celéri's cheeks were flushed, and her nostrils were wide. Her dark eyes danced with interest and amusement and something more he didn't want to acknowledge. He could feel heat rising in his own cheeks and stood, backing away to put more distance between them. The last time he and Celéri had been in close proximity Merry had been with him. He wished she was with him now.

"That's *not* why I brought you here," Eynon blurted.

"Why not?" said Celéri. She leaned back on the bench, rested her shoulder blades against the edge of the table, and took a deep breath, causing her chest to rise and fall. After licking her lips, she ran her fingers through her short dark hair, then took another breath, softly sighing as she exhaled. "Come closer," she said, patting the bench beside her. "It's *so* nice having someone my own age around instead of being stuck with all those *old* people, especially Umbrose's relatives. They're scary."

"Umbrose's relatives?" asked Eynon.

"The wizard assassins," said Celéri. "Períkulōs and Sikárias are his mother and father while Perkússos is apparently his uncle." She bent a finger to further encourage Eynon to sit beside her, but he remained standing.

"Why were they all on the ground?" asked Eynon. "When I *ad hoc* gated in, only you, your uncle, and Gwýnnett were standing."

"Really?" asked Celéri. "I have no idea. I had my back to the spit and wasn't hungry, so I had no reason to turn around. You say they were all on the ground?"

"And not moving," said Eynon.

"Odd," said Celéri. "I wonder if Gwýnnett poisoned them?" She stretched again, running her palms along her sides and down the outsides of her thighs. "That would be her style, wouldn't it?"

"So I've heard," said Eynon. "I felt bad about gating away without checking to see if any of them were injured, but Magister Callidus told me a squad of powerful wizards would be arriving to investigate shortly. I'm sure they'll revive the others on the Tempest Isles if Gwýnnett didn't kill them."

Celéri shrugged, unconcerned if the wizard assassins lived or died.

Eynon rummaged in his back and brought out a length of dried meat and something round wrapped in broad green catalpa leaves. He held both items out to Celéri. "Would you like something to eat?" asked Eynon. "I know that drinking a healing potion often makes me hungry. Have some venison jerky and sweet cakes. The cakes were baked by my next-door neighbor back in Haywall. They're soaked in honey and delicious."

"I mention poisoning and you immediately offer me something to eat," teased Celéri. "What am I supposed to think about *that?*"

"Ummmm..." said Eynon. He hadn't considered the awkward juxtaposition.

Celéri didn't give Eynon time to recover from his embarrassment. "If you want something *really* delicious," she said, "you'll take me over there." Celéri pointed to the pair of beds—each large enough for two— arranged against the far wall of the cabin.

"It's a very kind offer, but..."

"But what?" said Celéri. She tried to nudge Eynon closer with a tendril of solidified sound, but he blocked it.

"That's not why I want to talk to you," Eynon blurted.

"We can talk after..." said Celéri. She used two tendrils of solidified sound to try to bring Eynon closer this time. Both were intercepted. The atmosphere inside the cabin changed. It felt charged with magic like the air after a summer thunderstorm. Celéri saw Eynon stand straighter. His jaw tightened and his face grew stern. Celéri thought he looked more like Magister Callidus than an inexperienced wizard her own age.

"Would you please just *stop!*" said Eynon. "You don't have to attempt to seduce everyone around you. Especially when I think I might actually *like* you if you stopped trying so hard."

"Don't you *want* to be seduced?" asked Celéri.

"Not by someone who's so insecure she wants to be a wizard emperor," said Eynon. "Magister Callidus told us you'd said that was your ultimate goal."

"Most of the time I don't know what I hope to accomplish in the next few hours, let alone any sort of long-term plan," said Celéri. "Sometimes I want to be in charge of everything—and sometimes I have no idea *what* I want. It can be confusing."

"I think that may be one of the first honest things you've ever said to me," said Eynon. "It's also something we have in common. I'm trying to figure out what it really means to be a master mage, though sometimes I just want to go back to Haywall and milk cows. I'm often confused too, but I'm trying to do my best. Being the master mage of Dâron is a huge job with big responsibilities, so I'm talking to all the master mages on this side of the Ocean to get their advice on what it takes to do the job well."

"Why would you bother bringing me here then, if I'm as confused as you are?" asked Celéri.

"Because there might be things we can learn from each other," said Eynon. "You've been trained for years in a Roma military mage school while I've had only a few days of formal training from my mentor, Ealdamon, and a lot of making it up as I go along."

"Ealdamon?" asked Celéri. "As in Ealdamon's *Epigrams?*"

"That's right," said Eynon. "He believes in putting his apprentices through extreme testing."

"So do the Roma military mage instructors," said Celéri. "Something else we have in common." She motioned Eynon closer yet again. He circled to the other side of the table and sat on the bench opposite Celéri with her flying disk on the table between them.

"Before we talk further, I want to clarify things," said Eynon. "Some of my friends didn't want me to talk with you because they think you're as power-mad as Sírénae and as dangerous as Umbrose and the wizard assassins."

"And you don't?" asked Celéri.

"I thought you might be as scared and as overwhelmed as I am," said Eynon. "We both try too hard. My fireballs are way overpowered. I don't know my own strength or how to control it." He smiled at Celéri. She extended her right hand and squeezed Eynon's left, smiling back. Eynon gently pulled away and put his hands in his lap.

"I was and still am scared," said Celéri. "Learning I could *ad hoc* gate changed things, though."

"The mark of a master mage," said Eynon. "I had no clue what it meant, growing up on a farm on the far border of Dâron. You grew up in the capital of the Western Empire with all the magical resources of the Imperium to draw on. Part of me envies you—your libraries must be amazing."

"They are," said Celéri, "but the Imperium's military mage training involved very little reading. It was all drill and exercises to help us throw larger fireballs and more powerful lightning blasts. Magister Callidus gave his more competent and talented students books to read on advanced mathemagical topics, but our instructors were more like the equivalent of twenty-year veteran centurions in the legions, substituting magical equivalents for a legionnaire's gladius and scutum."

"Doesn't the Imperium have scholar wizards?" asked Eynon.

"Of course," said Celéri. "Mostly ones whose fireballs can't start a campfire. Unfortunately, they usually stick to their towers and academies, separate from where we battle mages practice. There's a famous scholar wizards' school in Roma Mater near the Tiber housed in a tall white building faced completely with mammoth, mastodon, and elephant tusks."

"The original ivory tower?" asked Eynon.

"You've heard of it?" said Celéri.

"In a manner of speaking," Eynon replied. "On this side of the Ocean the term is used for anywhere scholars gather away from the day-to-day concerns of the kingdom, like Dâron's Valley of the Towers or Tamloch's Institute in Bhaile Pónaire."

"I wonder what it would be like to live that sort of life..." Celéri mused. Her eyes drifted up to the ceiling without seeming to focus on anything before returning to meet Eynon's.

"I'd love to spend time in a great library studying wizardry and history and geography and..." Eynon began.

"I'd love to do the same," broke in Celéri. "Maybe we could do that together?"

"I thought you wanted to be an emperor?" said Eynon. He brought his hands back up to the tabletop and gave Celéri a tentative smile.

Celéri waved a hand, dismissing his words. "I say a lot of things I don't really mean," she said. "I'm still trying to figure out *what* I want."

"So am I," said Eynon.

Celéri lowered her gaze and extended her arm to place a hand on top of Eynon's. "You could have *me* if you wanted."

Eynon didn't pull away, allowing Celéri to keep her hand where it was. "I like you," he said, "but I'd like to get to know you better before..."

"...you sleep with me?" asked Celéri.

"That's jumping six squares ahead of ourselves," said Eynon. "Let me put it a different way. I like you—but I'm not sure *you* like you yet. I don't want to get in the way of you learning to like who you are."

"What do you mean?" Celéri looked directly at Eynon then turned away as he returned her gaze.

"It's like one of my older cousins back in the Coombe," said Eynon. "She was really pretty, but her appearance changed very quickly. She shifted from an awkward, plain-looking foal into a graceful and beautiful filly in less than a year." He watched Celéri's eyes, saw she was paying attention, and continued. "She was painfully shy and didn't know how to handle all the new attention she was getting."

Celéri nodded and motioned for Eynon to continue. She shifted her hand to hold his and squeezed.

"I was too young to really understand what was going on," said Eynon, "but the gossip in Haywall was that my cousin would take anyone who asked up to the hayloft or for a walk in the woods."

"Are those euphemisms?" asked Celéri, smiling.

"Oh yes," said Eynon. "And most of what people said back in the Coombe was quite a bit—earthier."

"I'm sure legionnaires are every bit as *earthy* as farmers," said Celéri.

Eynon proceeded with his story. "Looking back, it seems clear my cousin wanted reassurance that people liked her, and the only way she knew how to do it was to lead with her body and beauty. It gave her some control, making her popular on the outside while she was still shy on the inside."

Celéri nodded again. "What happened to her?" she asked.

"My mother told me my cousin spent the first half of her wander year camping alone in the mountains east of the Coombe," said Eynon. "After that, I'd heard she'd worked on farms at several baronies along the Rhuthro, keeping her head covered and her face dirty."

"To hide her beauty?"

"I assume so," said Eynon. "Mother said she was glad my cousin wasn't euphemisming anymore."

"There's no such word," said Celéri.

"I know, but I wanted to make you smile."

Celéri grinned. "You succeeded. Is there a happy ending?"

"Yes," said Eynon. "A young man from Wherrel, a village west of Haywall, knew my cousin from before her appearance changed. They'd played together when my cousin visited an aunt who lived next to the young man's family. He started *his* wander year several months after my cousin started hers. It took him some time to find her, but when they reconnected, my cousin realized he had loved her since before she transformed. They were friends who then became lovers and life partners."

"That's sweet," said Celéri.

"They have the cutest three-year-old daughter now," said Eynon. "The little girl has a small churn to make her own butter. I used to bring her mugs of cream before I left on my own wander year."

"It sounds like I could learn something from your cousin," said Celéri. "Will you introduce me to her?"

"That depends," said Eynon. "Will you try to conquer the Coombe if I gate you there?"

"No," said Celéri. "The Coombe sounds just fine as it is. I'm more interested in conquering the capital cities of kingdoms and provinces, if I'm going to conquer anything."

"The beginnings of wisdom?" asked Eynon.

"Don't patronize me, hayseed," said Celéri. She was still grinning, so Eynon knew she was teasing.

"Getting back to the reason I found you..." said Eynon.

"Kidnapped me," teased Celéri.

"It's difficult to kidnap a master mage who can *ad hoc* gate away wherever and whenever she wants to," said Eynon.

"You have me there," said Celéri. She eyed the beds, leaving an unspoken *and you can have me over there as well* unspoken.

Eynon intentionally ignored her intent. "Will you teach me a favorite spell of yours and share a few morsels of your newfound wisdom?" asked Eynon. "I'm serious about trying to learn from every master mage on this side of the Ocean."

"Except Umbrose?" asked Celéri.

"Except him," Eynon confirmed.

Celéri released Eynon's hand, pushed her bench back, and stood. So did Eynon. He watched her test putting weight on her previously injured foot and saw she no longer seemed to be in pain. She took a few steps toward the cabin's door then stretched—to unkink her muscles, not to seduce—and turned to Eynon. "What sorts of spells are you interested in?" Celéri asked.

"Ones you've found particularly useful," said Eynon. He moved around the table and followed her.

"I'm proud of my offensive magic," said Celéri as she reached the door. "And don't say anything you might regret."

Eynon thought better of the comment he'd been about to make and shook his head in negation.

"Blast!" said Celéri as she stepped outside. "I forgot my flying disk."

"I'll get it," said Eynon. He turned and it only took him a few strides to snatch Celéri's flying disk up off the table. His own was on his back, lightly resting on its shoulder straps. Eynon notice a thin sliver of light showed in the surface of the flying disk and realized that must have been where the spear had pierced it and continued on to stab through Celéri's foot. He stepped outside, closed the cabin's door, and handed over the disk.

"Thanks," said Celéri.

"Will it still work with a hole in it?" Eynon asked.

"Probably, but why take the chance," Celéri answered. She held the flying disk up and generated several laminated layers of solidified sound over the spear-damaged section. The cut edges seemed to melt together, repairing the damage.

Eynon watched her carefully. He'd never been taught how to make a flying disk. Nûd, at Ealdamon's request, had found one for him in a storeroom in the depths of the castle at Melyncárreg. *Maybe the steps for making a flying disk are described in one of Rōlin and Peregrína's recipe books of magic,* he considered.

"That should do it," said Celéri after running her fingers over the smooth skin of the now-healed cut. She slid her arms through the straps of her flying disk and shrugged it onto her shoulders. She looked up at Eynon—he was more than a foot taller than she was—and extended her hand. "Come down to the river and I'll show you a spell I came up with myself."

"Great," said Eynon. He took her offered hand and let her guide him. The afternoon was warm, and the sky was cloudy. Eynon's experience with the weather in this part of Dâron made him think they were in for a thunderstorm in a few hours. *Celéri is a lot like a that sort of storm,* Eynon mused. *She's powerful, beautiful, changeable, and from what I've heard, sometimes quite angry. I hope she stays friendly—but not* too *friendly—for the rest of our time together.*

When they got to the eastern bank of the Rhuthro, Celéri stopped at the narrow stretch of sand and small stones where travelers could pull their boats partly out of the water and tie them up on tall hardwood stumps left in place for that purpose. The western bank, not more than a hundred feet away, was steep and lined with boulders, scraggly bushes, and opportunistic pines finding odd bits of soil to grow in. Celéri dropped Eynon's hand, took a deep breath, and pointed.

"See that big rock," she said, indicating one of the largest boulders, a sharp-edged square piece of rock twice as big as one of the huge barrels of cider Eynon and Merry had been transporting to Tyford months, or was it lifetimes, ago.

"It's hard not to," said Eynon. He looked upslope and saw bare rock of the same composition thrusting out of the mountain and knew the boulder must have originally started there before falling to rest by the river.

"Don't say anything while I'm working my spell," said Celéri. "I need to concentrate, and concentration is the purpose of the spell. I'll make my constructs visible so you can see what I'm doing, but you'll want to keep them transparent if you use this spell in battle."

Eynon nodded, not wanting to speak and distract Celéri.

"You might want to make sure you've got your shield up," she said. "There may be shards of rock flying out at high velocities."

Inclining his head again, Eynon did as instructed, creating a broad spherical shield reinforced against impacts.

"First, I make a long cone of solidified sound," said Celéri. "The end close to us should be the size of a mammoth, and the far end, next to the target, should be as small as the tip of a scribe's quill." Without waiting for Eynon to acknowledge her words, Celéri generated a translucent cone along the lines she'd specified. It stretched from where they were standing to terminate in the center of the boulder across the river.

A sudden silence made Eynon realize he no longer heard the familiar background sounds of frogs croaking, crickets chirping, or birds singing. Even the ongoing rush of water in the river seemed softer. He checked to make sure there were no boats upstream. It wouldn't do to have unsuspecting travelers caught in whatever display of power Celéri had planned. Eynon was pleased no boats were in sight.

"Next, I generate one of my biggest fireballs and send it into the cone," said Celéri. "The cone has to be especially strong, so the fireball doesn't blow it out. All my fireball's energy will be focused on the cone's tip." She squared her shoulders and looked over at Eynon. "You may want to brace yourself," she said.

Eynon did, sending rods of solidified sound behind him to reinforce his spherical shield. He watched as Celéri opened a congruency and summoned a ball of fire as broad as the cabin was tall. She sent the flaming mass of energy flying down her cone, using a plane of solidified sound shoved behind it to ensure none of its power came back up the cone to fry them. The burning sphere passed along the length of the cone like a rat through a rattletail, bulging but not breaking its bonds of solidified sound.

"Bam!" shouted Celéri as the entire force of her giant fireball, focused down to the width of a needle, slammed into the boulder.

Eynon expected the huge rock to explode into shards rocketing out in all directions. Instead, in a definitely underwhelming display, the boulder simply disintegrated into a collection of dust and granules that slid into the river and were carried downstream by the current. He looked over at Celéri. She looked back and shrugged.

"Sorry," she said. "It's the first time I actually tried the spell at full size. Smaller fireballs on rocks the size of my fist do explode most of the time." Celéri saw Eynon raise a hand to point to his mouth. "You can talk now," she said.

"Good," said Eynon. "That was impressive. I can see it being very useful, with or without explosions."

"You say the sweetest things," said Celéri. She put a finger to her chin and bent her legs, giving Eynon a tiny curtsy, followed by a hip shimmy.

Eynon raised one eyebrow and shook his head.

"I'm still trying too hard?" asked Celéri.

"In my opinion," said Eynon. "You're likable enough without the constant attempts at seduction."

"Lots of people seem to enjoy being seduced," Celéri replied.

"Are those people the sort to be good life partners?" asked Eynon.

"There are times when I just want to have fun," said Celéri. "I can find a life partner later." She moved to stand next to Eynon and leaned her head against him. "Working powerful magic gets me excited. We could have a good time together back in the cabin, or even here on the shore if you'd like."

Eynon stepped away until Celéri was a few feet distant. "Thank you for teaching me that spell," he said. "Devising it was a clever piece of wizardry."

"You're trying to teach me something, aren't you?" said Celéri.

"Consider your recent demonstration a metaphor," said Eynon.

"If I try too hard things may disintegrate?"

"Something like that," said Eynon. "Are there any other spells you'd like to teach me?" he asked, changing the subject.

Celéri paused and considered before her face brightened and she responded. "Yes," she said.

"Another one of your own creations?" asked Eynon.

"It is," said Celéri. "This one's based on lightning, but it's a matter of subtlety, not power."

"Show me?"

"Gladly," said Celéri. "But you'll have to drop your shield first and it might be better to work this spell back in the cabin where we're less likely to be disturbed." She looked upstream, checking for boats on the river.

"Lead on," said Eynon. "This one sounds intriguing." He let Celéri take his hand again and guide him back up the gentle rise to the cabin's door. They entered and Celéri sat on the side of the wide wooden bed, patting the mattress to indicate Eynon should sit beside her. He looked uncomfortable at the prospect.

"I won't bite," she told him. "This is to teach you a new spell."

"In that case," said Eynon. He lowered himself to sit beside her, keeping a dozen inches between them.

"Some scholar mages believe our brains work by having tiny bursts of lightning jump from place to place inside them," said Celéri. "They call them sparks of insight."

"I've heard that," said Eynon. "One of my cousins had Caesar's sickness. He'd have fits from time to time and the local hedge wizard told us it was from thunderstorms inside his head."

"That's not a bad analogy," said Celéri. "A huge fireball can vaporize a boulder, but a tiny bit of lightning can have a similar effect on a human mind."

"How so?" asked Eynon.

"Let me show you," said Celéri. She put her hands on his temples, triggered her spell, and lowered Eynon carefully as he sprawled back, unconscious.

"I told you I wanted to take you to bed," said Celéri. "One way or another."

Chapter 40

Master Mages Assembled

The assembled master mages of Orluin agreed on Laetícia's plan for their attack on the wizard assassins. It wasn't because she had the most experience in magical combat—it was because she was Occidens Province's spymaster and was thought to have the most insight into their opponents' likely actions.

Laetícia's plan started by gating everyone into a cave on the side of a hill overlooking the Tempest Isles Grand Harbor, the same cave where she'd gated Eynon several weeks earlier. She hoped things would go better for her team this time than they had when Eynon was attacked by Sírénae's wizards and dragons.

"Amber and Knútr, do your best to be undetectable and scout out the section of beach where we saw the wizard assassins and the others," Laetícia commanded. "Callidus, stay with me and coordinate our defense and communications. Verro, you're on offense. Get as close to the beach as you can and be ready to cause as much damage as necessary. Callidus and I will be your backups."

The other master mages nodded. Verro tilted his head as if to ask a question.

"Yes," said Laetícia. "Be ready to gate in Uirsé and her healers if the situation warrants them." She looked around the cave's tight confines. "Ready? Go."

Amber and Knútr left first, sailing directly out of the entrance to the cave on their flying disks and immediately disappearing.

Verro paused and spoke to Callidus. "Any updates before I jump into the forge fire?"

Callidus shifted the interface for the bug that Eynon had sent back to its original location. Only two figures were standing on the beach. "We can hope that Uirsé's skills will be needed for our opponents more than for us," he said.

"It could still be a trick," Laetícia cautioned.

"I'll keep my guard up," said Verro. Faster than a bolt from a crossbow, he flew from the cave to execute his portion of their mission.

"Can our bug focus on Períkulōs, Perkússos, and Sikárias?" Laetícia asked Callidus.

"Not at present," Callidus replied. "Our bugging spell is designed to pay attention to sound and motion, so it's only paying attention to Gwýnnett and Pixo at present."

"Blast!" said Laetícia. "I'll have to add more capabilities next time, to give us more control."

"If there is a next time," said Callidus.

"Aren't you cheerful today," said Laetícia.

"Just being realistic," said Callidus. "We're going up against three, or rather four, very powerful, sneaky, and deadly mages."

"You're counting Umbrose?" asked Laetícia.

"I am," said Callidus. "I've had to work with him for years and needed, or at least wanted, a long hot soak in a caldarium after every interaction."

"I'm sorry," said Laetícia. "How much of Sírénae's megalomania was due to Umbrose, do you think?"

"It was all hers," said Callidus. "I saw that firsthand. Umbrose was simply a willing dagger in her fist, ready to strike where she directed."

"Like the rest of his family, then," said Laetícia. "They serve the wills of others—in exchange for generous fees."

"We can be thankful for that," said Callidus. "Those three wizard assassins could have been the secret rulers of the entire Imperium if that was their desire." He stared out the cave's mouth. "I wonder," he said, addressing Laetícia. "How do we know that they aren't?"

"For the same reason Umbrose wasn't a power behind Sírénae, I suppose," Laetícia replied. "They're professional killers who want to stay out of messy political machinations, preferring to practice their arts for the highest bidders."

"If that's the case, can't we just pay them more?" asked Callidus.

"Perhaps," said Laetícia. "But it would have to be quite a bit more. Let's see how things play out."

Callidus felt something buzz in his ear. It was a small cowrie shell placed there, one of a set of six enchanted by Laetícia to help the master mages stay in touch. He heard Amber's voice as the Bifurland master mage reported.

"We see seven bodies on the beach," said Amber. "They're not moving. A couple of big, armored beasts—"

"Glyppos," said Callidus.

"A couple of glyppos, then, are further up the beach annoying four black dragons."

"Annoying?" asked Callidus.

"Smacking them with something like spiked maces on their tails," said Amber. "The dragons don't appear to be amused. One looks ready to flame them."

"That's probably Mégàrotáxus," said Callidus. "She's recovering from dislocation sickness and is probably short-tempered."

"The other three black dragons must be the wizard assassins' mounts," said Laetícia.

"Provided by Gertrude of Mainz," said Knútr. "I recognize them from the Roma garrison at Septéntriacastra." The Nordland wizard's speech had a similar, though subtly different rhythm compared to Amber's.

"Are you absolutely sure the people flat on the ground aren't moving?" asked Laetícia. "Can you use distance viewing lenses to see if they're breathing?"

"We'll try to get closer and check," said Amber.

"Don't bother," said Verro.

The bug's interface in front of Callidus shifted to show Verro standing over a black-clad body.

"The wizard assassins—are they dead or alive?" asked Laetícia.

"Alive, it seems," said Verro. "I got close enough to see that their chests are still going up and down, slowly. Admiral Pixo is in shock and Gwýnnett is smiling like my brother Túathal did when he was having one of his bouts of madness. She's pacing back and forth on the sand, singing what sounds like a child's rhyme about yellow apples."

"Confirm the bodies are real and not illusionists' constructs," said Laetícia.

"And remove any magestones you find," added Callidus.

"We're here," said Amber as the Bifurland and Nordland master mages canceled their camouflage illusions and allowed themselves to be seen. "We can help search." They immediately began to check the clothing of the people on ground, starting with Períkulōs, Perkússos, and Sikárias. The northern master mages removed the wizard assassins' silver-handled obsidian dagger magestones while Verro gated out to bring Uirsé and her team of healers to the Tempest Isles.

Laetícia and Callidus *ad hoc* gated to the beach. The Occidens Province spymaster took a black onyx magestone from Umbrose and removed Hibblig's new magestone, while Callidus found his old friend Pixo and gave him several sips from a wineskin he carried on a cord over his shoulder.

"What happened?" Callidus asked Pixo.

"I don't know, I don't know, I don't *know*," said the admiral. "If I'd had a slice of meat, I'd be like *them*," he said, pointing at Sírénae, Túathal, and the others.

Amber held Perkússos' wrist. "His breathing is slow, but his pulse is fast," she said.

"There's blood in their mouths," added Knútr, who was kneeling beside Sikárias.

"Don't touch any fluids," said Laetícia, no stranger to poisons herself.

"There are morsels of meat beside them on the ground," said Amber. "I'll save them in spheres of solidified sound."

"Good," said Laetícia. "Uirsé may be able to identify the specific poison used, though I doubt it. The wizard assassins are reputed to have protected themselves from every poison known to the Imperium."

Gwýnnett changed the course of her pacing and approached Laetícia. In a child-like voice she sang, *"Yellow apples, yellow apples, from the Caiman Island come. Prickly branches, burning skins, unknown to the Imperium."*

Laetícia was spared any need to respond to Gwýnnett by the arrival of Verro by *ad hoc* gate, accompanied by Uirsé and two of her healers perched around Verro's flying disk. She reviewed the scene at a glance and stood over Túathal, her former king, checking every vital sign she could without risking damage from contact poisons.

"Get healing potions down their throats," Uirsé instructed her assistants. "They can't hurt and might help."

"Bind them before you dose them," said Callidus.

Amber and Knútr nodded and *ad hoc* gated back to King Bjarni's steading to fetch what was needed. They returned in the time it would take to recite three of Ealdamon's shorter epigrams, holding steel manacles reinforced with solidified sound they'd specifically constructed to bind mages stripped of their magestones. Without a magestone a wizard should theoretically be no more powerful than any normal human being, but with the wizard assassins they didn't want to take any chances.

As each person on the ground was bound, Uirsé's assistants poured healing potions down their throats.

Once the poisoning victims' wrists and ankles were circled in steel, Amber and Knútr paused to look at their slack faces more closely. "Their eyes are moving rapidly under their lids," the Bifurland master mage remarked.

"As if they're dreaming," added Knútr.

"Or terrified, and dying," said Uirsé. "I've seen similar reactions in patients who are paralyzed or whose minds have been damaged by eating the wrong plants." The master healer stopped by Túathal and went to her knees to examine a slice of roast pork that had fallen from her former sovereign's fingers. She sniffed and shook her head. "I don't understand," she said. "There are poisons that have similar effects, but they all have distinct odors, and I'm not smelling anything familiar."

Such scents-less violence, thought Callidus, realizing what Celéri would have likely said. Being a wiser mage, he kept silent.

"Gwýnnett's responsible, I'm sure," said Laetícia. "Verro, get her to repeat the song she sang me. Uirsé should listen, too."

Verro stepped close to Gwýnnett but didn't touch her. Instead he caged her in walls of solidified sound. "Sing for us, Princess," he instructed. "Tell us! What did you do?"

Gwýnnett sang her *yellow apples* song again. Some of the madness left her eyes and she held her hands out to Verro. "I solved your assassin problem for you," she said. "And I stopped Sírénae, Umbrose, and Túathal as well. Will you put in a good word for me with your son? I'm so very tired of all this dreary camping and hate having sand between my toes."

Verro stared at her, but didn't step away, so she took that as an invitation to continue. "Please ask Nûd to let me return to my suite in the royal palace at Brendinas. I want my flavored ices, I want my servants, I want my fine clothes, and most of all, I want my feather bed. Could you ask him for me, please, please good mage? Have pity on your nephew Dârio's loving mother!"

Laetícia felt for Verro, bound by kinship ties to this horrid woman. Gwýnnett always put her own comfort and status first. Laetícia expected Verro to tell Gwýnnett her earlier actions still merited a prison cell, but he surprised her.

"Comforts you desire and comforts you shall have, Princess," said Verro. "Removing several threats to the Orluin Alliance has earned you that."

Gwýnnett beamed, swelling up with anticipation, already imagining a return to her former privileged life.

"However," said Verro, "I could never advise Nûd or Dârio to allow you within a hundred miles of where food is prepared. Today's events have shown the utter folly of such a course."

"But," said Gwýnnett, deflating as her hopes disappeared with a louder metaphorical pop than a dozen mages *ad hoc* gating at once.

"But you should be glad to have your life—and comforts—in exile," said Verro. "We'll consult with Eynon's cartographer friends, Rōlin and Peregrína, to identify some suitably remote island and set you up there in luxury. We could even arrrange for Túathal and Hibblig to be exiled with you if you'd like."

Gwýnnett moved her chin left and right and waved her hands in strenuous negation. "No, *please,* good master mage, I want to be alone—except for servants, of course."

"Of course," said Verro. "That can be arranged." He escorted Gwýnnett to sit on a rock not far from where Pixo rested, glaring at her.

Verro imprisoned Gwýnnett with a sphere of solidified sound that would both keep her in and keep Pixo out, should he try to punish Gwýnnett for her attempt to poison him.

Behind Gwýnnett's back, Laetícia and Callidus shook their heads and offered rueful smiles. Gwýnnett, Túathal, and Hibblig were Verro's problem, and Eynon's, should he choose to express an opinion. The two Roma master mages needed to deal with Sírénae and Umbrose, while the wizard assassins were a problem for leaders on both sides of the Ocean. Valentius with Sírénae's former legions in Valentia and Quintillius, Laetícia's husband, the governor-general of Occidens Province would likely have a say. The opinions of Valens, Emperor of the South, and Phraátēs, Emperor of the East, would have even more weight in determining the ultimate dispositions of Períkulōs, Perkússos, and Sikárias.

Laetícia looked over at Amber and Knútr. The pair of gold-robed mages had finished their work immobilizing the poisoning victims and were speaking softly to each other a dozen steps down the beach. *I expect King Bjarni and Queen Signý of Bifurland, plus their counterparts in Nordland would likely contribute their thoughts on how best to address what Northern Emperor Flavia Drusilla and her puppet Gertrude of Mainz had done as well,* Laetícia considered. *If the wizard assassins lived, it would be an apt form of justice to send them back against their original employers—but that was not her decision to make.*

Uirsé and her assistants shifted from person to person on the ground, checking to see if their first doses of healing potion had helped. The master healer didn't look happy when she stood up and walked over to join Verro, Laetícia, and Callidus. Amber and Knútr shifted to be part of the conversation as well.

"Their heartbeats are slower, and their breathing is closer to normal, but I still have no idea how to counteract the whatever poison Gwýnnett used," Uirsé told the master mages. "It would be different if I had one of those *yellow apples* she's talking about to analyze, but without one, I'm not sure what I can do."

"Do we need to do anything?" asked Knútr. "Wouldn't it be better for everyone if their condition didn't improve?"

Uirsé stared at the Nordland mage. "I don't know how things work in your part of the world, but here we try to heal, not harm."

Verro put an arm on Knútr's shoulder. "On this side of the Ocean we try not to antagonize the people who put us back together after warriors and enemy wizards try to take us apart," he told the gold-robed mage.

"Isn't *that* a battle axe to the brain," Knútr replied with a sigh, using an expression that the others hoped was an idiom rather than a literal expectation.

"I could bring back one of those *yellow apples* if Gwýnnett points out where she found it," said Verro. "It sounds like that would help."

"It certainly would," said Uirsé. "How long do you think that would take?"

"Not more than an hour," said Verro. "I've already been to Caiman Island where we initially exiled Gwýnnett, Túathal, and Hibblig. Gwýnnett and I can gate there now."

"Excellent," said Uirsé. "The sooner I have a *yellow apple,* the faster I can formulate an antidote."

"Be careful," said Callidus.

"I can protect myself from caimans," said Verro.

"It's not caimans I'm worried about," said Callidus.

Verro looked over at Gwýnnett and nodded. He was about to retrieve Gwýnnett and leave when a cacophony of screeches, bellows, and roars assaulted their ears. It grew louder and the master mages watched as Thraxa flew toward them, beak snapping, pursued by a pair of glyppos who were in turn followed by an angry black dragon.

"Mégàrotáxus!" shouted Callidus.

The dragon didn't seem to hear her name and was in literal hot pursuit of the glyppos who were waving their spiked mace tails wildly behind them, trying to discourage the dragon from approaching too closely. Thraxa launched herself into the air and was about to land on top of the poisoning victims, but Laetícia covered them with a hemispherical shield of solidified sound and the snow gryffon slid off away from the prostrate people.

Callidus, who had more experience with glyppos, generated a vertical plane of solidified sound and slammed it forward directly into the glyppos to slow their charge, deflecting them closer to the water of the harbor. Mégàrotáxus finally noticed Callidus—a familiar face as the favorite rider of Xaxidiánus—and didn't release the blast of flame she'd been stoking.

To everyone's surprise, the waters of the harbor roiled, and a massive wedge-shaped head filled with sharp white teeth came up, opening wide and targeting the glyppos. The beast slid its bulk up on shore and shifted its neck and jaw, trying to swallow the glyppos whole.

"Blast it, Még!" shouted Callidus, amplifying his voice with a cone of solidified sound.

The dragon, pleased to have an approved target to flame, released jets of fire that didn't so much as discourage the black and white-scaled leviathan sea dragon as surprise it. A creature of the Ocean, it wasn't fond of fire and abruptly reversed course, slipping back under the surface of the harbor.

Mégàrotáxus preened while Callidus complimented her. The pair of glyppos were ponderously trotting away toward the eastern end of the island while Thraxa had disappeared into the nearby trees.

"That's enough excitement for one day," said Laetícia, releasing a long breath.

"Maybe for you," said Verro. "I've still got to take Gwýnnett to Caiman Island and come back with a *yellow apple.*"

"And be quick about it," said Uirsé who was busy offering sips of wine to her frightened assistants.

Verro realized he'd dropped the sphere of solidified sound holding Gwýnnett in place when his attention had been distracted. He looked over to see if he'd have to hunt her down and saw she was collapsed on the sand in front of the rock where he'd left her. "Could you check on Gwýnnett please, Uirsé?" he asked. "She'll be easier to transport on my flying disk if she's standing."

"Gladly," said Uirsé. "Try to bring back a few twigs, leaves, and bark from the tree as well—but don't touch anything. We don't know if it's a contact poison."

"I'll treat the tree with almost as much caution as I'll treat Gwýnnett," said Verro.

"That's wise," said Uirsé. She held something under Gwýnnett's nose and helped the now-revived woman to her feet, walking her over to Verro and helping her onto his flying disk.

Verro held on to Gwýnnett's shoulders and Tamloch's master mage whispered into her ear. "Be on your best behavior on this trip or I'll recommend exiling you to a frozen island north of Bifurland populated exclusively with hungry white bears." He couldn't hear Gwýnnett's reply but sensed her grudging nod and considered that a sufficient answer.

Chapter 41

Waking Up Together

Eynon woke up slowly, feeling like he'd had one too many mugs of Applegarth's Best hard cider. He could feel Merry's warm body cuddled up against him, skin to skin, and decided he could postpone opening his eyes for a few minutes. He felt soft lips kiss his and kissed back languidly, still half dreaming. There'd be time for passion when more of his brain decided to function. His red and blue magestones reassured him by their comforting presence around his neck.

"You're awake," said a voice that wasn't Merry's.

Surprise burned through his internal fog. He opened one eye and saw a tousled mass of dark hair on the pillow beside him. "What?" he mumbled, jerking himself upright. Eynon rolled out of bed, realized he was naked, and grabbed the nearest thing at hand to cover himself, which turned out to be the bed sheet. Once removed, it showed Celéri, also naked, except for the silver choker around her neck bearing her obsidian magestone. She stretched like a cat in a sunbeam and held her arms out to Eynon.

"Come back to bed," she said. "I promise you'll enjoy it."

Eynon tossed the sheet back over Celéri and saw his shirt, small clothes, and wizard's robes laid out neatly on the cabin's second bed. He crossed the intervening distance between the beds, stepped into his small clothes, pulled his linen shirt over his head, and regarded Celéri with the same wariness he'd give a hungry wolf or a rabid badger. "What did you do to me?" he asked, raising his voice as if trying to be heard on a battlefield.

"Sadly, nothing," said Celéri.

"That's not what I mean," said Eynon. "You were going to show me a new subtle lightning spell."

"I did," said Celéri. "It knocked you unconscious. That's what it does. I'd only practiced it on small animals, so I wasn't exactly sure what would happen."

"Wait," said Eynon. He stared at Celéri's body, revealed as much as hidden by the drape of the sheet. "Nothing?" he asked.

"Nothing," said Celéri, adding a soft sigh.

"But I woke up naked," said Eynon.

Celéri smiled up at him. "I did take off your clothes—and mine," she admitted. "I wanted us both to be comfortable. Weren't *you* comfortable?"

"That's not the point," said Eynon. "You knocked me out and took advantage of me. How do I know your spell didn't give me amnesia?"

"You mean you don't remember our night of shared passion?" teased Celéri.

"Stop that," said Eynon. "It's not funny."

Celéri frowned. "Be that way," she said. "What's the last thing you remember?"

"We were sitting on the bed," Eynon replied. "You put your hands on my temples—and that's the last thing I remember."

"You don't have amnesia then," said Celéri. "After you fell back unconscious, I did take your clothes off, and mine Then I cuddled into your shoulder, pulled the sheet up over us, and fell asleep." She looked out one of the cabin's three windows. "From the angle of the sun it's late afternoon. We've only been in bed together for an hour or so."

"That's not the point," said Eynon. "How would you feel if I knocked *you* out and you woke up naked in bed next to me?"

"Happy?" said Celéri.

"What if I was old and ugly, with liver spots, wrinkles, and missing teeth?" asked Eynon. "Would you still be happy?"

"Not so much," Celéri admitted. She looked up at Eynon, then averted her eyes. "You think I'm ugly?" she said in a small voice.

Eynon was impressed. In the space of a few sentences, Celéri had turned the tables on him so that now *he* was on the defensive, not her. Her ploy might have been more effective if Eynon hadn't had a younger sister. He decided he wouldn't play her game. "Yes," he said. "You're ugly—at least you act that way on the inside. You're treating me like less than a person, like a thing, and I don't appreciate it."

Half a dozen different reactions flashed across Celéri's face in succession: anger, frustration, desire, confusion, fear, and finally—remorse. Tears rolled down her cheeks.

Eynon wanted to hold Celéri and help her deal with her emotions, but he held back, knowing she had to work things out for herself. When her tears finally stopped, he leaned across the narrow space between the beds and held up one of the far corners of the sheet so she could dry her eyes.

"Sorry," said Celéri. She sat up, her knees bent, keeping the sheet covering her from shoulders to ankles.

"For?" asked Eynon, leaving the word suspended in the air between them.

"For taking advantage of you after I demonstrated my spell," said Celéri. She dabbed at her eyes again, not looking at Eynon, and a flood of words flowed out from her quivering lips. "For not treating you with respect—for trying to manipulate you—for crying—for not knowing what you want from me—for not knowing what I want from myself." She took a deep breath and lifted her chin, facing Eynon. "For everything," she concluded, looking away again.

"Thank you," said Eynon. "I accept your apologies—for everything."

Celéri's small hand inched tentatively out from under the sheet. Eynon extended his arm and took it, giving her hand a gentle squeeze. Celéri offered Eynon an uncertain smile. When he returned it, her smile grew larger. "Are we still friends?" she asked.

"We're starting along that path," said Eynon. "And your *friend* would appreciate it if you'd get dressed now."

Celéri began to drop the sheet but stopped herself. "Please pass me my clothes," she said. "And turn your back."

Eynon turned to retrieve Celéri's underclothes and purple wizards' robes from near the pillows on the second bed where he was sitting. He tossed them over and stood, facing away from her. Then he gathered up his own sky-blue robes, intending to don them shortly. As he stepped toward the other end of the cabin, he reinforced his tight shields as Verro had taught him. Eynon thought Celéri was sincere about wanting to be his friend but didn't want to hear Merry say *I told you so* if he was wrong.

When they were both fully clothed, Eynon returned to the table and sat on one side, motioning Celéri to sit across from him as they had before. He reached into his pack and put a strip of venison jerky, the leaf-wrapped sweet cakes, and his leather flask on the table between them. "I think we would both do well to eat something," Eynon told her. "I recommend starting with the sweet cake." He pulled back the leaf wrappings and slid the honey-drenched treat toward Celéri, licking his fingers when he'd done so.

Celéri broke off a piece of one of the cakes, put it into her mouth, and began to chew. Her eyebrows rose, along with the corners of her mouth. "You're right," she said. "Your neighbor's sweet cakes are delicious." She grinned at Eynon, ate the rest of her cake, and proceeded to lick honey from her own fingers.

"Help yourself to some cider to help wash it down," offered Eynon, pointing to his leather flask. Both of them drank, then shared some venison jerky.

"My hands are sticky," said Celéri when they'd finished. "I need to wash them off."

"We can walk down to the river," said Eynon.

"It's easier to bring the river to us," said Celéri. Eynon watched as Celéri made a pair of congruencies stacked a foot apart over the table between them. The smaller, upper one was the size of her palm while the lower one was twice as big. Water flowed down from the upper congruency and disappeared into the lower one without a drop landing on the table. Celéri put her hands into the stream of water and rubbed them together until the sticky honey had dissolved. When she'd finished, Eynon mimicked her motions and did the same.

"That's very convenient," said Eynon after Celéri had canceled both congruencies. "You have a lot to teach me. I can be very creative with magic, but part of me will always be a farm boy used to carrying water in buckets."

"Every new wizard serving Roma's armies learns how to open congruencies to provide the legions with water," said Celéri. "More advanced training teaches us how to open fixed gates for supply wagons."

"It's a good thing wizards like Magister Callidus couldn't open gates across the Ocean to supply Sírénae's invading forces," said Eynon. "We wouldn't have outlasted them if they weren't running out of food." He didn't mention that Fercha and Mafuta *had* developed gates across the Ocean, even if they were quite narrow.

Celéri's eyes lost their focus. She seemed to be looking at a point above Eynon's head. He recognized that her brain was working furiously considering some complex problem. His parents and sister had complained about it when he had that same look, after all. "I wonder if it's possible to set up relays of fixed gates from one side of the Ocean to the other by anchoring ships at intervals," she said after her attention to her surroundings resumed. "I'll have to ask Uncle Pixo." Her brow furrowed. "That might not work," she said. "He was always complaining about resupply problems when his ships were under sail."

"Sounds like a great question to ask Magister Callidus and your uncle," said Eynon. "Would you mind if I ask *you* a question?"

"Of course not," said Celéri.

"What was that spell you used to knock me unconscious?" he asked. "You said it involved subtle lightning, but then your fingers touched my temples and..."

"...you were out like a dimmed wizard lamp," said Celéri. "I hadn't really thought that through."

Eynon wondered if she had indeed thought it through and had planned all along for him to be unconscious so he could end up naked in bed with her, but he didn't allow his reservations to show on his face. "Can you explain what you did *without* using me to demonstrate it this time?"

"Gladly," said Celéri. "Simply put, I sent a *very* small burst of lightning into the front of your brain, from one temple to the other. It acts like pulling the clutch out on a waterwheel, disconnecting your mind temporarily."

Eynon touched his head and gave her a concerned look.

Celéri held her hands up. "I tested the spell before I used it."

"But you told me I was the first *person* you'd tried it out on!"

"The chickens seemed fine after I did it to them," said Celéri.

"You only tested the spell on chickens?"

"And rabbits," said Celéri. "And squirrels."

"What happened to your other test subjects?" asked Eynon.

"When I used too much power the chickens stopped clucking and started peeping," said Celéri. "I think they'd mentally regressed to chicks, though with chickens, it's hard to tell."

"So if you'd used too much power by accident you could have reset my brain and turned me back into an infant?" said Eynon. He tried to keep his voice from getting louder but didn't completely succeed.

"I was *very* careful," said Celéri.

"Still," said Eynon. "What happened when you tried more powerful bursts of lightning?"

Celéri didn't answer.

"What happened?" Eynon demanded. "I know you tried it."

"Moderate bursts turned chickens into chicks," said Celéri. "More powerful bursts left their bodies intact, but their brains were gone."

Eynon was about to ask Celéri how she could tell, given how stupid most chickens were, but he truly didn't find anything humorous about what she'd done to him. Still, what was done was done, and his mind seemed unharmed. *It won't help to let Celéri see my anger,* he thought. *Not if I want her to turn her back on her previous companions.*

Celéri looked at Eynon like a dog that didn't know if it would be struck or stroked.

Taking a long, slow breath, Eynon smiled at Celéri. He remembered what Magister Callidus had told him about Celéri earlier and changed the direction of their conversation. He reached out, took Celéri's hand, and spoke to her softly. "Nora told me you lost both your parents," he said. "That must have been hard."

Celéri lowered her eyes and didn't respond. Eynon squeezed her hand, and she broke the silence. "Nora talks too much."

"I think she was trying to help us understand why you always seem to have something to prove."

Celéri replied in a monotone. "My parents died in battle," she said. "They were both mages supporting one of Sírénae's legions in the mountains between Nárbo and Éberria."

"Magister Callidus told me about them," said Eynon. "He said they were two of his best."

Celéri looked up and smiled.

"He also told me they were killed by wizard assassins hired by Flavia Drusilla."

"What?" said Celéri. Her face looked like a thunderbolt. "Períkulōs, Perkússos, and Sikárias killed my parents?"

"Callidus thinks so," said Eynon.

Celéri tried to stand but Eynon held on to her hand. She glared at him across the table. "I'll kill them," she said. "I'll blast them to a crisp and make chamber pots from their skulls."

"Think things through first," said Eynon. "You don't want to attack three powerful wizard assassins on your own."

"Let me go," said Celéri. She pulled her hand from Eynon's grip and stood. "They didn't murder *your* parents!" She pushed back from the table, retrieved her flying disk from farther down its surface, and slid her feet into its foot straps.

"Don't!" said Eynon, rising himself. "You can't just—"

"Try and stop me!" said Celéri. The pop as she *ad hoc* gated away echoed in Eynon's ears for three heartbeats before it died.

Chapter 42

Verro and Gwýnnett

Verro had made sure Gwýnnett was standing in front of him, not behind him, before *ad hoc* gating them both to Caiman Island. He released her upper arm, establishing only the minimal level of touch necessary for their transition, and was pleased when Gwýnnett quickly stepped off his flying disk and onto the sand, increasing the distance between them. Nearby, a trio of caimans was working flesh from the carcass of the giant sea turtle Túathal had killed earlier and a pair of equally dead horseshoe crabs were staining the white sand with a dark ichor spreading out from their tailless bodies.

Gwýnnett noted that Brünedíxés, the western dragon who had brought Sírénae, Umbrose, and Celéri to the island, was no longer present. *Good,* she thought. The dragon had been easily fooled by Umbrose, Sírénae, and Celéri, but coping with Verro would be challenge enough for her now.

"Take off your clothes," said Verro.

"What?" said Gwýnnett. After a brief pause, she looked at Verro, tilted her hip, and smiled at Tamloch's master mage. "Here? I can think of more comfortable places if you want to dally. Sand gets into everything, don't you know?"

"You misunderstand," said Verro. "It's not *your* body I'm concerned about—it's mine. I want to ensure you don't have more exotic poisons hidden on your person that you can use on *me.*" He looked Gwýnnett up and down, then gave his head a small shake.

"You don't like what you see?" asked Gwýnnett.

"Asps and rattletails may have a certain beauty without them being desirable traveling companions," said Verro. "Get on with it."

"Right out in the open?" asked Gwýnnett.

"Yes," said Verro. "And don't protest too much. I know you have no more modesty than an actor behind a screen doing a quick change of costume between scenes."

Gwýnnett flashed him a frown.

"And no, I'm not turning my back," Verro added.

"At least actors get a screen," grumbled Gwýnnett.

"Here," said Verro. He generated a translucent cylinder of solidified sound five feet high and four feet in diameter around Gwýnnett. "I've made you a screen. Toss your clothing over the top."

"Very well," said Gwýnnett. Only her neck and head were visible above the cylinder's walls. She gave Verro what he thought she thought was a seductive smile—it wasn't—and tossed her overdress toward the wizard.

Verro caught it with tendrils of solidified sound and shook the garment, which was lightweight and utilitarian, appropriate for someone exiled to an island far to the south of Tamloch and Dâron. Using planes of solidified sound he pressed the fabric, looking for anything hidden in the folds of the dress. He found nothing.

The same wasn't true for the next layer of Gwýnnett's ensemble. He found a clamshell wrapped in large leaves in a pocket of her underskirt. Unwrapping the leaves with more probes of solidified sound revealed it contained a thick creamy liquid. Verro wrapped the leaves back around the clamshell and surrounded the potentially dangerous item in a sphere of solidified sound the size of two fists. He'd pass it along to Uirsé for her to analyze.

The underskirt also held a dozen bright red barbed seed pods. Verro created a second sphere to isolate them, double checked that both spheres would remain in place until he dispelled them, and slid them into a commodious pocket in his wizard's robes.

"Keep going," said Verro. "I need to inspect everything you're wearing."

"You've got everything I collected," said Gwýnnett. "You have the sap and the castor beans."

"Forgive me if I don't take your word for that," said Verro. "I've lived with my brother long enough to be cautious about such statements. I've protected your delicate modesty—now I need to protect my person from your poisons."

"The castor beans *are* a poison, I'll admit," said Gwýnnett. "But I'd need to process them to produce anything dangerous. The sap, on the other hand, is something new to me. I collected it so I could examine its properties if I ever returned to Brendinas."

"Less talking, more undressing," said Verro.

A white linen shift soon sailed over the top of the cylinder. There were few places to hide anything in the simple garment and Verro confirmed it was only fabric. "Now the rest of it," he said.

"You want my small clothes?" said Gwýnnett, her voice rising on the last two words.

"Yes," said Verro. "I want to make sure you're not concealing *anything* on your person. Remember, I'm the one who will decide if you go into exile on an island north of Bifurland populated by hungry white bears, or in a more civilized location."

"If you insist," said Gwýnnett. She tossed her small clothes into the air.

Verro intercepted them and they were just like the linen shift, holding nothing dangerous, *beyond,* Verro considered, *Gwýnnett herself.* He returned all her garments to her, draping them over the side of the cylinder, and waited for her to dress. When she'd done so, he dispelled the cylinder. "Let's find that tree you spoke of," he said. "We'll need more of those yellow *apples* for Uirsé to inspect so she can cure the wizard assassins."

"I don't see why you want to," said Gwýnnett. "Aren't we all better off with them paralyzed?"

"That's not a matter for me to decide without consulting the other master mages," said Verro. "Períkulōs, Perkússos, and Sikárias are citizens of the Imperium, so what happens to them is likely up to Quintillius and Laetícia, but I expect all the master mages of Orluin will contribute to a discussion about what to do."

"I'd just kill them outright," said Gwýnnett.

"I'm sure you would," said Verro, "just as you'd poison me if I gave you a chance."

"Not before you returned me to civilization," said Gwýnnett. She waved a hand away from the beach and toward the forest. "I think the *apple* tree is that way."

She began walking and Verro followed several paces behind. Large, blue-striped lizards scuttled about ahead of them, retreating toward the beach to bask. The forest, such as it was, wasn't thick by the standards of the Orluin kingdoms. They soon reached a clearing Gwýnnett remembered and just beyond it was the tall, broad tree with the small, yellow, apple-like fruits she'd collected earlier.

"Are these the *apples* you used to poison the wizard assassins?" asked Verro.

"They are," said Gwýnnett. "I don't recommend touching them—and make sure none of the tree's sap gets on your skin. I saw it paralyze and start to digest a spider when I was here earlier." Gwýnnett didn't think it was worth mentioning that *she* was the one who put a drop of sap on the spider.

"I'll be careful," said Verro. "And I'll collect some of the sap as well. Uirsé may find it useful in her analysis."

"Uirsé has no appreciation for the subtle application of the poisoner's art," said Gwýnnett.

"No," said Verro. "She's too busy trying to cure people who've been poisoned."

Gwýnnett made a face at Verro. She looked like a small child unhappy at being sent to bed early as a punishment for some minor misdeed.

Verro shook his head in response and used tendrils of solidified sound to detach several of the yellow *apples* from the tree, storing them in another sphere of solidified sound. He used a similar technique to collect several drops of sap from a few of the tree's thin branches after removing spade-shaped leaves.

Gwýnnett noticed that the blue-striped lizards avoided the tree and kept their distance. *I'm glad I never had to eat one,* she mused, remembering the one she'd killed on her previous trip through the forest. *I wonder if any larger animals live here?* she considered.

As if in response to her unspoken question, she heard twigs breaking nearby and her nose was assaulted by a stench far worse than that of a wet dog who'd been nosing about in a garbage pit. While Verro was focused on collecting samples, a creature the size of a short-faced cave bear, covered in matted hair and sporting claws the size of daggers shambled toward them. Gwýnnett saw it freeze when it saw them. She coughed to get Verro's attention.

"We have company," she said.

"I smelled it," said Verro. He finished collecting the last drops of sap and stored the spheres of solidified sound with that liquid and the apples in pockets of his wizard's robes. He turned and observed the creature. "That's an odd beast, to be sure."

"With claws like that, do you think it's dangerous?" asked Gwýnnett.

"Only to glyppos who bother it while it's feeding, I expect," said Verro. "Look at its teeth. I expect it's a fruit eater."

"You're right," said Gwýnnett. "It doesn't seem too bright, but at least it's avoiding *this* tree." She pointed at the tree with yellow *apples*. "Why isn't it moving?"

"Perhaps it's trying to hide," Verro suggested.

"From what?" asked Gwýnnett.

"Let's not stay here to find out," said Verro.

"Back to the Tempest Isles?"

"I think not," said Verro. "At least not immediately. I need to collect someone in Nova Eboracum before we return there." He removed his flying disk from his back and placed it on the ground in front of him, then stepped on it and set his feet into its leather straps.

Gwýnnett arched an eyebrow as if to say *what do you want me to do?*

"Stand in front of me facing forward like you did before," said Verro. "Not too close. I'll *ad hoc* gate us north."

Gwýnnett complied. "Will you leave me there?" she asked. "The Roma have hot baths and excellent cooks. They know how to live in comfort."

"No," said Verro. "You'll be coming with me back to the Tempest Isles eventually. The master mages assembled there can decide what to do with you."

"I hope eliminating the threat of the wizard assassins can count for *something*," said Gwýnnett.

"I expect that *will* weigh on the scales in your favor," said Verro. "Just stay on your best behavior when we get to the city."

"I will," said Gwýnnett. "I promise." She kept a mental reservation to promise to do what was in her own best interest but didn't allow that thought to show on her face, not that Verro could see it with her back to him.

Verro's flying disk rose a few feet above the forest floor and with a pop the two of them gated away.

* * * * *

No one was present in Laetícia's study when they appeared. Verro surprised the guards on the landing outside, but they were used to strange happenings and one of them agreed to escort the new arrivals to the suite in the governor-general's palace where the person Verro wanted to see was currently living.

Verro asked the guard to keep his eyes on Gwýnnett and knocked sharply on the suite's door. "If the two of you can tear yourselves away from catching up for lost time, I need to talk to you," he said.

"Go away," came a gruff male voice from the other side of the thick wooden door.

"See what they want," said a lighter voice. "I should probably visit my mother anyway. We can only spend so much of our day horizontal."

"Standing up is overrated," said the gruff voice, "but give my regards to Carys."

Verro heard footsteps approaching the door, then a bolt being slid back, then the clank of latch being lifted. The door opened and Verro saw Damon—Master Mage Ealdamon—standing before him wearing only heavy, unlaced boots and a loincloth. "Having fun?" asked Verro.

"Obviously," said Damon.

Spotting Astrí in the room, Verro waved to her. "Good to see you," he said. She moved to stand beside her husband. "Do you have something to keep him busy for a few hours while I visit my mother in Brendinas?" she asked Verro. "He can be tedious when I bring him along."

"Why should he be any different when visiting his mother-in-law?" asked Verro. He smiled at Astrí, then at Damon, to make it clear he was teasing.

"Whatever you do, please don't get him killed," Astrí instructed. "I have plans for him."

"And I have *plans* for you," Damon told Astrí.

"Hello, Gwýnnett," said Astrí when she noticed Gwýnnett under guard in the hall. "Back from your exile so soon?"

"It's a long story," said Verro.

"And I have to be off," said Astrí. "Put your robes on and go with Verro and Gwýnnett. You can tell me what it's all about when you get back—after."

"Yes," said Damon, shaking his head and looking like he'd just been fed a teaspoon of alum. "After can't come soon enough. I'll be with you in a few moments. Where's our next stop?"

"The Tempest Isles," said Verro. "We need your wisdom to help decide the future of empires."

"Of course you do," said Damon. He returned a few seconds later wearing his blue wizard's robes and carrying his flying disk. He put his disk on the stone floor next to Verro and Gwýnnett. "Let's get on with it," he said. "The future waits for no man."

Verro stared at Damon. "Are you quoting yourself?" he asked.

"I don't think so," said Damon. "I'll have to remember that one for the next volume of *Ealdamon's Epigrams*."

Chapter 43

Merry and Berrt

Merry looked out along the valley of the Rhuthro from her high vantage point atop Fercha's tower. A light breeze was ruffling her hair and making the fabric of her wizards' robes gently ripple. She noticed both her hands were clenched and consciously relaxed them, willing herself to tamp down her desire to shake Eynon until whatever was loose inside of his head reconnected. *What could he possibly think he'd learn from Celéri?* she wondered. *The Roma wizard was no more mature than a just-hatched chick.*

She shifted her head to gaze northwest in the direction of Seven Mile Cave, the place where she'd found Berrt, the troll from the Short-faced Bear Clan, and established her sanctum. Not for the first time, Merry wished *she* could *ad hoc* gate. *That must be it,* she considered. *Eynon thought Celéri worthy of his attention because she was a master mage, and master mages can* ad hoc *gate.*

Merry mentally measured the distance to the top of a mountain at the edge of her vision and prepared herself for a line-of-sight gate in the direction of the cave, then stopped. *If Eynon values master mages so highly, I'll prove myself to be one,* she decided. *Small steps first. I'll try gating back to my sanctum. Every wizard can generate an emergency gate, after all, so it will be a good test. Perhaps I can jump off Fercha's tower without my flying disk to put my life at risk?*

She leaned her head over the tower's parapet, saw sharp rocks poking out of the river below, and decided jumping off was not the action she would opt for. *It wouldn't prove anything, anyway,* she realized. *Master mages can* ad hoc *gate without their lives being threatened. Still, jumping to her sanctum would surely be easier than trying to jump to the Tempest Isles directly.* She shook her head. *I might end up in the middle of the Ocean with no sense of where to find the closest land if I tried to jump directly to the Tempest Isles. Better to try something shorter as my first* ad hoc *gate attempt.*

Merry stepped onto her flying disk, closed her eyes, and visualized the cavern where she'd established her sanctum. She thought about how much of an idiot Eynon was and how much she wanted to prove herself, but that didn't help her—she remained anchored to the stones of the tower. Then she considered when she'd learned how to line-of-sight gate at the park in Nova Eboracum. *That style of gating won't help me with my eyes closed,* thought Merry. She opened her eyes for the time it took to blink and closed them again, reminding herself she needed to sharpen her focus the way she did when turning a broad sunbeam into a narrow rod of tight light.

She began to take long, slow breaths, filling her lungs through her nose and letting the air out between her lips, feeling the discipline of doing so quiet her brain and center her. She sensed her magestone and sent slow pulses of its magic through her with the same rhythm.

Her thoughts, unbidden, turned to times she'd taken a coracle out on the river, found a secluded, well-shaded spot, and read books until her head was full of wonders. Merry smiled. *Books can take me anywhere.* Holding her calm joy in her mind, she pictured the cavern deep inside Seven Mile Cave where she'd established her sanctum, put her hand to her magestone, and willed herself to travel there.

The sudden change in temperature surprised Merry, though in hindsight, she realized it shouldn't have. The cavern where she now found herself was decidedly cooler than standing in the sun on top of Fercha's tower had been, and there wasn't any wind in her new location. She opened her eyes, looked around, and realized she was *not* standing in the circle she'd inscribed to mark her destination, but instead had transported herself to arrive a few feet away.

"I *didn't* emergency gate!" she said. "I really did *ad hoc* gate. That makes me master mage!"

"Is that a good thing?" asked a familiar deep voice. Berrt was standing by the entrance to the cavern.

Merry noticed that Berrt's magestone was no longer inserted into his beard. Her new friend had crafted a setting for that egg-sized piece of sparkling quartz, inserting it into a torus of gray chert that he'd hung on some sort of cord around his neck. After appreciating how easy it now was to see around her, she realized her sanctum, far from being a dark cave, was well-lit by wizard lamps floating at intervals around the space. "It's a *very* good thing," she told Berrt. Merry stepped over to stand beside the troll and hugged him with such exuberance that Berrt lifted her off her feet as easily as if she were a child's doll and spun her around to help her celebrate.

"Congratulations," he said after he'd put Merry down. "I'm not quite sure what it means, but I'm happy for you."

"It means I now have equal standing to any other master mage in Orluin," said Merry.

"Can *you* teach *me* now?" asked Berrt. "You were looking for a master mage to instruct me."

"I could and will, but I haven't been a wizard all that long and I just became a master mage," said Merry. "You need someone with more experience in magic as your teacher." She gestured at the lights around her sanctum. "Not that you've been slow about learning new spells, it seems."

"Light spells come easily to me," said Berrt. "It was always so dark here in Seven Mile Cave that I treasured the light from the small fires I made to cook snakes, small game, and fish. I want to make every chamber in the entire cavern complex bright—except when the light bothers sleeping bats."

"Are there lots of bats here?"

"Tens of thousands of them," said Berrt. "Millions, maybe. I didn't put lights in their sleeping caverns. I don't really like going in those caverns anyway."

"Don't like bats getting in your hair?" asked Merry.

"No," Berrt replied. "I don't like guano getting between my toes. There's a layer of white sludge several inches thick in there and it smells."

"It sounds like you're wise to avoid their sleeping caverns then," said Merry. "I'll have to remember *not* to bring Ace, my familiar, with me when I visit you in the future," she added. "He's a rockhound and loves to eat bats."

"A rockhound?" asked Berrt.

"Ace is difficult to explain," said Merry. "Sometimes he looks like a rock, sometimes like a dog, and sometimes like a large flying squirrel."

"That does sound difficult to combine in one creature," said Berrt. "I guess I'll just have to wait to meet him."

"I think Ace will like you, once he gets to know you," said Merry.

"And I expect I'll like Ace as well, so long as he doesn't eat too many bats. These eat insects and cut down on the number of bugs that bother me when I leave to look for rabbits."

"It's a good thing when various species don't get out of balance," said Merry. "I'll make sure Ace keeps his appetite in check when he comes with me on visits."

"I appreciate it," said Berrt. "What will you do now that you're a master mage? Is there a school for master mages?"

"There's not a formal school," said Merry, "but Eynon—he's my partner—is getting lessons from other master mages." She paused and frowned. "*All* the master mages on this side of the Ocean."

"Is something wrong?" asked Berrt.

Merry's frown didn't leave her face. "You could say that," she replied. "Eynon is off getting master mage lessons from Celéri."

"Who's that?"

"A young Roma woman from the Western Empire three thousand miles away," said Merry. "She's one of the battle wizards in Sírénae's invading army and only learned how to *ad hoc* gate a few weeks ago. Before that she tried to spy on us when we were gathering honey."

"She's your enemy?" asked Berrt.

"I'm not sure," said Merry. "I don't even know if she knows which side she's on—it may change with the angle of the sun in the sky or the phase of the Moon."

"That sounds like a common state for young people your age, be they your kind or mine," said Berrt. "Not that I'm ever likely to have children of my own."

"Teen years can be a trial, and not just for parents," said Merry. "Why don't you think you'll ever have children?"

"I'm alone here," said Berrt. "My people dispersed and went into hiding to avoid your people. I've been too afraid to roam around in search of other trolls to court and mate, since we've been hounded and persecuted for centuries, in the Imperium and here in Orluin once we took our ice boats to these shores." He shook his head. "There weren't many of us to begin with, and if we can't meet and mate there will soon be fewer still."

"I might be able to help you find others of your kind," said Merry. "Do you know about my people retreating to caves to hide from Sírénae's invasion?"

"Of course I do," said Berrt. "Several hundred of your people occupied the outer caverns here at Seven Mile Cave, forcing me to go deeper into the cave complex to avoid them. It was a challenge to get enough to eat." Berrt rubbed the furs covering his abdomen. "Thank goodness for fish in the lake six miles in."

"There's a lake down here?" asked Merry.

"Indeed there is," said Berrt. "The fish that swim in it are blind, but they were still drawn to my torches. That makes them easier to catch."

"You'll have to show me this lake—later," said Merry. "Let me get back to how I can help you. I heard from my friend Dârio—he's king of Tamloch, that's the northern kingdom, and he led quite a few people to safety in a very large cave complex far to the south of here."

"If he's king of a northern kingdom, why was he in caves to the south?"

"Dârio used to be king of Dâron," said Merry. "That's the kingdom your cave is located in. Now my friend Nûd is king of Dâron and Dârio is king of Tamloch."

"It sounds complicated," said Berrt. "It also sounds like you're someone with friends in high places."

"You're right on both counts," said Merry, "but the important thing is a story Dârio told me about when he was hiding from invaders in caves. He said that food was disappearing from the supplies they'd brought at a faster rate than they'd expected. He thought it might be his own people taking more food than they should, but what if it was some of *your* people taking food so they could have something to eat, since they couldn't go out to forage? I could help you find that cave complex and perhaps locate more of your people."

"That would be wonderful," said Berrt. "But wouldn't your people be afraid of me? I don't want farmers with pitchforks or soldiers with spears chasing me. I went through too much of that just to get to Seven Mile Cave."

"I'm sorry you had to endure such mistreatment," said Merry. "People are afraid of what they don't understand, and you do look somewhat frightening to my people." She gave Berrt a long look. "I think we could make you look less fearsome rather easily, if you don't mind," said Merry.

Berrt shrugged his massive shoulders.

"Good," said Merry. "Then it's time to take you home to meet my parents."

* * * * *

Berrt had been surprised by Merry *ad hoc* gating him to Applegarth, but unlike a dragon with disorientation sickness, he recovered quickly. The troll mage looked much less threatening after a quick bath in the river, using hot water initially provided by Merry and soon controlled by Berrt himself after Merry taught him how to access congruent heat sources. Mabli, Merry's mother, gave him several bars of apple-blossom scented soap and Berrt scrubbed himself with a fleece until years of dirt and grime from living in a cave were rubbed away. He looked much younger now, perhaps only in his early twenties.

Merry and Mabli worked together to cut Berrt's hair using a combination of sheep sheers and scissors, leaving it trimmed back to hang just over his big ears. While they were practicing their sartorial skills, Derry, Merry's father, found small clothes and a tabard big enough to fit Berrt that had belonged to one of his more muscular baronial guards. Adding a dark blue hooded cloak completed Berrt's transformation from a fearsome troll into a far-less-threatening, even somewhat handsome, individual. His nose and brow were still on the outer edge of the human norm, but both features were largely hidden in the shadows of his hood. To Merry and Berrt's surprise, the entire process had only taken an hour and a half.

"Now we can go after Eynon—and Celéri," said Merry, after nodding her approval at Berrt's appearance. She hugged both her parents and informed them that she'd be *ad hoc* gating away in a moment. Berrt put his giant tortoiseshell flying disk on the flagstones of the courtyard at Applegarth and Merry placed her flying disk beside it. She took Berrt's hand in one of hers, waved to Derry and Mabli with the other, centered her thoughts, and popped out, leaving a small circle of dust spinning behind.

Chapter 44

Celéri's Vengeance

Celéri appeared on the beach at the Tempest Isles beside the spot where she'd been sitting earlier. The other master mages were gathered a dozen feet away, deep in conversation with her Uncle Pixo. Their voluminous robes blocked her view of the beach behind them.

"Where *are* they?" shouted Celéri. "Where are the wizards who killed my parents?"

Pixo turned and stepped toward Celéri, his arms outstretched. Laetícia, Amber, and the other master mages present watched her with concern. Callidus was about to speak when a black silk scarf reinforced with steel wire held by Períkulōs encircled his throat. Perkússos used his scarf to do the same to Amber while Umbrose wrapped a thin rope around Knútr's neck and began to twist it tight. Sikárias, holding her own black scarf, seemed to take particular pleasure in choking Laetícia. Simultaneously, Sírénae, applying force more directly, had circled Uirsé's neck with her forearm, squeezing her biceps to deprive the master healer of life-giving air.

Distracted by her uncle's attempt to comfort her, Celéri didn't realize what was happening for a few crucial seconds. When she finally realized the other master mages were being attacked, she wasted precious time trying to determine how to stop Sírénae, Umbrose, and the wizard assassins without injuring their victims, whose faces were already turning the dark blue of the dragon on Dâron's flag.

Celéri had finally decided to generate an extremely bright sphere of light to blind the attackers, making them more vulnerable to her next, more targeted spells, when Eynon gated beside her, wrapped his arms around her waist, and *ad hoc* gated them both away without pausing to the notice the attacks elsewhere on the beach.

Admiral Pixo turned and took in what was happening with the insight of a seasoned military commander. He immediately understood

Sírénae to be the weakest of his potential opponents and ran toward her as quickly as his gamy leg would allow, tucking his body low and rolling into the deposed emperor and the healing mage with the full weight of his body and accumulated inertia, knocking them both to the ground. He accomplished his purpose and Sírénae was forced to release her hold on Uirsé as they fell.

Callidus, Amber, and Knútr were still struggling against the garrotes around their necks. Laetícia grasped the scarf held by Sikárias, trying to prevent it from completely cutting off her air supply. She twisted her head from side to side, lashing Sikárias with the beads at the ends of her braids and marking the wizard assassin's face with small pocks where they struck.

On the beach behind the attackers, Hibblig and Túathal were slowly rising to their feet. The healing potions that had revived the others were working on them at last. They looked at each other, nodded, and moved toward the master mages under attack, whose struggles to breathe were diminishing as the last bits of air left their lungs.

* * * * *

"Let me go, you fool!" shouted Celéri as she and Eynon appeared in the sky a hundred feet above a broad, slightly domed expanse of exposed limestone surrounded by thickly forested mountains. "I've got to go back to the Tempest Isles and kill those thrice-blasted wizard assassins!"

"We need to talk first," said Eynon.

"I don't need to have a conversation with a wizard known for acting without thinking," said Celéri. "You're not the one to hold me back—and you've cost me the element of surprise. I could have taken all of them if you hadn't gated me out."

"You don't need to kill them," said Eynon. "They've done enough that Imperial justice should accomplish the end you seek."

"If you believe that, you're a bigger fool than I'd thought," said Celéri. "They're the emperors' tools, operating in the shadows, but under the protection of one emperor or another."

"Then they'll face justice at the hands of the Orluin Alliance," said Eynon. "Bjarni, Nûd, and Dârio will deal with them if the Roma won't."

"Only if they're alive to do so," said Celéri. "All three of those monarchs are targets for assassination."

"We won't let that happen," said Eynon. "They're all unconscious and we can imprison them so they can't do any more harm."

"You're missing a key bit of information," said Celéri. "The wizard assassins are already awake and attacking the other master mages. We have to go back *right now* to stop them."

"What?" said Eynon. "They're awake?"

"Yes, fool!" said Celéri. "We stand a good chance because they don't have their magestones—yet. But that could change quickly, and your friends, and mine, are in trouble."

"Don't we need to make a plan first?" asked Eynon.

"To the depths of the Ocean with planning," said Celéri. "I just want to kill them!"

Celéri *ad hoc* gated away, followed by Eynon before the air could flow in to replace the space she'd vacated.

* * * * *

Merry and Berrt appeared on the flagstones outside the door to Farnam's cabin up the Rhuthro from Applegarth. She opened the cabin door and was disappointed to find it empty and only one of its beds unmade. She'd hoped to find Eynon and Celéri there, since it was a favored spot for Eynon to hold long, private conversations. It appeared, however, that Eynon and Celéri had done more than just talk. She returned outside and gave Berrt a smile, of sorts.

"Eynon's not here," she said.

"Your mate?" asked Berrt.

"Yes," said Merry. "My so-called partner in life. He's been completely obtuse lately."

"An angle of more than ninety degrees?" asked Berrt. "That's not right."

"It certainly isn't," said Merry. "I'll show him there's another master mage in Orluin he has to learn from."

"I'm sure you'll be an excellent teacher."

"Thank you," said Merry. She glanced at her left hand as a familiar ring decorated with an apple design began to vibrate. It was the first gate ring Eynon had made. Merry removed the ring and expanded it to a two-foot diameter as the air outside the cabin echoed with the ring's three clear chimes.

"Merry," said Eynon from the other side of the interface. "I need your help."

"I'm sure you do," Merry replied.

Eynon expanded the gate ring to an eight-foot diameter and stepped through to join Merry and Berrt. He hugged Merry, released her, finding her response to his hug less enthusiastic than usual. After stepping back from Merry he extended his hand to Berrt. "Nice cloak," he told the troll. "Is this your new wizard friend?" Eynon asked Merry.

"Yes, this is Berrt," said Merry. "He's a natural talent as a wizard and is very strong as well." She was about to tell Eynon she could now *ad hoc* gate but he interrupted her. "We don't have time to talk," he said. "We have to stop Celéri."

"Stop her from doing what?" asked Merry.

"I'll tell you when we get there," said Eynon.

"Get where?" asked Merry.

"The Tempest Isles," said Eynon. He looked at the trees near the clearing and cut a heavy branch from an oak with a plane of solidified sound, trimming it into a makeshift club and conveying it to Berrt on tendrils of force. "You may need this," he told the troll. Then Eynon gathered Merry and Berrt beside him and motioned for them to board their flying disks. He held their hands and *ad hoc* gated all three of them to a cave above the beach on the Grand Harbor at the Tempest Isles. It was the same one where he and Laetícia had observed Sírénae's invasion fleet where they'd stopped to ride out a storm *en route* to Orluin months earlier.

* * * * *

Verro, Damon, and Gwýnnett *ad hoc* gated unto the beach twenty yards away from where the struggle was in progress. They watched Laetícia, Magister Callidus, Amber, and Knútr fall to the sand and saw Túathal and Hibblig—their loyalties to Orluin proving stronger—stab Umbrose and the wizard assassins from behind with their makeshift pointed horseshoe-crab-tail swords. Unfortunately, all four wizards were wearing hardened leather under their robes and the sword strikes bounced away without doing significant damage.

Períkulōs and Perkússos whirled around and grabbed Hibblig and Túathal by their robes. They tugged the two together, then bounced Hibblig's head against Túathal's before pushing the stunned pair to the ground, claiming their horseshoe-crab-tail swords in the process. Verro and Damon readied offensive spells while Sikárias reclaimed the wizard assassins' and Umbrose's magestones from a pouch on Laetícia's belt. All four of them had their magestones returned in time to interpose shields of solidified sound between themselves and Verro's lightning bolts as well as Damon's focused force beams of tight light.

A few feet distant, Pixo held Sírénae's throat in the crook of his elbow while his legs were wrapped around her waist, pinning her to the sand. Uirsé's chest was expanding and contracting, but her eyes hadn't yet opened. The admiral squeezed his arm, trying to remove at least one player from the *shah mat* board while not drawing attention to himself from the wizard assassins, who were more attentive to Verro and Damon. Gwýnnett, meanwhile, slowly stepped back from her traveling companions, hoping not to be caught in whatever spells the wizard assassins sent in return.

Sírénae, now unconscious, didn't see Verro and Damon trapped inside four concentric ten-foot diameter spheres of solidified sound, each sphere cast by a different opponent. In time to the motions of the nodding head of Períkulōs, Umbrose and the wizard assassins rapidly shrank the diameter of their spheres from ten feet to five, then four, compressing Verro and Damon into contortions to avoid being crushed.

In a well-practiced maneuver, Sikárias generated a congruency linked to the near vacuum a thousand miles up inside the contracting spheres, exhausting any air within them so rapidly that neither Verro nor Damon were able to open their own congruencies linked to a more breathable atmosphere. In seconds, the two master mages' bodies went slack and fell into an interwoven pile at the bottom of the shrinking spheres.

"Take their magestones!" Perkússos shouted to Umbrose after the contracting spheres disappeared.

"Yes, uncle," Umbrose replied. He collected Damon and Verro's magestones, then moved on to gather up the magestones belonging to

Hibblig, Laetícia, Amber, Knútr, and Callidus, who were all lying inert on the sand. He joined his parents and uncle with his trophies and gestured toward Pixo, Uirsé, and Sírénae. "What shall we do about them?" he asked.

"The admiral and the healer may still have their uses," said Períkulōs. "Let them live for now. As for Sírénae, I'll leave her status up to your discretion. Revive her or kill her as you wish. I'm sure a case can be made for either outcome."

"True enough, father," said Umbrose. "She's given me plenty of reasons to wish her dead, not least of all threats to feed me to her former pet, but she may yet have her uses. Perhaps you can consult your clients and see what *they* would prefer?"

"There's no love lost between Flavia Drusilla and Sírénae," said Sikárias.

"But Gertrude of Mainz was technically one of Sírénae's protégés," said Perkússos.

"I don't know if that would make Gertrude less or *more* likely to want Sírénae dead," said Umbrose.

"Keep her alive until we get confirmation then," said Períkulōs. "Remember, we still have to eliminate the kings of Dâron and Tamloch."

Sikárias pointed to Laetícia's prone form a few steps away on the sand. The Occidens Province spymaster's chest still rose and fell, but her eyes were closed. "True enough, but we've made progress on our commission. For one thing, we have a hostage Quintillius values every bit as much as his children," she said. Waving beyond Laetícia to Amber and Knútr, she added, "Plus a way to guarantee the cooperation of Bjarni and Signý as well."

"We're ahead of schedule then," said Perkússos. "Do we need to wait for the royal weddings before we kill Nûd and Dârio or can we eliminate them now and get back across the Ocean sooner, rather than later?"

"I vote for now," said Sikárias. "They're probably both already at the Great Falls, so they won't be hard to find."

"But none of us know how to *ad hoc* gate there," said Períkulōs.

"The healer can take us," said Perkússos. "And if she can't *ad hoc* gate us there herself, we have maps and can interrogate a few locals to get directions if we have to ride our dragons. They should have had enough rest to manage the trip."

"Let's get on with it then," said Períkulōs.

"What about the master mages?" asked Umbrose.

"We bind them and take them with us," said Sikárias. "I've got some sleeping potions to ensure they don't cause us any trouble. Our dragons are strong enough to manage the extra weight."

"And we could make a lot of money ransoming the master mages back to their kingdoms," said Perkússos.

"Though once we kill the two kings, who would pay the ransoms?" asked Períkulōs.

"Flavia Drusilla might find uses for captive master mages," said Sikárias. "She has potion makers who can bend even master mages to her will."

"Sounds like a good reason to round up Gwýnnett and bring her along, too," said Perkússos. "Flavia Drusilla's potion makers might learn something from that one." He spotted the princess a hundred yards from them trying to hide behind a far-too-small rock.

"All in all, we've done quite well," said Sikárias. She motioned her family members closer and hugged Períkulōs, Perkússos, and Umbrose each in turn. "Now," she said, indicating her husband and brother-in-law. "You two get our dragons. Umbrose and I will administer sleeping potions and bind the master mages."

The others nodded—then the sky exploded. A shockwave like Vesuvius erupting knocked Umbrose and the wizard assassins to the sand. Above them, a human shape that sparked like a fiery bird glowed in red-hot fury and an amplified voice resounded with words meant for the wizard assassins.

"You killed my parents! Prepare to die!"

Celéri had taken time to link a congruency not to the corona of the Sun, but to its core. A measure of star stuff no larger than a grain of pollen pulsed inside a shell of solidified sound that barely seemed able to contain it. With a scream of inchoate anger Celéri threw the burning sphere toward Umbrose and the wizard assassins—its power was so great it was likely to turn the entire beach for hundreds of yards into a plain of molten glass.

The sun core fireball never struck, however. Eynon appeared, flew near Celéri, and generated a congruency that intercepted the burning sphere on its downward trajectory and sent it through to a point above the waters a dozen miles to the north. They saw the results of it striking the Ocean, sending up an immense column of superheated steam.

"Why did you stop me!" shouted Celéri. "They all deserved to die!"

"You would have killed everyone on the Tempest Isles with that blast," said Eynon. "Including yourself. Did *you* want to die?"

"I'd have gated away before that happened," said Celéri.

"What about your uncle and his sailors?" asked Eynon. "What about the master mages? You would have vaporized them all."

"I didn't think about them," said Celéri.

"That's right, you didn't," said Eynon. "And now we have to focus on holding off four powerful mages." He generated a sphere of solidified sound around himself and Celéri, blocking the energy of lightning strikes simultaneously sent up from Umbrose, Períkulōs, Perkússos, and Sikárias.

"Leave me alone," said Celéri. "I have to avenge the deaths of my parents."

"By dying yourself?" asked Eynon. "You will, if you persist in trying to take on Umbrose and the wizard assassins without help."

"Who will help me?" asked Celéri. "You?" She shook her head while using her own magic to strengthen the sphere around them. "You just keep trying to *stop* me."

"Stop you from killing yourself and other good people, perhaps," said Eynon. He put a hand on her forearm and *ad hoc* gated them both to the cave above the beach where he had transported Merry and Berrt not long before. Eynon disguised the cave's entrance with illusions so he and Celéri could observe what was happening on the beach without being seen themselves.

Celéri pulled away from Eynon and stared down at Umbrose and the wizard assassins. They seemed to be congratulating each other on forcing Celéri and Eynon to retreat. "Thank you *so* much," she told Eynon. "You've lost me the element of surprise."

"Maybe not," said Eynon. He explained what would soon be happening and watched Celéri smile. She looked like a house cat who had just recruited a panther to deal with a quartet of hungry rats in the pantry.

"Did you *plan* this?" Celéri asked.

"No," said Eynon. "But I did use your Sun-core fireball for our advantage."

"How long do we have?" asked Celéri.

"Not long," said Eynon. "We'll have to make ourselves invisible and collect everyone from the beach. There should be room for all of them in the back of this cave. It's high enough above the Ocean to be safe, I hope. Then I'll figure out how to reclaim our master mages' magestones from Sikárias. The important thing is for us to move quickly."

"I can move faster than the wind when I need to." She glanced at Eynon and shook her head. "I expect you think I'm always acting too fast without taking time to think things through." She laughed. "My parents gave me my name because I arrived so quickly on the day I was born," she said. "Celéri means swift."

"We'll need every bit of your speed," said Eynon. "Look to the north. It's coming already. You get Uirsé, plus your uncle and his sailors. I'll get the remaining master mages and Gwýnnett."

"What about Sírénae?" asked Celéri.

"I think you know what I'd say," said Eynon.

"Fine," said Celéri. She stamped her foot on the center of her flying disk and gave Eynon a look that would have curdled milk. "You'd give sweet cakes to a man who robbed you."

"Probably not," said Eynon. "But I wouldn't starve even a thief in my custody." He tapped a ring on his left hand and spoke into it briefly, then turned to Celéri. "Ready?" he asked.

"Ready," she replied. Both Eynon and Celéri disappeared from sight but not from the cave. Then, in a rapid series of *ad hoc* gating by the pair of young master mages, the unconscious bodies of everyone on the beach save for Umbrose and the wizard assassins appeared farther back inside the cave. Uirsé, who was *not* unconscious, began to tend to the others.

Eynon and Celéri made themselves visible again and stood in the entrance to the cave high on a hill near the beach, watching the Ocean to the north. Above them, on the summit of the hill, they heard the bellows and grunts of large beasts that puzzled Celéri, though they made Eynon smile.

Below, on the beach by the Grand Harbor, Umbrose and the wizard assassins stood back-to-back in a defensive posture, awaiting an expected magical attack.

"We can take the pouch where Sikárias put the master mages' magestones when she first sees what's coming from the north," Eynon told Celéri. "That should be enough of a shock to distract her attention."

"I'd rather slit her throat while her focus is elsewhere," said Celéri.

"No sweet cakes for you," said Eynon.

"Wait," said Celéri. "What about the wizard-assassins' dragons?"

"I've seen to that," said Eynon, holding up his left hand. "They've been warned."

"Good," said Celéri.

The two young wizards watched as a wall of water taller than Laetícia's tower in Nova Eboracum swept down toward the Tempest Isles' Grand Harbor with the speed of a charging war elephant. In the seconds when Umbrose and the wizard assassins were frozen in shock, Eynon—making himself invisible with illusion magic—gated in and took the pouch holding the master mages' magestones from the belt around the waist of Sikárias. He immediately *ad hoc* gated back to the cave above the beach and was pleased to see Celéri holding three obsidian magestones.

"You got them?" said Eynon.

"For all of them except Sikárias," said Celéri. "I didn't want to risk bumping into you."

"That was wise—for once," said Eynon, smiling at Celéri.

"As if *you're* known for your wisdom," Celéri replied. "Look!" She pointed at the beach where the tidal wave, focused by the geometry of the Grand Harbor, grew even larger as it swept relentlessly down on the beach. Sikárias only had time to surround herself and her family members in a reinforced bubble of solidified sound before the wall of water struck. It crossed the quarter-mile strip of land forming the southern border of the Grand Harbor without losing any of its power, carrying rock and coral and trees and vegetation along in its wake. The bubble holding Sikárias and her family spun like a child's top and rode the crest of the wave far to the south before passing out of the young wizards' sight, even augmented with distance-viewing lenses of solidified sound.

Eynon pointed up and Celéri's gaze followed his arm to spot four dragons circling overhead, well away from the great wave's awful reach. "Merry warned them," Eynon announced. "She also warned Pixo's fleet at the east end of the Tempest Isles and got the glyppos to safety. They're grazing on the side of the hill above us."

Off to the east another flying creature circled. This one was smaller than the dragons and the white of her fur and feathers was lost against the background of clouds.

Celéri nodded and noted just how close the top of the wave had come to their cave. A scant twenty feet below them the hill had been scraped clean. "How did you know we'd be above the water in this cave?" she asked Eynon.

"I didn't," he replied. "I just figured I could protect us with shields of solidified sound if your Sun-core fireball had even more energy than I'd expected. Imagine what would have happened if it had struck the beach."

"I don't want to think about it," said Celéri. She gestured to draw Eynon's attention to the scene on what had been the beach below them. The land at the southern end of the broad fishhook forming the Grand Harbor was gone, replaced instead by open water and an isolated arc of land to the west.

"So much for the Grand Harbor," said Eynon.

"Roma wizard engineers can build it back," said Celéri.

"If you say so," said Eynon.

"Do you think we've seen the last of the wizard assassins?" asked Celéri.

"Of course not," said Eynon. "But it will take some time for Sikárias to get Umbrose and her fellow wizard assassins back to land, and by then we'll have all the master mages revived and ready for her. As a single wizard, I doubt she'll be much of a problem for us."

"I hope you're right," said Celéri. She stepped close and was hugging Eynon just as Merry floated down on her flying disk from the top of the hill to join them at the cave's mouth.

"Am I interrupting anything?" asked Merry.

Eynon stepped away from Celéri and rushed to pull Merry from where she hovered. He embraced her with an enthusiastic vigor comparable to the energy of the giant wave. Shaking her head, Celéri turned and walked deeper into the cave, but Eynon and Merry didn't notice her departure. After a long minute, Merry finally broke their connection and took a deep breath.

"You held me so tight I could barely breathe," Merry told Eynon. "I guess you're glad to see me, but is that any way to treat a master mage?"

"What?" said Eynon, holding Merry at arm's length so he could look her up and down with new eyes.

"That's right," said Merry. "I can *ad hoc* gate now."

"I'm *so* glad!" said Eynon. He put his arms around Merry, pulled her close again, and they kissed, oblivious to all around them.

Chapter 45

Berrt to the Rescue

"Ahem," said Celéri. She had returned from observing Uirsé and her Uncle Pixo reviving the master mages farther back inside the cave.

Eynon and Merry stopped kissing but didn't break their hug.

"We still have to deal with Sikárias, Umbrose, and the other wizard assassins," Celéri continued, sounding enough like Magister Callidus instructing erring students to make Eynon smile.

"Ummm," said Eynon as Merry distracted him by kissing his neck.

"Stop that," Celéri commanded. She glared at Eynon. "You told me I had to rescue Sírénae from the great wave—now we have to rescue, or at least *find* the wizard assassins to make sure they're not lost out on the Ocean."

Merry sighed and stepped back from Eynon while continuing to hold his hand. "I suppose we must," she said. "I expect they'll never be more vulnerable than they are now if we can locate them. We don't have any idea how far the wave could have carried them."

"They don't have much choice except to return here to the Tempest Isles," said Celéri. "I've seen my uncle's charts and there's no other land for hundreds of miles in all directions."

"I guess we don't want them to drown," said Eynon.

"Though Sikárias *does* still have her magestone," said Merry. "We saw her create a protective bubble, but do you think she has the strength to *fly* everyone back here?"

"Or the power to *ad hoc* gate them all back?" asked Eynon. "Four people at once must be challenging."

"You gated two glyppos," said Merry. She wagged a finger at Celéri. "And *she* gated a *dragon!*"

"I'm sorry, I didn't know about disorientation sickness," said Celéri, making her words sound like more of a protest than an apology. She smiled at Eynon and frowned at Merry before continuing. "But that's not important right now," she said. "The key thing is that we might have four unhappy wizard assassins appearing on the beach in the near future."

Eynon rubbed his chin. "Can you gate back to a place if it no longer exists?" he mused.

"What do you mean?" asked Merry.

"If the only place on the Tempest Isles Sikárias has ever been was the beach..." he began.

"And since the beach is gone now," Celéri continued. "She can't gate back."

"Are we certain of that?" asked Merry.

"No..." said Eynon, drawing out the word.

"And are we sure she can't *fly* them all back?" Merry added.

"No," Eynon repeated.

Celéri nodded to Merry. "Then we'd better take steps to find Sikárias and the others," she said.

Merry squeezed Eynon's arm. "Before they find us."

"If we're going after the wizard assassins, you should probably leave their magestones with Uirsé," Eynon told Celéri.

"I already did," Celéri replied. She moved to stand beside Eynon, opposite Merry. "Now, handsome," she said, squeezing his other arm, "What's our plan?"

Eynon took a deep breath. It was one thing to insist on planning and quite another to devise a plan. His face was growing red from Celéri's attentions along with Merry's. He opened and closed his mouth a few times before he finally spoke. "We'll have to search for their bubble of solidified sound."

"How do you suggest we do that across miles of open Ocean?" asked Merry.

"Perhaps with a grid search?" said Celéri. "I learned about them in school. They're part of the training program for scout wizards."

"I thought you were a battle wizard," said Merry.

"I'm both," said Celéri.

"How does a grid search work?" asked Eynon. "Do you super-impose a grid over an area and search each square methodically?"

"It sounds like you went to scout wizard school," said Celéri.

"You know I didn't," said Eynon. "But I am a student of geometry, and it just made sense. I can generate the grid lines using illusion magic."

"I don't know if we need a formal grid," said Merry. "There are three of us. We can simply search far, middle, and near distances along the line of the great wave."

Eynon and Celéri nodded.

"I'll take the far search," said Merry. "I can line-of-sight gate and get there faster."

"I'll do the middle distance," said Eynon, thinking he often found himself in the middle between these two capable women.

"Leaving me to search nearby," said Celéri.

"But not too near," said Merry. "That wave was powerful."

"Thank you, Magister Merry," said Celéri. She raised an eyebrow to indicate her reaction to Merry's advice.

Merry smiled instead of frowning, however. Hearing a Roma refer to her as a magister somehow made her new status as a master mage seem more real.

Celéri shook her head and disengaged her hand from Eynon's arm. "Remember to scan for the presence of a dagger-shaped obsidian magestone," she said. "That will be harder to hide than a bubble of solidified sound."

"Right," said Merry. "And what should we do once we *find* the wizard assassins?"

"We should rendezvous back here in the cave every hour," said Eynon. "With luck, some of the other more experienced master mages will be revived soon and can both help us with the search and advise us on how to deal with Sikárias and the others."

Before the three young wizards could fly off, they heard a deep voice bellowing from the top of the hill.

"Merry," shouted Berrt. "Is everyone safe?"

In part to test her new abilities, Merry *ad hoc* gated to the summit of the hill above the cave and returned with Berrt, who bowed when he met Celéri, holding his huge wooden club across his midsection as he did. The Roma wizard nodded back, then—impressed by the size of the weapon and the person wielding it—smiled at the troll and bowed in return.

"The glyppos have eaten all the grass above," Berrt told Merry. "I'm going to lead them to forage on what passes for grass down on what's left of the beach."

"That sounds sensible," said Merry. "Watch out for dragons."

"Those dragons?" asked Celéri. She pointed off to the northwest where what had been the far end of the fishhook of land forming the Grand Harbor was still above water. Four dragons were clearly sleeping on the rocky, sun-warmed strand like a quartet of napping cats.

"Not much of a threat there, I suppose," said Eynon.

"There may still be dangers about," said Merry. "Be on your guard."

"I will be," said Berrt.

Merry returned Berrt to the glyppos and was back in seconds. "Ready to start our search?" she asked.

"Let's get on with it," said Celéri.

The three young mages stepped onto their flying disks, flew out of the cave, and set off for the far, middle, and near distances.

* * * * *

Merry didn't spot the wizard-assassins' bubble or sense the dagger-shaped obsidian magestone around the neck of Sikárias at the far distance. Eynon's search of the middle distance was likewise unsuccessful, but Celéri's search nearer to the Tempest Isles was a different matter.

For most of an hour, the young Roma wizard saw nothing as she peered down at the deep Ocean waters below her, until she spotted a long, dark shape of immense size—a sinuous shadow—moving toward the shore at great speed. When rows of black, upward-pointed neck plates broke the surface she recognized the creature for what it was. The outline of the massive sea dragon, what she'd called a leviathan, was unmistakable.

The huge aquatic dragon was accelerating its bulk toward what was left of the beach to the east of the now-vanished shore. Celéri could see the two glyppos grazing on sea grass and suspected they were the leviathan's intended prey. While appreciating that even sea dragons had to eat, she knew Eynon and Merry would be displeased if the leviathan ate the glyppos and she couldn't tell if Berrt was close enough to the armored herbivores to be at risk himself.

The well-muscled troll mage intrigued her, and she wouldn't like to see him end up in a leviathan's belly.

From her present position half a mile from shore, Celéri *ad hoc* gated outside the cave on the hillside and sped down to the remains of the beach. She saw Berrt below with the glyppos. He seemed to be practicing his shield spells, casting walls and hemispheres of solidified sound, then dispelling them. His back was to the Ocean and she could tell he couldn't see the sea dragon rushing in toward him and the grazing glyppos.

Should I alert Eynon and Merry? Celéri considered. *There's no need,* she decided. *Discouraging the leviathan shouldn't require their assistance.*

She couldn't have been more wrong. Before Celéri could alert Berrt the great sea dragon's huge head reached the shore and its vast mouth opened, disgorging a spiked bubble of solidified sound holding Sikárias and the others. Sikárias immediately launched a lightning blast at Celéri, catching the young Roma wizard unprepared and leaving her senseless, falling a dozen feet from her descending flying disk onto yielding sand and vegetation.

Berrt stood frozen for a moment, torn between defending the glyppos from the hungry leviathan and protecting Celéri from Sikárias and the wizard assassins. Thinking quickly, the troll mage launched an exploding light spell a thousand feet into the air where it burst into a rapidly expanding dandelion head of red, blue, green, gold, and purple brilliance.

His pyrotechnics held the attention of the wizard assassins and the leviathan alike. Even the glyppos looked up and blinked before returning to cropping grass. Berrt saw Umbrose, Sikárias, and the other wizard assassins rush toward Celéri, their daggers out, ready to kill her and take her magestone. With a pop of air, he suddenly found himself standing above Celéri's prone form and raised his club to protect her.

Celéri was shaking off the shock of the lightning blast. She opened her eyes and lifted her upper torso on one elbow. She saw Berrt standing above her, ready to take on four attacking wizards with a few novice spells, his wits, and his club.

Berrt set himself to counter the wizard-assassins' attack. Behind them, he saw the glyppos shift to defend themselves from the leviathan's snapping jaws. There was nothing he could do to help the big beasts now. He had to protect Celéri—and himself. Berrt created a plane of solidified sound on the beach behind the wizard assassins, placing it a few inches below the surface and lifting up a substantial quantity of fine sand in the process. He moved the plane until it was above the wizard assassins, then dispelled it, raining sand down upon them.

Sikárias had set her protective shields to form a wall between her family and Berrt, so they didn't stop the sand from falling into their eyes and hair from above. The wizard assassins paused to regroup. While they were distracted, Berrt threw his sea-turtle shell flying disk toward them. It caught Perkússos in his midsection, doubling the man over and taking him out of the fight, at least temporarily. Berrt reached for Celéri's flying disk, which had fallen nearby, and repeated the same maneuver, using her disk to incapacitate Períkulōs.

With a crack of thunder and a blinding flash, Sikárias sent a blast of lightning toward Berrt. To his own surprise, he blocked it with his non-conducting wooden club and sent that weapon spinning back along the lightning bolt's path to strike Sikárias on the forehead. Her body fell to the sand, limp, but moaning.

Umbrose moved to Sikárias and removed her magestone, placing the chain around his own neck. "Sorry, Mother," he said. "My need is greater." He blocked a rock thrown by Berrt with a swipe of a giant hand formed of solidified sound, then extended that hand to grip Berrt and pin his arms to his sides. Umbrose glared down at Celéri. "It's a shame my family didn't kill you when they killed your parents," he said, squeezing Berrt harder and making the troll's face turn as red as Celéri's rising anger.

Celéri tried to stand but couldn't. Her legs wouldn't respond to her mind's commands. Maintaining control of Berrt, Umbrose approached and stood over Celéri and held his dagger near her throat.

"First, I'll deal with you," he said. "Then those annoying young Dâron wizards."

A piercing and all-too-familiar screech rooted Umbrose in place as wings battered his arms and a sharp beak cut the thong holding his mother's magestone around his neck. *Not again!* thought Umbrose.

Clever girl, thought Celéri as she watched Thraxa carry the magestone off to the top of the hill above the cave.

The hand of solidified sound gripping Berrt vanished and the troll mage, after a few seconds to compose himself, bent to wrap his hands in the folds of the robes around Umbrose's shoulders. He lifted Umbrose off the ground, shaking him like a terrier shakes a rat until the dagger flew from the spy mage's grasp. That task completed, Berrt released Umbrose and batted Umbrose's skull from side to side half a dozen times with his massive palms, rendering the spymaster unconscious before he hit the sand.

"Thank you," said Celéri. She extended her hand to Berrt and allowed the troll mage to assist her in regaining her feet. He bowed to her, but she didn't return the bow. Instead, she wrapped her arms around him and held him tight.

Chapter 46

Leviathan

Eynon and Merry spotted Berrt's signal and promptly *ad hoc* gated back to what remained of the beach. They got there in time to witness the troll mage's fight with the wizard assassins but were distracted from their observations by the great sea dragon attacking the glyppos. The sea dragon was massive, every bit as large as Viridáxés and Zûrafiérix, but its proportions were different. Its neck was longer, its body was more streamlined, and its tail extended back for tens of yards before terminating in massive horizontal flukes like a whale's. It was well-adapted for the Ocean, with webbing between the digits of its claws. Like the pictures of sea wolves Eynon had seen in bestiaries, it's coloring was fitting for an Oceanic predator as well, with black on its back and white on its belly. Rows of black plates grew out from its head and neck and its teeth were like a collection of greatswords as long as Governor-General Quintillius was tall.

After a moment to take in the sea dragon's impressive proportions, Merry acted quickly and began to herd the two ponderous herbivorous glyppos toward the hill where Berrt had been watching them, out of reach of the sea dragon's snapping jaws. Unfortunately, the sea dragon was reluctant to lose such a large potential feast. Using its four flipper-like limbs, it pulled its massive body up on the shore and stretched its long neck to pursue its retreating quarries.

Eynon reacted promptly as well. Triggering the personal tight shields Verro had taught him to construct, he hovered ahead and above the sea dragon's gigantic head, generated a tremendous fist of solidified sound, and used it to deliver a firm bop on the aquatic invader's huge snout. His blow was hard enough to drive the sea dragon's head halfway to the sand on what was left of the shore and gave Merry time to drive the glyppos closer toward the hill.

The sea dragon responded by whipping its head up, smacking it into Eynon, and sending the young mage arcing skyward. Eynon generated a wide wing of solidified sound and warped its trailing edge to transform his parabolic arc into a *loop de loop* that returned him to his original position above and in front of the sea dragon. The sea dragon seemed uncertain. It shifted its head until it was level with Eynon, then it opened its jaws, roared with as much noise as an onrushing tidal wave, and lunged for him.

"STOP!" shouted Eynon, his voice rising in pitch involuntarily.

The sea dragon paused. "What did you say?" it asked with words that sounded more like a squeal than a bellow.

"I told you to stop attacking me," said Eynon.

"You can talk?" said the sea dragon.

"You can talk?" Eynon replied.

"Hmmm..." said the sea dragon. "Maybe it's not really intelligent, just repeating my words, like a bird."

"What do you mean, maybe I'm not intelligent?" asked Eynon. As he floated on his flying disk, he put his hands on his hips and stared at the sea dragon. Eyes bigger than chariot wheels stared back.

"I retract my statement," squealed the sea dragon. "Clearly, you can generate unique utterances, even if your voice is so low I can barely make out what you're saying."

Eynon experimented with an amplifying and transforming cone of solidified sound for a few seconds then spoke again, his voice moderated by the cone to sound even higher than a young child's. "Is this better?"

"Very much so," said the sea dragon. Its voice was like a mosquito's whining, which was quite incongruous to Eynon for something so huge. The young wizard generated similar constructs of solidified sound to lower the pitch of the sea dragon's speech. "Why are you keeping me from my food? It's so seldom I get to eat anything that lives on land."

"I hadn't thought about it that way," Eynon replied. "I grew up raising cows for milking and its my first instinct to protect large grazing animals."

"Like wisents?" asked Merry a second after she line-of-sight gated over to float beside her partner.

Eynon turned to Merry and shrugged. "You have me there," he said. He showed Merry his pitch-shifting constructs and she constructed a set of her own.

"Please don't eat the glyppos," she told the sea dragon. Pointing toward Berrt she said, "My friend considers them his pets."

"Oh," said the sea dragon. "I don't eat pets. I have a pet sea turtle named Shelly."

"Because it has a shell?" asked Eynon.

"No," said the sea dragon. "Because her name is Nichelle. Shelly is just my pet name for her." The sea dragon's long red tongue extended and circled its jaws before returning to its mouth. "But where are my manners? I'm usually such a solitary individual, I don't have much opportunity to use them." The plates on its head and neck flexed and it dipped its head. "My name is Marímnemossocétûx, but you can call me Tûx. What are your names?"

Merry replied. "Pleased to meet you, Tûx. I'm Merry." She tilted her head, appreciating the sea dragon's black and white color scheme and noting a small patch of black—two triangles conjoined to a circle—amidst the whiteness where the sea dragon's neck met its massive body. She waved her right arm toward her partner. "This is Eynon." Then she extended her left arm up the beach. "The big person standing over there is our friend Berrt and the smaller one in purple robes is Celéri."

"You're all small from my perspective," said Tûx. "What about the ones on the ground?"

"They're not friends of yours?" asked Eynon. "You carried them back here from out on the open Ocean."

"Friends?" said Tûx. "They're not friends of *mine*. They slid their spiky ball into my mouth when I was chasing tuna and I came here to use my impact with the shore to dislodge it." Tûx's head moved in a slow figure-eight as if the sea dragon was preening. "It worked, too."

"You're lucky," said Merry. "The people inside that spiky ball are wizard assassins from the Imperium, here to cause trouble and kill *our* friends. They could have caused you harm if they stayed inside your mouth."

"They certainly were an irritation," said Tûx. "I tried to crush their ball, but the spikes on it hurt my soft palate. I felt like an oyster dealing with a grain of sand in its shell."

"Without a means to form a pearl around it," said Eynon. He'd never seen an oyster but had read about them and the famous stones they produced.

"Berrt stopped the wizard assassins before they could cause more trouble," said Merry. "Now we have to figure out where we can imprison them so they can't escape and threaten us further."

"I know of caves with air deep beneath the Ocean," said Tûx. "Shelly goes in them sometimes and told me about them. Maybe you could use those caves as a prison?"

"Maybe we could," said Eynon. "That would make it much more difficult for the wizard assassins to escape."

"Well then," said Tûx. "I've been of service to you. Do you have any suggestions on ways for me to get some land animals that *aren't* pets for me to sample?"

Merry looked at Eynon. "Wisents?" she asked.

"Too small," Eynon replied, aware of Tûx's huge bulk. "How about mammoths?"

"Or mastodons or elephants," said Merry. "Good idea."

"We can make arrangements to deliver a big land animal to you," Eynon told Tûx. He extended his arm and pointed to the north. "In the meantime, the large fireball that created the tidal wave probably left lots of stunned fish in that direction."

"It probably *cooked* a good many of them too," added Merry.

"Fascinating," said Tûx. "I seldom get cooked food except when I take the time to drag a swordfish down to one of the black smokers far to the east of here. That's seldom worth the effort, but if there are fish already cooked close at hand, I should take advantage of the opportunity to savor them."

"Very good," said Eynon. He reached into his pouch and removed a pair of communications rings. "I'd like to give you a gift so we can stay in touch," he told the sea dragon. Using their own pair of rings, Eynon and Merry demonstrated how the communications rings functioned.

He flew closer to Tûx's head, then stopped, unsure of where to put the ring so the sea dragon could use it.

"I like gifts," said Tûx. "All the more so because I so seldom get them—and that tiny thing glitters so nicely. Is there some sort of problem?"

"I don't know where to put it," said Eynon. "We wear our rings on our fingers or on chains around our necks, but the webbing between your claws makes that difficult and I wouldn't want to put it over one of the plates on your head. You'd have no way to keep it in place once it expands to serve as a communicator."

"Did you say chains?" asked Tûx. "I can find chains." The great sea dragon reversed direction and slid back into the Ocean with a surprisingly small splash, given its bulk.

Eynon returned the ring to his pouch. He and Merry flew over to Berrt and Celéri, pleased to see Umbrose and the wizard assassins remained unconscious.

"That was impressive," Eynon told Berrt.

"Thank you," said the troll. His arm was draped around Celéri's shoulders.

"He's magnificent, isn't he," Celéri added, making it a statement rather than a question. *And he* ad hoc *gated to save me,* she thought.

"I'm glad the two of you are getting along so well," said Merry. She glanced at Eynon and was happy to see him smiling back at her rather than looking at Celéri.

"It looks like our new sea dragon friend may be able to help us with a place to imprison the wizard assassins," said Eynon. He jumped when Laetícia dropped an illusion concealing herself, Verro, Callidus, Damon, Amber and Knútr.

"And where might that be?" Laetícia asked.

Eynon was pleased to see his fellow master mages had recovered—mostly. Several of Laetícia's tightly woven braids had come out and Damon's hair, what little was left of it, looked like a squirrel's tail caught in a rainstorm. "In a cave deep under the Ocean," Eynon told Laetícia. "Without their magestones the wizard assassins wouldn't be able to escape it."

Verro rubbed his chin. "And it would be difficult for anyone to mount a rescue expedition in such a location."

"But not impossible," said Damon. His face looked like he'd be much happier if he was back in the governor-general's palace in Nova Eboracum in bed with Astrí.

"I think it would be advisable *not* to return them to the Imperium," said Magister Callidus. "There would be too many temptations for one faction or another to arrange their release and free them to take further commissions."

"You have a point," said Laetícia. "And that sea dragon would be a formidable jailer."

"Tûx," said Merry.

"That's short for Marímnemossocétûx," said Eynon.

"I'm surprised the two of you didn't convince the wizard assassins to quit their current occupations and retire to manage vineyards in Dâron's southern provinces," said Damon.

"Give them time," said Laetícia. "I have important—and pleasing— news to share, by the way. Quintillius reached me while I was recovering."

"Do tell," said Merry. She nudged Eynon with an elbow.

"Oh!" said Eynon. "Let me share *my* news first. Merry can *ad hoc* gate."

"Wonderful!" said Laetícia.

"We're always glad to have another master mage in our number," said Verro.

Amber said nothing but moved close and hugged Merry before stepping back again. Knútr clasped Merry's forearm and released it. Damon nodded his approval, then glanced from her to Eynon and grinned for the flap of a hummingbird's wings.

"I'm pleased for you," said Magister Callidus. "When I saw you could line-of-sight gate I expected it wouldn't be long before you learned how to take the next step."

Merry smiled and gave a small bow. "Thank you, everyone. I look forward to learning from all of you." She extended her hands toward Berrt. "This is *my* new apprentice," she said.

"No," said Celéri. "He's mine."

Merry leaned back and held up her palms as if to say *let's postpone this discussion.*

Before Laetícia could return to sharing her news, the master mages' attention shifted back to the beach as Tûx reappeared. The sea dragon lowered its head and its great dark eyes regarded them. A massive chain with links as thick as Eynon's legs hung from Tûx's neck.

Merry clapped. "Where's the anchor that chain attached to?" she asked.

"I left it embedded in a whale's skeleton," came the sea dragon's reply. "Will this serve?" Tûx asked Eynon.

Eynon smiled. "Quite well," he said, removing the communications ring from his pouch. He expanded it until it was three feet in diameter and boarded his flying disk to lift himself, so he was next to the chain around Tûx's neck. He generated a congruency *through* one of the links, slipped the enlarged ring onto the link, and canceled his spell, leaving the ring hanging from the chain. "This should do it," he told Tûx. "When you want to reach us or answer us when we contact you, just lean forward so you can see the ring at the end of the chain." He rose to Tûx's ear and whispered the phrase to trigger the communications ring. "You'd be welcome to attend the double royal wedding at the Great Falls on Midsummer's Day if you can get there," Eynon added. "Just ring me to let us know you're coming."

"Understood," said Tûx. "I've never been to any sort of wedding, let alone a royal one. It's nice to have new friends. I'm glad I didn't eat you."

"So am I," said Eynon with unfeigned enthusiasm. "Now go get yourself a nicely cooked fish dinner."

"An excellent idea," said Tûx. The great sea dragon lumbered across the beach and into deep water of the Tempest Isles' Grand Harbor, a broad line of bubbles fading off to the north marking its progress.

Chapter 47

Laetícia's News

"Well," said Merry to Laetícia, "what's your news?"

"I need to see to a few important details first," Laetícia replied. "Callidus, would you assist me on transporting some guards from Nova Eboracum?"

"With pleasure," said Magister Callidus.

The pair of Roma master mages popped away and returned several times, bringing pairs of legionnaires in full kit with them with each trip. The new arrivals were put to work binding and guarding Períkulōs, Perkússos, Sikárias and Umbrose. Callidus gated his last pair to the cave above them and helped transport Sírénae, Hibblig, Túathal, and Gwýnnett back to the beach once their hands had been bound. Gwýnnett sat in the sand, sobbing. Hibblig and Túathal stood silently, but Sírénae was quite creative in spouting invective aimed at Callidus and Laetícia.

"Do you want to do the honors or should I?" Laetícia asked Callidus.

"I will," said Magister Callidus. "You have one more person to bring here."

"Indeed I do," said Laetícia. She disappeared and as air rushed into the space she had occupied, Callidus applied a gag of solidified sound to Sírénae, stopping her tirade.

Eynon whispered to Merry. "I wish he hadn't done that quite so soon. I was expanding my vocabulary."

"Not me," said Merry. "But I used to hide in a corner of Taffaern's Inn on trips to Tyford. The patrons thought I was lost in my books, but I was paying attention. I also used to listen in on my father's guards and retainers when they were drinking and gambling. The Roma do seem to have more words for body parts and unsavory personal habits than the folk of Dâron do, though."

"Maybe you could teach me some of these words the next time we're alone together," Eynon suggested.

"The next time we're alone together we'll have better things to do than study words and their meanings," said Merry.

"You have a point," said Eynon. He put his arm around Merry's shoulders, and she leaned into him, enjoying the warmth of his body along with the heat of the sun beating down on the Tempest Isles. Before more than a few seconds passed, Laetícia returned to the beach with her husband Quintillius beside her.

Several of the newly arrived guards slapped their right fists against their chests and shouted, "Ave Imperator!"

Eynon and Merry exchanged a quick look. Damon shook his head slowly and allowed the corners of his mouth to raise in a smile, while Amber gave Quintillius a small nod of respect. Verro spoke. "I can guess at one part of your news, at least," he said.

"Yes," said Laetícia. "I shared what the wizard assassins said about Flavia Drusilla and Gertrude of Mainz as captured by the *bug* Eynon left here on the beach. Emperor Valens of the South and Emperor Phraátēs of the East found it compelling evidence of Flavia Drusilla's treason and Gertrude's complicity. With support from the First Citizen in Roma, Quintillius was declared Emperor of the West, filling the position Sírénae's banishment had left open. Flavia Drusilla and Gertrude have been taken into custody and transported to Roma Mater to stand trial."

Smiling, Laetícia rose more than a foot on her flying disk until she was at a height where she could kiss her tall husband without him bending down. Quintillius hugged her and swung Laetícia back and forth with such enthusiasm that her feet slipped out of the stirrups of her flying disk, which clanged to the ground. After enough time to recite the alphabet, he gently returned Laetícia's feet to the sand and helped return her flying disk to its usual spot on her shoulders. "I couldn't have done it without you, my love," he told her.

Laetícia grinned up at Quintillius. "I know," she said. "We make a good team."

Eynon reached down to squeeze Merry's hand, and she squeezed back, echoing the Roma couple's sentiments by their connection. They were so caught up in their own feelings, they didn't see Celéri squeeze Berrt's hand in much the same way, though the expression on the troll's face was more confusion than composure.

"Does this mean you're both leaving Orluin?" asked Merry.

"The capital city of the Western Empire is Nárbo," said Quintillius. "It must be our new home."

"But now that we have effective gates across the Ocean it will be easy for us to return to Nova Eboracum to visit with our friends," said Laetícia.

"And Occidens Province *is* still part of the Western empire," added Quintillius.

"Who will be the new provincial governor-general?" asked Verro.

"General Machaera," said Quintillius. "She led the invaders' army at the Battle of the Abbenoth."

"At least she was wise enough to surrender when her troops opted to support Valentius over Sírénae," said Magister Callidus. "I'm sure she'll do a fine job."

"I'm glad you think so," said Quintillius, "since I want *you* to be her master mage. You know the leaders of Orluin and are well respected."

"Thank you, I think," said Callidus. He bowed to Quintillius. "The emperor honors me."

"No need to feed me sugar-drenched manure, Callidus," said Quintillius. "Machaera will need your good advice to keep her from antagonizing Dârio, Nûd, Bjarni, and the various clan chiefs, to say nothing of Orluin's master mages. I'm counting on you."

"Right," said Callidus. "I don't promise to stay in Nova Eboracum once snow starts falling, though. It's too easy to gate down to Valentia and stay warm."

"Valentius will need your good advice as well," said Quintillius. "At least until his father retires and he becomes the new Emperor of the South."

"Is that outcome certain, Quin?" asked Callidus. He winked at Quintillius. "I thought the incumbent emperors and the First Citizen had to give their approval for any such appointment and consult with the Imperium Senate."

"Stop baiting him, Callidus," said Laetícia. "You know quite well how *de facto* is different from *de jure*."

"And the Imperium Senate won't stand in the way of appointing whomever Valens, Phraátēs, and I determine should be Valens' replacement," said Quintillius.

"Not if they know what's good for them," said Damon under his breath.

"Who will be the new Emperor of the North?" asked Knútr. "Not that anyone wouldn't be an improvement over Flavia Drusilla."

"You can be sure the new Northern emperor will *not* be a foe of Nordland," said Quintillius. "I'll see to that. My experience in Orluin has taught me the value of other perspectives and independent kingdoms. If anything, I expect trading relations with your realm will be strengthened."

"I'm glad to hear that," said Knútr. "And I'm sure King Harald will be as well."

"Good," said Quintillius. He turned to stare at Sírénae, and his cheeks turned darker as blood flowed to them. "And as for *you*," he said.

"Temper, Quin," said Laetícia.

Quintillius paused and took three long, slow breaths, mastering his anger. Laetícia nodded. "As for you," he told Sírénae, "the emperors have decided to remand you to imprisonment at the School of Good Governance in Roma Mater where you will serve as an example of *poor* governance for the remainder of your life."

"That doesn't sound too bad," said Eynon.

"It will be for Sírénae," said Laetícia. "She's so full of her own self-importance that thousands of students criticizing her decisions in courses year after year will be like daggers peeling off bits of her skin."

"And rubbing salt in the wounds," added Callidus.

"I see," said Eynon.

"She will also be displayed in a cage at festivals and parades," said Quintillius.

"Probably next to Flavia Drusilla and Gertrude of Mainz," said Laetícia.

"I thought the Roma killed traitors?" said Merry.

"Common traitors, yes," said Quintillius. "But death is too good for emperors who betray our trust. Dishonor cuts them deeper and is far more instructive."

"Don't you risk making them martyrs?" asked Eynon.

"Killing them outright would be more likely to make them martyrs," said Laetícia. "We've found presenting all the evidence against them in a public trial, then displaying them in cages with all their crimes enumerated on signs beside them to be more effective."

"Can people like Sírénae Accipiter, Flavia Drusilla, and Gertrude of Mainz truly feel shame?" asked Knútr.

"Perhaps not," said Laetícia. "But losing the fawning approval they'd become used to receiving can be painful all on its own."

"I've changed my mind," said Eynon. "Now that you've described it I can see that the punishment fits the crime."

"Doesn't there have to be a trial to establish their guilt first?" asked Merry.

"Sírénae has already been tried and convicted *in absentia*," said Quintillius. "As for the others, the testimony of the wizard assassins' candid admissions makes their convictions certain—but we *will* try them."

"The forms must be followed," said Callidus.

Eynon sighed loud enough so everyone heard him.

"There's a reason statues of Blind Justice in courtrooms hold both scales *and* a sword," said Quintillius.

"In the Coombe we just banish people who can't get along," said Eynon.

"Sírénae banished herself to Orluin and see how much trouble *that* caused," said Laetícia.

Eynon nodded.

"What about them?" asked Merry, indicating Hibblig, Túathal, and Gwýnnett.

"They're citizens of Dâron and Tamloch," said Quintillius. "That means their fates are for Nûd and Dârio to determine."

"We can get them," said Eynon.

"And Jenet and Bonnie, too," said Merry. "They're probably ready to think about something other than their upcoming wedding day after tomorrow."

Eynon took Merry's hand and before any of the others could advise them the pair had gated away.

Off to one side, Berrt and Celéri were standing close together, talking softly. They were so focused on each other they didn't notice the two glyppos—one with a yellow flower behind an ear—had stopped moving up the hill and had returned to the beach. The larger of the two beasts quietly stepped close to Berrt and positioned its armored head directly behind the troll. The other glyppo did the same for Celéri. When the larger one nodded, both glyppos snapped their heads up at the same time, catching Berrt and Celéri squarely on muscles the Roma would call *gluteus maximus*.

The two mages' mouths opened, and their eyes were as big as turkey eggs as they both rose five feet into the air from the impact. When they fell back down the glyppos' heads snapped up again, launching Berrt and Celéri even higher. Callidus and Laetícia took pity on the two wizards, intercepting them with tendrils of solidified sound as they rose and shifting them a few feet away from the playful glyppos.

Berrt bowed to Laetícia, not realizing the irresistible target his posture made. The larger glyppo lunged forward, smacking Berrt on his rump and sending him rolling down the beach. Celéri retrieved her flying disk and Berrt's turtle shell, gaining enough altitude to avoid being pushed over by the second glyppo. She tossed the turtle shell to Berrt. He boarded it and lifted off until he was far enough above the glyppos to be out of range of playful attacks from either of their ends. Head butts are one thing but impacts from the glyppos' spiked tails would be truly dangerous.

Floating above the larger glyppo, Berrt leaned down and rubbed the beast's head with his knuckles. "It's not playtime, Butthead," Berrt told the glyppo. "You and Buttercup should go crop sea grass and we can play later."

The glyppos snorted and turned to follow Berrt's recommendation.

"You've given them *names?*" said Celéri as she watched the glyppos depart.

"Of course," said Berrt. "They have distinct personalities."

"So I see," said Celéri. "And apparently quite low senses of humor."

"Head butts and pratfalls *are* funny, I agree," said Berrt.

"But not when we're the butts of the joke," said Celéri. She rubbed her posterior and made a face. "How could you tell one glyppo was male and the other female, by the way? It seems to me all the relevant parts of their anatomy are tucked up under their belly armor."

"How do you think I could tell?" asked Berrt. He put his arm around Celéri's shoulder and adopted a stilted tone. "When a momma glyppo and a poppa glyppo love each other very much..."

"Stop!" said Celéri between giggles. "I get it—and I'd like to *see* it sometime. I expect it would be... inspiring."

"Don't look at me—I'm too old for you."

"I like older men."

"I'm not a man."

"Of course you are—and more of a man than most."

"But I'm going to leave soon on a quest to find more of my kind," said Berrt.

"And I'm coming with you," said Celéri.

"I doubt I could stop you if you've made up your mind to join me."

"See," said Celéri. "I knew you were wise."

"Our attraction wasn't covered in my study of philosophy."

"Perhaps you should consider the wisdom of a more hands-on approach in the future," said Celéri. She rubbed her *glutes* and wiggled her eyebrows at Berrt.

Before anything could progress further, Eynon popped in with Nûd and Bonnie on his flying disk. Seconds later Merry appeared with Jenet and Dârio.

Jenet crossed the distance to where Laetícia and Quintillius were standing and gave them both hugs. "Did you tell them the good news?" she asked.

"We did," said Laetícia.

"You'll still be able to attend our weddings, won't you?" asked Jenet.

"We need to get to Nárbo soon, but not so soon that we can't join you for your celebrations," said Laetícia.

"Especially now that it's a matter of imperial diplomacy," teased Quintillius.

"Our thanks for eliminating the assassins planning to kill us," said Nûd.

"Are they the ones wearing black leather over there in the sand?" asked Dârio.

"What gave it away?" asked Bonnie. "The legionnaires guarding them?" She smiled at Dârio.

"You're still a subject of Tamloch, at least until the weddings, so show more respect to your king," said Dârio, smiling back.

"I'd respect you more if you had a better appreciation of the obvious," said Bonnie.

"I'm glad to see the four of you are getting along so well," said Laetícia, "but Eynon and Merry brought you here for a reason." She gestured toward Hibblig, Túathal, and Gwýnnett. "We've determined how to deal with Umbrose, Sírénae, and the wizard assassins. They're Roma and our responsibility. However, the kings of Dâron and Tamloch must pass judgment on these three."

Nûd and Dârio exchanged their previous smiles for guarded expressions. This was serious business.

Eynon spoke, breaking the mood. "I expect this could take a while, so before we get started, and before Tûx returns, does anyone know where I might find an elephant?"

Chapter 48

Standing in Judgment

Amber informed Eynon about the young rogue mammoth with impressive tusks who had been trampling crops on garths near Bjarniston in Bifurland. It took only a few minutes to *ad hoc* gate Eynon there and together they located the troublesome beast. Eynon transported the mammoth back to the Tempest Isles and with Amber and Merry's help, got the destructive rogue to the spit of land to the west that had once formed part of the enclosure for the Grand Harbor. After cautioning the Roma dragons basking there *not* to eat the mammoth, the mages returned to the beach to join the others.

In their absence, Nûd and Dârio had stepped a few paces away to consult with Jenet and Bonnie, their soon-to-be spouses, along with Laetícia and Quintillius. When Eynon, Merry, and Amber returned, the two royal couples moved to stand in front of Hibblig, Túathal, and Gwýnnett. The new emperor of the West and Laetícia stood to the side, observing.

Nûd nodded to Hibblig. "Step forward, wizard," he commanded. Hibblig did so, his head held high. The king of Dâron thought he saw hints of fear in Hibblig's eyes, so he thought Hibblig must be merely feigning a lack of concern for his fate. "You conspired with Gwýnnett against your kingdom and all Orluin. The price of treachery is death."

Hibblig's eyes went wide and his jaw dropped, leaving his mouth gaping open. He realized he must look like a startled fish and closed his jaw so quickly everyone on the beach could hear his teeth snap together. "Your Majesty," Hibblig pleaded. "My mind was not my own." He pointed to Gwýnnett. "I was enthralled by her potions."

Beside Nûd, Dârio's head moved slowly side to side, not in negation, but in a sad acknowledgment of his mother's use of potions to control others. Hibblig noticed Dârio's motion and misinterpreted, thinking the king of Tamloch didn't believe him.

"She *made* me do it!" Hibblig exclaimed, his voice rising.

From his position between Callidus and Verro, Damon spoke. His voice sounded like a wagon wheel in need of grease. "You always were a horse's ass, Hibblig."

Hibblig was about to offer a reply, but in an atypical show of good judgment, stayed silent.

"Grandfather," said Nûd. His single word carried both affection and authority. Damon nodded and turned out both his palms indicating the older mage now acknowledged Nûd was no longer his servant, but his king.

Hibblig shifted from foot to foot, digging his boots slightly deeper into the sand on the beach as his eyes darted across the individuals standing before him, looking for anything that might be cause for hope. He saw Bonnie lean close and whisper in Nûd's ear.

"I am reminded that you attacked the wizard assassins when they attacked the master mages," said Nûd. "You were *not* under Gwýnnett's control at that point, and I will assume that better reflects your true loyalties..." Nûd paused.

Hibblig rubbed his hands together in front of him then realized what he was doing and clasped them behind his back.

"Therefore," said Nûd, "I won't have you executed. From this day forward you are exiled to live among the Southern Clan Landers. If you ever return to Dâron—" Nûd glanced at Dârio, then Quintillius, then Amber. "—or Tamloch or Occidens Province or Bifurland, your life is forfeit. Do you understand?"

Hibblig's head bobbed like a pigeon's. "Yes, Your Majesty," he said. "Thank you, Your Majesty."

Before Nûd could wave Hibblig back, Bonnie asked her husband-to-be a question. "Will you return his magestone? He'll just craft another in the Southern Clan Lands anyway."

"He can have it," said Nûd. "From what I've heard from Eynon, Brùtha of the Falcon Clan could use more mages to help clear land in the new Southern Clan Lands' territories to the west. That should keep Hibblig busy and out of trouble for a few decades."

"I'll be sure to let Brùtha know that's your intent when I deliver Hibblig to his exile," said Eynon.

"Excellent," said Nûd. "That will be all, Hibblig. Now get out of my sight before I change my mind."

"As you command, Sire," said Hibblig. The now-humbled wizard turned and walked several paces off to one side.

"You were hard on him there at the end," Bonnie whispered to Nûd.

"I know," Nûd replied. "Not that he didn't deserve it. Being a king isn't all feasts and flowers, I'm afraid."

"You're like my Advanced Congruent Mathemagics professor at the Institute," said Bonnie. "Both tough *and* wise."

"Would that I truly was tough," whispered Nûd. "And as for wisdom, only time will tell if I have it."

"You do, my love," said Bonnie. "Of that I have no doubt."

"Thank you," said Nûd quietly.

With Hibblig's departure, only Túathal and Gwýnnett stood awaiting royal judgment.

Nûd's conversation with Bonnie completed, he turned to Dârio and saw his cousin's shoulders rise and fall. Dârio sighed, loud enough for all to hear.

"I'm sorry," said Nûd. "It's hard to be responsible for the fates of your own parents."

Jenet put a hand on Dârio's arm. He smiled at her and returned to facing the prisoners. "It's harder still to have such a pair *as* my parents," he said. "If not for the love and care I had from Prince Dâri, Queen Carys, and Duke Háiddon, who knows what kind of man I might have been?"

Jenet squeezed Dârio's upper arm. "Would it be better for me to sentence them?" she asked.

"Or me, cousin?" added Nûd.

"No," said Dârio. "They're my responsibility." He caught Verro's attention. "Would you be kind enough to ask Uirsé to join us, please? I need her counsel."

"Of course, Your Majesty," said Verro. He disappeared with a pop and moments later floated down from the cave with Uirsé. Admiral Pixo rode behind the master healer on her flying disk. The three of them landed near the royal couples. Dârio beckoned Uirsé closer and whispered together with her before she stepped back. He didn't seem pleased to hear what she told him.

"Túathal," said Dârio, his features appearing as unyielding as stone. "I count it my great good fortune that I never knew you were my father."

"That was a mistake on my part," said Túathal.

"One of many, brother," said Verro.

"Perhaps," Túathal replied. "But if I'd enlisted Dârio in my plans to make him king of both Dâron *and* Tamloch far earlier, I doubt he'd be passing judgment on *me* today."

Verro stared at his brother and shook his head. The expression on his face made him look like a man about to put down a beloved dog infected with the foaming sickness. Verro's jaw tightened, and his mouth formed a thin line. He faced the royal couples. "Please excuse me, Your Majesties. I'll return in a moment," he told them and popped away again, returning seconds later with Fercha beside him. He held Fercha's hand and stood straighter, as if her presence gave him added strength. "She deserves to witness this," Verro told everyone assembled. Nods of agreement followed his statement. "Do what you must," he told Dârio.

Dârio faced Túathal. "Your treachery is greater by far than Hibblig's," said the young king. "And we all know the penalty the laws of Tamloch impose on traitors."

"Death," whispered Knútr. The wizard was correct, for the laws of Nordland and Tamloch were alike on that point.

Túathal stood impassively, waiting to hear Dârio's next words.

"I have also heard that you, like Hibblig, attacked the wizard assassins," Dârio said after a pause. "That is no small weight on the scales in your favor. And sages much wiser than I have told us disaster is sure to follow from patricide, no matter if a son knows he's killed his own father or not."

"Don't even *think* of marrying your mother," said Jenet. She smiled at Dârio, and he smiled back without even glancing in Gwýnnett's direction.

"I won't, my love. And no matter how much I think justice should be blind, I won't be plucking my eyes out, either."

"See that you don't," said Jenet.

Eynon leaned close to Merry and whispered in her ear. "What are they talking about?" he asked.

"It's from the plot of a famous Athican play," she said. "I read it in a bookshop in Tyford and will tell you about it later."

"Thanks," said Eynon. "Maybe we can see it performed in a theater together when we explore the Imperium."

"Shhh," said Merry. "Dârio's talking."

"Túathal, your previous actions made it plain you weren't thinking clearly, and your mind had slipped into madness," said Dârio.

With a small nod, Túathal acknowledged the truth of Dârio's statement. "I'm feeling much better now," Túathal replied. "I think it was all the exercise and simple food I had when you left me on the Caiman Isles."

"Without any of Gwýnnett's potions," muttered Hibblig.

"What did you say?" asked Dârio.

Hibblig repeated himself, using a herald's projecting voice.

"I thought as much," said Dârio. "That's why I asked Uirsé if her healing magic had some way to ensure you retained your sanity," he told Túathal. "Unfortunately, she informed me her skills were better at healing bodies than minds."

Túathal's eyes shifted to Uirsé, then back to Dârio. "I assure you, I'm as sane as you are and intend to stay that way."

"Mere words, brother," said Verro. "Words alone aren't good enough."

"Then what?" asked Túathal. "Can any of you guarantee *you* won't go mad? What if you eat the wrong mushroom, or consume a slice of rye bread cut from the wrong loaf? *Ergot ergo insania,* as the Roma say." His eyes locked first on Verro and Fercha, then on Nûd and Bonnie. "Madness also runs in families you know. How can you be sure both of you proud monarchs might not slip into madness with the right provocation? Is there to be no mercy for my own journey—and return—from walking that path?"

"You make a good point," said Dârio. "Bring the last prisoner forward."

Gwýnnett had been trying to slip away, moving along the edge of the beach, but Amber and Knútr intercepted her and brought her to stand in front of the kings, beside Túathal.

"You're a traitor, too," said Dârio, addressing Gwýnnett. "Can you give me any reasons why I should not have you executed?"

"I'm your mother!" Gwýnnett blurted.

Dârio hands clenched into fists, then he raised one of them to his forehead for a moment as if trying to summon memories from his childhood. Jenet touched Dârio's arm and he lowered his hand. His lips pressed together in a tight line for a moment before he opened them and spoke. "I may have come from your body, but you have *never* been a mother to me," he said. "I was always nothing more than a pawn in some devious game of *shah mat* you and Túathal were playing." Dârio glared at Gwýnnett. "Try again," he said.

"Because I'm a woman?" asked Gwýnnett.

Dârio shook his head.

"Because I love you?" said Gwýnnett, not sounding hopeful.

This time, Dârio almost laughed and shook his head again.

"What do you want from me, then?" said Gwýnnett. She stamped her sandal-clad foot on the sand.

"I want you to become a healer," said Dârio.

"I don't understand," said Gwýnnett. "I'm not a mage—how can I heal?"

"You may not be a mage but your skill with potions *not* based on wizardry has been strong enough to disrupt the course of two kingdoms," said Dârio. "Uirsé says her healing potions can't guarantee Túathal's madness won't return, but maybe if your life depends on it, you can craft potions without using magic that will ensure he stays sane."

"If I do this, will I be allowed to return to my rooms at the palace in Brendinas?" asked Gwýnnett. "Will my wardrobe and servants be returned to me?"

"What if he allows you to keep your head on your shoulders for another year," said Jenet. "How does *that* sound?"

Eynon looked at Merry and the two of them knew each other well enough to be sure they shared an identical thought. *Why weren't Túathal and Gwýnnett simply being sentenced to live in the*

same undersea prison where the wizard assassins would soon be sent?
Then they heard Dârio's next words and realized the king of Tamloch's
solution was even better.

"After speaking with the emperor of the West and his consort,"
said Dârio, nodding to Quintillius and Laetícia, "I think it would
be prudent to send Túathal to join Sírénae as a prisoner at the
School of Good Governance in Roma Mater, where he can serve as an
example of a poor king alongside her example of a poor emperor."

"What about me?" Gwýnnett protested.

"You'll be going with Túathal," said Jenet.

"Where you stay so long as you can maintain Túathal's sanity,"
said Dârio. "If he returns to madness, you'll both be sent to join the
wizard assassins in their undersea prison."

"That's called an incentive," said Jenet.

"I'm told the apartments for noble prisoners at the School of
Good Governance are quite comfortable," noted Quintillius. "Will
you be wanting one of your own, or would you prefer to share with
Túathal?"

Gwýnnett's expression made her preference obvious.

"There are excellent potion masters—both mages and non-mages—
in Roma Mater you can consult to improve your skills," said Laetícia.

"And if you devise potions that can *help* rather than harm others,"
said Dârio, "it might convince me to revise your sentence from a
lifetime in prison to something shorter."

"Like only twenty years," said Jenet. She smiled at Gwýnnett, but
Gwýnnett didn't smile back.

Gwýnnett, Túathal, and Hibblig were led over to stand by the
legionnaires guarding the wizard assassins.

Dârio looked and Nûd and the cousins shook hands. "That concludes..."
said Dârio.

"One moment," said Quintillius, interrupting. "With your indulgence,
there are two more matters of business we Roma have to cover."

Nûd and Dârio waved for the emperor to continue.

"Admiral Pixo, step forward," said Quintillius.

Pixo moved away from Uirsé's side and presented himself.

"Admiral," said Quintillius. "You served Sírénae loyally, even though I think we both know that loyalty was misplaced."

"As you say, Your Imperial Majesty," said Pixo.

"Look around," said Quintillius. "The Grand Harbor of the Tempest Isles is in need of some repair, don't you think?"

"A few more stones here and there should do it," said Admiral Pixo. He smiled at Quintillius.

"More than a few," said Quin, smiling as well. "I think it's a big job, and I'd like you, an experienced officer, to manage the harbor's restoration—with help from a corps or two of wizard engineers, of course. The Tempest Isles are part of the Western Empire, so I can assure you, you'll have the resources you need. What do you say?"

"I am honored to serve," said Admiral Pixo. He struck his right fist against his chest in a salute.

"Excellent," said Quintillius.

"Now that gates across the Ocean are possible, these islands will be even more important," said Laetícia. "I expect there will be dozens of long-distance gates to and from here. The Tempest Isles will be a center for shipment of bulk cargo between Orluin and the Imperium."

"I expect you're right," said Admiral Pixo. "We'll get things shipshape here as fast as possible."

"And hire local islanders to do some of the work for pay?" asked Merry.

"That sounds better than waiting for them to put spears in our backs," said the admiral.

"I'll leave those details for you to work out," said Quintillius. "Now where has your niece gotten to?"

"Cel-ér-i!" shouted Pixo.

Celéri and Berrt rode up on the necks of the two glyppos, tossing out a spray of sand that almost hit the kings and emperor. Pixo was wise enough to step out of the way before he was crushed by Buttercup.

"I'm here," Celéri announced. From her perch on Butthead's neck her eyes were only a few inches above the emperor's.

"You've been summoned here to face Imperial justice," said Quintillius.

"Maybe I'll pay as much attention to you as I did to Sírénae," said Celéri. She saw Thraxa perched on the hill above the cave and waved to her. The snow-gryffon screeched a reply.

Laetícia touched her husband's arm and whispered, "Remember the first rule of a centurion, dear."

"Yes, my love," Quintillius whispered back.

"I can hear you," said Celéri. "I'm very good with listening spells."

"I know," said Laetícia. "We shouldn't have whispered. Quin and I have an assignment for you that I think you'll be glad to take on."

"What is it?" asked Celéri. She patted Butthead's neck and reached out to quickly squeeze Berrt's near hand.

"Why don't *you* tell her, Merry," said Laetícia. "It was your idea."

"You want to give me an assignment?" Celéri asked Merry.

"It's not so much from me as from Berrt," said Merry. "He'd asked me to help him find more of his kind, but I'm busy helping sort things out here in Orluin, so I thought if you'd be willing to put your capabilities as a master mage at Berrt's disposal, the two of you would be sure to be successful."

"I expect we would at that," said Celéri. "What do you think, Berrt?"

"I'd like it very much," said the troll mage. "When do we start?"

"Not until after the wedding," said Merry.

"You're both invited," said Bonnie.

"Our glyppos, too?" asked Berrt.

"We'll see," said Jenet.

The sound of massive amounts of displaced water from the north made everyone on the beach turn to face Tûx as the great sea dragon slid its huge head up on the sand. Tûx spoke, addressing Eynon.

"You were right about the cooked fish," said the sea dragon. "They were delicious. Is that mammoth for me?"

"It is," said Eynon, "but you might want to alert the black dragons near it about all the cooked fish to the north."

"I'll be glad to tell them," said Tûx. "And just to confirm, I would *love* to attend the royal weddings!"

Chapter 49

Wedding Errands

Running errands to help with their friends' weddings was different for Eynon and Merry than such tasks would have been for individuals who weren't master mages. Eynon and Merry started by *ad hoc* gating to the Coombe so they could transport Eynon's parents and his sister Braith from Haywall to the Inn at the Falls.

When the pair popped into the courtyard beside Eynon's home, Chee and Ace, the young mages' familiars, were overjoyed to be reunited with their wizards. Chee jumped on Eynon's shoulder and scolded his wizard at great length for leaving him behind. The raconette scampered from shoulder to shoulder, digging his small claws into Eynon's neck in passing and calling out a string of *chee-chee-chee-CHEEs* loud enough to prompt Eynon to protect his hearing with small ear coverings of solidified sound.

Ace, in his dog form, circled Merry's legs a dozen times before leaping into her arms and lapping her face with his long, wet tongue. Merry snuggled Ace close to her chest, telling him over and over that he was a good boy and she'd missed him and that she was now a master mage and wouldn't it be fun going on more adventures together. Ace barked with excitement and launched himself away from Merry in his winged form so he could take several turns around her head from above before returning to the ground and pressing his furry side against her shins.

"I think they're glad to see us," said Eynon.

"What gave it away?" asked Merry as she leaned down to rub Ace's back.

Everyone recognized that wasn't really a question. "Ace and Chee were no trouble at all," said Braith. "Felix and I went flying together and Chee rode on Ace's back to follow us. We flew all the way to the quarry at Wherrel."

"Felix and I?" teased Eynon. "You mean it wasn't just a one-time thing, you *hiding* in the hay barn with him?"

"If you must know, we did more than hide," said Braith.

"Do tell," said Eynon.

"As another younger sister," said Merry, "Don't expect to get an answer to that question."

"Oh, I'll tell him," said Braith. "As you well know, we were also trying to get help for our neighbors when the Southern Clan Landers invaded."

"I'm sure that was the only reason you were in the hay barn," said Eynon with a smile. "With Felix being so tall and you so short, did you have to stand on a milking stool to kiss him?"

Merry gave Eynon a playful shove on the shoulder Chee wasn't currently occupying.

"Height differences don't matter when you're horizontal in a hayloft," said Braith.

"True enough," said Eynon. He grinned at Braith and Merry.

"Mother and father are at the milking barn," said Braith. "I'm sure they'll be back soon, since someone will be certain to inform them you've arrived."

"News travels fast in small towns everywhere," said Merry.

"And here in Haywall, it travels faster than it would through a communications ring," said Braith. "I can see them leaving the barn now."

"Good," said Eynon. "We're here to take you all to the Great Falls, where I know you'll be pleased to be reunited with your swain, once Felix is finished helping Laetícia and Mafuta with a special project."

"What sort of project?" asked Braith.

"Installing congruencies to get food, water, and air to the undersea cave that will be used for holding dangerous prisoners," said Merry.

"And remove their wastes," added Eynon. "I'm glad we didn't have to deal with any of that."

"The Roma are pretty responsible about handling such details," said Merry.

Eynon looked at Braith. "I'm confident Felix is good at handling lots of things."

"You're right about that," teased Braith. "I'll get the whole story out of him when I get to the Great Falls."

After a series of hugs, Eynon's parents were at the Inn at the Falls talking to Doethan and Princess Ruth while Braith set off exploring in hopes of finding Felix. Shortly thereafter, Eynon and Merry transported Merry's parents, Baron Derry and Baroness Mabli, to the Grand Falls from Applegarth.

They didn't have to gate in Salder, since Merry's brother was in charge of food and drink for the celebrations and had been at the Great Falls for days. Salder was ably assisted by Taffaern, the innkeeper and former Barrel Knight, from Tyford as well as Tannis and Tibbo from the Blue Whale Inn in Riyas. Cooks and brewers from nobles' kitchens in Brendinas, Riyas, Bjarniston, and Nova Eboracum also contributed, with Merry's father seeing to the delivery of three huge tuns of aged Applegarth cider to the falls for the upcoming festivities.

Eynon also gated in Rōlin and Peregrína from Three Mountains Valley. They immediately found the proprietors of the Inn at the Falls and began to question them about changes to their hostelry so they could reflect any updates in a new travel book they planned to publish as a supplement to their atlas of Orluin.

Those tasks accomplished, Eynon and Merry approached the two royal couples who were standing next to a table covered in detailed lists of things to do for the wedding that would impress the senior quartermaster of a Roma legion with their comprehensiveness. Chee and Ace temporarily abandoned their wizards to frolic with Béryl, Bonnie's owlberron familiar. The trio made their way along a wide path from the inn to the Great Falls to reach an outcrop of stone where Rocky, Nûd's wyvern, was soaking up the sun on his black hide while being gently washed by mist spraying up from the vast descending cascades of water.

"What would you like us to do next?" asked Eynon after he confirmed the familiars were fine.

"Yes," said Merry. "Who can we fetch for you?"

"Brùtha of the Falcon Clan and any of her Southern Clan Lands' associates she wants to bring along," said Nûd. "I want to make sure Dâron stays on good terms with her and her people."

"It will avoid so many potential problems in the future," added Jenet.

"And from what I understand about the Southern Clan Landers, giving them easy access to good farmland to the west while still enabling them to live in the mountains will likely discourage any raids on the Coombe or Dâron's other nearby territories," added Bonnie, who had been studying the geography of her new kingdom.

"That was good thinking on your part," Dârio told Eynon and Merry. "Not that problems with the Southern Clan Landers will ever be completely eliminated."

"But now they're *my* problems, not yours, right, cousin?" said Nûd.

"I'm sure there will be plenty of problems to go around for all of us," said Dârio.

"Just so long as nothing goes wrong with our wedding ceremonies," said Jenet as she leaned down and ticked off a task on one of her lists. "I want everything to be perfect."

"I'll be happy if only wine, not blood, is spilled at the party afterwards," said Bonnie. "I read up on royal weddings at the palace library in Brendinas and at the wedding of Dâroth the Thirteenth several centuries ago the family of a jilted fiancée brought swords under their robes and..."

"...you can finish sharing that story *after* our weddings," said Jenet. "Listening to such things is definitely *not* on any of these lists and besides, guards from three kingdoms and Occidens Province will be on hand to provide security and prevent any violence."

"Along with more wizards in one place than have ever previously assembled on this side of the Ocean, I expect," said Merry. "What could go..."

Merry's words ended abruptly when Eynon put his hand over her mouth. "Don't say it," he said. "My mother always cut my father off when he began to utter that phrase. She told him the universe considered it a challenge." Eynon pulled his hand away from Merry's mouth with a small shout of pain. "You *bit* me," he said.

"You deserved it," said Merry with a smile. "Though I am sorry for what I started to say." She nodded to the royal couples.

"One more thing before you're off to fetch Brùtha," said Bonnie. "There's space on the island above the falls for more people to witness our weddings and the four of us decided we'd give our friends a chance to bring anyone—especially people who aren't nobles—to join the festivities. Is there anyone you'd like to invite?"

"The innkeepers at the Dormant Dragon down the Brenavon from the capital," said Eynon. "And their children."

"Távi and the urchin gang from Nova Eboracum who helped spy for us," said Merry. She looked at Eynon and the two of them came up with a new name simultaneously. "The dough ring man!" they exclaimed together.

"He's already here," said Jenet. "Laetícia brought him. She said her children insisted he attend. He's been feeding dough rings to all the people working on wedding preparations."

"Wonderful," said Merry.

"Is everything ready with the oversized communications ring so Viridáxés and Zûrafiérix can watch?" asked Eynon.

"Yes," said Nûd. "Fercha—I mean, my mother—has tested the pair of rings you gave her, and they work well."

"It's too bad Viridáxés and Zûrafiérix can't join us in person," said Eynon. "Zûrafiérix is still incubating her clutch of eggs. Maybe they'll be able to attend *our* wedding?" he suggested to Merry.

"Whenever we decide to have it," Merry replied.

"After we tour the wonders of the Imperium and finish our wander years?" asked Eynon

"Perhaps," said Merry. She took Eynon's hand and squeezed it.

"In case you were curious," said Dârio, "we also arranged for a communications ring so the dragons and legionnaires down on Valentia could witness the weddings. It wasn't practical for Kârkingórēx, Brünedíxés, and the other western dragons to fly up for the festivities."

"That was very thoughtful," said Eynon. "I should have remembered to set something up."

"Magister Callidus saw to it," said Bonnie.

"I hope you don't mind, but I invited Tûx to the weddings," said Eynon. "I don't know if the sea dragon can swim to the Great Falls in time..."

"Or even tolerate fresh water," said Merry.

"But given Tûx's role in helping us imprison the wizard assassins, I didn't think you'd mind," Eynon completed.

"Mind?" said Nûd. "Tûx is certainly welcome!"

"But not *on* the island," said Jenet.

"We have room for more guests, but not *that* much room," said Bonnie.

"Tûx can join us below the falls," said Dârio.

"We should set up another communications ring for Tûx to use to watch the ceremony from a distance, if necessary," said Merry.

"I'll put my grandfather on that," said Nûd. "It might keep Damon out of trouble."

All six of them laughed at that unlikely prospect. Chee and Ace heard the laughter and took that as a signal to return to their wizards, with Béryl trailing a few steps behind them. The owlberron stood between Nûd and Bonnie and affectionately spread her wings around the royal couple.

"Sometimes I wish *I* was a wizard and had a familiar," said Jenet.

"So do I," said Dârio. "Nûd's not a mage, but Rocky might as well be his familiar."

"It's not the same," said Nûd.

"We could invite one of your warhorses to the wedding," Jenet told Dârio.

"That's a great idea," Dârio replied. He rubbed his chin and thought for the time it took to draw three breaths. "On second thought, let's not. You'd probably make him wear a diaper so that nothing soils our special day—and Rocky might decide to eat him."

"I think I can guarantee that second possibility won't occur," said Nûd, "but diapers on horses are undignified."

"No horses," Jenet told Dârio. "If you want someone familiar, I'll have my sister Linette keep you company."

"Promises, promises," Dârio replied.

"I think you and your familiars should get on with retrieving Brùtha and other guests before I toss my husband-to-be off the cliff and into the river," said Jenet. "This will still be a big production with only *one* royal wedding."

"Go," said Nûd, smiling and waving Eynon and Merry away. "I have *no* interest in being king of both Dâron *and* Tamloch."

"I think a double royal wedding will be much more fun, don't you, Eynon?" said Merry.

Eynon nodded enthusiastically. "It's definitely time to go," he said. "May all the items on your list be crossed out before tomorrow!" With that, the two young wizards boarded their flying disks, ensured their familiars were ready, took hands, and gated out, leaving the royal couples to their work.

Chapter 50

Brùtha's Warning

Eynon and Merry found Brùtha and Máclaesh, another Falcon Clan wizard and her husband, in their new territories. They were using constructs of solidified sound to clear trees and brush from bottomlands along the Tríúnávon to prepare them for planting. It was readily apparent that the rich, alluvial soils along the banks of the river were fertile and should help the Southern Clan Landers feed themselves effectively in the future, without resorting to raiding.

I hope, thought Eynon. He remembered the name of the river from a label on the wall map at Travelers' Rest, Rōlin and Peregrína's home in Three Mountains Valley. It was as wide as the Moravon at Tyford and was formed from two major rivers joining in far western Dâron. Hundreds of miles downstream it would flow into the Mormoráfon, the great river that drained the center of the continent of Orluin. *Maybe someday I could float down its length on a boat or raft with Merry?* he mused before turning his full attention to the Southern Clan Lands' wizards.

The master mage of the Falcon Clan still wore the brown robes with red-ochre trim and black feathers around its neckline that she'd worn when she and four other wizards had attacked Eynon and Merry at the quarry in Wherrel. A handsome falcon perched on her shoulder and eyed Chee and Ace imperiously. Chee hid behind Eynon's hood and Ace gave a low growl before Merry put a hand on her familiar's head to quiet him.

Brùtha's next actions relieved any tension remaining in their meeting. Extending her hand in friendship, Brùtha grasped Eynon's hand, then Merry's, with a smile. Máclaesh did likewise. "I'm sorry I doubted you," Brùtha told the young wizards. She waved her arm to encompass everything around her. "These lands are quite good, and your ring gates will allow us to *live* in our mountains while farming these flat plains here in the west."

"More like the middle west," said Eynon. "Orluin extends for quite a distance until you reach the western Ocean. There's a map at Three Mountains Valley that..."

"What Eynon is trying to say," said Merry, interrupting, "is that he's pleased you and your people like your new lands and ring gates. After the weddings we can make more ring gates so it will be easier for all of your varied clans to have easy access to your farmland."

"That will be helpful," said Máclaesh. His large, dun-colored falcon familiar had the same look of focused intelligence as her wizard.

Brùtha was pleased to be invited to the double royal wedding, and doubly so to learn she would be gated to the Great Falls instead of having to fly the distance herself. She led Eynon and Merry a few hundred yards away to higher ground where the beginnings of a settlement were taking shape. Eight different buildings were under construction. Smooth stones from the river were piled into walls, their chinks filled in with thick clay. Various clansfolk were drying grass to serve as roofing thatch and eight wizards were floating in birchwood roof beams on tendrils of solidified sound to support it.

Merry noticed that the people working on each of the eight buildings wore different colored tartans, and each of the eight wizards assisting had a different kind of familiar riding with them on their flying disks or perched on their shoulders. She saw a raccoon, a polecat, a weasel, and a wolf with the wizards at the four farthest buildings. Closer at hand were a tawny gold mountain lion, a badger, and a raven so large she mistakenly thought it was an eagle at first glance. It took a second look to realize one of the four nearer wizards, wearing a green and white plaid kilt, had an eight-foot rattlesnake with diamond-patterned scales coiled around his torso and upper arms.

Disguising a shudder with a shrug, Merry decided to keep her distance from *that* wizard. A dozen yards away from the village toward the river, she saw a broad-shouldered man with a big nose and a protruding brow who reminded her of Berrt. He wore a short-faced bearskin over his tunic and was nearly as hairy as the bearskin himself, with a beard so long he forked it and tied the ends behind his back. The man was seated on a short, upturned length of log and spinning a mass of river clay on a horizontal wheel with a foot treadle. Beside him were a dozen ceramic storage and cooking vessels—pots, urns, and amphorae—waiting to be fired in a kiln, or by magic, Merry wasn't sure. Then she realized Brùtha was introducing her to the man.

"Merry, Eynon, this is Jaymes, though everyone calls him Hairy," Brùtha was saying. "He's in the Mountain Lion Clan, but we don't hold it against him. He's a true artist with clay."

"Pleased to meet you," said Eynon, sticking out his hand.

Hairy held up a clay-covered palm and nodded in greeting. Eynon nodded back and withdrew his hand. He and Merry bowed to the artisan and admired his handiwork.

Merry turned to Brùtha. "Would it be allowed by your customs for Jaymes to come to the wedding?" she asked. "There's someone there I want him to meet."

"If he wants to come, I won't stop him," said Brùtha. She smiled at Jaymes. "Though I would recommend giving him time to clean up first."

"Always wanted t'see the Great Falls," said Jaymes. "And I'll e'en warsh m'kilt as well as m'face 'n' beard if you'll give me a wee moment to g'reddy."

"That won't be a problem," said Eynon. He waved at the collection of crockery. "Would you like me to fire these for you while I wait?"

"No, m'lad," Jaymes replied. "They need to dry and I need to paint and glaze them before they're fired." He tilted his head and looked at Eynon and Merry. "Would either of you two wee wizards know if there's any good clays near the Great Falls? I'm always lookin' for new clays."

"That's not my area of expertise," said Merry, "but I'd be glad to introduce you to someone who might know."

"That'd be a welcome kindness," said Jaymes. "Thanks from me t'you." He stood and wiped his hands on his bare legs, revealing that he wasn't wearing anything below the waist. Merry hid a smile, wondering if Celéri had seen Berrt similarly attired, or perhaps more accurately *not* attired. "I'll go warm up some water," said Jaymes.

"I can help you with that," said Eynon. He followed the hairy potter to the riverbank, carrying the man's kilt, which had been draped over a tree branch to keep mud and clay off it, along with him on a rod of solidified sound.

While Eynon and Jaymes were seeing to warm water and bathing, Brùtha, urged by Máclaesh, took Merry aside for a private conversation.

"I know I should have told you sooner," said the chief of the Falcon Clan, "but I couldn't bring myself to tell the man who injured so many Southern Clansfolk."

"Please tell me," said Merry. "It sounds important."

"It is," said Brùtha, as Máclaesh made circular encouraging motions with his hands nearby.

"Remember those four brothers exiled from Dâron?" asked Brùtha.

"Of course I do," said Merry. "The one-time heirs to the Mastlands' barony on the Rhuthro. They've caused us no end of trouble."

"They're planning to cause still more," said Brùtha. "They've hooked back up with Grúgàch..." She paused and spat on the ground. "...and from what I heard they plan to disrupt the double royal wedding."

"What can four brothers and one wizard do?" said Merry. "There will be more guards and more wizards at these ceremonies than ever before assembled in Orluin."

"I don't know," said Brùtha, "but my sources tell me it's something about a massive fireball being set off *behind* the Great Falls. I don't understand it—how can you even get behind the falls? And wouldn't all that water just quench a fireball before it could do much damage? I'm just letting you know what I heard from someone close to Grúgàch."

"Thank you for the warning," said Merry as she noticed Eynon and Jaymes walking up from the riverbank. "You can ride on my flying disk, if you'd prefer not to travel so close to Eynon when we *ad hoc* gate to the Great Falls," she told Brùtha.

"You're a thoughtful young woman," Brùtha replied. "I'll take you up on your offer."

"Should we invite anyone else from the Southern Clan Lands to attend the weddings?" asked Merry as she quickly switched from thinking like a spymaster to a diplomat.

"No," said Brùtha. "If you did, then every clan would want their own representative."

"And this way, as the only Southern Clan Lander mage attending, your power and prestige are greatly enhanced," said Merry.

Brùtha nodded and smiled. "Precisely," she said. "You'd make a good clan chief."

"I *am* a baron's daughter," said Merry. "What about Jaymes?"

"It's not an issue," said Brùtha. "Everyone likes him—and they know he's only interested in clay, not power."

"Good to know," said Merry. "I'll be sure to introduce him to someone from near the Great Falls to help him find new clays once we arrive." She asked Brùtha a final question. "Is there anything you need to do before we leave?"

"No," said Brùtha. "Máclaesh can keep things humming while I'm away. There's a reason why I married him. He's competent."

"Interesting," said Merry.

"What's interesting?" asked Eynon as he and Jaymes reached Merry and Brùtha.

"Brùtha and Máclaesh are married—to each other," said Merry.

"I'm in favor of marriage," said Eynon. He smiled at Merry.

"Later," Merry replied, waving to Máclaesh.

Ace and Chee were called back from investigating the amphorae and cooking vessels near the potter's wheel. They hurried over and found their usual spots by Merry's legs and on Eynon's shoulder with only traces of clay on their fur to mark their explorations.

Brùtha joined Merry on her flying disk and Jaymes—in a clean kilt, with a clean beard *and* a clean bearskin—climbed behind Eynon. With a double *pop!* they disappeared. Only Máclaesh and the diamondback rattlesnake marked their departure.

Chapter 51

More News

The three wizards and the potter arrived near the Inn at the Falls a heartbeat later. The inn, which was technically on Tamloch territory, but by long convention considered a neutral site, was decorated with hundreds of yards of fabric in Dâron's royal blue and sky blue, side by side with equal amounts of Tamloch's green and gold. Every window was draped with bunting in the hues of the two kingdoms. The pillared porch running across the inn's front façade was covered in colorful swoops of cloth and stunning arrangements of fresh flowers that must have been donated from half a thousand gardens.

More than a dozen huge tents were set up nearby, some for food, some for attending dignitaries, including the deep purple standards of Occidens Province and Bifurland's black and gold. Beside the Bifurland banner, close to a smaller tent, was an unfamiliar red, white, and blue standard that likely belonged to Nordland, Eynon and Merry decided, given Knútr's presence on the Tempest Isles earlier. They decided they had to include a stop in that kingdom when they crossed the Ocean to explore the wonders of the Imperium—at some point *after* the weddings.

Merry shared Brùtha's warning with Eynon in a series of quick whispers. She saw his ears turn red from the intimacy of the whispers, which tickled his ears, then saw his face turn pale as the import of the warning sank in.

Chee, oblivious to Eynon's worries, jumped on Ace's back. The two familiars flew off to see what tidbits of food they could snag from a trestle table set up at one end of the inn's porch. It was loaded with breads, cheeses, fruits, and sweet cakes to fortify the people going about wedding party business and there were enough people around it that Eynon and Merry hoped their familiars would be circumspect in their poaching.

Brùtha spotted another kilt-wearing woman—Arminta, the leader of the Northern Clan Landers—and immediately set off to talk to her, thanking Merry for *ad hoc* gating her as she walked away. Eynon wondered if it was wise to have two such effective and potentially dangerous leaders connect, but knew it was too late to worry about such things at this point. There was plenty of land north of the Tríúnávon and south of the Inland Seas to provide the Northern Clan Landers with good farmland of their own if Brùtha told Arminta about the gate rings Eynon and Merry had given *her* clans.

Jaymes seemed overwhelmed by all the people bustling about preparing for the wedding, so Merry expediently introduced him to Captain Rood, the Tamloch officer in charge of the militia guarding her kingdom's territory north of the Great Falls. If anyone would know someone familiar with sources of clay in the vicinity, it would be Captain Rood.

"Pleased to make your acquaintance, Jaymes," said the captain. A broad smile crossed her sun-darkened face and made her seem much less threatening than the battle scars on her arms might otherwise have promised. "You're a big'un, aren't you?" she said. "Got some troll in you, I'd bet. My mother used to say we had some troll blood in our family, back a few generations. *Trolls have a feeling for the earth*, she used to tell me, so it's no surprise you're a potter looking for good clay."

After what the captain said, Merry was even more interested in having Jaymes meet Berrt, but she couldn't find her troll-wizard friend and assumed he was off with Celéri doing who knows what. *Who am I kidding?* thought Merry. *I think I can make a pretty good guess at what.* Captain Rood, meanwhile, had continued talking.

"It's my uncle Cassius you'll be wanting to talk to," the captain told Jaymes. "He knows everything about clay, even though he left Roma territory to marry my poor aunt Celin and isn't a proper western Tamlocher. He made bricks with clay from deposits along the Abbenoth, he did, and he always tells me it near broke his heart when Roma nobles covered up walls built of his good brick with marble. *Nothing's more honest than a well-made brick,* he says, if you ask him, and sometimes even when you don't."

Jaymes and Merry were impressed with Captain Rood's unceasing torrent of words. They rivaled the immense volume of water going over the falls. Eynon, more used to such speech from experience with various relatives and townsfolk back in the Coombe, inserted a question the way a person cutting down a tree might hammer in a wedge to ensure the trunk didn't land on their cottage.

"Do you know anything about the tunnels behind the falls?" Eynon asked. "Merry and I have been in them, but we need to specifically get to any tunnels below the island *between* the falls."

"Goat Island, you mean," said Captain Rood, "though I expect after tomorrow it will be called Wedding Island." She uncharacteristically paused to take a breath and rubbed her chin to encourage thought. "Aye, there's a map of at least *some* of the tunnels at the inn," she said, "but I doubt it will be much help because the folk who live down there keep modifying and extending them. The map was probably out of date a week after it was inked."

"People *live* in those tunnels?" asked Merry.

"Some might call them people," Rood replied, "and I'd be one of them, but I said *folk*. Troll folk. I told you they have an affinity for the earth. *Best tunnelers in Orluin,* my mother used to say. *Best miners, too, especially the young ones.* 'Why is that?' I'd ask her when I was still a girl. She'd say *Because they're minor miners,* then she'd laugh and feed me a slice of bread dipped with honey. *Trolls know rock,* she told me. *They chew up stone and spit out bricks,* though she didn't really say *spit,* if you take my meaning."

"I do," said Eynon. "Where at the inn might we find this map?"

"Last I knew it was in the library," said Captain Rood, "but I can't remember where my predecessor, Captain Shaw, might have filed it. Probably inserted behind the cover of one of those big atlases we imported from the Imperium. *Maps with maps,* Captain Shaw told me—but it doesn't matter. I can trace you out the main tunnels in the dirt once I find a stick. I was very fond of maps when I first joined the army."

Merry line-of-sight gated away for a moment. She found a stick that would serve beneath a green-leafed maple tree growing far enough away from the inn that it didn't spoil any guests' views of the Great Falls and was back before Captain Rood could utter more than a dozen words. "Here you go," said Merry as she handed the stick to the captain. They stepped over to a bare patch of ground where the grass had been worn away by too many passing feet.

Soon, a drawing that looked like a child's doodling with chalk on slate appeared in the dirt. Eynon and Merry recognized the tunnel that came up inside the inn and the one leading directly behind the curved Tamloch falls. They saw a large chamber that looked like it was beneath the island.

"What's that?" asked Merry as she pointed to the chamber.

"On the map it was labeled *Hall of the Mountain King*, though we don't have any mountains worthy of the name nearby," said the captain.

"Perhaps it was constructed for a troll king who lived on—or *in*—a mountain before coming here?" Jaymes suggested.

"That's as good an answer as any," said Captain Rood. "Now I'd best be getting on with introducing you to my Uncle Cassius, then it will be time to make my rounds to make sure my soldiers are doing their jobs as guards instead of napping."

"An officer's work is never done," said Eynon. "Thanks for your help."

"It's no trouble, none at all," said Captain Rood as she led Jaymes toward one of the big tents. She turned away but continued talking, focusing her words on Jaymes. "Whatever you do, don't mention the baths behind the inn," she said. "They're mostly brick but King Túathal covered up all the solid brickwork with marble and…"

Finding themselves alone, despite all the comings and goings around them, Merry gave Eynon a hug.

"How do we stop what might happen?" asked Merry.

"We now know the general layout of the tunnels behind the Great Falls," said Eynon. "You could hide an army down there."

"We only heard about Grúgàch and the four Mastlands' brothers," said Merry. "That's not an army."

"There were a lot of unhappy Southern Clan Landers after I accidentally blew up that mountain," said Eynon. "Maybe they joined the others?"

"I'm sure Brùtha would be aware of any such thing and would have told us about it," said Merry. "What I want to know is how those obnoxious Mastlands' sons got out of prison in Riyas."

As if to answer her question, Cáinta, the mayor of Riyas, and Sórcha, her chief secretary, approached. "Begging your pardon, good wizards," said Cáinta. "Might I have a word with you?"

"Of course," said Eynon. "How may we be of service?"

"It's more a matter of what we can do for you," said Cáinta. "Isn't that right, Sórcha?"

The chief secretary shifted from foot to foot and didn't look up, apparently finding blades of grass in the mist-watered turf utterly fascinating.

"Tell them," Cáinta ordered.

"Yes, mayor," Sórcha answered softly. She looked up at last and spoke to Eynon and Merry. "There was something I should have mentioned when you were in Riyas earlier," she said.

The two young wizards looked at Sórcha, waiting for more.

"Speak up!" said Cáinta. "Take responsibility for your oversight."

"It wasn't technically *my* oversight," said Sórcha. "It was the warden at the royal prison who..."

Cáinta silenced Sórcha with an upraised palm. "What my former chief secretary *should* have told you earlier was that two wizards broke four troublemaking Dâron men out of the royal prison in Riyas."

"*Two* wizards?" said Eynon. "Grúgàch must be one of them, but who's the other?"

"The warden only reported that one of the wizards was quite old and somewhat scruffy-looking," said Sórcha.

"With a long white beard?" asked Merry.

"I believe so," Sórcha replied.

"Merrillōn," said Eynon.

"Doethan's old mentor, yes," said Merry.

"We shouldn't have shown him how to make wide gates," said Eynon.

"That's water over the falls," said Merry, adapting a traditional maxim about bridges to fit the scene before her.

"Thank you for informing us, Mayor Cáinta—and Sórcha," said Eynon. "Merry and I are about to deal with those wizards and the escaped prisoners now, before they can interfere with the weddings."

"That sounds wise," said Cáinta. "Let us know if there's anything we can do to help."

"There is something you can do," said Merry. "Find Verro and let him know we're trying to stop a plot to ruin the weddings. Fercha will probably be with him, and if you see Laetícia, she should also be informed."

"We'll do our best," said Cáinta. "Won't we, Sórcha?"

"Yes, mayor," Sórcha replied. She followed Cáinta toward the inn's porch in search of the specified wizards.

"Shall we collect Ace and Chee?" Eynon asked Merry.

"Let them eat cake," said Merry. "Remember what happened the last time they were in the tunnels behind the falls?"

"They ran off and we had to chase after them," said Eynon. "Point taken. Do we go into the inn and retrace our path from last time?"

"Can't you just *ad hoc* gate us back?" asked Merry. "I wasn't a master mage then, so don't expect me to do it."

"I'd like to say it would be no problem, but those tunnels are a maze of twisty little passages, all alike, and I'm not sure I could gate us in accurately," Eynon replied. "Besides, before we go exploring behind the falls again..."

"I get your meaning," said Merry as she noticed Eynon shifting from foot to foot. "Let's gate to Riyas and use the gate in Túathal's bedchamber. I think that came out deeper behind the falls and closer to the Hall of the Mountain King below where the weddings will be held."

"Makes sense to me," said Eynon. He took Merry's hand and the two *ad hoc* gated away.

Chapter 52

Behind the Great Falls

Between the two of them, Eynon and Merry remembered the passphrase that opened the fixed gate from Túathal's sumptuous bedchamber to the tunnels behind the falls. The island where the weddings would take place was midway between the curved Tamloch falls and the straight Dâron falls so the two young wizards followed tunnels leading *away* from the ones they'd taken previously.

Eynon had planned ahead and used Túathal's garderobe, so he wasn't challenged by an intense need to relieve his bladder due to the constant, high-volume flow of water nearby. After twenty minutes of walking and several twists and turns, they were close to the large chamber below the island that Captain Rood had traced out with her stick. Eynon put a finger to his lips, then pointed to his ears. Merry understood his intent and they both cast the listening spell Merry had taught Eynon on the trip down the Rhuthro when they'd first gotten to know each other.

Their augmented ears immediately heard voices ahead.

"If you're just going to use fireballs, I don't see why you need *us* here," said a voice they recognized as belonging to Fox, the most intelligent of the Mastlands' brothers, though in Merry's opinion, at least, that wasn't saying much.

"If y'canna use the brains of half a goose inside your head fer more than suet pudding, that's not *my* problem," said another voice.

Eynon nodded when he saw Merry mouth the word, "Grúgàch," without actually speaking.

"We need your help to protect us while we're working dangerous magic," came a third, creaky-sounding voice. "We'll be vulnerable to physical attack while we're concentrating on assembling close to a thousand timed fireballs and maintaining the gate that will get us out of here before this chamber *and* the island above it blow up."

"Merrillōn," whispered Eynon at the threshold of audibility. This time, Merry was the one to nod.

"Keep your crossbows at the ready and shoot anyone who comes down any of the tunnels leading into this chamber," Merrillōn continued.

"Are you done with that gate yet?" asked Grúgàch.

"Don't get your smallclothes in a twist," said Merrillōn. "We all want this gate coming out at your tower, not in the middle of the Ocean."

"Just be quick about it," said Grúgàch. "I'll need your help to stabilize these fireball spells that need just one more word to trigger them."

"What's the word?" asked Fool, the least intelligent of the Mastlands' brothers, and that was saying something.

"Watch the tunnels and don't ask stupid questions," said Grúgàch.

"Fine by me," said Fox. "You're the one with the gold. You make the rules."

"And don't forget it," said Grúgàch.

Eynon and Merry exchanged glances that proved they were both glad Chee and Ace hadn't come along. Leaning in to whisper in Merry's ear, Eynon said, "I'll handle Grúgàch and his fireballs— you deal with Merrillōn and the Mastlands' brothers."

Merry kissed Eynon's cheek. "You always give me the fun jobs," she whispered back. "Invisibility first, or distraction first?"

"No distraction," Eynon replied. "We don't want to risk Grúgàch losing control of his fireballs."

"I'll follow your lead," said Merry. "You've followed mine often enough."

"On three," said Eynon. He stepped back from Merry and held up three fingers, slowly lowering first one, then two, then three.

Both young wizards disappeared, using their illusion powers to render themselves invisible. Stepping like stalking cats, they tiptoed into the chamber and saw that Grúgàch had assembled hundreds of smoldering red fireballs, each the size of an apple, inside a large sphere of solidified sound. If they'd heard the enemy wizards' prior conversation correctly, it would only take a single word to detonate every fireball simultaneously, bringing down the roof of the chamber and potentially causing the island above to crumble and be washed down over the falls.

Along the far wall of the chamber, Merrillōn was putting the finishing touches on a temporary gate that would allow Grúgàch, the four Mastlands' brothers, and himself to escape before the massed fireballs were triggered. The brothers were presently on guard at the four tunnels that entered the chamber at the cardinal directions. Their crossbows were cocked and ready and their senses were on high alert for any signs of attack.

Eynon and Merry didn't give them any reason to react. They heard Merrillōn chant the last words needed to make his temporary gate spell snap into place. A squat gray stone tower atop a steep cliff was visible on the other side of the interface. It appeared to be truly isolated, with no signs of habitation for tens of miles.

"That's done," said Merrillōn. "What do you need me to do for *you?*" he asked Grúgàch.

"Nothing, *now,*" said the Southern Clan Lands wizard. "You could have helped me stabilize individual fireballs, but it's too late for that." The hundreds of apple-sized balls of fire magic inside the sphere of solidified sound Grúgàch maintained were pulsing now. "Get the guards to the gate—we'll only have seconds before these blow."

Eynon could sense the building energies inside the sphere Grúgàch held. Waves of red-orange light splashed against the chamber's walls from the primed fireballs. They seemed filled with more potential explosive force than Celéri's congruency linked to the corona of the Sun. Indeed, each of the hundreds of fireballs were connections to the Sun's corona just waiting for a single word before they opened. That word was *not* the word Eynon was about to utter, which was "Now!"

Before he could speak and alert Merry to attack, dozens of screaming trolls wearing black bearskins charged into the chamber from three of the four tunnels. They carried short spears and lindenwood shields. The Mastlands' brothers shot their crossbow bolts in a panic, without taking time to aim. Three bolts ended up embedded in wooden shields. The fourth wedged into the shinbone of an older and larger troll, whose spear tip was washed with gold. The shield he carried was painted with a highly realistic depiction of the snarling face of a crowned short-faced cave bear. He bellowed in pain and anger, nearly doubling the volume of the troll newcomers' previous screams.

Amid the confusion, Grúgàch nearly lost control of his sphere containing the primed, but not triggered fireballs. He staggered toward the temporary gate Merrillōn had created.

Eynon thought, then acted. He surrounded the sphere of solidified sound Grúgàch had created with a larger, thicker sphere of his own.

"Down!" shouted Merry. She didn't wait for the others to follow her instruction. Instead, she slammed Merrillōn, the Mastlanders, and the new troll-folk arrivals flat to the floor of the chamber with a plane of solidified sound descending from the chamber's ceiling with the force of a falling mammoth.

For the tiny fraction of the time it takes a heart to throb a single beat, Eynon held the power of what seemed like nearly a thousand exploding suns inside *his* sphere as the original containment sphere maintained by Grúgàch was consumed in white-hot flames. Before Eynon's strength gave out, he shoved the sphere through the open temporary gate.

Seeing it gone, Merry disrupted the careful balance of the gate, causing it to close with the finality of a cell door slamming on a prisoner held for life in solitary confinement. The chamber was darker and quieter now, without trolls' war cries or the pulsing red glow of the primed fireballs. For a dozen breaths nothing happened. The trolls were the first to rise, with the large troll shot by a crossbow removing the bolt from his shin and holding the bloody point before him, ready to skewer Fox, who remained on the floor with his brothers.

Grúgàch rose next and cast around, using his magic to locate other magestones. "There you are," he told Eynon as he released a blast of lightning in Eynon's direction. Merry tried to interpose a plane of solidified sound between Grúgàch and Eynon, but she wasn't fast enough. The blast struck Eynon squarely in the chest— and flowed down his tight shields until its charge dissipated into the stony ground beneath Eynon's feet.

Stepping toward Grúgàch, Eynon was about to blast the shaggy Southern Clan Lands' wizard in return when he saw the massive arms of a troll encircle the wizard's chest, strip the leather bracer holding his magestone from his arm, and lift Grúgàch off his feet. Grúgàch struggled in the troll's dragonclaw-like grip, with his legs kicking ineffectually beneath him.

"I am Barrt, King Under the Mountain, at your service," said the large troll to Eynon. "I've long thought that wizards should deal with wizards, but it seems to me that you've already done your part."

"By not allowing your captive to blow up the falls?" asked Eynon.

"True enough, but he's not *my* captive, he's yours," said King Barrt. "I'm just holding him temporarily."

"Thank you for your able assistance and the aid from your people," said Merry. She waved a hand at the trolls holding each of the Mastlands' brothers' captive.

"Yes, thank you," said Eynon. He turned to face Merrillōn, who slowly got to his feet with a formidable troll standing beside him.

"Don't hurt me," Merrillōn pleaded. "I'm just a poor, tired old man. I won't cause any trouble."

"Don't believe him for an instant," said Merry. "Take his magestone."

King Barrt nodded to the troll by Merrillōn and that worthy removed the white haired wizard's magestone and tossed it to Merry.

"Doethan can determine your fate," said Merry. "You were *his* teacher. You can be his problem."

"You are most merciful," said Merrillōn.

"That remains to be seen," said Eynon. "Doethan may have other ideas."

The trolls bound Grúgàch and Merrillōn's hands and did the same to the Mastlands' brothers who glared as much at Grúgàch as they did at Eynon, Merry, and the trolls. Fox tried to speak, but Merry covered his mouth and the mouths of his brothers with thin sheets of solidified sound. She'd heard everything she'd ever wanted to hear from her unneighborly neighbors who had once lived along the Rhuthro.

Eynon took a healing potion from his pack and handed it to King Barrt. The injured troll took it gratefully and nodded his appreciation to the young wizard.

"How many of your folk live here behind the falls?" Merry asked King Barrt as the healing potion closed his wound.

"Several hundreds," Barrt replied. "These tunnels are an important refuge for my people. We've expanded them extensively over the years."

"So I've gathered," said Merry.

Before the king could reply, the ground around them shook like a wet dog flinging off water. The floor of the chamber briefly undulated beneath them.

"How far away was Grúgàch's tower?" Eynon asked Merrillōn.

"Several hundred miles to the southwest, deep in the mountains," Merrillōn replied.

"What did you do to my tower?" asked Grúgàch.

"What tower?" said Merry with a smile. "I don't think you *have* a tower—at least not anymore."

"Blast you!" said Grúgàch.

"You tried that already, and failed," said Eynon. "I also think you know what happened to your precious tower—precisely what *you* planned to do to the Great Falls and the royal wedding island."

Grúgàch lapsed into a litany of calumnies attacking Eynon's character, parentage, and personal habits. Merry let him go on long enough for the Southern Clan Lands' wizard to start repeating himself before slapping a thin sheet of solidified sound across his mouth as well.

"You were sharing details about your refuge here, O King," said Merry. "Tell me, do you by any chance know a young troll named Berrt?"

"What sort of trouble has my wayward son gotten into now?" asked King Barrt.

"You'd be surprised," said Merry. She was surprised as well, since Berrt had obviously been far from truthful with her about his background.

"Or maybe not," added Eynon, smiling at Merry. "You'd be a-*maged* at what Berrt's gotten into."

Merry shook her head and wagged a finger at Eynon, who kept smiling.

"By the way," Eynon continued. "How would you like to attend a double royal wedding? I'm sure I could get you an invitation."

Chapter 53

Midsummer's Day Morning

Midsummer dawned with delicate solar rays of Tamloch gold shining through crystaline skies of Dâron blue, ushering in one of the most beautiful mornings in Eynon's memory. The day was even more lovely because Merry was beside him in a feather bed on the third floor of the Inn at the Falls and because four of his friends were scheduled to be wed when the Sun reached its zenith at noon.

Merry rolled toward him and put an arm over his hip without seeming to wake.

"Now?" whispered Eynon, saying the word he hadn't said in the chamber below the island.

"Uh huh," said Merry, demonstrating she hadn't actually been asleep at all.

"I can't think of anything better to do before a pair of weddings," said Eynon.

"More kissing, less talking," said Merry.

Eynon was pleased to follow Merry's recommendation. The day was off to an excellent start.

* * * * *

Time passed... pleasantly.

Merry disentangled herself and pulled back just enough to see Eynon's eyes. "Up for another?" she asked.

Eynon looked down his torso, then looked up and nodded. "I am," he replied. "Twice seems appropriate, given that we have a *double* wedding to celebrate."

"What did I say about less talking?" teased Merry.

The sounds of water going over the falls provided an eminently suitable accompaniment for the noises coming from their comfortable bedchamber.

* * * * *

Dârio woke to find Jenet pacing across the imported Eastern Empire carpet at the foot of their bed as a shaft of dawn light pierced a window, illuminating the contours of her delightfully female form through her thin sleeping gown.

"What's wrong, my love? Is there anything I can do to help?"

"You can tell me I was foolish for trying to manage all the details of my own wedding," Jenet answered.

"Don't..." Dârio began.

"If the next word from your lips is *worry* the wedding is off!" said Jenet. "Of course I'm worried. There are so many details to juggle and I'm the one in charge of all of them."

"You may be in charge, but you've also selected competent, experienced subordinates to see that everything gets done to your satisfaction," said Dârio. "They all have checklists and every one of them has good judgment and the flexibility to adapt well to changing circumstances."

"You admire flexibility?" said Jenet. "Like the way my younger sister, Linette, is flexible?"

"Now I know it's just nerves," said Dârio. "You never bring up Linette unless you're feeling insecure and want me to tell you that I love you—which I do, from here to the Imperium and back. Come over and stand beside me so I can hug you."

"Oh no," said Jenet. "I'm not playing *that* game." She flashed a quick smile at Dârio. "First, it's a hug. Then it's a kiss. Then it's *more* kisses, and soon we'll be horizontal making love. There's got to be some sort of rule of etiquette against making love on your wedding day, at least *before* the wedding."

"You're making that up," said Dârio. "And we don't have to be horizontal if you don't want to."

"Harrumph," said Jenet. She paced over and faced Dârio with her hands on her hips. "I am not making it up," she insisted, her smile becoming simultaneously wider and more mischievous.

"At least let me hug you," he said. "What can that hurt?"

"Very well... my king," said Jenet. She stepped closer while Dârio shifted his legs off the bed and stood up. "You may hug me, if that is your royal will."

"We have time," said Dârio. "My royal will is to help you forget about all the wedding details filling your head for half an hour. Does that meet with the approval of my future queen?"

Jenet's smile transformed into a grin, and she threw herself into Dârio's arms, pulling his head down so she could whisper in his ear. "Could we make it an hour, my love?"

"It would be my pleasure," said Dârio.

"Mine, too," said Jenet. "Mine, too."

* * * * *

Bonnie felt a sunbeam on her eyelids and a warm form next to her on the bed. She sighed without opening her eyes. She remembered back a few months ago when she was only in love with the magic of mathematics, or was it the mathematics of magic? The distinction didn't seem all that important to her at present and the term *mathemagic* combined both nicely. Today was her wedding day. *I never would have dreamed I would have fallen in love with anyone, especially someone as wonderful as Nûd,* she thought. *And for him to turn out to be the king of Dâron? What are the odds of that?*

She forced her brain to stop trying to calculate those odds and smiled. *Nûd will be a good king,* she mused. *He has the potential to be a great one. I hope a can be a queen who is worthy of him.* She thought about her days as a student at the Institute in Bhaile Pónaire and wished there were graduate-level classes for her to take that would teach her everything she needed to know about being a queen. She always did well in her classes, but the only grades she'd receive for being Nûd's wife, queen, and consort would come from Nûd—and the people of Dâron.

Her eyes still closed, Bonnie rolled over to give Nûd a kiss. She leaned in, puckered her lips, and kissed—a *beak!* Bonnie's owlberron familiar emitted a high-low squawk-growl and left the bed to perch in an open window where the sunlight was streaming in.

"Béryl, what are *you* doing in bed with me?" exclaimed Bonnie. "No familiars on, or especially *in* the bed! That's a rule!"

Nûd's voice came from a few feet away. He was sitting in an over-stuffed chair near the foot of the bed. "I gave her permission," Nûd told Bonnie. "She wanted my warm spot."

"What if *I'd* wanted your warm spot?" asked Bonnie. "No, what I want is you! What are you doing way down there? I wanted to kiss you and wake you up the best way. You should have told her you were in charge."

"Béryl is six-hundred pounds with a bear's hind paws and an owl's beak and talons," said Nûd. "I wasn't going to argue with her."

"You're a king," said Bonnie. "You rule all of Dâron. Do you mean to say you're going to allow a mere owlberron to defy you?"

"There's nothing *mere* about an owlberron," said Nûd, "and as for defying me, remember—she didn't defy me. I gave her permission to take my warm spot."

"But why would you do such a thing?" asked Bonnie.

"Have you ever heard the phrase, *never give an order...?*"

"*...you know won't be obeyed,*" Bonnie completed. "I take your point."

"Consider it a lesson in being a king or queen," said Nûd.

"I was just thinking about that," said Bonnie. "What do you think the odds are of you getting back into bed?"

"Pretty high," said Nûd as he got up from his chair. "Do you think my spot is still warm?"

"Only one way to tell," said Bonnie as she patted the side of the bed.

As Nûd moved to get into bed and confirm whether or not his spot was still warm, Béryl looked at him, looked at Bonnie, and smoothed down her ruffled fur and feathers before launching herself out the window in search of small rodents and accessible beehives. The thought passing through her brain, if it could truly be properly translated, was something like, *there are lots of ways to celebrate and they can have theirs.* Given the peculiarities of owlberrons' combined avian and mammalian reproductive physiologies, mating was not a pleasure for Béryl or her partners. *But a field mouse dipped in honey fresh from the comb is a joy beyond measure.*

* * * * *

"Our son is getting married," said Verro when he'd propped his head up on one elbow.

"I'm so sorry we couldn't give him more parental attention," said Fercha as she adjusted the bedsheets to cover what she wanted to cover while revealing what she wanted Verro to see.

"We only kept our distance to protect him," said Fercha. "And now Nûd hates me."

"He doesn't hate you," said Verro. "He just doesn't know you very well."

"Nûd resents me," said Fercha. "*My* mother was more of a mother to him than I was, at least while she was in Melyncárreg."

"If my brother had learned about Nûd he would have had him killed," said Verro. "We did what we needed to do. Nûd is a sensible man—he'll realize that and give us a chance to build a relationship with him. Once he and Bonnie have children, you'll be Nana Fercha, and I'll be Grampa Verro. That will help."

"Reminding me I might be a grandmother in the not-so-distance future *isn't* helping," said Fercha.

"Don't forget, that will make Carys a great-great-grandmother," said Verro.

"The Old Queen would like that," said Fercha, allowing the corners of her mouth to turn up. "I was talking to her yesterday. The proprietors at the inn gave her a room on the first floor so she doesn't have to climb stairs. She's excited about the prospect of developing a series of Queen Lessons for Bonnie."

"With Jenet as a guest lecturer?" teased Verro.

"Probably not," said Fercha. "Bonnie and Jenet are friends, but Jenet has so many advantages, being raised as a duke's daughter, that Bonnie feels inadequate by comparison."

"While Jenet's understanding of mathematics is limited to arithmetic, algebra, and keeping manorial accounts," said Verro. "She has no idea of the complexities involved in Bonnie's studies at the Institute."

"And *I* do," said Fercha. "I love it when we start discussing topological equivalences of non-Euclidean solidified sound constructs together. Bonnie's eyes light up, and so do mine."

"There's your answer, then," said Verro. "Nûd loves Bonnie. If Bonnie loves you, he'll learn to love you, through her, and potentially build an adult friendship with you, even if he'll never really think of you as his mother."

"I expect you're right," said Fercha. "But what we've given up still hurts."

"It does," said Verro. "Though I am beginning to really like Eynon, and I think the affection and respect is mutual. I hope he'll continue to seek my advice over the years."

"That's another thing," said Fercha. "My father."

"Don't get started," said Verro. "For all that Damon seemed to mistreat Nûd, our son has his head set firmly on his shoulders. The old man's approach may have been unusual, but it's hard to argue with his results. Nûd has a thorough grounding in all the skills of kingship without the swelled head that usually goes with wearing a crown."

"I know," said Fercha. "But it's still galling. He treated me much the same way and I left Melyncárreg as soon as I was able." She rested her head back on her pillow and put her palm on her forehead before she spoke again. "Interesting," she considered. "That may be another way for me to develop a relationship with Nûd. We've both suffered under Ealdamon's tutelage."

"So has Eynon," said Verro. "And look how he's turned out. I think Damon was wise not to train Eynon too rigorously. He's a once in five generations talent—maybe once in ten generations."

"I heard rumors he and Merry stopped a pair of Southern Clan Lands' wizards from blowing up Goat Island," said Fercha.

"I can confirm that," said Verro. "Mayor Cáinta told me that's what the two of them were up to. Why they didn't think to ask other wizards for assistance is puzzling, however."

"Between them, I don't think Eynon and Merry *need* assistance, even from us, for most situations," said Fercha. "There is one thing I'd like to dig into, however. Merry developed into a master mage by extension from using her emergency gating capabilities. If that's true, maybe *all* wizards have the potential to be master mages and *ad hoc* gate."

"I'd be very circumspect about exploring that possibility," said Verro. "We don't want too many mages with delusions of grandeur thinking they can escape consequences for their actions by *ad hoc* gating away."

"You have a point," said Fercha. She leaned forward and kissed Verro's lips. "Tell you what," she said. "If you help me learn how to *ad hoc* gate, I'll make it worth your while."

"What do you have in mind?" asked Verro.

Fercha artfully shrugged, causing the bedsheet to slip, and revealing exactly what she had in mind.

"I accept your offer," said Verro, returning her kiss and tugging the sheet down even further.

"We can take all the time we need," said Fercha.

"Don't we have a wedding to attend at noon?"

"Yes, but no one pays any attention to the mother of the groom."

"I plan to pay quite a bit of attention to her," said Verro.

"I'll hold you to that," said Fercha.

"If I told you that you had a beautiful body…"

"Would I hold it against you?" Fercha smiled and wrapped her arms around Verro's chest. "Of course," she said. "In fact, I already am."

* * * * *

"They gave us the room we had the last time we stayed at the Inn at the Falls," said Damon.

"I asked them to," said Astrí. "The bed is especially comfy, and they're next to my mother's room, so I can be close at hand in case she needs me."

"Old Queen Carys will have dozens of admirers across four generations hanging on her every word," said Damon. "Grandmothers are celebrated at weddings and great-grandmothers even more so. Dowager queen great-grandmothers like your mother are in a class by themselves. You'll be lucky to exchange a score of words with her today."

"Perhaps," said Astrí as she plumped a goosefeather pillow behind her back, then shifted to her side to face Damon. She put her hand on the curly gray mat of hair on his chest, which was as luxuriant as the hair on his head was sparse. "Have you considered my request?" she said, working her fingers down to stroke his abdominal muscles.

"You don't play fair," said Damon. His head fell back, indenting his pillow more deeply and he released a sigh that held depths of emotions held in check for decades. "What do you want?" he asked.

"You know what I want," said Astrí. "I want you to serve as Dâron's master mage with me in Brendinas, not off like a hermit in Melyncárreg, and give Eynon and Merry a year of freedom," said Astrí.

"A year?" said Damon. "This is like climbing an ice wall. I'll give them a year, then it will be two years, then a million barbarians on horseback will invade the Imperium and Eynon and Merry, riding on wisents—no, mammoths, will rout the invaders with illusions before making friends with them."

"You're too young to be that cynical," said Astrí.

"Young?" said Damon. "I've earned the lack of every hair on my head and every gray hair on my chest. You can stop playing with my chest hair and stomach muscles any time now unless you want to start something."

"What time is it?" asked Astrí.

"Do I look like a sundial?"

"A little," said Astrí. "Especially when your gnomon is standing up, like it's starting to now."

"Why did we ever separate?" asked Damon.

"You know why," said Astrí. "And you promised to do better, starting with..."

"...giving Eynon and Merry a year to explore the world together and serving as Dâron's master mage while they're away," said Damon. "I'll even live in Brendinas with you if that will make you happy."

"It will, dear," said Astrí. "Now let's see if I can get a better reading of the time so we'll know how long we have before I have to bathe and dress."

"Agreed," said Damon. "Maybe I'll even get a few more maxims for the second volume of my epigrams by keeping my ears open at the wedding?"

"At least that will keep you out of trouble," said Astrí. "And so," she said, moving her hand lower, "will this."

* * * * *

Princess Rúth and Doethan woke in their own bed in the royal palace in Riyas. There was a fixed gate from the palace to the Inn at the Falls in a side hall and they would take it a few hours before the wedding. It connected to an arrivals room at the Inn at the Falls, not the tunnels behind the falls where the fixed gate in Túathal's bedchamber came out.

Rúth had been assigned several important tasks by Jenet, but they were all items that could be done in advance and Rúth had seen to them days ago. She was looking forward to supporting Dârio and Jenet any way she could in the years to come, given certain constraints she had recently become aware of. Beside her, Doethan was snoring softly. Sunlight was filtering through his thick eyelashes and Rúth wondered why she'd waited so long to be with the man she'd loved since she first came of age. *If I had to do it over,* thought Rúth, *I should have defied my brother twenty years ago.*

She shoved Doethan's shoulder gently, causing him to open his eyes and stop snoring.

"Good morning, my princess, my sweet, my love," said Doethan. "Today's the day."

"It is indeed," said Rúth. "It seems like half of Orluin will be at the Great Falls to celebrate the weddings."

"Won't it be wonderful," said Doethan. His smile was like a sunbeam warming Rúth's heart.

"It will," said Princess Rúth. "And in six months or so, if all goes well, there will be yet another person to attend the next celebration."

"What do you mean?" asked Doethan as he rubbed sleep from his eyes.

Rúth put his hand on a spot below her navel and held it there with her own. "What do you think I mean?" she asked.

"Oh," said Doethan. "OH!" he repeated as the full realization of her words struck him and he hugged her. "That will be wonderful indeed!"

Chapter 54

The Procession

Kennig and Inthíra had created spectacular decorations with their illusions. Wizards from three kingdoms and Occidens Province had used their talents with solidified sound to build bridges of truly solid stone from the island to both Dâron and Tamloch territory. The illusionists had transformed the stolid construction of the bridges into sparkling white traceries resembling pastry chefs' spun-sugar confections. The cobbles of the paths leading up to the bridges reflected a hundred different hues and changed color each time a foot touched them.

Not to be outdone by the mages, the people of Dâron and Tamloch did their part to brighten their monarchs' nuptials. Ten-foot white birchwood poles lined the edges of the path from the inn to the bridge on the Tamloch side of the Great Falls. Alternating poles were wrapped with green and gold ribbons or dark and sky-blue ribbons, interwoven with fresh flowers. There were so many blossoms that guests walking to the island had to stop every few feet just to inhale and appreciate their scents. On the Dâron side, the poles were replaced with tall arches holding pots with living rosebushes covered in red, white, and yellow blooms.

After their earlier dalliance and the fun of bathing together—always a treat for mages since their magic ensures they have plenty of hot water—Eynon and Merry donned new sky-blue linen wizards' robes made for them by Merry's mother, Baroness Mabli, and friends from her baronial court. Eynon was impressed to see his robes were lined with red silk the color of his magestone, while Merry's robes were lined with purple silk so dark it was almost black.

A note with Merry's robes, written in her mother's hand, read: *Because you admire Laetícia and the Roma.*

"I must be growing up," Merry told Eynon. "I want to hug my mother instead of strangle her."

"Surely you exaggerate," said Eynon.

"No, I wanted to strangle her three or four times a week before we took our trip down the Rhuthro," said Merry. "She wanted a daughter whose highest ambition was to marry the son of another baron along the river and live close enough for her to visit her grandchildren easily."

"That doesn't sound much like you," said Eynon.

"True enough," said Merry. "It's the reason I preferred the company of my father to my mother."

"Derry is a remarkable man," said Eynon. "I knew that for certain when I met him on the first day of my wander year."

"And you set that old oak tree on fire," said Merry.

"I didn't know what I was doing then," said Eynon.

"And you do now?" teased Merry.

"I'd like to think so."

"I need you to do me a favor," said Merry as she straightened the collar and hood of Eynon's robes, making sure his red magestone with its gold chain and setting could be easily seen.

"Of course," said Eynon.

"You might want to ask me what it is before you agree," said Merry.

"I know you, trust you, and love you," said Eynon. "Whatever you want, I'll do it."

Merry stepped close and put her arms around Eynon, squeezing him tight. She brought her flying disk close with a tendril of solidified sound, shifted onto it, and lifted herself so it was easier for her to kiss him.

"What was that for?" asked Eynon when they broke their kiss.

"Everything," said Merry. "The favor I want is for you to make sure my mother doesn't see me cry when I hug her to thank her for these robes. Do you think you can manage that?"

"Easily," said Eynon. "I plan to hug her, too, and you can wipe your tears away on my robes while I distract her."

"Best partner ever," said Merry.

"You see the world's best partner whenever you look in a mirror," said Eynon.

The pair kissed gently.

A trumpet fanfare from outside their third-floor window provided a much-needed distraction. Eynon and Merry walked to the window, hand in hand, only to have Ace fly in with Chee on his back squeaking out a high-pitched *cheeeeeeeeee* as their two familiars made a circuit of their room and zoomed back out again the way they'd entered. The trumpet sounded once more, seeming to be close to the inn. The two young wizards spotted a man with a long brass horn just beyond the edge of the porch. Sunlight glinted off his polished instrument.

"Isn't that..." Merry began.

"The trumpeter who put the circus elephants through their routine at the Battle of the Abbenoth?" Eynon completed.

"It *is*," said Merry. "Jenet told me she'd asked Laetícia to have him play."

"When did you have time to talk to Jenet about musicians?" asked Eynon.

"Days and days ago," said Merry. "We'd better get moving. His fanfare is the signal for us to assemble."

They took another minute to watch hundreds, perhaps thousands, of guests walking across the bridge to the island. Eynon used distance viewing lenses of solidified sound to see similar throngs of people crossing over to the island from the bridge on the Dâron side. He was surprised to see so many children walking with their families—more children than all the people who lived in the Coombe, by his estimation. He mentioned his observation to Merry.

"Everyone wants to make sure their children see the ceremonies," said Merry. "It's a once in ten lifetimes event and they want their sons and daughters to be able to tell *their* grandchildren that they were there."

"Right," said Eynon. "It's like when three red-headed brothers married three red-headed sisters from two farms over back in the Coombe. Everyone for twenty miles in every direction showed up to wish them well and build them three new houses."

"Something like that," said Merry. "But these couples already have places to live."

"Places?" said Eynon. "They have *palaces!*"

"Exactly," said Merry. "The analogy only goes so far."

"Stairs or flying disks?" asked Eynon.

"Flying disks," said Merry. "But we're walking to the island. It wouldn't be right to fly in when the royal couples are at ground level."

The two wizards boarded their flying disks and shifted their positions from the third floor to the flagstones in front of the inn's wide porch in an effortless glide. Many of their friends were already lined up for the procession. Eynon and Merry greeted Valentius and Aleña, who were walking beside Emperor Quintillius, Laetícia, and their three children. Eynon had to fend off attacks from Tertia wielding a stick as her sword as he passed her. Princess Rúth and Doethan looked particularly happy, but Merry didn't have a chance to catch up with her old mentor. Doethan did mention that Verro and Fercha would be joining them shortly. Fercha was putting the finishing touches on a giant communications ring interface that would allow Viridáxés and Zûrafiérix to watch the festivities while they were caring for Zûra's eggs. Verro was helping her with fine tuning things from the dragons' end of the connection.

Salder rushed by and waved to Merry but couldn't stop to talk. Tannis, Tibbo and Taffaern were two, three, and four steps behind Merry's brother, respectively, carrying trays filled with mounds of iced sweet cakes that were sure to equal or possibly exceed to deliciousness of the ones made by Eynon's honorary aunt. Eynon knew he'd have to taste at least a few to compare them and see.

Closer to the bridge, he saw Queen Carys seated on a padded chair supported by four Dâron wizards and their flying disks, one positioned on each corner. Dozens of courtiers were crowded around the dowager queen as she floated a few feet off the ground. They were complimenting her and encouraging her to share stories from her youth—or at least that's what Eynon expected. From the smile on the Old Queen's face she seemed to be loving all the attention.

"She'll be with us for at least another decade," Merry noted when she saw where Eynon was looking.

"What makes you think so?" said Eynon.

"The prospect of great-great-grandchildren," said Merry. "She'll want to bounce them on her knee, or at least hold them, if her legs are failing."

"That would be nice," said Eynon. "I'd like to be a great-great-grandfather someday."

"You should live so long," teased Merry.

"Right," said Eynon. "You too!"

"I think we need to start with children first, before we get to great-great-grandchildren," said Merry.

"Let's worry about that *after* we tour the wonders of the Imperium," said Eynon.

"Well after," said Merry. "If your duties as master mage of Dâron allow."

"Don't forget," said Eynon. "You're a master mage of Dâron now, too."

"It wouldn't be fun doing the job in shifts," said Merry. "I want to explore the Imperium *with* you, not by myself."

"I feel the same way," said Eynon.

A loud commotion nearby interrupted their discussion. Axe blades clanged on brass shields at the far end of the porch as twenty Bifurland warriors escorted King Bjarni and Queen Signý to join the procession. The monarchs lifted their fists to acknowledge Eynon, Merry, and the other dignitaries near them. Amber floated over from behind the king and queen, nodding to Eynon and Merry. "Well done," said Amber. "I hear you averted a tragedy in the tunnels behind the falls."

"With help from the King Under the Mountain and his people," said Merry.

"Trolls assisted you?" said Amber. "Our tales talk of them stealing our livestock and taking human lives."

"These trolls *saved* lives," said Merry. "And you saw how Berrt, the troll mage consorting with Celéri, helped us defeat the wizard-assassins."

"He was a troll?" said Amber.

"He cleaned up well," said Merry. "It turns out Berrt is a troll prince, as well as a troll mage."

"Can troll mages be princes?" Eynon whispered to Merry. "Or is that restriction just a human thing?"

"How strange," said Amber, talking over Eynon. "Next you'll be telling me about some other impossible thing, like trees that walk."

"We haven't seen any ambulatory elms," said Eynon, "but here's King Barrt. We can introduce him to you, King Bjarni, and Queen Signý." Eynon and Merry presented King Barrt and were pleased when he received a warm reception, even if the Bifurland warrior guards did clutch their axe handles tighter when the troll king approached. Laetícia and Quintillius were quite gracious and invited King Barrt to visit them in the Western Empire if he ever crossed the Ocean. Princess Rúth said she'd be glad to assist in working out diplomatic relations between King Barrt's people and the kings and queens of Dâron and Tamloch, should that ever be welcome or necessary.

Barrt was polite but didn't speak at length until he noticed Jaymes standing with Brùtha and Captain Rood a dozen yards away. He rushed over and crushed Jaymes in a hug that resembled the sort given by the original owners of the bearskins they both wore. Eynon and Merry didn't try to listen in. Simple observation showed that the two trolls were obviously old friends reconnecting.

"I wonder if trolls hold grudges like Southern Clan Landers?" Eynon asked Merry.

"I'd guess not," said Merry. "Whatever Jaymes must have done to force him into self-exile seems to have been forgotten."

Eynon raised an eyebrow.

"Yes," said Merry. "I hope the same holds true for Berrt, though when it's fathers and sons it's always more complicated."

"I'm glad that part of *my* life isn't complicated," said Eynon.

"Not everyone is fortunate enough to have parents like yours," said Merry.

"I guess," said Eynon.

"Speaking of Berrt, have you seen him and Celéri?" Merry asked Eynon. "I really want to help Berrt reconnect with his father."

"I haven't seen either of them," said Eynon. "That worries me."

"Or rather, Celéri worries you," said Merry. "She's something of a hair-trigger crossbow or an easily sprung ballista."

"And about as destructive," said Eynon.

Chapter 55

A Double Royal Wedding

Eynon pointed toward the bridge. "Look!" he said. "The procession is moving." He flipped his flying disk up and slid it onto his back, then helped Merry make sure her disk was properly seated on her shoulders and the folds of her robes smoothed out before taking her hand and starting along the path. As they walked, he realized that Kennig and Inthíra's illusions went beyond just what he could see. Lovely music followed them as they walked between the white poles toward the bridge to the island.

Eynon was about to mention the sonic illusions to Merry when he held his tongue. Looking closer, he saw musicians with harps, flutes, viols, drums, and other instruments were spaced out along the path a few paces back from the poles. A fist-sized crystal on the ground in front of each of them was pulsing out a common rhythm of four even beats to ensure their playing remained synchronized and not discordant. "Fascinating," said Eynon.

"The cobblestones that change color?" asked Merry, who'd been looking down.

"The music," Eynon replied.

When they stepped onto the bridge an entirely new dimension of illusion surrounded them. Images flashed along the sides of the bridge, sharing scenes from the lives of the royal couples. Some of the scenes were clearly fabricated. It's difficult to make a life studying mathemagics at the Institute in Bhaile Pónaire or serving a grumpy old wizard seem romantic.

Speaking of grumpy old wizards, Damon and Astrí surprised Eynon and Merry by swooping over their heads and landing on the bridge in front of them. They stowed their flying disks and walked beside the young mages.

"Damon has something to tell you," Astrí informed Eynon and Merry.

Damon frowned at Astrí then held up his palms in surrender, giving in to his wife in some sort of extended battle the two were waging. "If I must," he told her. He shifted his stance to address Eynon and Merry. "I will fulfill the duties of Dâron's master mage while the two of you are off causing trouble in the Imperium," he said. "I won't like it, but I'll do it. I'll give you a year and a day from when you leave Orluin."

Astrí laughed at Damon's startled reaction when Eynon and Merry hugged him. Then they switched and hugged Astrí. Finally, they hugged each other. Quintillius, standing behind them, cleared his throat.

"You're not off to a good start on your visit to the Imperium if you're delaying the Emperor of the Western Empire on his way to a double royal wedding," said Quintillius, keeping his face serious until Tertia whacked his shins with her stick. Everyone laughed and they picked up their pace to close the gap that had opened in the procession.

Soon they reached the island and turned left, toward the falls, where a raised stage had been erected, with the rushing water thundering over cliffs behind it. A thick rock wall behind the stage protected anyone on it from the rising mist. Hundreds of chairs had been positioned near the stage for dignitaries. Farther back, thousands of sections of upturned cut logs provided additional seating. The end of the island opposite the stage had been permanently transformed by magic. It had been shaped by talented earth-working wizards into a vast bowl with bench seats of stone, like the Roma theatre built into a hillside in Nova Eboracum. It had room for ten thousand onlookers and would likely be a much-loved venue for dramatic and comedic works for centuries to come.

Every seat in the theatre was filled. All the cut log seats were occupied. Only a few hundred of the comfortable seats directly in front of the stage were still available, and they were being filled by members of the procession now stepping off the bridge and onto the island. Eynon and Merry didn't sit. They boarded their flying disks and took up stations above and behind the stage. Their roles were to use their illusion skill to project enlarged versions of Dârio, Jenet, Bonnie, and Nûd at twenty times life size so the guests at the very back of the island could follow the ceremonies as easily as those seated in the front rows. It was much the same sort of magic Eynon and Merry had used in Riyas when they'd created a duplicate of that city for Viridáxés to destroy at Túathal's command.

Fercha was on her flying disk by a communications ring expanded to a thirty-foot diameter and floating in front of and high above the stage, supported by three transparent cylinders of solidified sound generated by wizards from Nova Eboracum. Eynon and Merry saw the scaly faces of Viridáxés and Zûrafiérix on the other side of the interface and knew the dragons would be able to witness the event. Verro *ad hoc* gated from Bucket Island to join Fercha in the air as Mafuta, another highly experienced Roma wizard, rose to take Fercha's place so Fercha and Verro could descend to occupy seats of honor in the front row as the parents of one of the grooms.

Eynon saw a hand waving at him from near the back of the comfortable chairs. He used distance viewing lenses to zoom in and identified his sister Braith. She was sitting beside Felix, the tall young Roma wizard who she'd been snuggling with in the hay barn back in Haywall during the Southern Clan Landers' attack on the Coombe. Braith was wearing a new dress in a lovely shade of lavender that went well with the purple wizards' robes worn by Felix.

Not subtle, thought Eynon. *I wish you well, little sister. May you be as lucky in love as I am, and as our parents are.* He laughed to himself without letting it show on his face. *You could do a lot worse than Felix, but you're only fifteen and he's nineteen. He may break your heart, or you may break his, but you're both young enough to heal and move one.* Eynon laughed at himself this time. *Who am I to sound so old,* he mused? *I'm only sixteen myself!*

He was pleased to see his parents—and Merry's parents—sitting near his sister and smiled to notice the innkeepers from the Dormant Dragon Inn and their children a few rows behind them. Herophilos Bodégash, the apothecary, was seated a few rows over, holding a seat for Salder between himself and Uirsé. In the front row, Princess Rúth and Doethan wore big smiles. *They must be happy for the royal couples,* thought Eynon. Admiral Pixo sat next to Rōlin and Peregrína directly in front of Braith and Felix. Lléwys, Rōlin's squirrel familiar, kept peeking over Rōlin's shoulder and chittering at Chee, setting off a round of *chee-chee-chee-CHEEEs* from the raconette. Rōlin gave them each a walnut, quieting the pair and refocusing their attention.

Merry looked down at the stage. *They must have stripped all the gardens between Riyas and Brendinas to fill the stage with so many flowers,* she thought. Even floating above it, she could smell the sweet, blended fragrances of roses, daffodils, tulips, and a dozen more scents she didn't recognize. *I hope they've left room on the stage for the brides and grooms,* thought Merry. She examined the raised platform more carefully and realized its center was strewn with petals rather than bundles of cut flowers. There would be plenty of space for the royal couples.

Eynon and Merry were ready to assume their duties projecting their friends' images when Ace flew up from the back of the stage where the mist was rising from the falls. Chee was holding tight to the fur on the rockhound's back and their two familiars moved in a figure-eight pattern, circling Eynon and Merry in turn while *cheeing* and barking with exuberance.

Exchanging looks and shrugs, Eynon and Merry weren't sure how best to deal with the distraction until Eynon had the idea to project the illusion of a quartet of fruit bats above where Braith and Felix were sitting. Merry, grasping Eynon's plan, added the illusion of bunches of ripe grapes clutched in the bats' claws. Ace and Che were soon streaking away from the stage and toward the seats above Braith and Felix. When the familiars flew close enough to Eynon's sister and her Roma-wizard beau, Felix snared them in a ball of solidified sound and pulled them down so he and Braith could pet them and try to keep them out of trouble.

Laughter came from the assembled guests at the familiars' antics—then their laughs changed to gasps. Rising up from the falls were two winged black shapes, one larger, one smaller. Eynon and Merry immediately began to project the new arrivals. The smaller shape turned out to be Rocky, the wyvern who had initially befriended Eynon and later become Nûd's favorite mount and frequent companion. Nûd was riding on Rocky's back, with Bonnie seated behind him. Béryl, Bonnie's owlberron familiar, was keeping pace with the wyvern, flying just above and behind her wizard.

The larger shape was revealed to be Xaxidiánus, the senior-most Roma dragon in Orluin. Dârio and Jenet rode on his back, waving to the guests below. Merry had told Eynon that Magister Callidus had suggested using Xaxidiánus as part of the ceremonies when Nûd had insisted on flying in on Rocky's back. Jenet had protested that it wouldn't be fair for Nûd and Bonnie to *fly* in while she and Dârio merely rode in on horseback. Nûd was about to give in, reluctantly, when Callidus suggested they ask Xaxidiánus if he would be willing to convey them. The Roma dragon agreed, though he refused to be draped with wreathes of flowers.

Rocky expressed his own lack of interest in being painted a deep royal blue—the color of the dragon on Dâron's flag, as had been suggested by one of the more senior court heralds in Brendinas. The wyvern couldn't speak, but strategic nips from his sharp teeth at anyone carrying a paint brush were more than effective in showing his displeasure at the notion.

Landing simultaneously, Rocky and Xaxidiánus stretched out to make it easier for their riders to dismount. The wyvern and dragon then rose on beating wings and settled on the thick rock wall forming the rear of the stage. Nûd wore a short tunic of dark blue velvet over sky-blue hose and tall boots dyed to match his tunic. Silver piping and intricate patterns of silver braid ornamenting the tunic went well with his simple, highly polished true-silver crown.

Bonnie's ensemble complemented Nûd's. A gown of sky-blue velvet, cut something like an academic's formal robes, rippled around her body as she walked. It was long in the back but rose far enough in front to reveal her dark blue hose and sky-blue slippers. Silver piping in the same pattern used on Nûd's tunic graced her gown and enhanced the sense that the two were well matched. Her simple true-silver crown was the same style as Nûd's. Both fit the personalities of the individuals who wore them.

Keeping with a similar theme, Dârio's tunic was a rich green and covered with so much gold embroidery he practically sparkled.

He wore particolored hose with one leg green and one gold, with tall boots in contrasting colors. A gold-hilted sword in a gilded scabbard hung from a green leather belt around his narrow waist.

For all of Dârio's youth and virile beauty, Jenet made him seem a pigeon beside a peacock. Her bodice was green, worked with gold embroidery, and her skirt, made of alternating segments of green velvet and cloth of gold, both embroidered with thousands of tiny trefoils, made Jenet seem like the living embodiment of the Tamloch flag. Dârio and Jenet wore gold crowns, not ones of true-silver, but it was not lost on any observers that all four crowns were made in the same timeless style.

The two couples stood side by side on the stage, holding hands—their expanded images projected high above them. Before any words could be spoken, cheers erupted from all parts of the island. Chants of *Nûd, Nûd, Dâr-i-o* began, only to be replaced with antiphonal shouts of *Bon-nie Jen-et, Bon-nie Jen-et* and *Dâr-on Tam-loch*.

The cheers continued until Nûd and Dârio lifted their arms and lowered their hands to call for silence. Once the crowd was quiet, the cousins clasped forearms then shifted to hug each other. Bonnie and Jenet embraced as well, then all four hugged. Wild cheering began again until the two kings bid the cheering cease, at least temporarily.

Eynon and Merry amplified the monarchs' next words as they first spoke individually.

"I, Nûd, King of Dâron..."

"I, Dârio, King of Tamloch..."

And next said in unison:

"Call upon all assembled to witness our vows of marriage to our chosen partners."

More cheering started, but a dozen senior mages, recruited by Fercha and Verro, used their magic to soak up the cheers so the kings and their queens could still be heard.

Verro and Fercha stood. "We stand in witness," they said.

Duke Háiddon rose as well. "I stand in witness," he intoned.

Cáinta got to her feet. "I stand in witness."

Quintillius lifted Tertia to his shoulders so she could be seen, for it was the custom to have at least one young child as a witness. *"I sit on an emperor's shoulders, and I am a witness,"* shouted Tertia. *"I think this is wonderful and I'll never forget it!"*

The wizards were glad to allow the laughter that followed to be heard. More laughter resulted when Eynon and Merry amplified Tertia's next statement, "Now put me *down*, Pater!"

Nûd took Bonnie's hand. "I Nûd, take you, Bonnie, as my partner in life and love; to be by your side supporting you in times of joy and sorrow, in sickness and in health, and graciously accepting your support and wise counsel in turn. I treasure you as a scholar and a mage who works magic on my heart. I welcome you as my wife and queen of Dâron."

Bonnie spoke. "I, Bonnie, take you, Nûd, as *my* partner in life and love. I promise to support *you* in times of joy and sorrow, in sickness and in health, graciously accepting your support and wise counsel in turn. I welcome you as my husband and my king and hope I can be a queen worthy of the people of Dâron."

"You will, darling," whispered Nûd, unamplified.

"I want to study *you* even more than I want to study congruent topologies," Bonnie whispered in return.

Nûd hugged her and Bonnie hugged him back.

Dârio reached for Jenet's hand. She held it to her heart for a few seconds before he began. "I, Dârio, take you, Jenet, as my partner in life and love. I've loved you since I first saw you making mud pies from dirt by your father's stables."

"That wasn't dirt," whispered Jenet.

Dârio pressed his lips together to keep from grinning. "I promise to support you in times of joy and sorrow, in sickness and in health, graciously accepting your support and *depending* on your wise counsel in turn. I welcome you as my wife and queen of Tamloch. May our rule be better for us being together."

Jenet pulled on Dârio's arm until he bent down, and his head was even with hers. "I, Jenet, take you, Dârio, to be my partner in life and love. I've loved you since you actually *listened* to me when

I told you not to throw rocks at the hornets' nest above the door of the milking shed and carried my sister to the healer in your arms when *she* did and was stung. I promise to support *you* in times of joy and sorrow, in sickness and health, graciously accepting *your* support and wise counsel in turn as best I'm able. I further promise to tell you, in private, when you're being a fool if you promise to do likewise." Jenet took a breath and wiped away a tear. "I welcome..." She sniffed and repeated. "I *welcome* you as my husband and king— and I *know* our rule well be far better for us being together." She hugged Dârio's neck, and he lifted her off her feet, hugging her back and swinging her all the way around before returning her feet to the stage.

The mages suppressing crowd noises allowed sweet sighs from the guests to be heard but wouldn't let their loud cheers come through until after the royal couples kissed. Nûd, Bonnie, Dârio, and Jenet were leaning forward when a wizard—no, *two* wizards—popped into the sky above and behind the stage. It was Celéri, with Berrt standing behind her on her flying disk. The troll mage, who seemed to have no idea where Celéri had been taking him, jumped off and maneuvered his turtle-shell flying disk under him as he fell. Celéri amplified her voice and began to shout something inappropriate for the circumstances, but Berrt, now a hundred yards distant, covered up her shout with loud, exploding fireworks in the shapes of bright summer flowers.

Berrt's display was so beautiful the guests thought it must be part of the ceremonies. The two royal couples embraced and kissed while the assembled crowd cheered so loudly, they even drowned out the fireworks.

Eynon and Merry caught each other's eyes and tried to formulate an unspoken plan for dealing with Celéri, who had the unpleasant habit of always wanting to be the center of attention. Before they could come up with anything, the problem was solved to their satisfaction. A giant, scaly, black and white neck topped by the head of a sea-dragon shot up from the pool below the Great Falls. Tûx's hard nose accidentally smacked the bottom of Celéri's flying disk from all the force of its leap and sent Celéri sailing in a high arc far downstream.

Jets of water fountained up from the sea-dragon's mouth and painted half a circle of droplets high in the air from one side of the falls to the other. Eynon and Merry, assisted by Kennig and Inthíra, used their illusion powers to transform the droplets into a rainbow that remained above the island for more than an hour.

The sea-dragon rested its massive head on the wall behind the stage, causing both Rocky and Xaxidiánus to find other perches.

"Impressive!" Eynon said to Tûx. "That was quite an entrance."

"I told you I would attend," said the sea-dragon. "The Whale River does lead to the Ocean and eventually here. I'm a very fast swimmer, you know."

"Clearly, to make it here all the way from the Tempest Isles in so little time," said Merry. "We're quite pleased you made it on time."

"I couldn't miss it," said the sea-dragon. "These are the first weddings I've ever been invited to."

Chapter 56

Berrt and Celéri

"Should we check on Celéri and make sure she's not hurt?" Eynon asked Merry after Tûx slid back into the deep pool below the falls for a refreshing soak and shower.

"Well..." said Merry, pausing long enough for Berrt to fly over to them.

"I'm going to find Celéri," he told Eynon and Merry. "Tûx doesn't understand how fragile humans can be and Celéri was hit really hard, without any warning."

"Thank you," said Eynon.

"Better Berrt than you or me," Merry whispered under her breath.

Eynon reached into his pack and removed a healing potion from the assortment he'd been given. He shifted his flying disk closer so he could easily hand the flask to Berrt. "This should help if she's injured," said Eynon, smiling at the troll mage. "If she's in bad shape, ring Merry and we'll bring Uirsé. She's a master healer."

"That's very kind of you," said Berrt. "And greatly appreciated. I'll keep you informed."

Merry nodded as the troll mage flew downstream. *Falling from a height onto sharp rocks might teach Celéri a lesson,* she thought. *Though I doubt it.* She joined Eynon and the two young wizards descended to congratulate their friends.

* * * * *

Using his memory of Celéri's arc of travel, Berrt estimated her point of descent downriver with remarkable accuracy. He spotted Celéri's body lying on a large flat rock bathed in midsummer sun close to the Tamloch shore of the Whale River. Her wizards' robes were damp and clinging to her form. Celéri's eyes were closed, and she wasn't moving. A wave of fear larger than the wall of water that struck the Tempest Isles so recently nearly crushed him.

Berrt flew down to the rock as fast as a striking falcon. He was off his flying disk and kneeling by Celéri's side in less time than it would take

439

to recite an iambic couplet. Berrt took Celéri's hand and felt for a pulse. His own hands were trembling.

Celéri's eyes opened. "What are you doing?" she asked, staring up at Berrt.

"Checking to see if you're alive," Berrt replied, releasing a breath he hadn't realized he was holding.

"I assure you, I am," said Celéri. "I'm just resting—and drying my robes in the sun."

"Couldn't you do that with wizardry?" asked Berrt.

"That would require moving," said Celéri. "And magic," she continued. "Neither of which is appealing at the moment."

"Are you hurt?"

"Oh yes," said Celéri. "I have a collection of bruises that will make interesting patterns and colors when they've had a few days to develop. I was able to put up a spherical shield of solidified sound before I landed, so I don't have any broken bones, but I bounced around inside my shield several times, like a dried bean in a rhythm gourd."

"Ouch," said Berrt, still holding her hand.

"The bruises aren't what really hurts."

Berrt shifted to sit beside Celéri's on the flat rock. He continued to squeeze her hand, but didn't speak, waiting for her to say what she wanted to say on her own schedule.

Celéri's chest rose and fell in a long sigh. "What was I *thinking?*" she said. She looked over at Berrt, trying to sense if he was judging her, but the troll's eyes were warm and gentle. "I suppose I wasn't thinking, was I?" Celéri continued. "I do a lot of that." This time, she saw Berrt nodding.

"Drink this," he said, passing her the flask with the healing potion. She sat up long enough to drain the flask's contents then settled back against the flat rock's warm surface.

Celéri ran her tongue over her lips. "That's a well-made potion," she said. "It can't be one of Eynon's, so it's probably from Uirsé. That means you won't get to see the interesting patterns and colors of my bruises." She paused as if wishing to bear at least some physical signs of her misbehavior then shook her head. After a deep breath,

Celéri took Berrt's hand and put it over her heart so he could feel it beat. "Why aren't you telling me how thoughtless I've been?" she asked.

"Do I need to?"

"I guess not," said Celéri. "I'm telling *myself* over and over."

"Why did you try to disrupt the royal weddings?" asked Berrt.

Celéri pressed Berrt's hand tighter against her. Tears leaked from her tightly closed eyes. "I don't *know!*" she said. "I wasn't thinking. It just happened. *They* were getting all that attention. *They* were special, and I wasn't, so part of me wanted to show everyone how special I am. I'm a master mage, aren't I? I can do whatever I want. People need to pay attention to *me!*" Celéri sniffed and wiped her nose on the still-damp sleeve of her robes.

Berrt saw Celéri begin to tremble. "Are you cold?" he asked. "I can try to dry your robes with magic and warm you up."

"I'll just take them off," said Celéri. "It's a warm day and they'll dry faster if I spread them out."

"I don't think that's a good idea," said Berrt. "Let me try using magic." The troll mage had a knack for light and fire. He generated what looked like a small yellow sun in the air above them and fed it heat through a congruency. Soon Celéri's robes were dry, and they both were warm—perhaps even *too* warm.

"I really need to take off my robes," said Celéri.

"Leave them on," said Berrt.

"Don't you want me to take them off?" asked Celéri.

"No," said Berrt. "That would be too much of a temptation. You need me as a listener now, not a lover."

"Can't you be both?"

"Sometimes," said Berrt. "But not this time. Right now, I'm disappointed in you. You told me we were going to the royal weddings. You didn't say you were planning to disrupt the ceremonies and involve me in your thoughtlessness."

"What happened to you being a listener?" asked Celéri.

"I want to listen to you tell me how you plan to do better," said Berrt. "I want to hear how you plan to grow up."

"I *am* grown up!" Celéri moved Berrt's hand on her chest to illustrate her meaning.

"You have a woman's body, but you're behaving like a spoiled child," said Berrt. "I know you lost both your parents to the wizard-assassins. I know you're insecure in your new status as a master mage. I can see that you're using sex to get people to like you. It's clear you're acting immature to get attention, but what isn't clear is when you're going to realize what you're doing and start acting like a responsible adult."

"What do *you* know about being a responsible adult, mister hide-in-a-cave-with-your-philosophy-studies?" said Celéri. "I heard about where Merry found you. You'd still be living under a stone bridge below ground if you hadn't become a wizard."

"You have me there," said Berrt. "We're not all that different. My mother died giving birth to me and my father never accepted that I preferred reading to hunting. *'A king must lead with a strong right arm,'* my father said. *'The Short-faced Bears are the strongest of the troll clans and I won't have a son who prefers books to battles.'* That's why I left home behind the Great Falls and made my way to western Dâron with my library. I told Merry I wanted to find more of my kind, and maybe I do, but *not* my father's people."

"Your father is a king?" said Celéri.

"The king of twelve troll clans, yes," said Berrt. "Fewer than two thousand at last count, including children. They call him the Mountain King because our people originally came from the mountains of Nordland."

"You walked away from being a prince?" asked Celéri.

"I walked away to live the life I wanted to live," said Berrt. "Now I'm a wizard and it feels like I'm walking on cavern ceilings instead of floors. And then there's you."

"Me?" said Celéri.

"Yes, you," said Berrt. "I've never been with a woman, of your people or mine, despite all your enticements. It was just me in my cave with my scrolls and, with luck, a roast rabbit with wild onions for my dinner. Merry changed all that, but she and Eynon are so pair bound that I never even thought of her as a woman. You, on the other hand, made me want to mate with you from the first time I saw you."

"Then why haven't you yet?" asked Celéri.

"I want to—oh, how I want to," said Berrt. "But from years of studying moral philosophy, seeking the way to live a good life, I know I want a true partner, not a passionate dalliance for a day, a week, or a month. You don't know yourself and don't seem to *want* to. I've been *trying* to know myself since before I left home and even now, I'm not yet there. Self-understanding is hard!"

Celéri sat up and faced Berrt. "Why have you been following me around like a puppy, then?" she asked. "I thought you liked me."

"I *do* like you," said Berrt. "You draw me to you like a moth to a torch, even though my mind knows what's likely to happen when they intersect." He slapped his palm on the flat rock, making his hand sting.

"I draw you to me?" said Celéri.

"You know you do," said Berrt. "And I know you'll continue to act thoughtlessly and eventually drive me away, unable to cope with your childishness. But I still want to try to be with you."

"Wait," said Celéri. "What if I'm not happy with my own behavior? What if I *want* to do better? Would you help?"

"You're not saying that as a pretext to take me to bed?"

"Maybe a little, but I'm mostly sincere," said Celéri.

"That sounds like an honest answer," said Berrt. "Tell me, what do you plan to do to make up for your egregious actions at the wedding?"

"Offer a sincere apology to the royal couples and grovel a lot."

"That's a start," said Berrt. He gave Celéri a quick hug. "Maybe I can be your mentor in becoming more mature while you can be *my* mentor in magic?"

Celéri laughed. "For all my bravado I don't have a tenth the magical knowledge of mages like Magister Callidus or Laetícia," she said. "You could do a lot better."

"And I have all the maturity of a son who thought the answer to all his problems was to run away from home and lie to you about it," said Berrt. "Just ask my father for his opinion of how mature I am."

"One day I'll have to do that," said Celéri. "Given our respective situations, I'd say we're well matched."

"Probably so," said Berrt.

"Can I still try to seduce you?" asked Celéri as she slid her wizards' robes off one shoulder.

"Let's take that a day at a time," Berrt responded.

"I can live with that," said Celéri. "So you carry a torch for me?" she teased.

"I said you were *like* a torch," said Berrt.

"I'm hot stuff then?"

"Get up," said Berrt. "Time to fly back and grovel."

Chapter 57

Wonders of the Imperium

There were so many guests crowded into the large dining tents filled with refreshments that empty chairs and tables were hard to find. That wasn't a problem for Eynon and Merry. The two young master mages had generated chairs of solidified sound in a quiet location between two of the dining tents along with a three-legged table of solidified sound laden with plates holding sliced dough rings spread with soft farmers' cheese, a tray of thin iced cakes flavored with grated ginger, and large pewter mugs of chilled Applegarth cider.

Chee and Ace, their stomachs more than full of cakes, were sleeping under the table and using Béryl's belly fur as their pillow. Lléwys, Rōlin's squirrel familiar, had his head tucked into Chee's belly. The familiars made different sounds as they slept. The combination reached Eynon and Merry's ears as something like *hoo-grrr-ruffruff-chee-chitter-chit*.

Eynon and Merry had hugged the newlyweds and wished them all well more than an hour ago. They'd exchanged hugs and handshakes with Eynon's parents, Daffyd and Glenys, who'd be leaving soon through a ring gate to return to Haywall to help with the evening milking. Not for the first time, Eynon thought how glad he was that his daily schedule was no longer controlled by cows' udders. His mother and father weren't concerned about Eynon and Merry spending a year and a day across the Ocean exploring the Imperium.

"It will be just like you being off on your wander year, but a bit longer, since you started on the first day of spring and you say you'll be back by Midsummer's Day next year," said his mother after she'd brushed cake crumbs off the front of his robes.

"See if you can bring back a bull from one of those Southern Empire herds," said Daffyd. "The kind with a hump. I hear the cows they sire give especially rich milk."

"I'll try," said Eynon. He smiled at Merry after his parents walked away.

She smiled back and said, "I'll help you remember."

Then Merry's parents stopped by. Baron Derry was full of practical advice, like not drinking unwatered Roma wine, and not accepting the first price you were given by innkeepers. Like Eynon's father, he asked Merry for something. In his case, it was cuttings from apple trees that produced sweet fruit, since Derry wanted to try breeding more varieties of apples for eating instead of simply pressing them for cider. Merry's mother Mabli hugged Merry so tightly Merry squeaked.

"Moth-er," said Merry when she could breathe again. "I'll only be gone for a year and a day. And it's not like I'm going out on the steppes filled with horse-archer barbarians. I'll be in the civilized Imperium."

"You're a simple country girl from the Rhuthro valley," said Mabli. "I'm afraid all those city-folk will take advantage of you."

"I'm a master mage, mother," Merry replied. "I'll blast them to cinders if they try—or more likely *ad hoc* gate away before small problems turn to larger ones."

"That's what I worry about," said Mabli. "Out of the stew pot, onto the griddle. If it's not one thing it will be another and you'll be on the other side of the Ocean where there won't be anything I can do about it."

"I'll take good care of her, baroness," said Eynon.

"What's this baroness nonsense?" asked Mabli. "Prospective sons-in-law who've dined at my table should call me by my name, or perhaps it's time for you to call me Mother?"

"Mabli will be fine," said Eynon.

Derry took his wife's arm. "It's time for us to talk to Duke Háiddon, dear, and give these young people time to themselves." The two walked away with Mabli looking back over her shoulder until they'd turned the corner around one of the dining tents.

"Can we stay in the Imperium for *two* years?" asked Merry.

"You can try renegotiating with Damon if you want to, but I don't think you'll have much luck."

"Blast," said Merry. She took a sip of cider and smiled to see Berrt approaching. "Do you have an update?" she asked him as she and Eynon stood up to hear Berrt's news.

"Yes," said Berrt. "Celéri has decided to try to grow up and has asked me to help. In return she's going to teach me magic."

"Celéri?" asked Eynon. "A teacher?"

"I think we'll be good for each other," Berrt replied.

"In bed, maybe," muttered Merry.

Berrt laughed. "Maybe someday in bed, but not right away. That's part of our deal."

"You mean you haven't already..." Eynon began, then closed his mouth. Merry looked at Eynon, then at Berrt.

"No," said Berrt. "We've kissed and cuddled, but we're not lovers, yet. We may never be, but we do have things to learn from each other."

"Good luck with that," said Merry. She shook her head and frowned.

"I'll wish you both good fortune," said Eynon. He raised an eyebrow at Merry. "I mean that sincerely."

"Thank you," said Berrt. He rubbed his hands together a few times then wiped them on his robes. "There's one other thing," he said.

"What's that?" asked Eynon.

"Celéri wants to talk with you," said the troll. "She wants to apologize for disrupting the ceremonies. You were part of them, so she wants to apologize to you both. She's already groveled in front of the kings and queens."

"And what happened?" asked Merry.

"They forgave her," said Berrt.

"If Nûd, Bonnie, Dârio, and Jenet can forgive Celéri, I expect I can," said Eynon.

Merry crossed her arms over her chest and watched Berrt leave to fetch Celéri. Eynon thought Merry was feeling out of sorts because she was the one who'd found Berrt and now he wanted to spend time with Celéri. It was clear, even to Eynon, that Merry didn't think much of Celéri and Celéri's recent actions hadn't changed that an iota. Seeing Celéri approach them kneeling on her flying disk and bowing did make Merry stop and reevaluate, however.

"Mea culpa, mea culpa, mea maxima culpa," said Celéri with her head still down facing her flying disk.

"You don't need to do that," said Eynon.

"Speak for yourself," said Merry. "I'm enjoying this."

"Don't be that way," Eynon replied. He tugged on Celéri's shoulder and helped her stand, then step off her flying disk.

"I'm really sorry I disrupted the wedding ceremonies," Celéri began.

Merry stopped her by making a chopping motion with the edge of her hand. "Did you apologize to the kings and queens?" she asked.

"Yes," said Celéri.

"Did they accept your apology?"

"Yes," Celéri repeated. "But I have to help clean up the island tomorrow and transport all the workers who helped with the celebration back to their homes. *And* I have to take lessons in responsible wizardry from Magister Callidus for three months."

"That sounds about right," said Merry.

"I expect he's a good teacher," said Eynon. "Will he be teaching Berrt, too?"

"Probably," said Celéri, "though that wasn't a royal requirement."

"You're a citizen of the Western Empire," said Eynon. "Why do you feel bound to do what the kings and queens of Dâron and Tamloch tell you?"

"Because it's something I need to do in order to take responsibilities for my actions," said Celéri. "I'm *trying* to be more grown up."

"That's good," said Eynon.

"About time," muttered Merry.

"I also need to apologize to the two of you for being such a pain when we harvested honey together," said Celéri.

"There's no need to..." said Eynon.

Merry made the cutting motion again. "Let her speak," she said.

"It wasn't appropriate for me to try to seduce the two of you back at Applegarth," said Celéri. "Not that it worked."

"It wasn't exactly kind of us to gate out while you were asleep, either," said Merry. "I think we're square there."

"You did leave me some honey to take to the emperor," said Celéri. "That was nice of you."

"We're very nice people," said Merry. She waved her arm toward Eynon. "At least one of us is."

"Let us know if there's anything we can do to help you as you learn to behave more responsibly," said Eynon.

See, mouthed Merry to Celéri, causing the Roma wizard to smile.

"I'll be helping her with that project," said Berrt.

"You can begin by reconnecting to your father," said Merry. "He's talking to King Bjarni, Queen Signý, and the prince from Nordland. You might find their discussion worth your while, especially if you're serious about finding more of your kind."

Celéri nodded at Berrt.

"I'll take your advice, then," said Berrt.

Celéri took Berrt's hand. "Follow me," she said. "I know where to find them. They're busy draining a cask of mead behind the stage. There's a good view of the falls from there. You can consider problems of moral philosophy regarding rescuing three people going over the falls in a mead cask versus five."

"Philosophy always goes better *after* mead," said Berrt. "Lead on!"

Celéri led Berrt away toward the falls, looking like a terrier followed by a shaggy alpine mountain dog.

"I thought they were already sleeping together," said Merry.

"So did I," said Eynon, "but apparently not."

They each reached down to the table of solidified sound, had another sip of cider, and were considering *ad hoc* gating back to the feather bed in their room at the inn for a "nap" when they heard excited children's voices nearby.

"Mater! Pater! I see them!" shouted Seconda.

"Ave Eynon! Hello Merry!" said Primus.

"Béryl and Ace and Chee and a *squirrel* are with them!" piped Tertia, waving her stick in front of her wildly.

Quintillius and Laetícia were close behind their children.

"It's good to see you," said Laetícia.

"Good to see you, too," said Merry.

"Are you still planning on visiting us across the Ocean soon?" asked Quintillius.

"We are," said Eynon. "We want to travel and see the wonders of the Imperium."

"Which wonders?" asked Seconda.

"The Seven Ancient Wonders? The Seven Modern Wonders?" asked Primus.

"The Seven *Natural* Wonders?" asked Tertia. "Eynon and Merry can dive into Mount Vesuvius and drop gold rings into its *cal-der-a*. That's supposed to bring good fortune, you know."

"It brings fortunes to the merchants who sell tourists gold plated rings and call them solid gold," said Laetícia. She smiled at Eynon and Merry. "Seriously, what are your plans for visiting the Imperium."

"I'm not sure," said Eynon. "It's a long way to fly."

"Fercha and Mafuta have a working long distance gate across the Ocean, if you'll recall," said Laetícia. "The five of us will be taking it tomorrow, then I'll gate us to the imperial palace in Nárbo."

"The capital of the western empire," said Primus.

"They know, son," said Quintillius. "You'd be welcome to come with us through the long-distance gate if you'd like. Three cargo ships are carrying our belongings from Nova Eboracum to Nárbo in a few days as well, so you could also travel by sea."

"Though that voyage lasts several weeks, even with wizard-assisted winds," said Laetícia.

Tertia poked Lléwys with her stick, waking all four of the sleeping familiars and leading to a spirited chase involving various permutations of three children and four familiars gamboling on the grass between the dining tents.

When the parents and young wizards finished laughing, Eynon and Merry whispered together for a few seconds. "We've be very grateful to go with you through the long-distance gate across the Ocean," said Merry.

"Excellent," said Laetícia. "Meet us in the gardens at the governor-general's palace in Nova Eboracum at nine tomorrow morning, ready to go. It will be a tight fit, and you and Quin will have to duck your heads to get through it, but you'll be in the Imperium by mid-afternoon."

"It takes that long for the gate to function?" asked Merry.

"No," said Eynon. "Think about it. The world is a sphere. When the Sun is at mid-morning over eastern Orluin..."

"...it's mid-afternoon in the western part of the Imperium," said Merry. "I wasn't thinking."

"How were you thinking of paying for your expenses on your travels?" asked Quintillius.

"I hadn't thought about it," said Eynon.

"I have some money," said Merry.

"And I have a lump of gold in the bottom of my pack," said Eynon, just remembering that fact.

"What Quin is planning to tell you is that the Imperium treasury would be glad to cover all your expenses, within reason, if you'd spend a few days teaching our top wizard artificers how to make gate rings," said Laetícia.

"That's right," said Quintillius. "Valens, Phraátēs, and I will be glad to arrange guided tours of any wonders of the Imperium you'd care to visit in return for such instruction. I'm sure the new emperor of the northern empire will be glad to do the same."

"That would be *wonder*ful, I mean, great," said Eynon. "I'd be glad to teach your wizard artificers."

"We'd want royalties on every pair of gate rings made," said Merry.

Laetícia smiled at Merry and winked at Quintillius, as if to say, "I told you." "I think that can be arranged," she told Merry. "When we're across the Ocean I'll introduce you to someone who's a wizard at drafting up such agreements. Rumor has it his familiar is a shark."

"Thank you," said Merry. "You're going to be very wealthy soon, Eynon."

"I'm already rich," Eynon replied. "I have you in my life."

Merry pulled Eynon down to give him hugs and kisses that only stopped when the rambunctious children and familiars returned. Quintillius and Laetícia collected their brood and left while Béryl and Lléwys went off to find more peaceful environs with their wizards. Ace and Chee resumed napping under the three-legged solidified sound table.

"Well," said Merry. "We'll be in the Imperium tomorrow."

"About to begin new adventures," said Eynon.

"Where do you want to start, after we teach the wizard-artificers?"

"I was thinking we could visit the Great Pyramid," said Eynon. "We could start farther south and take a boat, just the two of us, traveling down the Nile."

"Like we did on the Rhuthro when we'd first met," said Merry. "I'd like that."

"So would I," said Eynon. He held Merry close with the thunder of the falls behind him, then released her, stepping back a few feet so he could see her eyes. He smiled at her.

Merry smiled back.

"Here's to new adventures," said Eynon.

"To new adventures!" Merry replied.

Please visit

www.CongruentMage.com

for more information about
Eynon, Merry and their friends

Sign up for the Congruent Mage mailing list on
the web site to get advance notice of future publications
and receive a free short story set in the author's
Xenotech Support universe.

XenotechSupport.com/mailing-list

MAPS

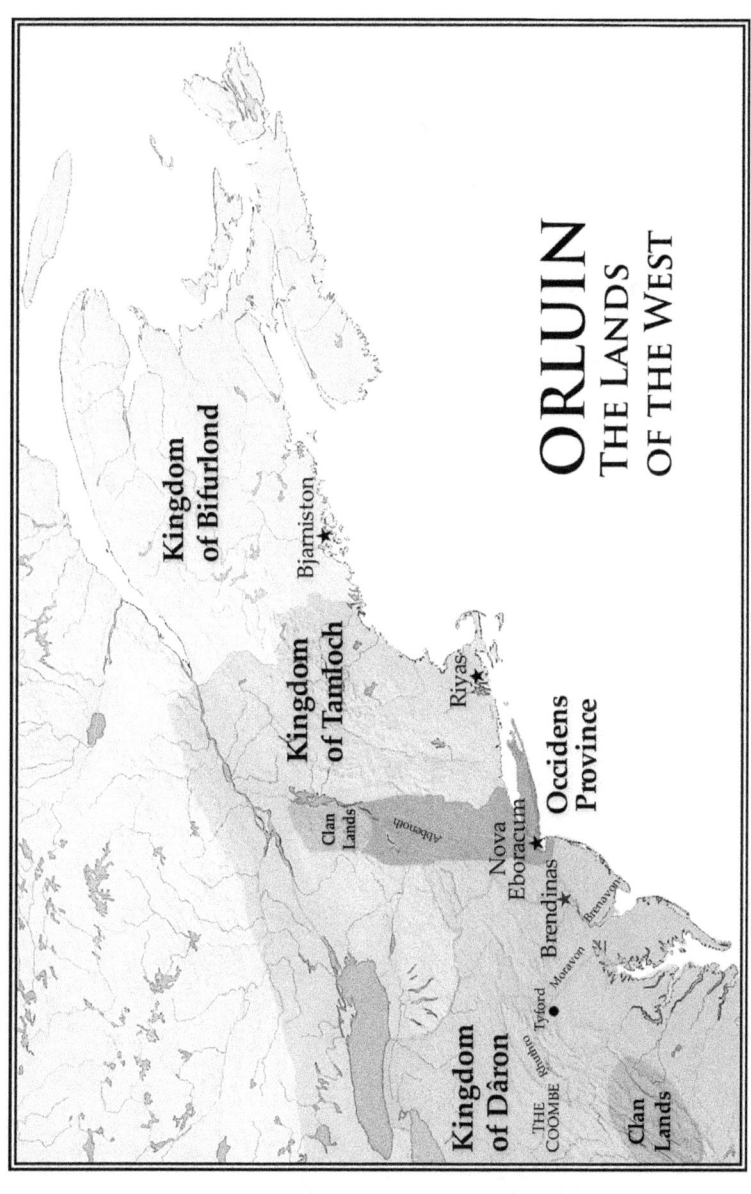

ORLUIN
THE LANDS
OF THE WEST

Kingdom
of Bifurlond

Bjarniston ★

Kingdom
of Tamloch

Rivas

Clan
Lands

Abbsroth

Occidens
Province

Nova
Eboracum ★

Brendinas ★

Brenavon

Moraven

Tyford

Sonno

THE
COOMBE ●

Kingdom
of Dâron

Clan
Lands

Larger color versions of these maps are available at:

CongruentMage.com/maps.html

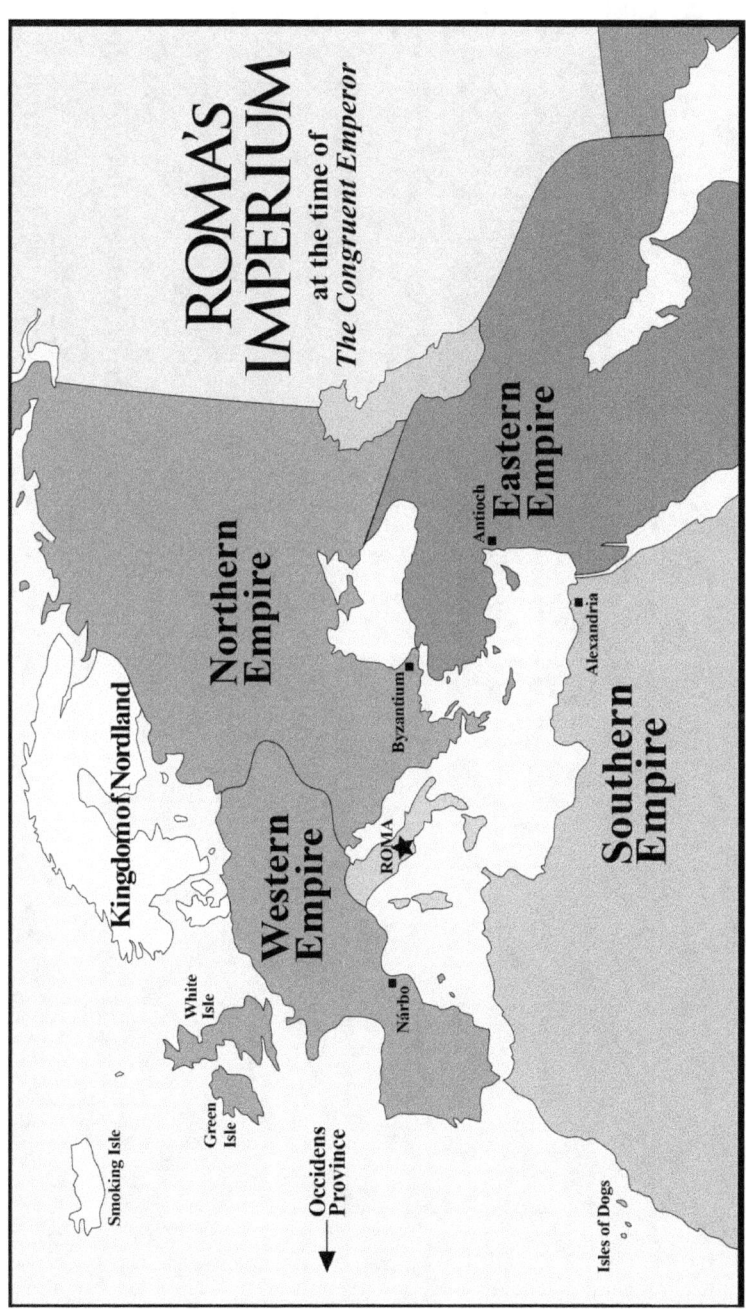

ROMA'S
IMPERIUM
at the time of
The Congruent Emperor

Kingdom of Nordland

Northern
Empire

Eastern
Empire

Western
Empire

Southern
Empire

Smoking Isle

Green
Isle

White
Isle

← Occidens
Province

Nårbo

ROMA

Byzantium

Antioch

Alexandria

Isles of Dogs

VALENTIA

Portus Aleña

THE CAIMAN ISLE

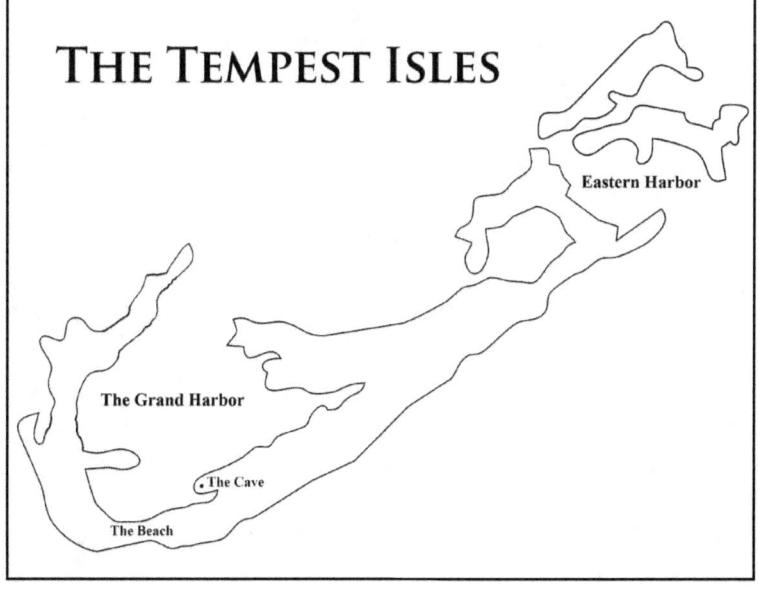

THE TEMPEST ISLES

Eastern Harbor

The Grand Harbor

. The Cave

The Beach